Death Comes to the Ballets Russes

DAVID DICKINSON

Constable
An imprint of
Little, Brown Book Group
Carmelite House
50 Victoria Embankment
London EC4Y 0DZ

An Hachette UK Company
www.hachette.co.uk

CONSTABLE • LONDON

www.littlebrown.co.uk

CONSTABLE

First published in Great Britain in 2015 by Constable

This paperback edition published in 2016

1 3 5 7 9 10 8 6 4 2

A CIP catalogue record for this book
is available from the British Library.

ISBN: 978-1-47211-376-4

Typeset in Palatino by Initial Typesetting Services
Printed and bound by CPI Group (UK) Ltd, Croydon, CR0 4YY

Papers used by Constable are from well-managed forests and other
responsible sources.

MIX
Paper from
responsible sources
FSC® C104740

For Krystyna and for Jane

1

Demi-pointe

Being on *demi-pointe* is like being on tiptoe. The ball of
the foot is in contact with the floor, and is supporting
the weight of the body. Sometimes this movement
is referred to as three-quarter *pointe*. When a dancer is
wearing *pointe* shoes, she can raise to *en-pointe*, where
she is actually using the tip of her foot to support her
weight on the floor.

New Year is the season of hope or despair. For the
young, the first day of January brings another chance
of true love, the prospect of a new job with new hori-
zons. For the middle-aged, it is the time when people
start to look back as well as forward, the time when the
first faint lines start to appear on what had been perfect
skin, the time funerals start to replace weddings and
christenings as the rite of passage. For the old, they
know that the aches and pains that have grown into
permanent fixtures are never going to go away now;
they know that time is not going to run backwards to

1

make them fit and healthy again; they know that each New Year might be the last and, more surely than ever, that death comes at the end.

For the gilded aristocracy of Europe, New Year always begins with a ball. In the perfectly sprung ballrooms of the Habsburgs and the Romanovs, from the Hofburg in Vienna to the Winter Palace in St Petersburg, aristocrats dress up and dance. Like the Roman god Janus, who gave his name to the month of January, the dukes and duchesses, the princes and princesses, the counts and countesses face both ways at once. They look back, secure in the knowledge that their family has left its mark on history across the centuries. They look forward, secure in the knowledge that their family will leave its mark on the centuries to come.

Princess Marie Golitsyn thought she must have the largest collection of jewellery boxes in St Petersburg. All of them, large or small, were open on her dressing table, their contents spilling over the sides and rolling away across the floor. She had jewellery boxes made with different kinds of wood, walnut and rosewood and mahogany. There were silver ones, boxes inlaid with silver or platinum; even a box shaped rather like a heart in the Art Nouveau style. The Princess had gold and silver ornaments, she had rubies and sapphires and emeralds and pearls. She had bracelets and chatelaines and carcanets and a couple of diadems left to her by her favourite aunt. There was a diamond tiara made by Fabergé, a present from her husband a few years before. The Princess discovered later that it was one of a pair. The other one had gone to her husband's mistress in Moscow.

Princess Marie was one of a vast throng of aristocrats in the Russian capital preparing for a ball at the Winter Palace. She had been at her dressing table for an hour and a half and thought she would be ready quite soon. The carriage was waiting outside in the snow. She could hear her husband pacing up and down the hallway. She knew that if she didn't finish her toilette soon he would be so drunk that it would be impossible for him to go to the palace at all. She decided on the triple ring of pearls and a dog-collar-style choker necklace. A series of diamonds encircled the top of her ornate dress from Worth in Paris. She added earrings and the Fabergé tiara, bracelets for her wrist and a sapphire star, the most valuable piece she possessed, pinned to her waist. Her fingers shone with the pure gold of a couple of rings believed to have been created in Paris at the end of the seventeenth century for a mistress of the Sun King. Princess Marie Golitsyn rose from the table and swept down the stairs. She left her jewels strewn all across her dressing table and the boxes lying around on the floor. The servants could pick them up later. That was what servants were for.

Ten minutes later she was handing her cloak to one of the attendants outside the Winter Palace. Ahead she could see the white marble staircase that led up to the gigantic galleries, each one as tall as a cathedral. Baskets of orchids lined the walls, flanked by enormous mirrors where the ladies could inspect their adornments and make final adjustments to their décolletage. Cossack Life Guards in scarlet tunics stood to attention every fifty yards. But for Princess Golitsyn and her cousin Tatiana, who lived next door, and for Princess Nathalie, her neighbour on the other side of the Fontanka Quay, the important people that evening were not their husbands or the soldiers or the lovers they would dance with under the glittering chandeliers. The important people were their sons.

The Russian capital St Petersburg had always been blessed with more than its fair share of dissolute and depraved young men, who spent money they did not have in the gambling clubs; young men who bought expensive presents on credit for the stars of the opera and the theatre; young men who spent lavishly on the pretty wives of their contemporaries they thought might be compliant. Most of these young men were bailed out by reluctant fathers and families. But as the New Year Ball of 1912 drew closer, two young men, Prince Alexis Kishkin and Prince Felix Peshkov, officers in the fashionable Preobrazhensky Guards, found that all the doors in front of them were shut. Their fathers and grandparents had closed ranks, refusing any further loans and insisting that the income the young men had inherited on coming of age be used to pay down their debts. The banks were under instruction not to lend the young men a single rouble. This was easier than it might have appeared, as Peshkov's father owned one bank and had considerable shareholdings in two others.

The young men relied on secret contributions from their mothers. 'We couldn't let Alexis starve.' In the dying days of 1911, the impoverished young men had hatched a daring scheme to restore their fortunes. The season for great balls in St Petersburg was approaching. The young men had often seen their mothers preparing for these evenings. The most difficult choice was never what clothes to wear, but what jewels should adorn them. Few women in Europe loved their gems like the aristocratic women of St Petersburg. The young men knew that special boxes and caskets would be brought out. Various combinations would be tried. The final decision was usually left to the very last minute.

As the carriages and the sledges sped across the snow to the New Year's Ball in the Winter Palace, the young men made their move. Characteristically they took one big gamble. They gambled that their mothers would not have put their jewels away. They would still be littered across the dressing tables and the dressing-room floors. They put on their most splendid uniforms and charged into three of the grandest houses on Fontanka Quay, the Belgravia of St Petersburg, home to Princess Marie Golitsyn and her cousin Tatiana and her friend Princess Nathalie. They brought six of their soldiers to act as sentries and lookouts. 'There's been a robbery!' they shouted as the butlers let them in. 'Tell everyone to stay where they are and not to move!' The young men sped upstairs and gathered pearls and diamonds, emeralds and sapphires, gold and silver, into three different saddlebags. Then they disappeared into the night.

The following week they took a train to Moscow. They consulted a dealer. He said it would be impossible to sell the jewels in Russia, as the authorities probably had details of every single piece by now. He advised taking them to Antwerp or London and selling them there. Prince Felix Peshkov had a special friend in the corps de ballet in Diaghilev's company the Ballets Russes. Peshkov knew the ballet was going to London after Monte Carlo and Paris. He knew his friend would take them if he asked her and sell them for a good price. Even regular dancers in the corps de ballet travel with enormous amounts of luggage, costumes, special outfits for particular roles, even scenery for the more exotic offerings. If anybody asked, the girl was going to say the jewels were fake and were needed for her part in *The Firebird*. Anastasia was a good girl. Prince Felix Peshkov knew she was a good girl. Didn't she live in a pretty little house he provided? Didn't she go to fashionable parties in the fashionable clothes he had bought her?

*

The lights went out very slowly in the Royal Opera House, Covent Garden. The stage was dark at first. Balakirev's music was filled with foreboding, a sad and tragic melody that set the mood for the ballet. As the curtain rose, a great room was revealed, with mauve and purple walls and a green ceiling. There was a fire with a dying glow and on a huge divan lay the sleeping figure of Thamar, Queen of Georgia, stirring uneasily in her sleep.

The date was 12 June 1912, and this was the London premiere of the Ballets Russes's *Thamar*, first performed in Paris. The year before, Diaghilev's company had taken London by storm. They had danced in front of the King and Queen. They had danced on a specially constructed stage at Strawberry Hill and been invited to all the finest society houses. Rupert Brooke had come down from Grantchester fifteen times to see them. A more puritan figure perhaps, Leonard Woolf, former civil servant in Ceylon, had been entranced. Harvey Nichols cleared their windows of the white cream and lilac of summer fashion and replaced them with hangings in the style of Léon Bakst, the artistic director of the company.

At the centre of the Ballets Russes was a pair of lovers. Sergei Diaghilev, thirty-nine years old, broad chested with a homburg hat tilted low over his eyes, a cane always in his hand, was the founder, impresario and inspiration behind the venture. His ballets were set to music by the finest Russian composers, from Tchaikovsky and Rimsky-Korsakov to Stravinsky. His sets and costumes, designed by Léon Bakst, brought an air of the exotic and the erotic Orient to the more restrained capitals of Western Europe. Diaghilev had met Tolstoy and conversed with Oscar Wilde. He, like most of the company, spoke hardly any English. French, the lingua franca of the Russian intelligentsia in St Petersburg, was also the language of the dance. Large, and running to fat because of his love of food, Diaghilev was believed by Osbert Sitwell to have only three words of English, 'more chocolate cake'.

Diaghilev was the foremost impresario of his age. His career began in St Petersburg with the launch of a magazine called *World of Art*. He organized a major exhibition of Russian portrait paintings, travelling across the vast country in search of forgotten artists and lost masterpieces. He had no home of his own. He lived in hotels where he sometimes left without paying the bill. He was neurotic, superstitious, disorganized. Rehearsals were a form of controlled chaos that somehow managed to come right on the night. For several years now he had refused to send letters, preferring the more immediate telephone or cable, which lent themselves better to panic and hysteria. In spite of all this he managed to run the finances, the publicity, the choice of ballets. He teetered permanently on the fringe of bankruptcy.

Diaghilev's favourite place in the world was Venice. Something about the watery city soothed his troubled spirit. Here, after all, his great hero Richard Wagner had composed the second act of *Tristan und Isolde* in the Palazzo Giustinian and died in the Ca' Vendramin Calergi on the Grand Canal. Like Diaghilev, Wagner's life was characterized by political exile, turbulent love affairs and repeated flights from his creditors.

Diaghilev loved the shimmering waters of the Grand Canal, the palazzos in their Gothic glory, the pompous grandeur and self-importance of the Doge's Palace, the sense that the entire place was a stage set waiting for one more performance, that opera singers or ballet dancers might suddenly drift out from behind the Hotel Danieli on the waterfront and perform in the great drawing room of St Mark's Square. His favourite hotel was the Grand Hotel des Bains on the lido, built at the turn of the century for Europe's rich, in flight from harsher winter climes. Diaghilev was consumed by the desire for artistic perfection. He was supremely Russian but now lived mainly abroad. To his great regret, he had never been able to take his Ballets Russes to St Petersburg. He had problems with the administration of the Imperial Theatre. He had enemies in the Imperial Court.

One of his famous ballerinas was very young when she joined the Ballets Russes and would later say that she always called Diaghilev 'Sergypops'. Diaghilev's paramour was the young dancer from the Imperial Ballet, Vaslav Nijinsky. He was already the most famous dancer in the world, apparently able to hang in the air and perform impossible leaps. He drew audiences into theatres like a human magnet.

When Thamar, Queen of Georgia, wakes, she waves a scarf through her window to entice a passing suitor into her castle. When the Prince arrives in his astrakhan cap and huge black cloak, she initially rejects his advances, but fervent dancing follows and the pair kiss. There is a wild Caucasian dance, a kaleidoscope of tossing sleeves and flashing boots where real daggers thud into the floor. The lovers embrace, then they leave the room and the Queen's followers continue dancing wildly. When the Queen and Prince re-enter, she suddenly stabs him and he falls through a secret panel into the river below. The Queen returns to the window to signal to a new victim with her scarf.

The Covent Garden audience gave the performance a standing ovation. The ballet wasn't long, but it was like no other ballet the audience had seen before. It was followed by another Diaghilev special, full of Eastern promise, called *Scheherazade*. When the stars and the corps de ballet came on stage for the final curtain call, there was one notable absentee. Originally it had been Adolph Bolm cast in the role of the Prince in *Thamar*, but he had been indisposed so an understudy had taken the role instead. The understudy did not appear to take his bow; his body was found below the trapdoor where the Queen had thrown him after she had stabbed him. But this was no mere Russian version of the ancient myth of *The King Must Die*. The understudy really was dead, stabbed through the heart with one of the daggers used in the dance, as he had been on the stage.

It was hours after the performance before they found the corpse. Sergei Grigoriev, the *régisseur* who was in charge of all administrative matters, found Diaghilev

9

taking a late supper at the Savoy Hotel with Nijinsky and Tamara Karsavina, the ballerina who had danced the title role in *Thamar*. They were on the second bottle of champagne.

'Sergei Pavlovich,' said Grigoriev, 'you must come back to the theatre at once! Something terrible has happened.'

'What is it? Can't you see I'm having my supper?' The other diners turned to watch the animated conversation in Russian.

'It's Taneyev, the understudy who took Bolm's place in *Thamar* this evening.'

'He's a promising boy, that Alexander Taneyev,' said Diaghilev. 'I promoted him to understudy Bolm myself.'

'Well, he won't be doing any more work as an understudy,' Sergei Grigoriev crossed himself three times as fast as he could, 'not now, he won't. He's dead. Stabbed through the heart with one of the daggers used in the ballet. We found him lying in a pool of his own blood.'

'My God, this is frightful. What an inconsiderate time to die, right at the beginning of a new season. This could ruin everything. Stupid English policemen tramping round the sets of *The Firebird* and *Le Spectre de la Rose* in their great boots. God in heaven, it doesn't bear thinking about.'

Diaghilev stopped for a moment to comfort Tamara Karsavina, who was crying quietly into her oysters. 'Calm down, child, calm down. You mustn't ruin your looks.'

Even his critics admitted Diaghilev was a good man in a crisis. By now he had lived through so many of them.

'Have you told anybody about this, Grigoriev?'

'What do you mean, told anybody about this? It's a quarter to one in the morning, for God's sake! There was only Misha, the stagehand, and myself in the opera house looking for Alexander. Everyone else has gone back to their hotels. Misha is waiting for me to come back.'

'So the authorities at the opera house know nothing about this? The English police have not been informed?'

'That's right.'

'Very well,' said Diaghilev, taking out his monocle and polishing it on one of the Savoy's finest napkins. 'This is the best I can think of for the moment. Go back to the opera house. Find a big trunk – I've seen plenty of them lying about at the back of the dressing rooms – and put Alexander in it. Close the lid. Lock it if you can find a key. Take it to that great storeroom in the basement that's full of bits of old stage sets and other junk. Nobody's going to find it in there, not for a while, at any rate. Then leave as quietly as you can.'

Grigoriev slipped away into the night. 'Just one last thing,' Diaghilev waddled at full speed to catch his colleague by the door.

'What's that?'

'Just this, my friend. Don't forget to throw away the key.'

Karsavina was still weeping softly at the supper table.

'What about that poor boy, Sergei Pavlovich? You can't just leave him in a trunk in that awful basement. What about his burial? What about his parents?'

'You leave that to me, Tamara. I'll think of something.

11

Come to think of it, we'll be out of London in another five weeks. Maybe they won't find the body until after we've gone.'

*

Diaghilev could well have been right about the body in the trunk not being discovered until after the Ballets Russes had left town. But there was one factor he had overlooked. Alexander Taneyev was not staying with the rest of the junior dancers and the corps de ballet in their hotel. He did have a room there, but he wasn't spending the nights in the hotel most of the time. He was staying with his uncle, one Richard Wagstaff Gilbert, in a large house guarded by two stone lions next to Barnes Pond and close to the River Thames. Gilbert was a financier with fingers in many of the City of London's tastiest and most profitable pies. When the young man didn't come home the first evening, Gilbert presumed he had gone to the hotel with friends and stayed there. At that stage he wasn't worried at all. Three days later, he moved into action. He sat on a charity committee with the Commissioner of the Metropolitan Police. The Commissioner was pressed into service. Gilbert was a trustee of the Royal Opera House and knew one of its principal patrons, Gladys Robinson, Marchioness of Ripon, a formidable society lady who used to move in the fast set around King Edward VII and Mrs Keppel. Oscar Wilde had dedicated his 1893 play *A Woman of No Importance* to Lady Ripon. By now she was a woman of considerable importance. She was a friend and supporter of Nellie Melba. The day after Richard Gilbert mobilized his forces, twenty policemen were sent to search the Royal

12

Opera House. They found the body just before the doors opened for the evening performance of *Carnaval*, *Thamar* and *Les Sylphides*.

Lady Ripon was in her box as usual. Her chauffeur drove her up to town every evening in her six-cylinder Napier motor car. The journey took about half an hour from her house in Coombe just outside London. No mention was made of the murder of Alexander Taneyev. Alfred Bolm was back dancing the role of the Prince in *Thamar*. There was no sign of Diaghilev. Lady Ripon had noticed that he was often to be seen during performances, watching from an empty box or peering round the curtain. She only heard about the incident the following afternoon when she received a telephone call from Richard Gilbert. Reports of the Russian's demise were already circulating in the City of London.

Lady Ripon had Russian blood in her veins. She was descended from the 11th Earl of Pembroke, who married Countess Catherine Semyonovna Vorontsova, on 25 January 1808. Catherine was the daughter of the prominent Russian aristocrat and diplomat Semyon Romanovich Vorontsov. Like many in her circle, Lady Ripon had a great many acquaintances and very few friends. After she heard the news, she invited herself round to the Chelsea house of the one Russian lady she knew in London to tell her the full story. Natasha Shaporova and her husband Mikhail had been based in the capital for a number of years. Natasha was in her mid-twenties and was one of the most beautiful women in London. Mikhail's father was one of the richest men in Russia. People said he was far wealthier than the Romanovs. Amongst his many financial interests was a large bank with branches all over Europe.

Natasha and Mikhail had just returned to London after a two-year spell in Cannes, where Mikhail had opened the Riviera office of the Shaporova Bank to cater for the needs of the wealthy Russian émigrés and their everlasting lust for expensive chips at the Casino in Monte Carlo.

'Well, Natasha,' Lady Ripon asked as she finished her story. 'What do you make of it, this death at the Ballets Russes? I expect the news will be all over town tomorrow morning.'

'I'm not an expert in these matters, Lady Ripon. Even Russians don't usually go round murdering each other at the end of the ballet. Do you think there will be a scandal?'

Natasha smiled a rather wicked smile as she brought up the subject of scandal. It looked as though she would rather enjoy it.

'Scandal? A scandal?' Lady Ripon was horrified at the thought that she might be caught up in such a thing. It might not be well received in Society.

'I tell you what the really interesting question is,' said Natasha, who was a devotee of the works of Conan Doyle.

'What's that, my dear?'

'It's this. Did the murderer intend to kill the understudy Alexander Taneyev? Or was the victim meant to be Alfred Bolm, who was on the programme to take the role? I don't suppose we know when Bolm cried off, do we?'

'God bless my soul! I'd never have thought of that. I have no idea what the answer might be. That'll be something the police will have to find out, I expect.'

Natasha started to giggle. Lady Ripon frowned.

Aristocratic young women weren't meant to giggle like schoolgirls.

'Forgive me, Lady Ripon. I've just thought of something. The police are going to have a terrible time. Diaghilev doesn't know a word of English. He speaks Russian or French. The top people in the Ballets Russes like Fokine and Bakst all speak French but not English. The make-up artists and the technical people they bring with them from St Petersburg don't speak French. They only know Russian. I met that lovely ballerina Tamara Karsavina when they were here last year. She doesn't speak English either – she and her friends always carried a note with Premier Hotel, Russell Square, Bloomsbury written on it to show the taxi driver where to take them. It's going to be chaos, pure chaos.'

'What am I going to do?' Lady Ripon was horrified at the prospect of her Royal Opera House and her Ballets Russes, as she always referred to them, turning into a Tower of Babel in the middle of Covent Garden. 'I feel so responsible, you know.'

Natasha Shaporova suddenly remembered a hotel in St Petersburg where she had danced with a handsome investigator from London some years earlier when she was still Natasha Bobrinsky. The investigator was at the end of a difficult case involving an English diplomat found dead on the Nevskii Prospekt and was returning to London the next day. Natasha recalled asking him where the most romantic place in the world to get married was. She never forgot his reply: 'There's only one answer,' he said, smiling at Natasha and feeling at least seventy years old. 'Venice. You get married in the Basilica of St Mark or, if you can't manage that, San Giorgio Maggiore across the water. You have your reception in the Doge's Palace. If that's not possible, I'm sure you could rent a whole palazzo on the Grand Canal. It would be wonderful. Mikhail's father and yours might have to throw quite a lot of money about, but the Venetians have been taking bribes for centuries. Anyway, you should all feel at home there.'

'Should we?' asked Natasha.

'Of course you should, whole bloody city's built on the water. Just like here.'

She had married Mikhail in the marble church of Santa Maria dei Miracoli in the heart of Venice. The investigator and his wife were among the guests at the reception in the Ca' d'Oro on the Grand Canal.

'I know what you should do,' cried Natasha. 'I know exactly what you should do!'

'What should I do, Natasha?'

'I've just remembered. I know just the man for you. I met him in St Petersburg years ago when he was investigating a murder. As far as I know he doesn't speak Russian but he speaks perfect French. At least he'd be able to talk to Diaghilev and Fokine and Bakst and that rather frightening-looking composer person – Stravinsky, I think he's called. My friend is one of the most distinguished investigators in the country.'

'And what is his name, my dear?'

'Why, he lives just round the corner in Markham Square, Lady Ripon. His name is Powerscourt, Lord Francis Powerscourt.'

2

Pas

Literally, 'step'. In ballet, the term *pas* often refers to a combination of steps which make up a dance (typically, in dance forms such as jazz, hip-hop, tap, etc., this is called a *routine*). *Pas* is often used as a generic term when referring to a particular suite of dances, i.e. *Pas de deux*, *Grand Pas d'action*, etc., and may also refer to a variation. The use of the word *pas* when referring to a combination of steps which make up a dance, is used mostly in Russia, and much of Europe, while in English-speaking countries the word *combination* is often used.

'Lady Ripon, my lord.' Rhys, the Powerscourt butler, coughed apologetically before his announcement. He always did. Powerscourt's wife, Lady Lucy, had a private theory that Rhys must have North American blood. The cough, she maintained, was the modern English equivalent of the Indians up in the hills sending smoke signals to their colleagues down on the plains.

It was three o'clock in the afternoon the day after Lady Ripon's conversation with Natasha Shaporova. The staff at the Royal Opera House had telephoned early that morning to make the appointment.

'Thank you for seeing me at such short notice, Lord Powerscourt. I don't think we've met. Mind you, I'm sure I have come across your charming wife about the town from time to time.'

Powerscourt thought she made it sound as if it was his fault they had not met before.

'And how may I be of assistance to you, Lady Ripon?'

Lady Ripon was tall with luscious brown hair, a very superior air and a lorgnette. 'I trust this conversation may be regarded as private, Lord Powerscourt. I have come in my dual role as Patron of the Ballets Russes and Patron of the Royal Opera House.' Powerscourt felt sure she would have accepted the patronage of any other organizations that bothered to approach her. She made it sound like a royal command.

'Of course.'

She told him the details of the murder at the ballet. 'It's important to us that the matter is sorted out as soon as possible. I and my people would like the matter cleared up in a week. Can you give me your word on that?'

'I beg your pardon, Lady Ripon. If you are asking me to give my word that I could solve this case inside a week, the answer is no. Definitely no. It's just not possible to say how long it will take to clear up a matter like this. I'm sorry.'

'My people will be disappointed, Lord Powerscourt. We had heard such good things about you. We had high hopes.'

Powerscourt wondered who 'my people' were and who she had been talking to. He decided that if she didn't want to tell him the names of her associates, he would just have to find out.

'Have the police been informed?' Powerscourt asked. 'And the newspapers? Publicity often helps in cases like this. People remember they may have seen something which could be useful.'

Lady Ripon snorted. 'The last thing we want, Lord Powerscourt, is for the common people to be reading sensational stories in the vulgar press and gossiping about them in the public houses. *The Times* and the other principal papers have been spoken to this morning. They will do as they're told. I felt we had no choice but to inform the police. The victim may be a foreigner of whom we know little or nothing but the reputation of British justice must be maintained. The police are under orders to be as discreet as possible.'

'I see.'

'Can I take it then that you will take on the investigation? I can tell my people that you will start work this afternoon?'

Lady Ripon rose as if to go.

'No, you can't do that, Lady Ripon. I suspect there will be great difficulties, certainly about the language. I don't know how many of the Ballets Russes people speak English. I need time to think about it. I need to talk it over with my wife.'

'I thought you agreed that our conversation was confidential, off the record. We can't have you discussing the matter with anybody you like.'

'My wife is not anybody, Lady Ripon. Nor is your husband. I shall let you have my answer first thing in

19

the morning.' Powerscourt rang the bell for Rhys to take Lady Ripon away.

Lady Lucy was fascinated to hear of her husband's meeting with the world of opera and ballet.

'Was she really frightful, Francis?'

'Do you know, I rather think she was. Somewhere between Lady Bracknell and the current Queen Mary with a hint of Lady Catherine de Bourgh.'

'I wonder if that isn't the key to her whole attitude.'

'You're way ahead of me, Lucy. What might this key be?'

'Well, I'm sure she is much less important now than she was under the previous regime. I never had anything to do with them, but Lady Ripon was a key player in that fast set around the late King, bed-hopping in the night, little cards left on every bedroom door with the name of the guest so people knew who they were going to visit, gentlemen expected to be back in their quarters by four thirty in the morning when the servants began moving about. Enormous meals. Expensive chefs from Paris. No expense spared to entertain a King. Some people are thought to have almost bankrupted themselves serving in the royal progress. Mrs Keppel was everywhere, always keen to have the last word and nobody daring to argue with her. Now I come to think about it, Lady Ripon was famous for a while for her role in the Duchess of Devonshire's costume ball back at the time of the Diamond Jubilee.'

'How did she become famous for dressing up?'

'That's the thing, Francis. Mary Queen of Scots was there and Queen Zenobia from Persia and a couple of Nelsons. Lady Ripon was one of three Cleopatras. But she was the only one who took her slave girl with her at all times.'

'I see,' said Powerscourt. 'And that's all gone now. The King is dead. Long live the King. Lady Ripon and her set must feel rather like Bardolph and Poins and Falstaff after Prince Hal gives up his naughty past and turns into a warrior prince. Edward the Seventh was the opposite of his mother. George the Fifth is very different from his father. Respectability, not dissipation and luxury, is the new order of the day. Rosebery told me at the time of the Coronation that the new King had spent most of the past seventeen years sticking stamps into his album in that dreary York Cottage up at Sandringham. God help us all.'

'Did you see her as a *grande horizontale*, Francis?'

'I'm not sure about that. *Grande* certainly. I can't quite bring myself to imagine Lady Ripon *horizontale*. I've always thought it referred to aristocratic mistresses in Versailles with loads of perfume and cupboards full of suggestive lingerie. Madame de Pompadour, Madame du Barry before she was sent to the guillotine, those sort of people.'

'So Lady Ripon might feel the need to put on airs, to throw her weight about now, precisely because she is much less important than she was before?'

'Exactly so, Lucy, exactly so. But I wonder who she meant by "her people". She referred to them more than once.'

'I'm sure she knows a lot of very rich men, Francis, like those financiers who bailed out Edward the Seventh. The only other thing I know about her is that she was one of the first society ladies to have a motor car and to install a telephone. She claimed, so I was told, that the telephone was much more discreet. No *billet-doux* left lying around for the servants to black-mail you with later on. Anyway, Francis, are you going to take on the case?'

'Well,' said her husband, 'I must admit that I was very tempted to tell Her Ladyship to go to hell. But I don't think I can refuse. Think of that poor dead dancer – he can't have been much older than our Thomas is now. Think of his family back in St Petersburg or Kiev or Moscow or wherever they live. I shall send a note round to the Royal Opera House, accepting the case and requesting an interview with Diaghilev in the morning. Maybe he's one of "her people". But I look forward to meeting him. I wonder what he's like. I do have one major problem with this case though.'

'What's that?'

'I really don't like ballet, Lucy. I never have and I never will. I can't stand it.'

*

The stage at the Royal Opera House in Covent Garden was a hive of activity. A couple of carpenters were high on their ladders adjusting the scenery. A make-up artist was putting the finishing touches to the complexion of one of the prima ballerinas. The girls of the corps de ballet seemed frozen in mid-pirouette, waiting for guidance. The choreographer, Michel Fokine, a young man, probably in his early thirties, looked as if he was, quite literally, tearing his hair out. He was swearing violently in what Powerscourt presumed to be Russian. Powerscourt learnt later that Fokine had one com-plaint, repeated over and over again: why in God's name did I leave St Petersburg with these stupid girls?

Another young man was staring hard at the scene. Powerscourt thought he must be a policeman. He had that slightly uncomfortable look people often have when they are transferred out of the uniformed branch.

'Excuse me,' said Powerscourt, 'are you connected with the opera or the Ballets Russes?'

'No, I'm not, sir. I'm a policeman. Sergeant Rufus Jenkins, at your service.' The young man bowed politely. 'And who might you be, sir, if I might make so bold?'

'My name is Powerscourt, Francis Powerscourt. I happen to be Lord Powerscourt but that isn't important. I have been asked to investigate a rather shocking murder that happened here a couple of days ago.'

'Why, my lord, that's why I'm here too. I'm the officer in charge of the police inquiry, so I am.'

'Forgive me if I sound rude, but are you the only officer on the case? In my experience Scotland Yard usually send an inspector to look into murder cases.'

'That's right, my lord. But that's what happens if you're English. English corpses get inspectors, so they do. Foreign dead get sergeants.'

'What would happen if you didn't come from Europe? Suppose you were a New Zealander or an African?'

'Empire dead would get a sergeant like me. Africans, I'm not sure what would happen to them. They might be lucky to get a detective constable, and that's a fact.'

'Have you been able to talk to anybody at all? Any of the witnesses?'

'This is bad, my lord, I know it's bad. Fact is, I don't speak a word of Russian. That lot on the stage, they don't speak a word of English. One of them, the bloke who seems to be in charge, tried to talk to me in what I thought might be French, but I don't speak bloody

23

French either. The office are busy hunting for fluent Russian speakers in the schools and over at the university, but they haven't found anybody yet.'

'Well, I can get by in French. I'll see if I can have a word with that man in charge when he's calmed down and they're not so busy with their rehearsal. You haven't come across a fellow called Diaghilev, by any chance? He's the head man of the whole thing. Big fellow. Astrakhan collar on his coat. Oiled hair. Monocle. Ring any bells?'

'I've not seen him at all this morning, my lord.'

'Lord Powerscourt! Lord Powerscourt! How very good to see you again!'

Natasha Shaporova was skipping down the aisle of the auditorium of the Royal Opera House. She was wearing a pale-blue coat and a rather raffish hat. Her feet, Powerscourt remembered from his time in St Petersburg, were clad in the usual high Russian boots. She looked as though she might be on her way to Ascot or Henley.

'Natasha, you look prettier than ever!' said Powerscourt. 'May I introduce my companion in arms, Sergeant Rufus Jenkins of the Metropolitan Police?'

Natasha Shaporova smiled at the young man. He was hers for life now.

'I heard about all this from Lady Ripon yesterday, about the murder and so on. I called at your house just now and Lady Powerscourt said I'd find you here. I've come to offer my services, Lord Powerscourt!'

'How nice to have you on board, Natasha. I feel happier about this investigation already.'

'I've come to help, Lord Powerscourt. When I was talking to Lady Ripon yesterday, I suddenly realized that there are going to be problems with the languages, Russians and ballet people not speaking English, and the English not speaking Russian. Well, I didn't know much English when we met before in St Petersburg, but I'm nearly fluent now. I will be able to translate Russian into English or French as you wish. I've lived here for a few years now. The last time we worked together, you had Mikhail as a translator. This time you can have me. I might not be so fluent but I like to think I'm better looking!'

'Thank you so much,' said Powerscourt. 'That's very kind of you.'

'Now then, Lord Powerscourt, why don't you wait here a moment and I'll go and speak to that fellow onstage. I think he's called Michel Fokine. He's quite a celebrity back home. Is there anybody in particular you'd like to speak to?'

'Well, yes, there is. I'd like to speak to Mr Diaghilev as soon as possible. I don't think I should talk to anybody else until I've spoken to him.'

'Very good. Hold on. I'm just going to set my brain to Russian – do you know, I don't think I've spoken it for a couple of months now. Mikhail makes me speak English at home. Says it'll be good for me. I'll be back in a moment.'

Natasha tripped forward to the edge of the stage. Powerscourt and Sergeant Jenkins stared in wonder as the corps de ballet began to move about the stage. It looked as if they were one single person, not fifteen.

*

The ballerina who had transported the jewels from the Fontanka Quay was not the only Russian with a mission in London that summer. Members of the Bolshevik Party, an extreme revolutionary sect, planning to take power and bring socialism to Mother Russia, had two reasons for sending a man to England. They were still sitting on the proceeds of a bank robbery they had organized in Tiflis several years before. A number of people had been killed in the shoot-out, but the haul had been enormous: 341,000 roubles. The only problem for those advocating the final liquidation of the capitalist system was that most of the money was in 500-rouble notes. And the authorities had the numbers. They could not be used or exchanged in Russia. Lenin, the leader of the Bolsheviks, and his follower Joseph Stalin had both been involved in the organization of the robbery. One of Lenin's disciples had a close friend in the Ballets Russes. So the notes were to go to London, where the disciple was instructed to contact as many revolutionaries as he could – Lenin had all the names and addresses – and enlist them in his mission. Between eleven and twelve o'clock one weekday morning, a guerrilla band of ten comrades were to take many thousands of roubles each into a series of different banks and change them into pounds. The day chosen was some days after the corpse was discovered beneath the trapdoor of the Royal Opera House. Lenin's friend was to make contact with his fellow revolutionaries, most of whom lived in working-class districts in the East End.

Lenin's disciple had a further mission. As well as the notes, concealed in the false bottoms of a trunk and a couple of suitcases, he was entrusted with another of Lenin's revolutionary tracts, proclaiming the inevitability of world revolution and describing the vanguard role to be played by the Bolsheviks. Cracow, Lenin's latest bolt-hole, was so infested with agents of the Russian Secret Service, the Okhrana, or local policemen hired to work on their behalf, that it was impossible to have anything printed in the city. Lenin's man was to have five hundred copies printed in each language and sent back to St Petersburg in the Ballets Russes luggage. The money to pay the printers was to come from the proceeds of the bank robbery.

*

Natasha was looking grave when she came back from the stage. Michel Fokine was shouting at the corps de ballet again.

'This isn't a very promising start, I'm afraid, Lord Powerscourt, Sergeant Jenkins. Fokine says that Diaghilev is in a terrible temper. It's not just the murder, apparently. His inner circle suspect he's run out of money and can't pay the bills. It's happened before, they say. Somehow or other he always manages to pull the squirrel out of the hat.' She stopped suddenly. 'Is that right? Squirrel, I mean? Something tells me it's not the squirrel.'

'Rabbit,' said Powerscourt with a smile. 'It's a rabbit out of the hat. But I'm sure it might have been a squirrel.'

Natasha laughed. 'One of the ballerinas said Diaghilev was going to see Lady Ripon. He got a lot of money out of her last year, apparently. He promises to bring Nijinsky down to her house to dance in front of her friends. She's built a little stage at the edge of her ballroom, they tell me. After Nijinsky has danced for his tea or his supper, she coughs up.'

'I suppose that makes sense,' said Powerscourt.

'Anyway,' Natasha went on, 'Fokine says we'll just have to wait. He's going to ring me when he's got some news. Nobody will speak until Diaghilev gives the all-clear. They won't even let you visit the scene of the murder without his say-so. Maybe we should all go and have a cup of coffee round the corner?'

Natasha took them to the Fielding Hotel near the Royal Opera House, where she and Mikhail often had supper after the performances. Sergeant Jenkins looked ruefully at Bow Street Magistrates Court across the way, as if he would have felt more at home giving evidence in court rather than consorting with prima ballerinas and temperamental impresarios.

'Natasha,' said Powerscourt, 'can you tell us about the ballet? I don't mean the composers or the choreographers or the artists, but the world of the dancers. What's that like?'

'Well, I don't know a great deal about the ballet, I'm afraid. I have a brother back in St Petersburg who knows all about it. He's a great ballet lover, what they call a balletomane. I can always ask him for more information. Let me see . . .' Natasha paused to help herself to a piece of chocolate cake.

'I think the ballet and the opera people all get trained at the Imperial Theatre School in Theatre Street in St Petersburg. I think they can go there as boarders when they're still quite young. They get a proper education, as well as being trained in their particular speciality, dancing or singing. Nijinsky was a pupil there – I remember my brother telling us that he was going to be the most famous ballet dancer in the world.'

'Do they get on with each other? The ballerinas?'

'You should try some of this cake, Sergeant,' said Natasha with a smile. 'It's really good. There's a bakery round the corner that's one of the best in London. In answer to your question, Lord Powerscourt, I don't think the world of ballet is an advertisement for brotherly love. Or sisterly love either. I don't think they have regular readings of the Sermon of the Mount at mealtimes.'

'Do they not get on with each other at all?'

'I think there is one word that explains so much about their behaviour. Jealousy. Just imagine, Lord Powerscourt. You've been friends with this boy or girl for a number of years. You're in the same class. You're sharing your schooldays. Then, one day, out of the blue, your friend is promoted. He or she is made up a grade. They can see their way right up to the top now, premier danseur or prima ballerina, the summit of your profession, the chance to make dramatic leaps all over the stage and heaps and heaps of money off it. But you, the one not promoted, may spend years stuck in the corps de ballet. You could be there until you take your pension. People are sometimes so possessed with jealousy that they do terrible things.'

'Stabbing each other to death with Cossack knives just used in a performance, perhaps?' said Powerscourt.

'I've never heard of anything that bad, but there are some terrible stories. One female dancer, who thought she was the one people came to see, was dancing with Nijinsky not long ago. At the end it was clear that the applause and the standing ovations that rang round and round were for him, not her. She's never danced with Nijinsky again.'

'God bless my soul,' said Powerscourt.

'Then there was another prima ballerina who found that her roles were drying up. She was cast in fewer and fewer ballets and her parts were getting smaller. She only found out the reason by accident. Another prima ballerina had gone to the choreographer Fokine we saw just now and told him that he, Fokine, must not put her rival in too many roles. She was consumptive. Too much dancing would be very bad for her health. Smaller roles, not too many performances, that was the secret.'

'It all sounds a bit like London gangsters to me – why don't we knife the boss of the gang next door?' Sergeant Jenkins was brushing chocolate crumbs off his jacket. 'I'm obliged to you, Mrs Shaporova, for the coffee and the cake. You were right about that. It's delicious. And now, if you'll excuse me, I have to get back to the station. My inspector may have found somebody who speaks Russian for me by now. I wish you both a very good day.'

Natasha Shaporova was also preparing to leave. 'I will let you know the minute I hear from Fokine, Lord Powerscourt. Do you have any plans in the meantime?'

'I do, as a matter of fact. I'm going to find out all I can about the gentleman Alexander Taneyev was staying with, Mr Richard Wagstaff Gilbert. In my rather disagreeable profession, Natasha, we learn a number of disagreeable truths. Jealousy may be one motive for murder. Money, especially money to be inherited, is undoubtedly another.'

3

Relevé

Literally 'lifted'. Rising from any position to balance
on one or both feet on at least *demi-pointe*, which is
heels off the floor, or higher to full *pointe* (commonly
for girls), where the dancer is actually balancing on the
top of the toes, supported in *pointe* shoes. Smoothly
done in some versions, a quick little leap up in other
schools.

'The buildings in the City of London are pygmies, just
pygmies,' Powerscourt said to himself as he made
his way up Lombard Street. The capital's skyline was
still dominated by the same landmark buildings that
had been there for centuries, St Paul's Cathedral, the
Monument, Big Ben. In New York, as his son Thomas
continually told him (as part of Thomas's campaign to
be taken there on holiday), there was a race towards
the stars. The 1890 World Building, at over 300-feet
high, had been overtaken by the Singer Building
in 1908, which had forty-seven storeys and rose to

612 feet. Its reign as New York City's tallest building didn't last long. It was surpassed by the Metropolitan Life Insurance Company Building, measuring 700 feet, a year later.

The London Building Act, Powerscourt remembered, prohibited buildings over eighty-feet high; that became law as a direct result of Queen Anne's Mansions, a block of flats in Westminster that were over 100-feet tall, which prompted many complaints – including from Queen Victoria herself, who objected to the new building blocking her view of her Parliament from Buckingham Palace.

Powerscourt was going to talk to his financier brother-in-law William Burke, who had risen to become very powerful in the world of money. Burke was sitting in a comfortable chair close to his marble fireplace. Powerscourt noticed that the portrait of Burke's wife – Powerscourt's sister – by the American artist John Singer Sargent, had now been joined by two further Sargents depicting the two eldest Burke daughters. The man's family is now growing on the walls of his office, Powerscourt said to himself, just as it did in real life when they lived in Chelsea all those years before.

'Francis,' said the financier, taking off his spectacles and putting down a great folder, 'how nice to see you. You've rescued me just in time.'

'Rescued you from what, William? Bankruptcy? Debtors' prison? The Marshalsea?'

'Sometimes, you know, from where I sit, those places can seem very attractive. I've got to decide whether to buy another bank or not. I've got to make a recommendation to the Board in two days' time. Do you know, Francis, I can't make up my mind.'

'I thought that you swallowed banks like other people might swallow a strawberry, William. You've been doing it for years.'

Burke laughed. 'It'll do me good to take my mind off it for a while. What can I do for you this morning? I sometimes think you only come to see me when you want information.'

'Richard Wagstaff Gilbert,' said Powerscourt. 'What do you know of the fellow?'

'Is he about to be recommended for a place on the Court of the Bank of England, Francis? A knighthood, perhaps?'

Powerscourt told him about the murder at the Ballets Russes and the fact that the victim had been staying with his uncle in a large house in Barnes guarded by two stone lions.

'I see,' said Burke, 'but before I tell you about Gilbert, does this mean that those bloody ballet dancers are back in town? The ones who were here last year? Ballets Russes, did you say? I was nearly bankrupted last summer with the wife and daughters going to see them over and over again. And for some reason, they had to have the most expensive seats in the house so they could see everything properly. I got so sick of hearing about Nijinsky every morning that I took myself off to a hotel for breakfast.'

'You'd better make a block booking at the Savoy for the fried eggs and bacon, William. They're back. They're here for about five weeks, I think. I'm surprised your women haven't begun pestering you already.'

Burke sighed. 'It could be worse, I suppose. Thank God they're not interested in racehorses. Now then, Richard Wagstaff Gilbert. I don't know a great deal about him. I know he's very rich. Some wag once said that there are basically three ways to get rich. Inherit it. Marry it. Make it at the gambling tables. Our friend has done two out of three. He inherited one heap of money from his mother. She was an American heiress whose family owned a lot of stuff in New York and Chicago. Hotels, was it? Jewellery shops? Grocers? I'm not sure. Richard Gilbert himself made another fortune at the roulette table and traded in diamonds for a while. I think he's involved with a lot of investment trusts. Some people don't care for him at all. They say he sails a little too close to the wind. Is that any good?'

'Very helpful, William, thank you very much. Are there any children, grandchildren perhaps, running round Barnes Pond with their nannies?'

'I've never heard of a wife and certainly never heard of any children either. Why do you ask?'

'Well, it's rather a long shot. You see, just at the moment I can't make much direct progress with this case. I can't talk to the man Diaghilev who runs the show. He's disappeared. But until he gives the all-clear, I can't talk to the dancers. I can't even see the place where the body was hidden.'

'I don't see, Francis, what this has to do with Gilbert.'

'Switch on your most suspicious mind, William. We investigators have to look for all sorts of things in our work: the how, the where, the why. In my experience, jealousy is a very potent weapon for murder, especially when love and marriage and fidelity are involved. But there's one other motive we meet much more often.'

'What's that?'

'Greed,' said Lord Francis Powerscourt. 'Simple, old-fashioned greed.'

*

Very few people in Paris had heard of General Peter Kilyagin. His neighbours thought he was a retired soldier. In fact, General Kilyagin was the Chief of the Okhrana, the Russian Secret Service in France. From his grand offices near the junction of the Rue de Monceau and the Boulevard Malesherbes in the fashionable eighth arrondissement, he supervised a staff of forty full-time officers and a small army of part-timers who ranged from waiters in the fashionable hotels and res-taurants to the manufacturers and shops dealing with weaponry and high explosives.

The senior ranks of the Russian military have always tolerated passions and obsessions of every sort. Mistresses, of course; hunting, music, yachting. But the General was the only one in history known for a passion for filing. This had started when he was in charge of the movement and accommoda-tion for his regiment. Everything was carefully filed. Everything had its place. When he took on his new post with the Okhrana, he was in his element. General Kilyagin was now an expert in the alphabet soup of the Russian opposition: SDs, FDs, SPDs, old Decembrists, anarchists, syndicalists, communists, Plekhanovites, Mensheviks, Bolsheviks. He kept on file every detail his team discovered about a suspect, great or small. He could find out in a moment where Lenin last had his hair cut or the address of some minor anarchist's mistress. He felt it was necessary, this vast network of surveillance that never slept. Russia was a very dangerous place, especially if you were a tsar or a senior government official. Tsar Alexander II, who had liberated the serfs, had been blown up by a terrorist bomb in the heart of St Petersburg. Grand Duke Serge, cousin of the present Tsar and Governor of Moscow, had been smashed to smithereens by a nitroglycerine bomb near the Nicholas Gate in the Kremlin in 1905. Only the previous year, the Russian Prime Minister Pierre Stolypin had been shot dead at the opera in Kiev. The Tsar and members of the Imperial Family were in the theatre to see him die. The opera was Rimsky-Korsakov's *The Tale of Tsar Saltan*. General Kilyagin liked to tell the tale of Stolypin's end. 'We told him,' he would say rather sadly, 'nobody could say we didn't tell him. We warned him not to go to Kiev. We said there was a plot to shoot him dead. But he didn't listen. The fool didn't even wear the bulletproof vest we gave him. He said it smelt bad.'

The son of the assassinated Tsar set up the Okhrana to stem the tide of assassination and revolution. Many of the opposition fled abroad to escape the clutches of the Okhrana. They didn't realize that the European network under the General's control could see as far – if not further – than the home headquarters in St Petersburg. The General's European Okhrana had very close links with the French Sûreté and its counterparts in Berlin and Vienna. They had officers in every major European capital. Their principal tactic was based on infiltrating the opposition groups. Sometimes they used *agents provocateurs*. They had a number of very attractive women on their books, prepared to sleep with a Bolshevik or a Menshevik, they didn't really mind which, or delve through his rubbish bins.

The General, oddly enough for a man in his profession, was not fond of violence. As a last resort he would call in his hard men, former soldiers of the Foreign Legion, who took their most reluctant prisoners to a chateau hidden deep in the mountains of the Cevennes. Some of the victims were never seen again.

He was a great believer in punctuality, the General. At precisely three o'clock in the afternoon, on the day Powerscourt met Natasha Shaporova again, a certain Captain Yuri Gorodetsky was shown into his office. The Captain was the senior officer in London who had a special appointment to see his boss.

'Good afternoon, Captain. I believe you have come on urgent business. You must have your hands full, with the Ballets Russes in town. They can be guaranteed to cause a certain amount of chaos wherever they go. God knows, they cause enough trouble every time they come to Paris. I don't think that rogue Diaghilev has paid his hotel bill from the time he was here three years ago.'

'I don't think he's changed, General. I don't think he'll ever change. I want your advice on a slightly different matter this afternoon, if you would.'

'Please, carry on.'

'I'm sure you remember that big bank robbery in Tiflis a few years back? The one where some people were killed and the Bolsheviks made off with an enormous amount of money?'

The General nodded. 'Not one of our better days, I fear.'

'As you know, the Bolsheviks couldn't get their hands on most of the cash. The haul was enormous, three hundred and forty-one thousand roubles. This was the snag. Most of the money, over a quarter of a million roubles, was in five-hundred-rouble notes. Most people have never set eyes on one of these. But the authorities knew the numbers. They sent them to every bank in Russia. Lenin organized a plot to cash some of the notes abroad. We managed to stop that. Now he's going to try again, in London this time.'

'Is he, by God?' said the General, taking a large cigar from the top drawer of his enormous desk. 'You've done well to track this plot down.'

'Thank you, General. There is a link with the Ballets Russes, as it happens. Lenin has a follower who works part of the time for the Ballets Russes, a member of Lenin's gang, currently holed up in Cracow. They spend a lot of time in the Café Noworolski apparently, reading the newspapers and planning the revolution. I don't think this contact brought the money with him. I suspect, but I'm not sure, that the banknotes were smuggled in by the Ballets Russes. Some of those female dancers take enough stuff with them to fill Selfridge's department store, or the Galeries Lafayette here in the Boulevard Haussmann. This is the important thing, General. Lenin's man has been meeting with a lot of home-grown revolutionaries in London. Our friends in the Metropolitan Police keep a very close eye on these characters. We believe that they are going to send a number of local revolutionaries in their best suits into a collection of banks across the City of London and the West End. Each man, we believe, will have a packet of five-hundred-rouble notes with him. They'll probably turn them into pounds or dollars – probably pounds, as that's the local currency. You could change those anywhere in Europe with no questions asked.'

'You have done well, Captain. Do you know when this is going to happen? And is it all meant to happen at once so the various banks haven't got time to warn each other?'

'I don't know how soon this is going to happen, General. I believe it is going to be very soon. Our English friends hope to get the answer to that question tonight. It was they who gave me all these details.'

'And what are the London police going to do? Do we know?'

'That is why I am here. Our English friends want to know our wishes. Should they arrest these people and put them in jail? Or should they watch and wait?'

The General took a long pull on his cigar. Outside, the noise of the children on the swings in the Parc Monceau floated in through the General's open windows.

'I can see the appeal of locking all those people up. It must be very tempting. But I'm always wary about sending these characters to prison. Even if you disperse them all over the country, there's still a risk. They go to jail knowing the trade they work in and a load of revolutionary nonsense. But think of the people they're going to meet, and the skills they could learn. You could be sent down as a carpenter and come back a burglar, or a lock picker, or a fraudster – maybe even all three. Perhaps you absorb even more revolutionary rubbish in the prison library. Is there another way round this problem?'

'I think the English police worry about publicity, General. The politicians would certainly want to lock them up. That would make them popular for a day or two. They would probably like to keep them locked away for a very long time. Suppose we just observe the operation? If we have witnesses in the banks, the police can pick up the revolutionaries any time they want and charge them with money laundering. We must have records of those bloody bank numbers in the files here.'

The General smiled a private smile as he thought of a night hunt through the grey cabinets in the long corridors down in his basement.

'Do we know what they're going do with the pounds or dollars once they've changed them?'

'No, we don't.'

'Suppose you're Lenin with that ghastly beard, holed up in his Cracow café with the newspapers and his Bolshevik friends. You wouldn't want to let your English colleagues keep the money for any length of time, would you? Their wives might spend it. They could get plenty of new friends in the pub standing everybody drinks. Maybe they could buy enough dynamite to build a few bombs.'

'How about this, General? Surely if you're Lenin, now on your fifth cup of coffee of the afternoon, you're going to get the money out the same way you sent it in. Pack it away in the Ballets Russes luggage. Next stop Paris or Monte Carlo. Plenty of banks in Monte Carlo near that great casino. You could change your new English pounds into any currency you liked in there.'

'Let's just act it through to see what the problems might be.' General Kilyagin was very fond of amateur theatricals. The shy members of his family always dreaded Christmas and the summer holidays. 'I'll be the banker. You're the Bolshevik from Bethnal Green.'

The Captain was already reaching for his wallet. 'You hand the money over,' the General went on, as his colleague duly gave him two English pound notes, masquerading as large numbers of roubles. 'Thank you very much, are you staying long? My goodness,' the General was peering closely at the note, 'we don't see these very often, even in London. Let me just check our current exchange-rate tables,' he rummaged about in his drawer. 'Here we are. That'll be eighty-four pounds six shillings and sixpence.'

As the General parted with two ten-franc notes, he slapped his hand on the table very hard. 'Damn,' he said very loudly. 'It's always good to rehearse these things. I see a problem.' The General rose from his desk and walked to the window. The children were still playing on the swings, their nannies gossiping in groups of three or four. 'I've got it!' he cried, sinking into his chair, thinking back to his days in the military. 'We funnel them, Captain, we bloody well funnel them!'

'Funnel them, General? Forgive me, I don't understand.'

'Sorry. The problem is the number of banks. It's a long time since I've been to London, but that bit round the Royal Exchange in the City, that's full of banks. I'm sure there are plenty more over in Mayfair and the West End. There must be a limit to the number of banks the Metropolitan Police can man, if you see what I mean. They could probably manage a dozen or so, but not fifty or a hundred. So they have to decide which twelve banks would suit their purposes, plenty of room to watch, that sort of thing. Then they cable all the other banks to tell them to tell any customers trying to change five-hundred-rouble notes: terribly sorry, sir, we don't have the facilities to change those here, but Blanks Bank round the corner can do it for you. Off they go to Blanks Bank, packed full of policemen in plain clothes. That's how the funnel works. What do you think?'

'I like it, General, I like it very much. With your permission I shall return to London. I'll send a cable to the Met before I go so they can set things in motion.'

'God speed,' said the General, 'and good luck.'

*

There was marble everywhere. It swept through the foyer of the Savoy Hotel and carried on for about a hundred yards to the suite of management offices at the end. A huge reception desk, manned by severe-looking men in frock coats, stuck out like the bridge on an ocean liner. Powerscourt thought these people could have been Roman senators in a previous life. Three other 'senators' in top hats swirled round the front doors, greeting the new arrivals like royalty, which they often were. A phalanx of footmen, lower in the pecking order than the senators, were also on duty. They stooped down from Mount Olympus to give directions to lost children or aged dowagers. Sometimes they escorted the new guests to their quarters in the electric lift. The Savoy was the only hotel in London which was totally powered by electricity. It was also the only hotel in the capital where all the bedrooms had their own bathroom attached.

Powerscourt and Sergeant Jenkins had been waiting for Diaghilev since nine o'clock in the morning. By a quarter to ten he had still not appeared. They had not been invited to his suite, merely told to await his arrival in the reception.

'What do you think he's doing, Sergeant? Is the man

still asleep? Eating breakfast in bed with bacon and eggs and cups of Russian tea?'

'I don't know, sir. I've never had breakfast in bed in my whole life and that's a fact. Come to think of it, I've never stayed in a hotel, either.'

'You will, Sergeant, you will. Lots of inspectors take their families to seaside hotels for their summer holidays. Your time will come.'

'I tell you one thing, my lord. You'll never guess where I went last night.'

'Go on, astonish me,' said Powerscourt.

'Why, I went to the ballet, my lord. I took my mama, as she doesn't get out that much since my father hurt his leg. She thought it was great.'

'You mean the Ballets Russes, I presume?'

'That's right. My mother was bowled over by Nijinsky. There's one dance, called *The Spirit of the Rose*, I think, where he does a great leap at the end and disappears right off the stage. It was amazing.'

'Were you as impressed by Nijinsky as your mum?'

'Yes, I was. But it was those girls in the corps de ballet who got me, my lord. Some of them were very beautiful. And they weren't wearing many clothes.'

'I'm told people don't wear too many clothes as a rule in the ballet.'

'Do you think I could ask one of them out, Lord Powerscourt? Tea in the Corner House, that sort of thing?'

'I don't see why not. If they won't come, then you just arrest them. Conduct your interview in the Corner House and then let them go for lack of evidence.'

A footman was approaching with a note on a silver tray.

'This has just come for you, sir. I believe Mr Diaghilev dictated it to one of our telephone girls. We always have one on duty who speaks French.'

'My art is more important than police procedures. I shall arrange another appointment when I have time. Diaghilev.'

'I say,' said the Sergeant, 'that's bloody rude.'

'It certainly is,' said Powerscourt, picking up his hat. 'I shall send a reply when I can think of something that will make him behave better in the future. It's not as if he's some bloody barbarian from the Russian steppes, after all. He wasn't brought up in the wilderness in Siberia like that holy charlatan Rasputin. St Petersburg is as sophisticated as any city in Europe. The man's well educated; he's been to university, he moves in the best circles in Paris and London. He just doesn't know how to behave properly.'

'Maybe them Russians don't think much of their own police force.'

'Maybe. We're going for a short walk, Sergeant. Shouldn't take long.'

'Where are we going, my lord?'

'We are going to the Royal Opera House, Sergeant. I don't care any more about what that man Fokine told us about not going to see the scene of the crime without Diaghilev's permission. Diaghilev can go to hell. We're going anyway.'

The head porters bowed as Powerscourt and Sergeant Jenkins left the sacred portals of the Savoy and headed off up Wellington Street in the direction of the Royal Opera House. They were just passing Covent Garden Market when Powerscourt stopped suddenly.

'It's old age,' he said, 'it must be. How could I be so stupid?'

'What's wrong, my lord?'

'It's the body, Sergeant, the body of Alexander Taneyev. Where is it, in heaven's name? Don't tell me Diaghilev's got it stashed away in his dressing room at the Savoy?'

'No, he's not. I must be getting old too, my lord. I meant to tell you first thing this morning. Our men took the body away the evening they found it. It's not very far away, actually. It's in the Middlesex Hospital near Oxford Circus. Some doctor or professor or maybe both is going to conduct the autopsy this morning, my lord. He'll be sending a written report, of course, but his office let us know that if we were to call in after two o'clock tomorrow, he would be able to talk us through his findings. Sorry about that, my lord, very remiss of me.'

'Don't worry. Good to know the autopsy is being carried out so soon.'

They made their way into the Royal Opera House through the works entrance at the rear, where the stage sets and other bulky items were brought in. A young carpenter brought them to the hole under the stairs where Alexander Taneyev, a Prince in Georgia, had jumped in at the end of *Thamar*.

'It's got very popular, this spot,' the carpenter said cheerfully, as he ushered them into the little room. 'I think they ought to charge people to come like they do at Madame Tussaud's. Mind you, Mr Diaghilev's had it all cleaned out and redecorated.'

There was still a strong smell of paint. The walls were pale blue. There were bare boards with no carpet on the floor.

45

'My God,' said Powerscourt. 'Who gave Diaghilev permission to tidy everything up? Why wasn't this room sealed off? Do we know what it looked like before, Sergeant?'

'As a matter of fact, we do sir. There were loads of mattresses piled up for the dancer to fall into. He was stabbed in the front. The killer appeared to have left nothing behind.'

'He might have left a hair behind, or something like that. He might have been blond, for heaven's sake. We'll never know now. Damn Diaghilev. To be fair to him it's perfectly possible he was told to leave everything as it was but the policeman didn't know that Diaghilev doesn't speak a word of English. Maybe it's a failure of communication rather than a deliberate attempt to destroy the evidence and cover up the scene of the crime.'

Powerscourt and the Sergeant went on a tour that took them round the scenery dock where the body was found, past the dressing rooms and up to the back of the main stage. Fokine was still shouting at the corps de ballet. Powerscourt wondered if it was the same complaint he had been making the day before.

'Tell me, my lord,' Sergeant Jenkins had noticed that Powerscourt's normal good humour seemed to have returned, 'they always emphasize on police courses how important it is to inspect the scene of the crime. You're meant to do it in person. Do you think it's very important?'

'I'm sure I've been told the same thing. Probably by a policeman, mind you.'

'Have you ever solved a crime or found the murderer by visiting the scene of crime?'

46

'Come to think of it, I'm not sure I have. Maybe they should revise the police manuals. What do you think, Sergeant?'

Sergeant Jenkins had been staring at the stage very hard. 'Sorry, my lord, it's those girls. Just look at that blonde one over there. And to think that some lucky bloke probably gets to pick that one up and throw her high in the air six nights a week. It doesn't bear thinking about. What was your question again, my lord?'

'Don't worry,' said Powerscourt, patting the young man on the shoulder. 'It's not important. It doesn't matter at all.'

*

Powerscourt had a standing invitation to tea at the Shaporova household any time after four o'clock. Natasha welcomed him with the finest English tea. Powerscourt was slightly disappointed. He had brought Sergeant Jenkins along because the Sergeant had told him that he, Jenkins, had always wanted to have tea from one of those samovar things. Never mind, Powerscourt said to himself: looking at Natasha for a while will take the Sergeant's mind off the corps de ballet.

Powerscourt told her about the disappearing Diaghilev and the repainted crime scene.

'Typical Diaghilev,' she said. 'Don't flatter yourself that you've been singled out for special treatment. It's perfectly normal, it happens all the time. Now then, I want to ask your advice, Lord Powerscourt. I've got a proposition to put before you.'

'Tell me more,' said Powerscourt.

'Well,' she said, pouring some more tea, 'you know how Diaghilev and Nijinsky are invited to all the best houses in London? Not just Lady Ripon; she and the Duchess of Devonshire are just the tip of the iceberg. Everybody wants to show the Ballets Russes people off in their own houses. So my plan is to invite the entire corps de ballet to lunch or tea here. Mikhail knows the Russian Ambassador quite well. I think the Ambassador owes Mikhail's bank a heap of money so he'll have to come. I can ask the priest in charge of the Russian Orthodox Cathedral of the Dormition of the Mother of God in Ennismore Gardens in South Kensington. That's The Assumption of the Blessed Virgin Mary to you heathens. Maybe he'll be able to rustle up a metropolitan or two to dress the set. We've got some icons praying away in a spare room upstairs. We'll give them an outing down here. Tea in the samovar, Russian food, lashings of vodka. Home from home in Chelsea Square. We'll make them our friends. I'll invite some Russian speakers to make them feel at home. What do you think?'

'I think it is a very cunning plan, actually,' said Powerscourt.

'I'm not sure I see why you call it cunning,'

'Well, if they are our friends, they may tell us things we wouldn't otherwise know. They could be like our spies in the Diaghilev camp. I presume you would wait until after the tea party before we start interviewing them?'

'I think it would work better that way, yes.'

'I tell you what, Natasha. It could be a great help if all these important people turn up – the Ambassador and a metropolitan or two. I've always worried that Diaghilev will simply instruct all his people to say as little as possible. He has the purse strings. He hands out the contracts. Do you want to spend the summer in Paris or not? You could ask your distinguished visitors to impress on the corps de ballet how important it is in the eyes of God and Mammon that they should cooperate fully with the English authorities. If they don't they could be stuck here in London for a very long time. They are ambassadors for the good name of the Tsar and Mother Russia, that sort of line. You follow me?'

'I do,' said Natasha with a smile. 'By the time you're through with this case, you'll be about as devious as Diaghilev, Lord Powerscourt. In fact, I suspect you already are.' She smiled.

'There is one thing I want to ask you about these interviews, Natasha. Do you think the girls would say more if it was just you doing the talking? If I wasn't there, in other words?'

Natasha clapped her hands three times and laughed. 'Goodness me, Lord Powerscourt, I don't think that is a good idea at all. For a start I might not ask the right questions. And the other reason is clear as daylight to a woman, but obviously not so clear to a man.'

'What's that?'

'You are an English milord. You are a member of the aristocracy. You know prime ministers and those sorts of people. These girls may be beautiful dancers but they are very young. Their heads may be turned. Maybe they will dream of becoming the mistress of an English milord. They can come and live in London. You must remember to wear your smartest clothes when you come to meet the girls. If you've got a real coronet in your dressing-up box, you'd better bring that too.'

4

Ballon

Ballon means 'to bounce', where the dancer can show
the lightness of the movement. This is a quality, not the
elevation or height, of the jump. Even in small, quick
jumps (*petit allegro*), dancers strive to exhibit *ballon*. A
dancer exhibiting *ballon* would spring off the floor and
appear to pause mid-air before landing.

George Walker was there. He was a docker. Albert
Smith was there. He worked on the railways. The
brothers William and Thomas Baker were there. They
were porters at Euston Station. Arthur Cooper was
there. He drove a bus. Henry Farmer was there. He
too worked in the docks. Frederick and Alfred Butcher
were there. They were miners from Kent. Joseph
Turner was there. He was a schoolteacher. John Jones
was there. He too was a docker. Walter Shepherd also
worked on the railways. Herbert Thatcher was there.
He drove a train.

These men were the twelve principal disciples of Lenin's revolutionary movement in London. The Bolsheviks weren't the only revolutionary group represented at the private meeting room in the Fox and Hounds in Rotherhithe. There were Syndicalists and Social Revolutionaries and Mensheviks, all united by extreme hatred of the capitalism that employed them at what they saw as minimal wages, maximum hours and very little concern for safety. For much of 1911 and 1912 they had been on strike or on the verge of a strike all over the country. Some of them wanted a minimum wage. Others, like the supporters of Lenin, wanted the complete overthrow of the capitalist system, an end to the power of the House of Lords, universal suffrage and the replacement of the monarchy by a Republic. Preferably all at once. Just as Christian Evangelicals believe personal salvation has to be experienced before true entry into the Church, so the Bolsheviks believed that conversion to the thinking of Karl Marx, principal saint in the Bolshevik religion, was a key part of being a true revolutionary.

Arthur Cooper, the bus driver and active trade unionist, called the meeting to order.

'Comrades,' he began, 'let me begin by thanking you all for coming to this meeting, especially when I didn't feel able to tell you what it was about.' He paused and took a long draught of his pint of mild and bitter. 'Now I can give you the full story. Very soon now we are all going to take part in a major assault on the capitalist system. We are going into enemy territory. We're going into the banks.

'Let me explain. Several years ago our colleagues in Russia organized what the capitalist Press would call a bank robbery in the Georgian city of Tiflis. You and I would say it was setting the people's money free. So tight-fisted were those bankers that they kept notes of all the numbers on the five-hundred-rouble notes. Five-hundred-rouble notes, comrades, are for so large a sum that no worker could possibly have owned one, let alone seen one. Those notes were indeed the fruits of the oppressing and exploiting class. Comrade Lenin and Comrade Stalin couldn't change these notes in Russia. They tried to change them abroad but were foiled by counter-revolutionary forces. Now it is our turn. We will have a series of bundles of notes, one for each man present, ready for distribution shortly. We will have prepared individual street maps with bank addresses so that you will all be going to different banks. This revolutionary action should start at precisely eleven o'clock. The reason for the coordination is to stop the capitalist bankers ringing up their collaborators and raising doubts about our plan. If the lackeys at the counter ask where the large note came from, you are to say that it was sent to you by the lawyers looking after the will of a rich relation in Moscow. Please ask to change the money into pounds. Please be polite. Revolutions are not won by guns alone. You are asked by Comrade Lenin to bring the money back here. We will organize its transfer to Lenin's current location to further the work of the revolution. I will try to answer any questions but I feel that revolutionary discipline should prevail. The less you know the better.'

Cooper looked round his little audience. Nobody asked any questions.

'Inside a week we shall further the cause of progress. Liberty, Equality, Fraternity! Let us close our meeting with "The Internationale".' The song had been used by socialists, communists, anarchists, democratic socialists, all the different varieties of revolutionary factions.

> *This is the final struggle*
> *Let us group together and tomorrow*
> *The Internationale*
> *Will be the human race.*

*

Powerscourt had suspected for some time that his wife Lucy slipped bad news into the conversation at times when he could not complain very loudly. They were just about to go to the theatre in a taxi when she announced that her Great Aunt Theodosia was coming to stay for a few days. She was a Stratton, this Theodosia, related to Lady Lucy on her mother's side, and very rich. Her family lived in a vast house with more servants than rooms on top of one of the largest and richest coal seams in the country. This aunt was extremely old, extremely deaf and extremely difficult. Powerscourt had once claimed that in any contest to find the most reactionary person in Britain, Great Aunt Theodosia would win at a canter.

'Why is she coming to stay with us, Lucy? Why can't she take a room at the Ritz or book a suite at the Savoy?'

'Honestly, Francis, she's a relation. People don't want to stay in strange hotels when they're as old as she is. They want to be in the bosom of their family.'

'What happens if the bosom of the family don't want them?'

'You're being unreasonable, Francis, you know you

are. Anyway, she has to come up to town on business. That's what she said, anyway.'

'What sort of business? Doctors? Wills? Solicitors? That sort of business?'

'You'll just have to wait and find out.'

Powerscourt remembered a previous conversation with Great Aunt Theodosia in the drawing room at Stratton Hall in Yorkshire. They may have been sitting on top of thousands and thousands of tons of coal up there, but the rooms were always freezing. The old lady would raise a topic and then use her victim's reaction to reveal the strength and depth of her prejudices.

'What about these women going about the place smashing things up?' she demanded after dinner. 'Suffragettes they call themselves, I believe. They'd certainly suffer if I were in charge, I can tell you. I suppose you approve of these monsters pretending to be proper women, Lord Powerscourt? It's the sort of thing fashionable people are said to agree with nowadays. Isn't that so?'

'Well,' said Powerscourt, realizing all too well that these waters were treacherous, 'I don't support their methods, Great Aunt Theodosia, but I do support their objectives. I think women should have universal suffrage. Wouldn't you like to have the vote yourself?'

'I most certainly would not, young man. Two of my relations sat in the 1832 Parliament when the Great Reform Act was passed and let some of the rabble vote. They sat for those splendid rotten boroughs which have, unfortunately, been abolished. But they voted against the changes every time they could. A great uncle of mine was in the 1867 House of Commons and he opposed the later reforms to let even more of the rabble vote. And I had three relations who voted with the Diehards last year when the House of Lords had to agree to a ridiculous Act cooked up by that wicked Asquith to rip up the constitution and limit the powers of the House of Lords. One of them wrote the closing speech for Lord Selborne: "The question is, shall we perish in the dark, slain by our hand, or in the light, killed by our enemies?"'

Great Aunt Theodosia stared at Powerscourt as if he were one of the ringleaders of this ongoing treachery over the voting system. He could still remember her final blast up there in the cold of Yorkshire.

'And another thing. They're not educated, most of the women in this country. I fancy some of the suffragette people may have learnt to read, but even those who can read don't spend their time following the passage of Bills through Parliament or the twists and turns of foreign policy. They read those dreadful magazines full of foolish gossip about film stars and people in the music hall. These women won't vote on the issues. They will vote on the looks of the candidates. Do you call that democracy?'

*

'Do you want to see the body? Some people don't.' Dr Thomas Harrison, the doctor who had conducted the autopsy was a small, sunburned man who looked as if he spent a lot of his life outdoors. Sergeant Jenkins was to tell Powerscourt later that the doctor loved walking in the Alps in spring and summer, returning with a fine tan and further specimens for his collection of wild flowers. He was in a small office next to the Middlesex Hospital morgue.

'Yes please.' Sergeant Jenkins sounded confident. This, in fact, would be the first corpse he had ever seen on duty. The doctor led the way. He nodded to the attendant to pull a body out of the trays on the wall.

Alexander Taneyev looked very peaceful and absurdly young.

'I've heard about you from my colleagues, Lord Powerscourt,' said Dr Harrison. 'They say you like complicated cases. Well, let me tell you, this is one of the most straightforward murders I have ever seen.'

'Really?' said Powerscourt.

'I'll show you the wound that killed him, if you like. Our estimated time for his death, based on the rigor mortis and so on, coincides with the timetable of the ballet. End of *Thamar*, down he leaps, the murderer is waiting, stabs him with one of those evil knives, that's the end of poor Alexander.'

'Have you seen the murder weapon, doctor?'

'I have indeed. The ballet people offered to let me hang on to one until all the formalities were complete. I said no. I didn't want one of those lethal instruments knocking about on my premises. I sent it straight back.'

'Could you describe it for us?' Sergeant Jenkins was keeping his eyes well away from the sight of the gaping wound.

'Of course. They told me it is a Cossack knife. It's very slim and incredibly sharp at the end. They're cleaned and sharpened regularly, I understand. The murderer knew enough about human anatomy to strike upwards from below rather downwards from above. The boy would have died immediately. It would have been very sudden.'

'Could you hazard a guess as to whether the murderer was a man or a woman, Doctor?'

Dr Harrison winced. 'Normally we associate death by knife wound with men. But we don't know much about the culture of these ballet people. It could have been a man or a woman. That dagger is so sharp, a child of twelve could have done it.'

*

Natasha Shaporova had hired a suite in the Fielding Hotel for interviews with the Ballets Russes. The girls wouldn't have to travel across an unknown city to a police station. They wouldn't have to change out of their costumes if they were in rehearsal. They would come in groups of three so they wouldn't feel too frightened or too alone. A samovar and a couple of miserable-looking icons had been imported from Chelsea Square.

The party for the corps de ballet in the Shaporova house the day before had been a great success. The Ambassador had turned up and made a splendid speech about the importance of proper behaviour and cooperation with the local police. It was, he assured them, rather like being invited to the country house of a rich relation you hadn't met before. You want to be asked back. This had gone down very well with the girls. The local priest had managed to enlist not one but two metropolitans. Powerscourt felt sure they must have heard about the quality of Mikhail's wines, which all came from the most prestigious vineyards in Burgundy and the Rhone valley. The holy men had glided about the room, crucifixes swaying by their waists, blessing the girls and reminding them of the church services in the cathedral. They led the gathering in singing traditional Russian hymns and folk songs at the end. Powerscourt had dressed the set, as he put it to himself, smiling at the corps de ballet like a benevolent uncle. Sergeant Jenkins had been bowled over by the beauty and the sheer numbers of the Ballets Russes dancers.

Powerscourt and Natasha had worked out a rough pattern for the interviews. She had borrowed a bilingual secretary with excellent shorthand from Mikhail's bank. Olga Penovsky was going to take notes in Russian and then type them up in English. Sergeant Jenkins was particularly pleased to be relieved of his note-taking duties.

Where were you when Alexander Taneyev jumped to his death? Did you hear anything unusual? Had you seen any strangers wandering round the backstage and the dressing rooms? When did you hear that there had been a murder? This was what Powerscourt called the first round. But, he had emphasized to Natasha, it was the second round that he was really interested in. For, as Natasha pointed out, it would have been virtually impossible for any of these girls to have carried out the murder. They were on stage at the time.

Do you have any particular friends in the corps de ballet? Do you like Mr Diaghilev? Do you like Michel Fokine? Do you like Nijinsky? What do you make of Alfred Bolm? Did he have any particular enemies? Did Alexander Taneyev? Why does Michel Fokine shout at you so much? Were there any feuds in the company that you were aware of? Is there anything you think the police ought to know?

After the first three interviews, Natasha gave Powerscourt a summary of what she had heard so far.

The girls had been sent to another room for coffee and chocolate cake and could be brought back if necessary before they returned to the Royal Opera House.

'It's more or less what you would expect, Lord Powerscourt,' she said, 'but there are one or two interesting bits. They're all frightened of Diaghilev. He seems very big to them. They were nearly all on stage at the time of the murder and heard or saw nothing unusual. Fokine shouts at them so much because he is such a good dancer himself and he thinks they are very slow to understand what he wants them to do. Deep down, I think they're quite fond of him. Alexander Taneyev was the same age as a lot of the girls. He didn't seem very interested in them. One of them wondered if Diaghilev fancied him. They all mentioned Diaghilev's affair with Nijinsky. 'He thinks we don't know, but he's wrong,' one of them told me. 'Everybody knows all about it.' The really interesting thing is this: they don't like Alfred Bolm at all. One of them blushed scarlet when his name was mentioned. Another looked down at the ground. Maybe he's tried to make love to them.'

Natasha stopped to drink her tea. 'One other thing, Lord Powerscourt, I nearly forgot. I think I can see now why Diaghilev was so quick to have the death chamber repainted and cleaned up. They all got hysterical when they heard about the murder the next morning. They didn't actually use those words, but that in effect is what they told me. One or two hysterical girls would be bad enough, don't you think, Lord Powerscourt? A whole crowd of them doesn't bear thinking about.'

By half past three the last dancer had left. The samovar was empty. Olga, the shorthand expert, had departed to her bank and her typewriters.

59

'Well,' said Natasha, looking at the notes she had scribbled down in the gaps between one group of three corps members leaving and the next trio arriving. 'Almost all of them are frightened of Diaghilev. One of them said she just gives him a big hug whenever she thinks he might be going to get cross with her. Apparently he's so taken aback he just laughs. But they are all worried that he will run out of money. One of the older ones remembers it happening before. There was a gap of a couple of months with no pay, which wasn't very pleasant for them. On the whole they're fond of Fokine. He usually apologizes after he's shouted at them, apparently. More black marks for Alfred Bolm. Nobody had a good word to say about him. I don't know what he has done. I'm certain that they could have told me but chose not to.'

'Do you think they would say more if they were on their own with you in your own house?'

'I don't know, I'm just not sure, Lord Powerscourt. Maybe some of the technical people will know more. They're usually aware of everything that's going on.'

'Even if all the girls hate Bolm, I'm not sure that takes us any further forward. Even if they did wish him harm, they couldn't have done it themselves. And I can't imagine any of them knowing enough about London to pop out and pick up a hired killer to stab him to death. We still don't know who the real victim was meant to be, for heaven's sake. Anything else, Natasha?'

She laughed. 'Well, there is one thing that will amuse you, Lord Powerscourt, as it doesn't reflect very well on London. Three of them complained about the market being so close to the opera house. That, they said, could never happen in St Petersburg. Imagine having to thread your way to the Mariinsky Theatre through rows and rows of beetroot and tomatoes and red cabbages.'

There was a very loud knock on the door. It was thrown open before anybody had a chance to say anything. The figure was wearing a dark coat with an astrakhan collar and a homburg hat. He was carrying a cane in his right hand and a sheaf of notes in his left.

'Sergei Diaghilev,' he announced himself in flawless French. 'I found I have a couple of moments to spare so I thought I would present myself. I gather you wish to speak to me. You, I presume,' he said, shaking his cane at Powerscourt's face in rather an alarming fashion, 'must be the man called Powerscourt.'

'I am indeed,' Powerscourt replied in French. 'Allow me to introduce Natasha Shaporova, wife of the banker Mikhail Shaporov, the head of the family bank in London.'

'Good,' said Diaghilev, bowing slightly to Natasha, 'bankers can be useful sometimes. They can also be very disagreeable at other times.' This was said with some menace.

'Won't you sit down, Mr Diaghilev? Would you like some tea?'

'I prefer to stand, thank you. I don't want any tea. I shan't be staying long. Perhaps you could give me some indication of what you wish to ask me?'

'What was your reaction, Mr Diaghilev, to the murder of one of your dancers at the Royal Opera House?' Powerscourt opened the batting.

'I regret it very much. My work goes on. I am an artist

and a collector and conductor of artists. Everything else is secondary to that.'

'Did you know the victim at all?'

'Of course I knew him. I hired him, you fool.'

'Do you know anybody who might wish to see understudy Alexander Taneyev dead? Or did you know anybody who might wish to see the man meant to dance the role that night, Alfred Bolm, dead?'

'These are ridiculous questions. I have no wish to make life difficult for the authorities here. But I am not prepared to speculate about members of my Ballets Russes. I am its artistic director. We have a reputation across Europe. I am not a policeman.'

'Mr Diaghilev,' Natasha was at her most charming, smiling at her visitor, 'is it true that you are going bankrupt? People are saying it all over London. Are they right?'

'This is preposterous!' shouted Diaghilev, banging his cane on the back of the nearest chair. 'I am not staying here to be insulted!'

With that, he turned on his heel and slammed the door behind him. They could hear him shouting in Russian as he made his way downstairs.

'Pity he didn't bother to say goodbye,' Powerscourt shook his head sadly.

'Rather a hasty exit,' agreed Natasha. 'Do you know, something tells me he won't be coming back to see us any time soon.'

5

Grand écart

Literally, great gap. Also known as 'spagat' in German
or 'splits' in English, is when the dancer opens his/her
legs in 180°, front or sideways.

Johnny Fitzgerald, Powerscourt's oldest friend and
companion in arms, was back in town. Ever since
the affair of the Elgin Marble he had lived mainly in
the country, supposedly researching a new book on the
birds of the Midlands. Lady Lucy had long ago established that Johnny's principal interest in the Midlands
was not, in fact, the local wildlife, but a rich widow
in Warwickshire. Lady Lucy had enlisted series after
series of interlocking circles of friends and relations in
the search for the identity of the lady concerned. She
was almost certain that her prey was a certain Lady
Caroline Milne, widow of the late Colonel Sebastian
Milne, formerly of the Life Guards and a previous
Master of the Harbury Hunt. Lady Lucy had been on
the verge of asking Johnny a number of times if Lady

Caroline was indeed the object of his interest, but she had resisted. If Johnny had wanted them to know, she reasoned to herself, he would have told them. All in good time, as her grandmother used to say.

'Well, Francis,' said Fitzgerald, 'I hear you're consorting with ballet dancers and that man Diaghilev. That's what they're saying round the town.'

'How very perceptive of you, Johnny,' said Powerscourt with a laugh. He gave Johnny the details of the case.

'And I presume that you have some delicious assignment lined up for me?' said Fitzgerald, who had visited many Valleys of Despair and Sloughs of Despond in previous cases with his friend. 'Lunch with the prima ballerinas? Dinner with Anna Pavlova if she's in town? That sort of thing?'

'I'm afraid not, my friend, I'm afraid not. Would that such entertainments were within my gift. Alas, that is not the fate I have in mind for you. But it could be worse.'

'What do you mean worse?' said Johnny darkly. 'Tell me the truth now.'

'There is a rich City businessman involved in the affair, Johnny. Name of Gilbert, Richard Wagstaff Gilbert. He lives in a big house in Barnes near the pond. He's very rich. He also happens to be a relation of the dead dancer Alexander Taneyev. He's his uncle. I want to know all about him.'

'Why? Are you looking for some hot investment tips, Francis? Buy Latin American copper, that sort of thing?'

'Well, you never know when that might come in useful. The first major problem in this case is this: who was meant to be the victim? The boy Alexander was the understudy. A much more famous fellow was meant to be dancing the part of the Prince, but he cried off. I know you're going to ask me why and when he vanished from the stage, as it were, and I can only say that I don't know yet. I haven't been able to talk to him. Relations with Diaghilev are a bit frosty at the moment, so that may have to wait even longer. Our friend in Barnes appears to have no children. We know Alexander was his nephew. How many more nephews, cousins, brothers or sisters does our man have? That would be interesting.'

'Francis,' said Johnny, looking sadly at his friend, 'you're getting too devious for your own good. It must be these Russians. I think you suspect that Alexander whatever he's called might have been Gilbert's heir. If that is the case, who might the new heir be? He would, certainly, have a strong motive for lurking round the bowels of the opera house with a nasty dagger in his hand. Is that what you want me to find out?'

'It is.'

'Why didn't you say so at the beginning? I'll get started right away.'

*

Sergeant Rufus Jenkins had recruited a couple of English assistants among the younger members of staff at the Royal Opera House. The elder boy, Jamie, had just started work when the Ballets Russes first appeared in London the year before. He was employed because his father was chief electrician. Jamie could even remember some of the ballet dancers' names, something the Sergeant thought might be beyond his powers. He, the Sergeant, had bought himself a little book that claimed to teach you how to speak Russian. The Sergeant realized very quickly that this would be hard work. French, as he used to say to his mother, had always been Greek to him at school. Why did the Russians have to have a different alphabet? Furthermore, why did they have to have so many letters – six more, by the Sergeant's arithmetic, than the English version? Why did 'Cc' sound like 's' in see and 'Pp' sound like a rolled 'r', for heaven's sake? It was enough to make a man despair.

Sergeant Jenkins' other recruit worked as a stage-hand and scene shifter and general dogsbody. Nicholas wanted to be an actor and this was the only job he could find that took him into a theatre. And it was Nicholas who provided the first burst of news from the world of the Ballets Russes, over a pint of bitter at the Lamb and Flag in Rose Street, known as the Bucket of Blood in an earlier century. Jenkins didn't want the Russians to see the connection between himself and his in-house spies, as he mentally referred to them.

'It was a fight, Sergeant, right in the middle of the stage, must have been about eleven o'clock this morning.'

'Not so fast, my friend. Who was on stage? What were they rehearsing? Who was fighting?'

'Well, from what I heard, I think they were running through a new routine for *Les Sylphides*.'

Nicholas had a pair of aunts who lived in Brittany, so he had picked up some idiomatic French, including a number of swear words, the precise meanings of which he was unsure.

'That choreographer who shouts at them all the time, Mr Fokine, he was doing his stuff.'

'And who was doing the fighting?'

'Two girls from the corps de ballet. One of them was that tall redhead called Kristina. The other one was a brunette and I don't know her name. I could point her out to you next time you're in the place, if you like.'

'That would be very kind. Was it like a boxing match? Wrestling maybe?'

'It was pretty fierce stuff. The brunette had apparently accused the one called Kristina of having given in to Bolm's advances. She denied it. There was a lot of shoving and a lot of biting. The redhead was trying to pull something out of her stocking when they were stopped. It might have been a knife.'

'A knife like the one used in the murder? One of those Cossack daggers?'

'God help me, I hadn't thought of that. It could have been, I suppose, but I'm not sure.'

'So who stopped it?'

'Mr Fokine and one of the big stagehands, one of the Russian ones, had to force them apart. The redhead had blood pouring out of her shoulder. The other one was limping. They were both taken away. Mr Fokine gave everybody else half an hour off. I saw him having a very large vodka all by himself in the bar. It's always open for the Russians that place, even at breakfast time.'

'Nicholas, you've done well. Please try to find out what they were fighting about. Maybe there's going to be another round.'

*

The early evening sun was still streaming through the great windows of Lady Ripon's drawing room at Coombe. She had just rearranged the flowers to her

67

satisfaction. Honestly, it was so hard these days to find staff who knew how to do things properly. She had already been to the ballroom where she had recently built a small stage for the ballet, the floor raked at an angle like the one at the Mariinsky Theatre in St Petersburg. Russian dancers always complained about the flat floors of London and Paris. Round the stage, twenty seats had been placed. Here at least the work had been carried out perfectly, probably because Lady Ripon had supervised every move herself.

She was wearing her rubies tonight, with the Nattier-blue taffeta dress. She had recently had all her jewels reset by Cartier in the fashion of the day, rather than the heavy gold settings of Victoria's time. The dining room was her last port of call with Crooks, the butler, in attendance. She was, as she told her maid later that evening, only just in time. The first problem was the table itself. 'Just look at those champagne flutes, Crooks. Can't you see they're in the wrong order? Sort it out, please. My word, you have to have your eyes about you these days.'

Lady Ripon turned her attention to the seating plan. Crooks held out the red leather pad with slits to hold the names and place settings of the guests and the order of precedence on the way into dinner.

'Good God, you don't expect me to be taken in to dinner by that fool Twiston-Frobisher, do you? I don't care if he isn't English, I must be taken in by Mr Diaghilev. It's my party and he's the guest of honour. I do believe Frobisher's the stupidest man in England. And you can't put Sir Ernest next to Lady Trumpington, he'll be bored to tears. And the Ambassador – he'll expect to be next to Mrs Sackville. He's been crazy about her for years.'

By eight o'clock all the guests had arrived except the Russians. Lady Ripon began to grow anxious. Her husband, an older and larger figure, was deep in conversation about cricket with the retired Brigadier who lived next door. By half past eight, Crooks the butler was whispering that the food could not be delayed much longer or it would spoil. He also pointed out that in the absence of Diaghilev and Nijinsky, the only appropriate person to take Lady Ripon in to dinner was Sir Felix Twiston-Frobisher. The guests were beginning to look at their watches in a pointed fashion by now. At ten to nine the butler reported that the chef and the sous chef were threatening to leave and take up another position in a house where their skills would be properly recognized. At five past nine Lady Ripon relented and was taken into dinner by the stupidest man in England. Half an hour later, as the lobster was being served, she had changed her mind. She was now sure that Sir Felix must be the stupidest person in the entire world.

Diaghilev came with the pudding. He was, he assured Lady Ripon, so fond of pudding that he would gladly forgo all the previous courses so as not to disturb the pattern of such an elegant dinner. Lady Ripon's spirits began to rise. They rose still further when she led the way to the little stage in her ballroom. It was lit entirely by candlelight. Nijinsky danced part of his role in *The Spirit of the Rose*. The guests were enchanted. Lady Ripon's Russian evening was saved.

*

Tap tap tap. Tap tap tap. Tap tap tap. Captain Yuri Gorodetsky's right foot was beating out a permanent rhythm on the wooden floor of his office. The Captain was normally a placid and peaceful soul. The uncertainties of military life had been replaced by a more regular occupation, even if that was being a secret service officer in pursuit of terrorists and revolutionaries. Captain Yuri Gorodetsky felt he had made a mistake – well, oversight might be a better way of putting it. He was walking up and down and waiting for the man who could reprimand him – who was also the man who could solve his problem – to speak to him on the telephone. The people in Paris had assured the Captain that General Peter Kilyagin, the man in charge of the Okhrana in Western Europe, was in his headquarters building. He had not yet gone home. He would be with the Captain in a moment.

'Gorodetsky! My dear fellow, how are you?' The General's voice was very loud, almost as if he was speaking from the next room.

'I am well, General. But I fear I may have made a mistake.'

'What's the problem? I'm sure we can sort it out.' At least the General seemed to be in a good mood. He had a fearsome temper and had once shouted at one of his subordinates for twenty-five minutes without stopping.

'It's about those revolutionaries trying to change the money from Lenin's bank robbery in Tiflis, General. You remember your plan to funnel them into twelve banks rather than let them spread out all over London?'

'Of course I remember. Bloody Bolsheviks from Bethnal Green. What's gone wrong?'

'I forgot one thing, sir. The bankers have spotted the problem and they want an answer tonight. Do they hand over the money – the English money, I mean. They say that if you can't change the money in Russia it's probably worthless. They suspect that the Russian authorities have cancelled all these notes.'

'What do they want us to do about it?'

'They want a guarantee that they will be fully recompensed for all the English pounds they may hand over tomorrow. You won't have forgotten, General, that we could be talking about a quarter of a million roubles.'

'I haven't forgotten. I'd be surprised if that amount of money goes on parade in the City of London tomorrow morning, mind you. I'm sure some of the notes will have disappeared, liberated on their journey, as our revolutionary friends might put it. Do you know, that's more than the annual budget for my whole department.'

'Mother of God!'

'Let me think for a moment, Captain. Don't go away. I'm just going to put the phone down for a minute.'

Captain Gorodetsky thought he could hear very faint footsteps coming down the line from Paris. Perhaps the General was marching around his office. General Kilyagin was tracking the bureaucratic route map he would have to use if he followed normal procedures for a question of this sort. This would involve not only the state bank, but also a number of different departmental bureaucracies. It would at some point enter the Winter Palace or the Tsar's Alexander Palace at Tsarskoe Selo in the country close to St Petersburg. At this time of year, the bloody Tsar might be on his yacht, or even going to Livadia in the Crimea on his special train, always accompanied by an identical special train to confuse the men with bombs. General Kilyagin felt certain that once his problem was inside the magic circle of Tsar Nicholas, his ghastly wife and the totally unpredictable Rasputin, any sensible request could be thrown out on a whim. Some grand duke might roll up and scupper the whole thing. General Kilyagin thought of phoning the Minister of Finance direct, but he thought the man might be drunk by this time of day. He was to say later that his mind was made up by a carriage on the Rue Monceau that performed a daring series of swerves to avoid running over two small boys who had wandered into the middle of the road.

'I've got it!' he yelled down the phone. 'Give the Bolsheviks from Bethnal Green the money! All of it. Don't hesitate. Pay up! Tell these miserable bankers that the Russian authorities will compensate them for every last pound or rouble they may have to pay out. You can give them my word on that!'

'Thank you for that, General, thank you very much. Would you like the English police to arrest the Bolsheviks and confiscate the English money? They're in receipt of stolen goods, after all.'

It was at this point that the General showed he was a master of strategy as well as a master of tactics.

'No, no, leave them be. Let's play this little game out right to the end. And let's take a leaf out of their Bolshevik book. Ask the English bankers to hand the money over in the largest possible denominations, hundred-pound notes if they've got such things. And for God's sake tell them to make a note of the numbers on the notes they hand over. We can circulate every bank in Europe with those numbers and arrest every Bolshevik who tries to turn them into any other currency, Polish zlotys or roubles or Swiss francs. There's only one proviso, Gorodetsky. You've got to keep your eyes on what happens to the money. The English revolutionaries will want to get rid of it as soon as possible. They will have to go to somebody who can get it back to Russia or maybe even to Lenin's café in Cracow in the Ballets Russes luggage. You've got to watch that luggage like a hawk, my friend. Like a hawk.'

'Should our English friends intercept the luggage before it goes on its travels?'

'I said we should play the game right to the end, Captain. We follow the luggage. We follow whoever picks up the money out of the luggage. We follow them wherever they go. At the point when the handover is actually happening, we arrest everybody. That would also be the time for our English friends to arrest the Bolsheviks from Bethnal Green if that's what they decide to do. If they arrest them any earlier, word will get to Lenin in his bloody café and the whole plan will be changed. We've got to play it long.'

6

Allegro

Meaning brisk, lively. A term applied to all bright, fast, or brisk movements. All steps of elevation in ballet fall under the term 'allegro' such as *sautés*, *soubresauts*, *changements*, *échappés*, *assmeblés*, *jetés*, *sissonnes*, *entrechats*, and so on. The majority of dances, both solo and group, are built on *allegro*. The most important qualities to aim at in *allegro* are lightness, smoothness and *ballon*.

Great Aunt Theodosia was definitely outstaying her welcome. She had been meant to go home the day before yesterday. She didn't go. She was meant to go tomorrow. Powerscourt could still hear the diatribe after supper in the drawing room the night before.

'Another thing, these dreadful trade units or trade unions or whatever they call themselves. They're always going on strike for more money, it seems to me, always. You can't open a newspaper today without reading about more of their antics. It's as if they think

74

they have as many rights to the fruits of their labour as their employers. What rubbish! You support those people as well, I suppose?'

Powerscourt wondered what it would be like to be the last liberal standing in an arena dominated by the Great Aunt. Probably like being the last gladiator left alive in the Coliseum before an emperor in a bad mood.

'Well,' he tried, 'I don't always agree with their methods. But I do believe in decent wages for these people. Most of them have wives and families to look after.'

'Stuff and nonsense! Stuff and nonsense! I blame Judge Williams myself. It's all his fault, if you ask me. I don't suppose you liberals even know who Judge Williams was, do you?'

Powerscourt shook his head.

'He was the fool in charge of those early trade unionists or whatever they're called. Your sort call them the Tolpuddle Martyrs, I believe.'

'What did he do wrong, Great Aunt?'

'Wrong? Wrong, you say? It's perfectly clear what he did wrong. He only sent them to Australia, didn't he? He should have had them all hanged, every single one of them. That would have been an example to the lower orders. Just think, we might have been spared Australia and Australians altogether if they hadn't sent the convicts there. Think of the money they'd have saved if they'd all been hanged. The cost of one piece of rope against a ship stuffed with sailors and jailors to guard the prisoners and months and months at sea! Have you ever met any Australians?'

Powerscourt admitted that he had not yet had the pleasure.

'Terrible people. Deplorable manners. Terrible accent,

you can't tell what they're saying most of the time! To think we could have been spared all that!'

*

George Smythe was one of those well-bred young Englishmen who always wear their clothes well. By day he wore them as a trainee at one of London's prestigious picture galleries, where he was expected to dress the set and persuade old ladies to part with the Raphaels in the attic. By night, in slightly different clothes, he was a man about town, often until dawn, for he loved parties. He was never at his best in the morning. He was also a cousin of Prince Felix Peshkov, the young man who had taken part in the daring jewellery raid on the mothers' collections before the ball at the Winter Palace in St Petersburg. The gems and precious stones were now in the luggage of the corps de ballet, where they had been stored by the Prince's Russian friend Anastasia. It had taken Anastasia, now in London as a member of the corps de ballet, a long time to call on George, whose address she had been given shortly before she left St Petersburg. Now she had entrusted a small, but – she hoped – representative selection of jewels to the aristocratic embrace of George Smythe, who was conducting a reconnaissance of possible buyers in Hatton Garden, London's diamond quarter. Anastasia had been left in a branch of Lyons Corner House at the far end of the street.

'Johnston Killick, traders in gold, diamonds and precious metals' seemed to George to fit the bill.

'Good morning, sir,' said George with one of those smiles you acquire at Eton and Christ Church.

'Good morning to you too sir,' said Mr Killick.

76

Each automatically began trying to work out if the other man was honest.

'And what can I do for you this morning, sir?' said Mr Killick, reminding himself that there was nobody more dangerous in London than the aristocratic con man, fourth or fifth sons perhaps, now on their beam ends, virtually sleeping rough.

'It's these jewels,' said George. 'These are a few of the best,' emptying his haul onto the counter and reflecting that the middle-aged like Mr Killick often had half a lifetime of crime behind them.

'My word, sir,' said Mr Killick, pulling out a glass and giving the precious stones serious inspection. 'These are fine indeed; easily the best I have seen this year.'

That's just the kind of thing the man would say, George Smythe said to himself.

'The whole collection – I presume you are interested in selling the whole collection? – is bigger than the samples you have brought this morning? How much bigger?'

George didn't like the word 'samples', as if he were selling dodgy carpets, but his upbringing kept him quiet.

'Fifty times larger maybe? A hundred times larger?'

'Great God,' said Mr Killick, who went over to the front of the shop and closed the door.

'I have to ask, where are they from? They do not look to me as though they were from this country.'

'They were a legacy, from my grandfather in Moscow,' George said. He and Anastasia had agreed this as a reasonable explanation of the jewels' origin.

'Were they indeed?' said Mr Killick, with the faintest hint of suspicion in his voice.

'And why did he not leave them to a granddaughter?'

George and Anastasia had not thought of this, but his time in the art world served him well.

'He didn't have any granddaughters, I'm afraid.'

'You don't have a copy of the will, I suppose?'

'I'm afraid not. All the papers are locked up in a Moscow bank.'

'From whence they are unlikely to depart for these shores, I presume, sir?'

'I'm afraid not.'

Mr Killick smiled, and George thought for a moment that Killick might be honest after all.

'Very well,' the jewel trader said. 'Can I ask you a question? Are you in a hurry to sell these items?'

'Yes,' said George, thinking of the departure dates of the Ballets Russes and the possibilities they afforded for concealment.

'Very well, I will tell you what my advice is. You will not like it, I fear. I shall keep the shop closed. I want you to go and bring me the entire collection back here. I shall leave some of the items English ladies like for my colleague here to see if he can effect a private sale in London. The rest I shall take to Antwerp, where European private buyers have different priorities in the matter of jewels. I shall be there for three or four days. I may have to travel to Berlin or Munich. Under no circumstances will I offer any of the items to Russian buyers. It is also of the utmost importance that the house of Fabergé here in London do not hear of it, for they would surely be in touch with their counterparts in St Petersburg.'

Killick paused. 'Have I forgotten anything?'

George Smythe stared hard at the jewel trader. 'Two

things, Mr Killick. One, how do I know that you will not disappear with my grandfather's legacy? And, second, how much do you think they will be worth?'

'I shall not disappear, sir. We have dealt with diamonds and precious stones for the coronations of most of the crowned heads of Europe here. If they disappear we should lose our good name and our honour, both of which are irreplaceable. I will not insult you by offering to post a bond in your favour with some local bank. Your jewels could be worth fifty thousand guineas; they might be worth twice that much. It is hard to say without examining them all. Either we trust each other, sir, or we don't. If you don't trust me, I wish you and your samples a very good day. But come, you must make up your mind. The trains to Antwerp are much worse in the afternoon.'

George Smythe never admitted that it was the mention of coronations that persuaded him. But it did. He shook Mr Killick by the hand, gave him his card, and set off to find Anastasia and bring the rest of the stolen haul.

The door of Mr Killick's shop remained closed for the rest of the day.

*

Richard Wagstaff Gilbert. Richard Wagstaff Gilbert. Johnny Fitzgerald said the name over and over to himself as he began his latest assignment for his friend Powerscourt. It had a certain ring to it. Johnny placed a couple of advertisements in the local newspapers asking for information about the gentleman in connection with a will from Brazil. There were people, Johnny knew, who placed great store in information received from these advertisements in the press, but neither he nor Powerscourt had much faith in them.

Instead he headed for a place his companion in arms would not naturally have associated with him, the financial district of London or, to be more precise, the wilder shores of the City of London. Lady Lucy had indeed been correct in her discoveries about lovers in Warwickshire. Lady Caroline Milne was the lady with whom Johnny was romantically inclined. She was also involved in trying to sort out the financial affairs of her late husband, Sebastian, a man quick over the hedges and fences of hunting country and equally quick, apparently, where money was concerned. Lady Caroline had told Johnny about her problems.

'Honestly, darling, I wonder if you could help me. There are all these papers in a locked drawer in Sebastian's study. I've had them opened and the solicitors took one look at them and said they were not qualified to give a judgement. Such investments, said the chief legal man, who's seventy if he's a day, are unknown in these parts. He gave it as his opinion that such transactions are seldom seen in Warwickshire. Honestly, darling, what's the old goat there for if he can't tell me what they mean? I've tried to read the wretched things, of course I've tried, but they're simply too boring to read. Could you take it on, Johnny? I'd be so grateful.'

Johnny might not have admitted it to himself, but he would have done virtually anything for Lady Caroline. He discovered that the late Master of the Harbury Hunt was a man permanently short of cash. Rather than selling a few thousand acres, he had dabbled in those investments always to be found in centres of finance, the ones that promise to bring forth a higher return, more ample rewards, than conventional stocks and shares. Well might William Burke and his fellows advise against anything offered at too high an interest rate, to Colonel Sebastian Milne and his ilk, high interest rate were the words they wanted to hear more than anything else in the world.

Most of Johnny's funds had prospered and grown in the care of William Burke. But he had a secret portfolio of his own. Johnny Fitzgerald liked investing in things he knew about. He had a considerable holding in the stock of the German camera and binocular company whose products he employed on his bird-watching missions. The same with a firm of American clothing manufacturers, whose garments kept Johnny warm in all conditions. Careful not to put all his eggs in foreign baskets, he also had shares in a couple of English breweries whose beer he liked. He told himself that Burke would feel the beer holdings balanced out the foreigners.

This morning Johnny was on his way to see the principal investment adviser to the late Colonel Sebastian Milne, a man called Sweetie Robinson, whose offices were close to, but not in, Chancery Lane. Johnny had had many dealings with him already over the financial affairs of the late Colonel. Cynics – and there were many, it has to be said – claimed that Sweetie felt he would be protected by the proximity of all these lawyers, silks and briefs available for hire like taxis at the great London railway stations. Of the origins of the name Sweetie there were many theories, the favourite being that he owned stock in all the sweet manufacturers in the capital, so much did he like their products. The other was that it was a term of affection bestowed on him by one of the many wives and mistresses who had graced his life, the endearment being passed down, as it were, through the female line.

'Johnny Fitzgerald,' Sweetie bawled as Johnny sat down in his office, 'how good to see you! I've got some papers for you by the way, don't let me forget them, about our mutual friend the late Colonel. Don't suppose the widow will like them, for they show a bundle of losses. Never mind, Johnny, I'm sure you'll be able to offer other forms of consolation!'

With that he guffawed and blew a vast cloud of smoke from his cigar. 'Now then,' Sweetie went on, what brings you to this lawyers' conclave today, my friend?'

'I want some advice, Sweetie, and I can't think of a better spot to get it than here.'

'I'm sure you've come to the right place,' said Sweetie, pausing to wave at a couple of silks on their way to glory in court. 'What do you need in the way of investments? I've had a couple of dodgy ones pass through here in recent days, I should say: mining for gold in the Peloponnese, on the grounds that there was so much gold about that the Spartans must have had a source for it. And –' Sweetie helped himself to a humbug from the bowl in front of him – 'what about this: advertisements for a fund to investigate turning water into wine. Man said if some uneducated carpenter's son could manage it at a wedding in the Middle East, surely it could not be beyond the wit of man to reproduce it here and now in the West End of London. Shares start at five pounds a pop. Few takers so far, I'm told.'

'Did the man offer the reverse?'

'I'm not with you, Johnny. Explain yourself, man.'

'Why, if they learnt how to turn water into wine, they could surely turn wine into water by the opposite process?'

Johnny was appalled at the thought of these alchemists being let loose in the vineyards of Burgundy or Bordeaux. It would be the end of the world as he had known it.

'Don't think there'll be many takers, as I said.'

'Well, that's a relief,' said Johnny, pleased that the vineyards of Europe had been reprieved. 'I want to ask you about a man called Richard Wagstaff Gilbert. What do you know of the fellow?'

Sweetie laughed and helped himself to a replacement humbug. 'Richard Wagstaff Gilbert, or Waggers as he's known in the less respectable parts of the Square Mile. I knew his past would come up and nip him in the leg one of these days. What's he been up to that I haven't heard about?'

'I'm afraid the trumpets aren't sounding for him just yet on the other side,' said Johnny, eyeing the humbugs suspiciously. 'It's just that I need to know what sort of man he is, how he makes his money, that sort of thing.'

Sweetie turned in his chair and looked out of his window. No cavalcade of lawyers could be seen to offer reassurance.

'Waggers, I'll tell you the thing about Waggers, as he's known in these parts. You know how some black-guards are often referred to as two-faced bastards, or even ruder words than bastards. Well, Waggers has at least four faces, probably even more that I don't know about. The surface Waggers – what you get when you open the parcel, if you like – is deep into investment trusts. He believes – and there are many who would agree with him – that these collective vehicles, these umbrella companies, holding a wide variety of stock in different parts of the world, are the way forward. There is no more tireless promoter of them than Waggers.

'Dig a little deeper and you find Waggers the promoter, Waggers the back-room boy, if you like; a man operating, almost in the darkness, to promote certain new issues. I know for a fact that he has been pushing the mining in the Peloponnesian venture. But – and this is the curious thing – he never invests himself. Not a sou or a mark or a franc or a rouble or even a dollar leaves his coffers for these attractive new ventures.'

'Do we know why?' asked Johnny. 'Is there a motive lurking behind the promotion?'

'Motive? Did I hear you say motive, Johnny? Do I detect the ghost of Lord Francis Powerscourt lurking in the shadows behind your shoulder? The great investigator himself?'

'Well, as a matter of fact, you do, Sweetie. And he doesn't like humbugs either. But come, before we move on to the last two Wagstaffs, is there a family Wagstaff? Little Wagstaffs in Little Lord Fauntleroy suits scampering around Barnes Pond? Any of those?'

'I see you are still at first base, my friend. Richard Wagstaff is single. His heirs, if you like to go there, and I feel sure you do, are all nephews, offspring of his two younger sisters. There was a daughter to one of them, but she died of some terrible illness.'

'Would you happen to have the names and addresses of these married Wagstaff sisters, Sweetie?'

'You can have them for a consideration, my friend.

The times are not so generous that a man can give valuable information away for nothing.'

'You shall have my consideration when I leave, Sweetie. I take your point. But what of the other Wagstaffs? We have only been introduced to two.'

Sweetie Robinson looked very serious all of a sudden. 'These are deep and troubled waters, my friend. The last two may hold the key to all the others.'

'You're speaking in riddles, Sweetie. Out with it, and you can have another humbug.'

'The third Waggers is an obsessive card player, so successful that few men who know him will play with Waggers for money.'

'And the fourth? What of the fourth?'

'The fourth is so dangerous that it could finish him off and end his position in society.'

'That sounds pretty serious, Sweetie. Tell me all.'

'It is. The fourth Richard Wagstaff Gilbert cheats at cards.'

7

Plié

Probably the most commonly known exercise performed in ballet. A *plié* is a bending of the knees, a bending action where the knees bend over the toes while the dancer's heels remain on the floor. A *demi-plié* is simply a small bending of the knees while a *grand-plié* is a full bending of the knees where the heels do actually come off of the floor. *Pliés* assist a dancer in many exercises performed, especially in jumping.

The real Francis Powerscourt was pacing about his drawing room in Markham Square. He was expecting a state visit from Lady Ripon and the prospect did not make his heart sing with joy. Lady Lucy had deserted him, saying that she would be going shopping in Sloane Street and trusted that the dreadful woman, as she referred to Lady Ripon, would be gone on her return.

'I don't expect it'll take long. I'm not sure if I'll be treated like the tenant of one of the farms on her estate or like a junior footman who has committed some unspeakable crime, like setting the forks out in the wrong order at a dinner party.'

'Lady Ripon, my lord.'

As she advanced into hostile territory, she managed to secure Powerscourt's favourite armchair by the side of the fire.

'Have you solved the murder mystery yet, Powerscourt? And if not, why not?'

Powerscourt protested that they had had little time so far, and that the language difficulty was proving to be a problem.

'I've always found, Powerscourt, in my experience in society, which is considerably wider than yours, that if you speak English loudly and often enough to these foreign persons, they will understand in the end.'

'Doesn't seem to work with the Russians, Lady Ripon. Perhaps it's the different alphabet and so on. Makes things even more difficult; a different sort of language, I think you'll find.'

'Stuff and nonsense. You haven't been trying hard enough. So you haven't solved the mystery and located the murderer. Pretty poor, if you ask me. So what exactly have you been doing?'

'Well, Lady Ripon . . .' Powerscourt had now established that in the Lady Ripon pecking order, he was the butler, personally responsible for some vast disaster on the catering front. 'We have talked to the corps de ballet through the good offices of Natasha Shaporova, whom I believe you know.'

'I do know Mrs Shaporova, and I have heard reports of these rather intimate gatherings where information is passed around with the tea. But they can't have done it, Lord Powerscourt. Even you must see that. They were on stage at the time. Were you talking of Mrs Shaporova's kind offer to help, Powerscourt? Are you carrying on with that young woman? It has been suggested to me, I have to report. It would explain your tardiness in detection. Are you carrying on with Natasha Shaporova, Powerscourt?'

'I am not, Lady Ripon, and I regard it as a gross breach of my hospitality to even suggest it in my house.'

'Oh well, I suspect you're far too old for her, Powerscourt. What, pray, are your plans for the future in this investigation?'

'We shall continue our work, Lady Ripon. I shall, of course, inform you of any developments.'

'I happen to have with me a most interesting development, as you choose to call it. I have in my bag –' a capacious vehicle it was too – 'an invitation from the Duke of Marlborough for Diaghilev's Ballets Russes to perform two or three short ballets at Blenheim Palace, one for the Duke and his friends in the Great Hall, and the other in the open air for the surrounding populace. And a generous fee! What do you think of that?'

Powerscourt wondered if the real purpose of this visit hadn't been to show off what was in her handbag. 'I shall certainly attend, Lady Ripon, it sounds most interesting.'

'You will have to find your place among the agricultural labourers and the poor of Woodstock, Powerscourt. I shall take great care over the guest list for the palace itself. Maybe you'll find more enlightenment among the rabble in the park than you have been able to do so far in the people of the Ballets Russes.'

*

Word reached Diaghilev in one of the dressing rooms of the Royal Opera House. There were a couple of cleaned and freshly ironed shirts to the side of the dressing table and a long purple scarf hanging on the back of the door. There was the usual chaos of make-up jars, cleansing lotion, cold creams and all the apparatus needed to make up a ballerina for her performance. Diaghilev and his choreographer, and Bakst his principal designer, were discussing a new ballet to be performed in Paris the following year. The note was handed to Diaghilev. He passed it round.

'This is ridiculous,' he said. 'These English must think we are some travelling circus, pitching our tents here and there as the will takes us. Or travelling monks, maybe, processing through Siberian villages with some mystery plays. What do you think, Fokine?'

'Well, Sergei Pavlovich, I had the good fortune to be briefed by the Duke's man of business last night. But his French was very bad, so I am not clear at all on many points.'

'What is this Blenheim Palace? Where is it? I thought the only palace here was that little one they call Buckingham with the toy soldiers marching up and down.'

'I believe,' Fokine was scratching his head now, 'that Blenheim was a battle in southern Germany that ended in an English victory. The General was made Duke of Marlborough and they gave him a palace as a thank-you present. The house was built in the early seventeen hundreds and is considered to be one of the finest in England.'

'Pshaw,' said Diaghilev. 'They speak of a performance in the open air for the surrounding peasantry. How are we to do that, in heaven's name? I think we should say no. Bakst, what is your view?'

'There are obviously great difficulties. But five thousand pounds is a great deal of money. And we have always argued, from the earliest times, that art should be brought to as many people as possible. We could at least aspire to that here.'

Bakst had always suspected that when Diaghilev referred to the widest possible audience he was referring to the workers by brain rather than the workers by hand. He, Diaghilev, really wanted the intelligentsia of St Petersburg and Paris to rejoice at his talents, rather than members of some mighty proletariat who travelled on foot or by bus rather than by barouche or taxi.

'The money is just a drop in the ocean,' Diaghilev said rather sadly. The gossip about his being on the edge of bankruptcy was pretty close to the mark. What really irked him was the prospect of leaving the Savoy Hotel and its luxury, high-class food available at all hours of the day and night.

'Is this place what we would call a palace, Fokine?'

'I do not think, if it is anything like the Buckingham, it will be what we could call a palace at all. It sounded to me like a superior sort of hunting lodge with great military honours displayed on the inside.'

'And they expect us to put on our art in a hunting lodge for five thousand pounds in all the uncertainties of the damned English weather? What do we do if it rains, in heaven's name? The colour would start to run out of your bloody costumes, Bakst, wouldn't it?'

Bakst laughed. 'Sergei Pavlovich, it would be a lasting reminder of the impermanence of art, the transient nature of beauty.'

'Do you think the bloody peasants will appreciate that? I bet their smocks don't disintegrate in the rain. I don't want to accept the offer, gentlemen. But I don't want to upset any of the English aristocracy. Some of them have enormous incomes from coal and investments. They could bail out our poor company and not notice they'd done it.' Diaghilev picked up the purple scarf and let it run through his fingers. 'Would these colours hold in the rain, Bakst? Don't tell me. I know what we are going to do. Fokine, can you get back in touch with the Duke's man of business? Tell him we are honoured by his invitation. It would be a great tribute to the Ballets Russes to perform in such an august location. Lay it on with a trowel, Fokine, you know how to do that. Just tell him the money is wrong.'

'What do you want me to say? Eight? Ten, for heaven's sake?'

'Let's not beat about the bush, gentlemen. Great art has its price. Tell him twenty-five thousand pounds.'

*

Captain Yuri Gorodetsky of the London branch of the Russian Secret Service, the Okhrana, had always suffered from anxieties about the telephone. There was nothing rational about his concerns – he had even read through a manual for one of the wretched objects and understood how it worked. But he wondered, often last thing at night after a couple of hefty swigs at the vodka bottle, if other voices might come out of it, Peter the Great come to upbraid the inhabitants about their slowness in building his great city St Petersburg, Tolstoy on the line urging all those connected by those strange wires to abandon the sins of the flesh and join him in the universe of love on the way to some provincial railway station. His tidings this morning, as he waited for the connection to General Kilyagin in Paris, were undoubtedly out of the ordinary run of secret-service intelligence.

'Gorodetsky, you old rogue,' the voice of his master boomed out of the phone with considerable force, as if the General himself was one of those night-time phantoms. 'What news of the Bolsheviks from Bethnal Green?'

'Good morning, General, the news is most unusual.'

'What do you mean unusual?'

'I mean, I don't think anybody could have predicted it!'

'Out with it, man. Have those pocket-sized London Lenins robbed the banks as well as changing their money?'

'It's nothing like that, General. They simply ran away.'

'What do you mean? Did they never even get as far as the bloody banks?'

'You're nearly there, General.'

'They got as far as the bloody banks and couldn't face going in?'

'Exactly so, General. Only one of them had ever been in a bank before and that had to do with his mother's funeral.'

'Hold on a minute, Captain. Did our funereal friend at least make it inside the doors?'

'On the contrary. His experience deserted him, or maybe it didn't. He told the leader afterwards that he was so overcome by the memories of his mother's death that he started running back to the East End as fast as he could go.'

'Do we have eye witnesses to this tragic story?'

'Mostly the head porters, sir, the men on guard at the entry to the banks. They're pretty formidable fellows and they claim they intimidated the revolutionaries so much that they didn't dare go inside.'

'Revolutionaries be damned!' The General was in full boom now. 'England is safe from the Communist International and all the other crackpot bodies these fellows belong to! It's as if the sans-culottes and the rest of the Paris mob took one look at the Bastille and simply ran away. It's unthinkable. Just imagine French history without the storming of the Bastille – they'd probably still have a bloody monarchy, for God's sake. This is the best news I've heard for a month, Captain. Are they regrouping, the Bolsheviks from Bethnal Green? Planning another assault by running away from the Bank of England with those pink-coated porters guarding the doors and the gold?'

'I understand there is a plan to try again, sir. They're going to go into a lot of smaller banks with very small deposits or to open accounts for themselves.'

'Sounds to me like they're joining the capitalist system, Captain. Any word in London about the ghastly Lenin with that bloody beard, in his Polish exile?'

'Not as yet, sir. I think they're not going to tell Lenin and his people for a while, if they tell him at all. One of the revolutionaries pointed out to his fellows that Lenin wasn't doing much for the revolution just now, holed up in that café in Cracow reading newspapers and writing pamphlets. That's hardly the first wave of the proletarian vanguard is it?'

*

'"The opening scene, a green forest glade of tall willows and beeches, joined by a rocky bridge, and in the distance the red glow of the setting sun. In the semi-darkness, a strange band of wood sprites, with olive-green bodies and large pointed ears emerged from the shadows, some hopping half upright, some gliding on all fours."'

It was breakfast time in Markham Square. Powerscourt was reading from the arts pages of his newspaper.

'What on earth is that, Francis?' asked Lady Lucy Powerscourt, who knew precisely what it was. She had been dreading this moment for days now.

'There's more,' said her husband, 'loads more . . . "Karsavina was dressed in a violet pleated peplum, decorated with silver leaves, her long hair loose and hanging down her back. There was one inimitable gesture, which made the whole ballet worth while: the burying of her face in the crook of her arm, a moving demonstration of her grief when Narcissus disdained her love. Nijinsky wore a fair Grecian wig, a white *chlamys* with one shoulder bare, and green and gold sandals with the legs cross-gartered."

'We know somebody else who was cross-gartered, Lucy, do we not? And his dress made clear that Malvolio had lost his wits at the end of *Twelfth Night*.

94

Has London lost its wits over these Russian dancers, Lucy?'

The dancers of the Ballets Russes had conquered Covent Garden and Lady Ripon's little theatre at Coombe. Now they were laying siege to Markham Square and Lord Francis Powerscourt – a reluctant convert, if, indeed, convert he was.

'I think that must be *Narcissus*, Francis, that ballet you were reading about. Your sister Burke and her daughters were raving to me about it only yesterday.'

'*Narcissus* be damned,' said her husband. 'I said I didn't care for it before they arrived. I still don't care for it now it's here, with all this fuss.'

Lady Lucy did not tell her Francis, but she had tickets for a box that very evening at the Royal Opera House, Covent Garden, entry despatched only yesterday by Natasha Shaporova, who seemed to have access to innumerable tickets, most of them, it had to be admitted, in the more expensive parts of the theatre. Lady Lucy had not yet worked out how to lure her husband into the building, but she was sure she could think of something.

*

The blinds were drawn in the back room of Messrs Neeskens and Sons, diamond and fine jewellers of Antwerp. Mathias Neeskens was an old man now, his eyes so weak that his grandchildren felt it was unfair to play hide-and-seek games with him as he could see so poorly. He had on his thickest glasses as he checked again through Mr Killick's haul.

'These are the finest jewels I have seen for years,' the old man said. 'You were right to bring them to me. My son Jacob runs the business now and he has a wider and younger clientele than me. But there is still nothing like a glittering diamond to cheer up an old lady. It makes them feel their dancing days may not yet be over and that it is worth dressing up once more.'

'Do you think you will be able to place some of them?'

'I believe I could place a fair number with my clients here. They come from all over Europe, as you know. We have a partner we do a lot of business with in Vienna. They are nearly as fond of jewels there as they are in St Petersburg. You said you believed there was a Russian connection, I believe?'

'I did, there was talk of a bank in Moscow and a grandfather. The bank is well known and very respectable.'

'I do not think these gems came from Moscow. These are jewels to adorn the aristocratic ladies of St Petersburg, not the wives of the rich merchants of Moscow. Jewels usually follow a king or a tsar or an emperor in Europe, as they hold the most glittering balls. It is different in America, my nephew Joshua tells me. He is on loan to an old firm of jewel merchants in New York before he returns to join our business here. He says that over there the most glittering jewels always go to those whose husbands or lovers have the most glittering bank accounts. It must make life easier, don't you think?'

'Indeed, Mr Neeskens. Now tell me your plan of action. I came here to place myself in your hands, after all.'

'Thank you. You were wise to do so. Tomorrow Jacob sets off to Vienna on a train so early he will hardly go to bed at all. I shall transact my business from here. For yourself I propose that you set off for Munich. I shall furnish you with the name of a firm we trust in that great city. They have wide contacts across Germany. We shall be in touch three evenings from now.'

*

Powerscourt might have been unwilling to visit Diaghilev's creations, but the same morning the Ballets Russes came to him just as he was about to go out.

'Monsieur Fokine of the Ballets Russes, to see you, my lord.' Rhys the Powerscourt butler coughed his usual cough when announcing visitors, 'Monsieur Michel Fokine.'

Fokine was a tall slim young man with dark hair and a dazzling smile.

'My dear Lord Powerscourt, please don't get up, and pardon me for calling on you out of the blue,' he began, settling down on the edge of the Powerscourt sofa and disturbing the twins' cat.

'How very nice to see you, Mr Fokine. The Ballets Russes are the talk of London,' said Powerscourt, waiting for the young man to declare his business.

'I have come to apologize for the lack of cooperation between our company and yourself and your associates, Lord Powerscourt. All I can say is that Diaghilev is a hard and occasionally erratic taskmaster. His thoughts are always on the ballets. I know he regards the murder as an irritant, a flea to divert him from his real purposes.'

'And what would you say they were, those purposes, Mr Fokine?'

'Well, Sergei Pavlovich wants to create the finest ballet company the world has ever seen. And it will be a Russian ballet company, for he is very conscious of the country he comes from, even if his creations are always seen in the lands of others. He does not work alone, Diaghilev, in spite of his love of publicity – which he says is always about the ballet and never about him. There are a group of people – writers, artists, musicians, set designers and costume designers, composers and so on – who form his inner circle. He leads but he always brings them with him. He has a craving for the new. He is, if you like, a dictator of whim, a dictator of passing fancies, of awful temper and a gift for making enemies where he need not and then being reconciled to them. I think he is the greatest impresario the world has ever seen. I know, for example, that I too will be out of fashion one day for Diaghilev and his ballets. Then I will also be cast on the scrapheap of Diaghilev's ambitions, like so many before me.'

'And what would you say is the reason for the Ballets Russes' success?'

Fokine suddenly began to pace up and down the Powerscourt drawing room, as if he were Powerscourt himself.

'Forgive me,' said the young man, 'I often think better walking up and down. Let me put it this way. Suppose your house here, Lord Powerscourt, is the world of ballet before Diaghilev came along. The composer lives in the basement. The librettist is in the attic along with the corps de ballet. The producer is in the other half of the basement. I, the choreographer, am in your study with the telephone I saw on my way upstairs. The set designer lives on the first floor along with the scene shifters. The other choreographer is on the second floor. So is Diaghilev. Nobody speaks to each other. Each prepares his part in the performance without any contact at all with the other elements. That is what Diaghilev changed. They may all still live in this house, but they talk to each other all the time now; there are non-stop meetings to build an integrated whole, here in your drawing room. It's this cooperation, this cross-fertilization of ideas, that has made the ballet what it is.'

'Were you surprised by the murder, Monsieur Fokine?'

'Of course I was, Lord Powerscourt. We all were. Jealousy, feuds, factions, temporary ganging up on somebody for no apparent reason; all these are commonplace in a group of people forced to live very closely together for long periods of time. I expect you could find similar displays of emotion in any other similar organization. But murder is something new. After an interval of six months or so, I expect Diaghilev to order somebody to compose the music for an opera about a murder, only it will take place in the seraglio of some Eastern potentate, with dramatic colours to be provided by Bakst and dance choreographed by me. The murder, if you like,' here Fokine stopped walking and resumed his seat, 'was the culmination of things that had gone before, but things that had always run their course without the terrible outcome of death on the stage.'

'So the death will not have come as a complete surprise?'

'That depends on how old you are, Lord Powerscourt. For the young girls who make my life difficult, it will have come as a complete shock. Many, I'm sure, will be wondering if their mamas or papas are going to arrive in London suddenly to take them home. I do not think they would want to go – the murder adds a certain spice to life. It gives people something else to talk about after Diaghilev's affair with Nijinsky or whether the company is bankrupt or not.'

'I was going to come to the bankruptcy in a moment, actually. But first, let me ask you this. Remember that we have only talked to the girls of the corps de ballet. The young men, it would seem, do not have the same appetite for tea from the samovar and the finest English cakes as the girls.'

'I wish I could help you there,' said the young chore-ographer, 'but the night of the murder I was waiting in the wings to make sure nothing went wrong. They were my ballets, if you like. So I wouldn't have noticed anything happening offstage. But there is one thing you should know.' Fokine paused for a moment to brush a speck of dust off his immaculate trousers. 'The girls would never know it because they never see it.'

'And what might that be?'

'That whole area backstage – there's nobody looking after it during the performance, no porter, nobody from the Royal Opera House staff. I've often wandered round there when one of my ballets is on next – I'm a great prowler, as you saw just now. There are all kinds of people scurrying about: dressers, make-up artists, people bringing messages for one of the stars, new props being delivered, new costumes. It could be anything or anybody.'

'I do have one question for you, Monsieur Fokine, and let me tell you how grateful I am for your visit here and the help you have already provided. I hope I may ask you more questions as the investigation develops. And I presume that you would not want Diaghilev to know of our association?'

'Diaghilev would have a major tantrum if he knew I was in touch with you, Lord Powerscourt. He is a possessive man and I, for the moment, am one of his possessions. Shouting, expulsion from the ballet, wish that I'd never been born, what a hopeless choreographer I am – that would just be for starters.'

'My question is this,' Powerscourt said, 'and it may not at first sight have much to do with the case in hand. But it may do. Is the Ballets Russes going bankrupt? Is Diaghilev – for the moment, anyway – completely broke? Bankruptcy has a startling effect – it ricochets around the place, crashing into all sorts of unexpected people and places. That information could be most helpful.'

'I'll do my best, my very best for you, Lord Powerscourt. Come to think of it, I wouldn't mind knowing about a bankruptcy myself.'

8

Partnering

In general, partnering is an effort by both the male and female dancers to achieve a harmony of movement so that the audience is unaware of the mechanics to enjoy the emotional effects. Also known as *pas de deux*, or dance for two.

For a male dancer, partnering includes lifting, catching, and carrying a partner, also assisting with jumps, promenades and supported pirouettes.

Scarcely were M. Fokine's elegant trousers from Paris out of the door when Rhys and his cough were in action one more.

'Sergeant Jenkins to see you, my lord.'

The Sergeant was in a state of high excitement. Powerscourt wondered if his red hair hadn't turned an even deeper shade.

'They've spotted him, my lord! They saw him coming through on the boat from Calais!'

'Sorry, Sergeant, who is this "he" you speak of? You make it sound like the Second Coming.'

'I don't think it's that, my lord. Not yet, anyway. My granny always says the Second Coming will never happen under a Liberal government. Don't ask me why. Sorry, my lord, my mate Charlie Watchett works in the "make sure they don't kill the King or the PM or members of the Cabinet watch out for foreign spies" bit of the police. He says the boys at Dover picked up a tip from the Frenchies that this messenger from Lenin was coming. They all think this Lenin person is pretty important. Charlie's boys watched the messenger walk onto English soil this morning.'

'Did they let him through, or did they arrest him?'

'Very cunning this, my lord, they let him through. Charlie and the lads are going to have to watch out for him in London.'

'Did he have a name? No doubt he has many names and many disguises, but which one was he using for the present?'

'Karl Lodost, Pole from Warsaw, my lord. Can I ask you a question, my lord? I know I should have found the answer by now, but I'm worried that some inspector will ask me about the man and I won't know a thing.'

'Of course,' said Powerscourt, repressing a smile. 'Fire ahead.'

'Who is this Lenin person everyone seems to get so worked up about?'

'Good question,' said Powerscourt, 'I'm sure Lenin, man of steel, isn't his real name either. He's a leader of a band of revolutionaries, one particular band of revolutionaries, as there are many more. They are people who want to throw out kings and emperors and parliaments and replace them with rule by the working class. He wants to overthrow the institutions of democracy and replace them with the rule of himself and his fellows. Quite how that would be better is not clear. Quite how it is to be achieved, this revolutionary heaven, is not clear either. Lenin is banned from Russia, where he comes from, and has become a wandering preacher of revolution, usually by pamphlet, across the face of Europe.'

'I see,' said Sergeant Jenkins. 'I believe we have a few of our own here in London, our own home-grown revolutionaries, or so Charlie tells me. He says he has to pinch himself to stay awake when he has to go to their meetings. They all carry on so. They keep on mentioning the name of some other bloke – Karl Marx, is he called? He seems to be the Top Prophet man.'

'You keep thinking of Karl Marx as Top Prophet, Sergeant, and you won't go far wrong.'

'But what's this messenger man doing here, my lord?'

'I haven't the faintest idea. Russia's troubles seem to have come a long way from home if they're ending up in Markham Square. New revolutionary Congress perhaps? They're always holding mass rallies, like the revivalist preachers they resemble. Only thing is that there are so few of them in any one country that they have to invite everybody they can think of from the entire Continent. They say the arguments about which city should host the meeting – London, Paris, Berlin, Vienna – can go on for months. Perhaps it's one of those. Maybe there's another pamphlet due from Lenin. They're great ones for pamphlets, these revolutionaries, Sergeant. I'd advise you to keep in touch with your friend Charlie. He may bring us further news, though I do find it hard to think of a link between Lenin and his friends and the Ballets Russes.'

*

Natasha Shaporova would have been the first to claim that she loved her fellow countrymen and women very dearly. But a little of that sisterly love was, if not abating, receding slightly from the shore. For the route from Covent Garden to her house in Chelsea seemed to her to have an Ariadne's thread strung out along the way. The girls from the corps de ballet came in ones and twos and threes and fours, all lured by the prospect of tea from the samovar and the icons on the wall and an occasional visit from the local priest and a place where Russian was the normal language. She had discovered one important thing, and she was going to tell Lord Powerscourt as soon as she could. At first, in those early meetings in the Fielding Hotel, the name of Alfred Bolm and the suggestion that he might have pursued some of the young girls had been a trickle. Definitely there, but a trickle nonetheless. Now it had turned into a torrent.

You couldn't get into a lift with the man. He wasn't to be trusted in a train or taxi or any form of wheeled transport. His presents had to be returned immediately, his other advances rejected. Natasha knew that none of these girls could have carried out the murder, but what about the other members of the company – the reserves, as she called them, who weren't on the stage that fateful night? Could one of them, carefully selected by her fellows for her skill with the dagger in the Cossack dance, have performed in a new adaptation below the stage?

Natasha also sensed that the girls had been turned homesick by the murder. In St Petersburg by now, the police would have arrested somebody, almost certainly the wrong person, but still an arrest. Now the plaintive calls grew in number. Why was London so big? Why were there so many people in it? Where was the sea? Why did the people always walk so quickly? Why did nobody speak Russian? Why hadn't the police arrested somebody? It was Diaghilev who had done it. It was Bakst. It was Fokine, his patience finally exhausted by the ballet girls until he could kill the first person he saw.

For Natasha, that last accusation was too unkind. The girls had gone and she and Mikhail had an important engagement. They were going to meet Lady Lucy and Lord Francis at the ballet.

*

Powerscourt had known it was coming. It was fruitless to resist. He had said how nice in what he thought was a friendly fashion to Lady Lucy in the taxi that brought them here to the evening performance of the Ballets Russes in the Royal Opera House in Covent Garden. She looked at him with deep but silent suspicion. Now he was in their box. He waved to Natasha and Mikhail in their box on the opposite side of the auditorium. He could hear the orchestra revving up. He remembered an old saying of his father's about going to the dentist: just remember when it starts that you're much closer to the end; to the whole visit being over.

There were garlands on the stage already and things hadn't even started. Now they had! They were off! The music seemed to be almost a lullaby. The curtains rose to reveal a small pack of ballerinas, as Powerscourt referred to them, apparently frozen on stage. He remembered this one from his last visit all those years before. They're going to start prancing about now, he told himself. Then that one in the outrageous costume will wake up on her high bed and she too will start prancing about. Round and about, up and down, forward to the front of the stage went the ballerinas. Powerscourt thought that it was like a moving harem, a tableau of female flesh on display. When the music stopped you could pick your girl. You might have to dance your way off the stage with her, but you could retire to some invisible box behind the curtains. But no. The music did not stop. Instead, as Powerscourt had prophesied, the one on the bed woke up. She too began strutting about. The others retired to the back of the stage, wares still on display, minimum clothing, maximum length of leg still available. It was a miracle the Lord Chamberlain, keeper of theatrical virtue in the capital, hadn't intervened. Any moment now, Powerscourt said to himself, the music's going to change gear and became more urgent, more dramatic. It did. And – Powerscourt felt on top of his form now – some bloke is going to appear and jump about. He did. The fellow appeared capable of some of the highest leaps Powerscourt had ever seen. The audience were on the edge of their seats. Powerscourt felt this chap could win Olympic gold for the high jump if he ever bothered. Only later was he to learn that his name was Nijinsky. Passion offered, passion rejected, passion offered again – yet more leaping about, higher still and higher, and at last the first ballet of the evening was over. Passion seemed to have been resolved as the high jumper and the sleeping one seemed to move off together. The applause was deafening. One ballet down, only two to go, Powerscourt said to himself. He felt quite cheerful. If he could sit through one of the bloody things, two shouldn't be a problem. The evening at the dentist's would soon be over.

*

That same evening another telegram arrived for M. Diaghilev at the Savoy Hotel in London. It came from Venice. The message was short and to the point: 'Regret, repeat regret that your outstanding bills with the Grand Hotel have still not been cleared. No repeat accommodation will be offered here until they are settled. Giulio Baggini, General Manager Grand Hotel Venezia.' The message joined its companions, unopened and unread, in the guests' letterboxes in the Savoy Hotel reception.

9

Danseur noble

A highly accomplished male ballet dancer. The female
equivalent is *Prima ballerina* (Italian) or *danseuse*
(French). A *danseur noble* is not just any dancer in the
world of ballet, but one who has received international
critical accolades from the dance community . . . Most
boys and men who dance classical ballet are just called
danseurs.

The excitement in the Servants' Hall at Blenheim was
almost palpable. The footmen and the chambermaids
and the gardeners and the coachmen and the chauf-
feurs hadn't been so excited since they learned that
their lord and master, the 9th Duke of Marlborough,
was to play an important role in the coronation service
of King George V. But this was something different.
The Duke's man of business had mentioned it to the
manager of the Bear Hotel in Woodstock. He had been
overheard by one of the barmen. The barman, in his
turn, told his brother, who kept a clothing shop in the

town, but who was married to a local girl whose sister was one of the chambermaids in the big house. The intelligence took strange shapes on its voyages. The Russian Ballet was coming to the palace. That was definite. There were varying attempts to guess the size of the company. Some said thirty. Some attested that that must be rubbish, there had to be at least a hundred of them. The Tsar was coming, said the monarchists below stairs. No he wasn't, said the others – the whole thing was run by a big man called Diaghilev who spoke no English but swore at everybody in Russian. On two points there was general agreement. The ballerinas would be very beautiful. And that it would be a triumph for Blenheim Palace, making it for a time the most famous big house in the country – which it was anyway, they acknowledged, but people needed to be reminded of it from time to time.

Upstairs in the Big House, the mood was different. Blenheim Palace had been built for a man said to have been the finest military commander in Europe. The building, constructed with such elaborate panache and sense of triumph, was one of architect Sir John Vanbrugh's finest achievements. The original Duke's successors had not inherited his military prowess, or his political skill. They were not even particularly good husbands. The 9th Duke of Marlborough, one Charles Spencer Churchill, had, as it were, won the Derby and the Grand National in one go when he carried off Consuelo Vanderbilt, daughter and heiress to the vast Vanderbilt fortune, acquired in the trains and steamships of New York, and a great beauty to boot. Hundreds of thousands of pounds from her dowry were poured into the fabric of Blenheim. She, for her part, bore him two sons. She also brought an American friend of hers to stay, one Gladys Deacon, reportedly one of the most beautiful women in Europe. Her services soon replaced those of the Duchess in the marital bed.

La Vanderbilt lived with this for a while but then departed. Perhaps the Blenheim train services weren't up to the standards she had been used to on the Vanderbilt lines in and around New York. And she refused to get divorced. The Deacon woman, who might have been convinced that her presence in the marital bed gave her the right of Duchess by virtue of position, as it were, was permanently annoyed, not to say livid, to be fobbed off with the title of Your Ladyship inside the household and plain Mrs Deacon without. It was this acute awareness of the inferiority of her position that roused her to battle stations when the question of the Ballets Russes reached the State Drawing Room of Blenheim Palace.

'Think of it, Charles, just think of how famous these Russian dancers will make us.'

'I don't understand. They're far too expensive. I could buy the winner of the Oaks for less than that.'

'Who cares about winning horses? People say this is the finest ballet company in the world. We could invite anybody who is anybody from London. The trains to Oxford from London run all the time. Think of the attention! Think of the newspapers!'

Her Ladyship did not say so, but she planned to be at the Duke's side at all times. Those photos should put that railroad woman from New York in her place.

'It's all very vague still, anyway. Nobody's even decided where the ballets should take place.'

'You mark my words,' said Mrs Deacon, preparing a

grand departure from the room, 'that if those dancers don't come, I shall be seriously displeased. To hell with the money. You've got loads of it tucked away for buying racehorses and things. I'm depending on you!'

'I'll think about it,' said the Duke to the departing figure. He knew only too well what serious displeasure meant.

*

Johnny Fitzgerald thought his friend Francis always gave him the worst jobs. Here he was, standing outside the house of a Mrs Maud Butler, youngest sister of Richard Wagstaff Gilbert, mother to one of the three surviving nephews who might inherit his fortune, aunt of the boy murdered at the Royal Opera House only a few days before. And he had already pressed the bell. What, in God's name, was he to say to the poor woman? He was shown into an immaculate drawing room with one or two Impressionists that looked like originals on the walls.

'Mr Fitzgerald, Johnny Fitzgerald,' a middle-aged woman with blonde hair and a winning smile was inspecting him closely. 'I think I know you. Aren't you a great friend of that Lord Francis Powerscourt who used to own half of Wicklow until he sold it to a Guinness years ago? And didn't you come to help us with the missing pictures of the ancestors that had disappeared off the walls?'

'How well remembered!' said Johnny. 'You must be one of the Butler daughters who lived in Butlers Court. There was a grocer man at the bottom of the thefts, if I'm not mistaken. And is Butlers Court still thriving? Not taken over yet by the rebels?'

'It's still there. But look, Mr Fitzgerald, we can't sit around here all day gassing about the old times. What brings you here today?'

Her hands suddenly shot up to her face. 'Forgive me, I know why you have come. It's about poor Alexander, isn't it? His mother may be here next week, poor Molly. She and I were never close, but you have to be on hand at times like this.'

'I'm afraid you may find the nature of my questions rather inappropriate at a time like this, Mrs Butler.'

'No, I won't. I know just how your friend Powerscourt thinks after watching him at work in Ireland. Alexander's uncle is a very rich man. Is Alexander his heir? If he is, or maybe if he is not, who else might stand to inherit Mr Gilbert's fortune? Am I right?'

'You are.'

'Some families play pass the parcel, Mr Fitzgerald. We play pass the inheritance round our children and their cousins. You can never tell who's going to win when the music stops. I know I shouldn't call him a wicked uncle at a time like this but I will, so there. He teases us. One year it's my Mark to inherit. Then it's poor Alexander, God rest his soul, then my two nephews Peter or Nicholas. I should tell you, Mr Fitzgerald, that there are now three nephews left in the hunt. Alexander was Molly's only son. She and that Prince of hers, they're all called Princes in St Petersburg, as far as I can make out, have three daughters living, no more boys. My sister Clarissa, Clary we call her, has two boys older than my Mark – Peter and Nicholas, they live near Oxford. Uncle Richard, the wicked old goat, never says who is his final choice. Oh no, that would be too kind on his relations. And he always said he was going to tie up his will so the money couldn't be shared out between the rival contenders. Heaven only knows how he would do that, but we are all sure he could and he would.'

'I think that makes the position very clear. Do you know who the current favourite nephew is, or was?'

'It was Alexander, no question of it. We all had a letter about it in the post a couple of months ago. Not that it didn't mean he wasn't going to change his mind.'

'Perhaps you could warn your sister that I shall be coming?' asked Johnny.

'Of course.'

'And your Mark? Is he still here with you?'

'No, Mark is at Oxford, failing, according to his father, to pay enough attention to his law books. He's had to stay behind after term to catch up on his studies. Mind you, he and his friends have hardly been there these last few days. They all keep coming up and down to see the Ballets Russes. I think they've managed to see every single performance.'

*

The telegram came the afternoon before. 'Eight o'clock a.m. Prepare to accept a call. K.'

Captain Yuri Gorodetsky, sole representative of the Okhrana in London, was ready at his command post near Holborn Station.

'Captain! Are you there? It is I, General Kilyagin, who speaks!'

Gorodetsky didn't think there could be many other Kilyagins booming at him down the phone.

'Yes, sir! Here, sir!'

'What news of the Bolsheviks? Have they departed from Bethnal Green to learn the rules of changing money?'

'Yes, they have, sir. They have been most diligent. The chief Bolshevik – can you have a chief Bolshevik, sir?'

'Bugger the chief Bolshevik, Gorodetsky, just carry on.'

'He changed some money into French francs. They've been going round local banks changing it in and out. The locals must be expecting a French invasion.'

'Stick to the point, man, for heaven's sake. When is the big day?'

'It's two or three days from now, sir. There's some question of one of the railwaymen being able to change his shift, and the others won't go without him.'

'Good! Excellent! And are our English friends going to funnel them into twelve banks as before?'

'It's down to six now, sir. And the banks have agreed to put their smallest porters on duty. The English police are ready and waiting, sir.'

'Carry on Gorodetsky, carry on.'

*

'Diaghilev strode up and down that train in Paddington Station, as though he was the Duke of Marlborough himself on some kind of state visit. He tapped with his cane on the windows of all the carriages where his people were. Then he boarded the train at the rear into his own first-class carriage.'

Michel Fokine was stretched out on the sofa in Powerscourt's drawing room, giving a first-hand account of what he and the Powerscourts were to refer to ever afterwards as 'The Grand Reconnaissance', the day Diaghilev took the first division of his people to check out Blenheim Palace and prepare it for ballet.

'We were all there,' Fokine went on: 'dancers, choreographers, musicians, set designers, painters, an acoustic man, even Stravinsky turned up for the day. And when we got to Oxford, no minor train, no branch line from the outer reaches of the Vanderbilt Empire for us: there were four horsedrawn carriages. Not a whiff of petrol in the air. Diaghilev, in the lead position now, must have thought he was back on his quest for ancestral portraits that took him all over Russia, horse and carriage conveying him from stations miles away to some crumbling heap with masterpieces in the attic.

'When they got there the steward – he's the man in charge of the whole estate, am I right?'

Powerscourt nodded, reluctant to interrupt the flow. 'Well, he'd lined all the servants up around that great front door, like Diaghilev was the King or something. He spoke perfect French, by the way, and he and Diaghilev got on like a house on fire.

'"Welcome to Blenheim," says the steward, embracing Diaghilev on both cheeks, "and welcome to the Great Hall." Diaghilev raised his cane as his eye took in the enormous room rising high up to the painted ceiling. Then he brought it crashing down and rapped the floor very hard. Then he waved it around.

'"Here! my friend," he said.

'"Here?" repeated the steward.

'"Here!" said Diaghilev, "we shall have one performance of our ballet! In this great chamber here! It will be wonderful." He summoned the other choreographer and a number of his people to work out the details.

116

'"About one hundred souls will watch the Ballets Russes in this magnificent room!" Diaghilev proclaimed, and then he embraced the steward and kissed him on both cheeks. "And now, my friend, we must find the other location. Did I not see a lake on the way in? Lead me to it!"'

Fokine sprang from the sofa suddenly and grabbed the longest poker from the Powerscourt fire irons. 'Now,' he beamed, 'I can be more like Diaghilev with this poker to serve as his cane!'

With that he moved rapidly to the door and began waddling on the spot.

'Here is Diaghilev, cane raised as a sign of leadership, progressing with his motley army of Ballets Russes people – carpenters, builders and God knows who else from the palace, a couple of tall footmen and a pair of curious chambermaids bringing up the rear. He is Joshua at the walls of Jericho, perhaps, or the Pied Piper at the gates of Hamelin.'

Fokine made his way to the back of the sofa. 'Here you have to use your imagination, Lord and Lady Powerscourt.'

He took up his position at the back of the sofa. 'This is what they call the Palladian bridge, designed not by the man from Vicenza but by architect Vanbrugh himself, with dining rooms beneath where you could take dinner at a level below the water line. In front of you is a great sweep of water, ending up in a shape bigger than a U and slightly smaller than an O. There are gates into the park at the far end. Behind you is more water, more lake, but not so good perhaps for the ballet. Ahead of me, beyond the bridge, is the path through the grounds that leads up to the great obelisk that commemorates the warrior's triumphs. Behind me is the palace, with scarcely a window unoccupied as the staff and perhaps the family watch the show.'

Fokine waddled to the middle of the sofa and struck the parapet in the centre three mighty blows. 'Neither water nor gold ran out, I fear to say, but a great silence descended on the gossiping attendants.

'"Here! Here!" Diaghilev cried, "is where the musicians shall play. Not on the bridge, but I can see in my mind's eye a great platform in the lake, secured on the bridge here, with the orchestra, and on a further platform, the dancers, with wooden tongues running out from their base, deep into the lake and towards the dry land."'

Fokine tapped his cane poker twice more on the parapet and pointed dramatically out towards the imaginary lake and the grass sloping down towards the water.

'"And on either side," Diaghilev said, virtually shouting now, "we have the audience in tiers of seats if our friends can provide them, or squatting on the grass, or standing at the back. All will be welcome. For the first" – and almost certainly the last – ' Fokine added in an aside – '"time in its history, the Ballets Russes will dance for free! For the first time in its history, the Ballets Russes will perform in the open air! I and my artists do not care if it rains. What is a little damp to interrupt a spectacle such as ours? Ever since we started, our company has tried to perform before the maximum number of people. Let them come from Woodstock! Let them come from Oxford! Let them come from the four points of the compass and enjoy our ballets! This is our thank you to the people of England for the welcome we always enjoy here. Let us cheer for the Ballets Russes! Let us cheer for the Duke of Marlborough who invited us here! Let us cheer for Blenheim Palace for the joy and the glory it is about to deliver."'

Fokine returned to his recumbent position on the sofa. 'Diaghilev then convened a series of meetings, with the steward ever present, with the carpenters, the acoustic men, who wanted to put a series of heavy curtains over the musicians to stop the sound disappearing into the heavens, with conductors, with me, with the dancers. Little working parties were established. As far as I know, Diaghilev is still there supervising everything. All I know is that the ballets will have the minimum number of dancers in case the platform begins to wobble. The most likely thing to happen then,' Fokine said with a smile, 'is that the dancers would start to giggle and would probably fall into the water.'

'Thank you for your performance, Monsieur Fokine,' said Lady Lucy, clapping his description of the scene at Blenheim, 'it was magnificent. Would you care for a drink after your efforts?'

'I'd love a beer,' said the choreographer, sinking back into the sofa, the poker still clutched firmly in his hand.

10

Cabriole

Meaning caper. An *allegro* step in which the extended legs are beaten in the air. *Cabrioles* are divided into two categories: petite, which are executed at forty-five degrees, and grande, which are executed at ninety degrees. The working leg is thrust into the air, the underneath leg follows and beats against the first leg, sending it higher. The landing is then made on the underneath leg. *Cabriole* may be done *devant*, *derrière* and *à la seconde* in any given position of the body such as *croisé*, *effacé*, *écarté*, and so on.

Mrs Maud Butler watched very carefully from her window as Johnny Fitzgerald made his way slowly down the street. Then she headed for the phone downstairs to talk to her sister Clarissa. She was at home.

'Clary,' said the sister in Chelsea, 'you'll never guess who I've just had in my drawing room?'

'I've no idea,' said the sister from Richmond, well used to bouts of excitement from her sister.

'It was that man Johnny Fitzgerald, the man who came with Lord Powerscourt to investigate the missing portraits! Surely you remember him? Perhaps you were away at school at the time.'

'I've heard about the paintings, I remember Mama talking about them and the people who came from London. What on earth was he doing in your drawing room, Maud?'

'That's just it, Clary, can't you see? They were investigators then and they're investigators now. They've been asked by somebody to look into Alexander's death.'

'Have they indeed?' said Clary. 'They haven't wasted much time. What did you tell them?'

'Well, I told them about Uncle Richard and his will and his always changing his mind about which of the boys he was going to leave the money to.'

'You told him what?' The voice from Richmond seemed to have gone up an octave. 'You didn't have to tell him a single word about that. You could have kept mum and said we had no idea what was going to happen to Uncle's will, we hadn't really thought about it. I think you'll find that most families don't think about each other's wills unless the person concerned has loads and loads of money.'

'Which is precisely what Uncle Richard has,' said the sister from Chelsea, sensing perhaps that things were going to move in her direction now. 'It's only natural for his sisters to wonder about his will.'

'But not to the extent that he changes his mind all the time. That you definitely did not have to tell him.' Richmond now trying to recapture the high ground that had looked like slipping away. 'That was a mistake.'

There was a gasp down the line. 'Oh, I say, Clary, I might have made another mistake. I told him that Mark had been spending a lot of time at the Ballets Russes performances. Well, he has. I'm sure they'd have found out away.'

'You told him that your Mark had been a regular at the Royal Opera House? You did? Well, you've just guaranteed that your son is high up on the list of suspects for the murder of his cousin. That's all.'

*

Charles Richard John Spencer-Churchill, 9th Duke of Marlborough, had been a creature of habit since his days in the military when he had served as an Acting Captain and been on the staff of Lord Roberts in the Boer War. His brief political career seemed to have drawn to a close since two short periods as a junior minister under Lord Salisbury and then his nephew, Prime Minister Arthur Balfour. The Duke did not usually breakfast alone – his mistress Gladys Deacon was accustomed to reading him selected extracts from the newspapers as he wrestled with his kedgeree. But today Mrs Deacon, mistress but not wife of his household, had sent word that she would be breakfasting in her rooms on the first floor. It had been the same yesterday and the same the day before.

The Duke had also seen minor but not negligible service in his own locality, serving twice in the past decade as Mayor of Woodstock, the little town that bordered on the Blenheim estates. Some of his fellow peers remained mayor of their local borough year in and year out, regularly returned by a grateful tenantry, but that was not to be the fate of

Charles Spencer Churchill. After two terms he was voted out.

At ten o'clock it was his custom to meet with his Steward to discuss the business of the estate. Every day now the Steward made the question of the Ballets Russes the last item on the agenda. Her Ladyship – she might not have been a Ladyship outside the walls of the estate, Mrs Deacon was accustomed to tell friends and visitors, but she bloody well was inside the walls of the Palace – posed the question the Duke thought he had settled once and for all. What was he going to do about the Ballets Russes? Was he going to employ them to dance in the palace or not? Each day, with declining levels of firmness, the Duke had said no. After his meeting, the Duke took some coffee and looked at the racing magazines.

Under the normal domestic regimen, the Duke and his partner would have luncheon together, but the 'together' element had also been disrupted by the authorities upstairs. The Duke, who had always had a dread of eating alone, especially in that triumphant dining room with its works of art proclaiming a military victory that he would never achieve, took himself off to The Bear Hotel in Woodstock and ate in state in a private dining room. The Duke firmly believed that his dread of solitary mealtimes was known only to himself, but he was wrong. Once in his cups at Monte Carlo, he had shouted to Gladys that if she didn't hurry up he would have to eat alone in that bloody great hotel dining room and that he would, therefore, be the only person doing so. The shame and the boredom, he had yelled through her dressing-room door, would finish him off. Mrs Deacon, unlike the Duke, did not forget very much, but she saved this information for particularly important campaigns, like invitations to Royal Garden Parties or inviting Diaghilev to Blenheim.

What does a Duke do in the afternoons? The 9th Duke of Marlborough was accustomed to walking his estates and checking on the recent work he had ordered. But that was difficult now because half the estate, the half running away from the house past the Palladian bridge up towards the obelisk was destined to be the home of dancing nymphs and the glories of the corps de ballet, if Mrs Deacon had her way. Even his new water garden failed to bring any cheer, the water spouting away in splendour into the late afternoon sun. And his customary large gin at six thirty sharp, the starting pistol for an evening's refreshment, failed to lift his spirits as he looked at a couple of his ancestors on the walls, destined, like him, never to shine as brightly as the 1st Duke of Marlborough.

Then it was that damned dining room once more, the footmen specifically instructed never to speak in Her Ladyship's presence, or – by extension of Her Ladyship's command – to him either. They glided in, taking this plate away and bringing another one in. They hovered discreetly about his glass, with this evening a bottle of his cellar's finest St Emilion. Even though he had perhaps been – in Lloyd George's memorable phrase – one of five hundred men chosen at random from the ranks of the unemployed to sit in the House of Lords, the Duke had been brought up to expect and to exercise some measure of power in his own and in the wider world. This was intolerable. The Duke knew that there was a siege in progress, but whether he was the attacking or the defending power he had no idea. His adversary, still taking her meals in solitary splendour upstairs, had no doubt on that question. The Duke was under siege and the Ballets Russes at Blenheim was the prize.

It was the guinea fowl that did it, a guinea fowl served with a rich cream sauce with truffles and mushrooms that finally destroyed the remnants of the Duke's resistance. He remembered eating a similar dish years before at some grand military dinner at the Carlton Club. He asked for pen, paper and envelope. He wrote out the terms of his surrender. But the lady in question did not abandon the field that evening. She made him wait until after breakfast the following morning.

*

Sergeant Rufus Jenkins had found his translator at last. She was a teacher, Anna Okenska, and plied her trade at one of London's leading public schools for girls. The students were delighted to hear that Miss Okenska would be away from school until further notice. Miss Okenska had the reputation of being very strict in class and even stricter in the matter of homework. Miss Irene Delarue, who replaced her, was always susceptible to diversions in class and bouts of generosity on the question of the prompt arrival of written work from home.

Sergeant Jenkins found Anna difficult at first, with her strict dark clothes and no apparent interest in important things like football. But their relationship began to thaw when they discovered a common love of the ballet, for Sergeant Jenkins had taken his mama again after that first rapturous evening. For some reason she only wanted to come when Nijinsky was dancing, or 'on the menu', as she put it.

Their task – and it was not a happy one – was to find the strangers whom M. Fokine had identified as wandering round the back of the Royal Opera House during performances. So far they had found two messengers bringing items from the corps de ballet hotel that had been left behind before performances; one drunk who was obsessed with the ballet but too poor to buy a ticket and too far gone to understand what was going on if he had; an eccentric accountant who passed by on his way home eager for a sniff of the world of the Ballets Russes (as his wife would divorce him if he ever went to a performance); and an old lady tramp, festooned with cast-offs, who came along to see if any useful clothing had been left behind. This person, Miss Olenska maintained in the face of all opposition, was Sherlock Holmes in disguise, since he often used disguise in such clothes and must be bored to death with those bloody bees in Sussex. There was also, one witness said, a middle-aged man in a long coat who looked foreign.

*

General Peter Kilyagin was staring moodily at a telegram from his masters in St Petersburg. His faithful deputy Major Tashkin was on the other side of the desk, waiting for orders. The Major usually dealt with the rougher side of things and kept in regular contact with the outstations of violence and torture.

'Why would Lenin courier London?' said the General crossly. 'You'd think they had no bloody money left for telegrams, wouldn't you? And then it goes on for nearly half a page: our assessment of the purposes of the visit; if this is meant to spark a signal of outbreaks of revolutionary violence across Europe; if it means that there is to be a revolution in England; if Lenin has plans to come to the English capital? I ask you. Have they nothing better to do back there?'

'It may depend on which faction of the Okhrana or which faction in the Winter Palace sent it,' said the Major, who would have liked nothing better than to get his hands, literally, on Lenin and sweep him off to one of his special offices where the nearest neighbours were ten kilometres or more away.

'It is hard to tell who the hell is sending the bloody messages sometimes,' admitted the General.

'But the answer's obvious, surely,' said the Major. 'He's come to find out about the money. Have they got it or haven't they? That's all. Come to think of it, General, have they got the money or haven't they? You've been in touch with our man in London, surely?'

'Any day now, Major. Maybe later today we'll hear about the money. I think they'll get it myself. The interesting thing is what are they going to do with the money when they've got it. If you were in charge, at long range, of a group of people about to come into such enormous sums, what do you think they'd do with it?'

'That depends on the hold Lenin has on them, doesn't it? They could steal half of it for themselves. They could steal most of it for themselves. I can't see the whole total going straight to Comrade Lenin out there in Cracow, I just can't see it.'

'Think of it another way, General. This courier can't expect to bring the money back himself, can he? He'd be picked up at every customs house between here and Warsaw. So what is he doing?'

The General laughed. 'Paranoia perhaps, Major. Imagine you are Comrade Lenin, on the run most of the time, forced to take up residence wherever our secret police or somebody else's secret police may keep an eye on you but won't actually pick you up and send you back to Russia. I can never understand why somebody's secret police doesn't just kill the bugger and be done with it. It might bring forth a howl of squeals and wails from the liberal Press and parliamentarians, but across the whole Continent, honest law-abiding citizens could sleep more easily in their beds, even if they'd never heard of the Lenin person in the first place.'

'You don't suppose Lenin wants to do something with the money once his man has got it?'

'Do what? Order a few hampers of the finest food from Fortnum and Mason's for immediate delivery to that café in Cracow? God knows. Why did he send the money to London and not to Milan, for God's sake? Does he have a better way of getting it out of London that we don't know about? That could be anything or anybody: Duke's family with left-wing daughter going to Marienbad to take the waters, dozens and dozens of bloody trunks, all stuffed with useless clothes you could hide the money in?'

The General looked at his telegram once more. 'I'll just have to send the usual reply. I must have sent it so many times they'll think it's the last version, come again by mistake.'

The General picked up a pad in front of him. 'Here we go again. "Important intelligence germane to your inquiry expected this office within twenty-four hours. Will send details once received. Yours, Kilyagin."'

*

128

Lady Ripon called shortly after seven o'clock in the morning, as if she expected the world to be ready for action.

'Powerscourt!' she bawled. 'Some of your people must have been talking out of turn. There's been a leak. The story is all over the *Daily Mail*. I've talked to the proprietor already. He says all the journalists in the capital will be onto the story by lunchtime, if not before. What do you propose to do about it?'

Powerscourt felt slightly annoyed at having his morning disrupted with such a rude message.

'You didn't feel able to tell your Press lord's friends to pull the story from their pages and instruct all the rest of the newspapers to do the same? Surely you're capable of that, Lady Ripon?'

'I did think of that, believe me, but I could hear one of his men in the background saying that it could prove very good for circulation. I think the man said that nobody's going to check what's written about St Petersburg, it's too far away.'

'Give me half an hour, Lady Ripon. I'll have a plan. And you might ask the chairman and the general manager of the Royal Opera House to be ready to appear in public later this morning. Don't bother with the Ballets Russes – I'll talk to them, but I doubt very much if they'll put in an appearance. Anyway, the journalists won't speak French, let alone Russian.'

'This is the very devil, Lucy,' he said to his wife who was sorting out a slightly earlier breakfast. 'The journalists have got wind of the murder at the opera house. Every one of them will be sniffing round the bloody story now. Dead dancer from foreign parts slain in the heart of theatreland. It doesn't bear thinking about.

I'm off to the study and that better telephone line. I'm going to get hold of Rosebery and Patrick Butler from *The Times*.'

Rosebery was an old friend of the family and a former Foreign Secretary and Prime Minister. He could tell you the name of the oil that lubricated the passages of power in Whitehall and Westminster. Patrick Butler had been involved in a previous Powerscourt investigation as a young editor in the provinces, and was now deputy home editor of *The Times*. Powerscourt told them all he knew, including about Johnny Fitzgerald's interviews with the dead Alexander's aunt.

Rosebery's advice showed his experience in handling cases of this kind. 'You've got to keep them concentrating on St Petersburg, the theatre school he will have attended, the performances he will have taken part in at the Mariinsky Theatre. Order up a couple of ballerinas who knew him well to give glowing accounts of his personality. Find a translator who can do the business for them to be interviewed about four o'clock this afternoon wearing their skimpiest tutus. That should take care of the next morning. Once the vermin get hold of the English angle, English mother and two aunts living here in London, you've lost control of the story. You've had it. They'll print anything. One last thought: say there's a talk of a memorial night for him, some scholarship, maybe, to his theatre school in St Petersburg.'

Patrick Butler agreed totally with keeping hold of the story. 'It's the devil of a job for the participants, Lord Powerscourt. Here's what I would suggest. Chairman and general manager of the Royal Opera House on parade at the Royal Opera House this morning. On

130

the proper stage, with the journalists sitting in the front rows of the stalls. That'll help to keep them quiet. What is needed is a lot of sonorous verbiage that means nothing but sounds good: Anglo-Russian relations, bereaved families, St Petersburg in mourning. You could write that sort of stuff with your eyes closed, my lord, pretend you're an orotund bishop whose best choirboy has been found murdered in the choir stalls. And, most importantly, say there will be a conference every morning at eleven and another at four o'clock, beginning today, and at the same times every day and afternoon after that. Book a couple more ballerinas – I presume the supply line must be almost inexhaustible – and the Russian Ambassador for tomorrow afternoon. Couple of aged metropolitans with enormous beards for the day after. Now, I'd better go and organize the ring round the newspapers or the journalists won't turn up.'

Powerscourt began drafting speeches for the chairman and the general manager of the Royal Opera House. There was, of course, one flaw in the preparations for the morning of mourning in Covent Garden, and that was the man who had raised the alarm in the first place, Richard Wagstaff Gilbert, with his large collection of investment trusts and wide experience cheating at cards across the river in Barnes. Powerscourt arranged to meet him at his home in Barnes at eleven o'clock in an attempt to keep him out of the picture for the events of the morning. The English end had to be stopped for as long as possible. Keep it out of the papers for a week or so, Patrick Butler had told him, and the journalists won't be interested in any uncles – alive or dead – after that.

At eleven o'clock Powerscourt the speechwriter was on parade on the stage of the Royal Opera House. The journalists had their notebooks open and pencils ready. Powerscourt's representative in Covent Garden was Lord Roderick Johnston, chairman of the Royal Opera House and a dozen other companies:

'. . . a sad day indeed in the long history of friendship between our two countries . . . young life, so full of promise, so brutally cut short . . . extend our deepest sympathy to the ballet authorities in St Petersburg and to the theatre school where the young man learned his trade over so many years . . . sympathy and condolences to the bereaved family who live, we understand, just off that great artery of life in the Russian capital, the Nevskii Prospekt . . .'

*

The other Powerscourt was being shown to a seat in the residence of Richard Wagstaff Gilbert, whose walls were filled with a fine collection of English landscapes.

'Mr Gilbert,' Powerscourt began, 'how kind of you to see me at short notice this morning. Lady Ripon asked me to look into the sad affair of your nephew. Let me say how sorry I am. It must be terrible to have the joy of a dear relative come to stay, only for that stay to be so tragically cut short.'

*

'Our capital has been graced in recent years with many musical delights from your great country. Only last year did we first make acquaintance with Monsieur Diaghilev's Ballets Russes . . . think I can say without exception that we have fallen in love with that ballet, so

132

original, so full of life, and that the love affair continues with as much passion today as it showed that first day they danced in London . . .'

*

'Thank you very much for coming to see me, Lord Powerscourt,' said Gilbert. 'It is much appreciated. He was such a dear boy, Alexander, so much loved by all who knew him.'

There was something about the way Richard Gilbert looked at you, Powerscourt thought, a combination of slyness and a leer, that left you thinking his main objective was to get the better of you, or to win you over to some shady deal.

'There is this morning, Mr Gilbert, a press conference at the Royal Opera House with the chairman and the general manager telling the journalists what has been going on and outlining the opera house's plan for keeping the Press in touch in the days ahead. We, Lady Ripon and I, did not feel that the strain of those journalistic enquiries, the constant questioning of your staff at work and the people who look after you here, was one that it would be fair to subject you to at this time.'

*

'Let us not forget,' the chairman was nearing the end of the speech now, 'the wider context in which this affair sits, the close relations between our two countries and the joint role we play in international affairs . . . These are troubled times, with the threat of war, which seemed so impossible before, now threatening to darken the lives of all the countries on the continent of Europe. Let us hope that the flame of friendship between England and Russia, which does so much to keep peace alive in our time, may burn brighter yet because of this tragedy . . . may it serve to bring about a happy state where the people by the Neva may live at peace with the people of the Thames and people all over Europe, and that the forces working for international peace may be stronger tomorrow than they were yesterday . . .'

*

'I am grateful for that, Lord Powerscourt,' said Richard Gilbert, 'truly I am. It has always been my policy to avoid the limelight; to work, if not in the shadows, in the quiet places.'

Powerscourt could see that for once the man was speaking the whole, unvarnished truth.

'I am an old man now, Lord Powerscourt. I have no children of my own. But the nephews and their parents have always been a source of great delight to me.'

I'll say amen to that, Powerscourt said to himself, and a great deal of playing rather wicked games with them and their families.

*

'. . . thought I would outline to you gentlemen some of our proposals for keeping you in touch with this terrible crime.' The general manager was on his feet, the pens still moving rapidly across the notebooks. 'We propose to hold a conference with you every morning at this time to bring you up to date with events, bringing in representatives of the police and

134

the Ballets Russes as appropriate . . . happy to answer questions except that the Ballets Russes, who will probably be represented by their principal choreographer, Monsieur Fokine, are not with us this morning. He will be speaking in French . . .' There was a deep sigh from the journalists, a sigh of regret for not paying enough attention to French lessons at school, and a cry of pain at the thought of trying to extract money for the services of a French translator from a miserly news editor, but the general manager threw them a lifeline. 'We shall of course be offering the services of translators in French and Russian as required . . .'

*

'There has been a change in our plans, Lord Powerscourt. Originally my sister in St Petersburg was going to come and bring Alexander home in person. But that has proved difficult to organize and, obviously, a cross that my sister does not feel able to bear. We have engaged a courier from Thomas Cook to bring the boy home, starting the day after tomorrow. He will be away for at least ten days.'

*

'Our daily programme will include another conference at four o'clock here at the Royal Opera House. This afternoon we will be pleased and proud to offer you the Russian Ambassador, who asks you to remember that his only comments on the terrible affair will be made here this afternoon. Otherwise he regrets to say that the pressure of business is such that he will be unable to answer individual requests for comment or interview. And the following afternoon we shall have senior spokesmen, not as yet finalized, but definitely coming from the Russian Orthodox Church, to speak of Alexander Taneyev . . .'

*

'I'm sure that is the right thing to do,' said Powerscourt, 'to commission Thomas Cook to take the body from London to St Petersburg. I think you are all very sensible, Mr Gilbert. I have made that journey a number of times and it is a very tiring business, particularly the final stretch when you feel surrounded by the vast size of Russia. Are your other nephews going to the funeral?'

'Alas, no, the pressure of work or study is too great for them to be away so long. If you feel you need to be in touch with the family in St Petersburg, I have arranged that Lady Ripon could leave a message at the embassy there. They have very kindly given permission. The Ambassador is a former partner of mine at whist.'

Powerscourt took his leave a few minutes before the press conference broke up at the Royal Opera House. The general manager had done his job very efficiently, and two or three of the better brought-up journalists made a point of shaking him by the hand as they left. The one thing they had to be thankful for, as Patrick Butler of *The Times* had pointed out, was that there were unlikely to be many entries in the London telephone directories in the name of Taneyev.

11

Second position; *seconde*

Second position of the leg – the dancer stands with feet turned out along a straight line as in first position, but with the heels about one foot apart. The term seconded generally means to or at the side.

Second position of the arm – raises your arms to the side. Keep your arms slightly rounded. Lower your elbows slightly below your shoulders. Make sure your wrists are lower than your elbows. Keep your shoulders down, your neck long and your chin up.

Captain Yuri Gorodetsky was very worried about what his master in Paris would say when he heard the news. The call was booked for four o'clock on the afternoon of the great gathering at the Royal Opera House. As ever, the call came through on time. The General did not. As usual he was in the building but nobody knew precisely where he was. Messengers would be sent to search for the missing leader. Gorodetsky always wondered what it was that caused the delay. Did the General pop down to his basement to check the ordered ranks of his files? Did he nip into the library to catch up on the latest newspapers from Moscow and St Petersburg? The answer was none of these. The General merely felt that his presence would carry more weight if people had to wait around to talk to him. Being wanted, as it were, he would be more wondered at.

'Gorodetsky!' he boomed at last. 'What news of the Bolsheviks?'

'Good news, General, in one sense.'

'What do you mean "in one sense"? Give us a clear message, man, for God's sake!'

'They have changed the money, all of it. Our English colleagues, I have to say, were appalled at the way their fellow countrymen treated the revolutionaries. They all gave them a terrible rate of exchange, about two-thirds of what it should have been according to the published rates in the English papers.'

'There can't be that many people wandering round London wanting to buy that amount of roubles in large denomination notes, can there?'

'You're probably right there, General.'

'Is that the good news in the sense you referred to earlier, Gorodetsky?'

'No, it is not, General.'

'What is it then?'

'It's this. They've put all the money into an English bank account. The Central Provincial, Ludgate Circus branch, now holds tens and tens of thousands of English pounds. The chief Bolshevik, Arthur Cooper, had opened the account a few days before. He arranged for all his colleagues to meet him there. This caused a certain amusement among our English colleagues, General, but each Bolshevik had to watch as the chief cashier, operating from a private office, counted all the money and made the appropriate entry in his ledger.'

For once the General saw the joke. 'One load of money stolen from a bank in Tigris, being watched as it is counted into the vaults of another bank in the City of London, eh? What was the point? I've heard of robbing Peter to pay Paul, but this is robbing Peter only to put the money into a different Peter in another country. God help us all!'

'You don't think they've changed sides, do you, General? Seen the light?'

'I bloody well do not think that for a moment, Captain, and if you make that suggestion again you'll be counting the damned daffodils in some isolated Siberian hovel before I've finished with you!'

'Yes, sir, sorry, sir. Perhaps they want to buy something? Something to further the cause of world revolution, sir?'

'Ludgate Circus sounds a pretty odd place to me to be starting the world revolution. But come, let's think. He's a crafty bugger, that Lenin. He knows that if he transfers the money to Cracow or anywhere else in Russia there'll be more secret police waiting for him to come out of the bank than he has supporters. So what's his game? It has to be something he can buy in England and he must know how on earth he's going to get it out of England. Isn't that so?'

'Guns? Some kind of armaments, sir?'

'I can't see those boys going round buying guns. They enlist some poor soldiers or sailors in their cause and then use theirs. It's not weapons they're after.'

'Maybe Lenin's going to retire, sir? This is the golden egg for himself and Mrs Lenin to change direction. Perhaps they're going to go to America to start a new life.'

'New life be damned! The only new life that bastard wants is in Russia, and would lead to you and me being confined in the St Peter and Paul Fortress for the rest of our lives, or in that bloody daffodil village in Siberia. He's good for the employment prospects of counter-intelligence officers like you and me, Gorodetsky, I'll say that for him. Where would we be without Lenin, for God's sake?'

'Where indeed, sir? Our English colleagues are going to ask around the Russian community in a general sort of way about what Lenin might want to do with the money.'

'Good. We've got to find an answer to this one, Captain. I can feel the pressure coming from St Petersburg when I send in my next report. We're going to have bloody Lenin for breakfast, lunch, tea and supper for a long time to come.'

*

It might have been Lady Ripon's random fire into the ranks of the authorities that produced the Inspector. It might have been Lord Rosebery's more discreet applications of pressure in a world he knew so well. But when Powerscourt returned to Markham Square early that afternoon, there was a visitor waiting in his drawing room, twirling his hat in his hands.

'Good afternoon, my lord. Dutfield at your service; Inspector Matthew Dutfield of the Metropolitan Police. Also on the case is my interpreter Anna, transferred to my care by some Anglo-Russian banking house, currently reading up on the details of the case. Red hair, my lord, English by birth, loves everything Russian.'

'Are you the reinforcements, Inspector?'

'I suppose you could say I am. I was pulled off a nasty case of armed robbery to join your team, my lord. I've been doing my homework with Sergeant Jenkins.'

Matthew Dutfield was a tall thin young man with a mop of unruly brown hair and a winning smile.

'And I have news for the case, sir. The Commissioner's assistant received news from his colleagues that the Duke intends to give in to Diaghilev's commands for money. The great ballet performances at Blenheim Palace can go ahead.'

'That's good news indeed. Excellent news. I look forward to it. But isn't there one piece of police work that we could use to our advantage?'

'What's that, my lord?'

'Well, if my memory serves me right, don't the local police force have to give permission? There has to be adequate transport, no risks to public order, sufficient police available on the day to make sure things progress smoothly, that sort of thing?'

'You're right, sir, you're absolutely right.'

'I don't see why we can't use that to our advantage,' said Powerscourt. 'If the Ballets Russes don't behave at this end, then we block the performance at the other end. This could be the key to unlock Diaghilev's ban on our talking to his senior people. That has been the major block in this investigation. Until now we've made little bits of progress here and there, but until we can talk to those people we're operating largely in the dark.'

'I see what you mean, my lord. Begging your pardon, but could I use your telephone? It's just that the Assistant Commissioner seemed to have some sort of instant connection to Diaghilev's people – maybe it's this Lady Ripon woman – but if I can talk to him right now, he might be able to press a few buttons for us.'

'You carry on, Inspector, down the stairs and first door on the left.'

Powerscourt wondered if it was the shame of putting a Sergeant on the case that forced the Metropolitan Police to produce an Inspector. Maybe the thought of all those conferences at the opera house had forced their hand. It wouldn't take long for one of the journalists to ask if it was normal to put police sergeants onto murder cases involving distinguished artistic people from foreign countries. That, he said to himself, was probably the answer.

Inspector Dutfield was back in a few moments. 'Whoever got hold of that key into Diaghilev's inner circle has done us a great favour, my lord. Maybe they warned him that police cooperation at both ends of the Oxford Road was necessary. They're all going to speak to us, preferably after the event at Blenheim; all of his top people, and that's official. Even Diaghilev himself, apparently.'

'I wonder if I might leave that one to you, Inspector. The man stormed out of a meeting with Natasha Shaporova and myself earlier in this inquiry and stomped off down the stairs.'

'Begging your pardon, sir, but aren't you forgetting something? I've been reading up as much as I can about these ballet characters, and from what I can see they're all pretty volatile, liable to have a tantrum and threaten to leave in the morning, and then be best friends at lunchtime. And they're Russian as well. They're a pretty emotional lot. Can you tell me, my lord, of a successful English novel where the heroine throws herself under a train at the end? Dorothea Brooke? Elizabeth Bennet?'

'Do you know,' said Powerscourt, 'that thought had never occurred to me. How interesting.'

'Let me tell you, my lord, how I intend to proceed. I've earmarked a couple of pages in my new notebook here for each one: Benois, Bakst, Stravinsky and so on. I'm not just going to ask them about where they were on the night in question, I'm going to ask them what they knew of the whereabouts of the others. That way, if they're telling the truth, we can check all their alibis. Is there anything you'd like me to ask them, my lord, while I've got them in the witness box, as it were?'

'Well, you should remember that Monsieur Fokine, the choreographer, is sort of on our side. He volunteered his help a few days ago and he's most useful. Get him to give you an impression of Diaghilev at the Palladian bridge in Blenheim Palace. He may need a cane or a poker to make it work, but it's very entertaining. Now then, I think you should include Alfred Bolm, the man who was supposed to have been dancing that evening.

'And the reserves, if you like – the girls and the men who were not down to dance that evening, but were presumably acting as understudies in case somebody got ill. Sergeant Jenkins is working his way through the stagehands and so on.

'You ask, Inspector, if I have any special question I would like to ask these top men from the Ballets

Russes. Well, there is. It may seem way outside the scope of our inquiry, but I would like you to ask it anyway. Who were the next great stars going to be? Who were the next people to become as well known as Nijinsky and Anna Pavlova?'

*

George Smythe, trainee art dealer by day, part-time jewel broker for Anastasia from the corps de ballet and party-goer by night, hated being disturbed early in the morning. The fact that it was a telegram did not register with him at all at eight fifteen in the morning. His long and expensive education had included no training in the question of telegrams. The place of origin, Berlin Central, did not rouse him either. It was only when he saw the figure halfway down the form that he woke up. In excess of forty thousand English pounds. George ran a hand through his hair and sat down in his living room, strewn with abandoned shoes and neckties from the night before, to read the thing properly.

For the attention of: George Smythe, 74 Albemarle Street, London.

From: Elias Killick, of Johnston Killick jewel brokers, Imperial Hotel, Berlin.

'Delighted to inform you all jewels disposed of at respectable prices. Total of forty-thousand pounds. Would you wish monies sent direct to Moscow Bank or brought back to London? Direct transfer by far the safest option. Please advise by three o'clock this afternoon. Regards. Elias Killick.'

George Smythe hadn't dressed as fast as this since he overslept in Oxford and almost missed the last paper in his finals. A cab swept him to the Royal Opera House in less than ten minutes. He found Anastasia waiting to rehearse in an hour's time and dragged her off to a quiet corner of the Fielding Hotel.

'Look, Anastasia,' he began, 'that jewel man Killick has sold the lot. They're worth about forty thousand pounds. Can you believe it? It's marvellous news, don't you think?'

Anastasia shook her head, as if she too had been out late the night before. 'Tell me if I've got this right. The man Killick has sold the jewels? Is that true? For forty thousand pounds? Holy Mary, Mother of God!'

'That's right. It's fantastic!'

'Where is he now, the man Killick?'

'He's in Berlin. The thing is, Anastasia, we've got to decide how to get the money. Killick says they can transfer it direct to that Moscow bank you told me about. Nobody will know. You won't have to hide it in your luggage going back to St Petersburg or whatever you were going to do with it.'

'We're not going straight home – we've got engagements in a couple of other places before we get back to St Petersburg.'

'But can't you see, this is the safest way to get the money back to Russia.'

'I promised Prince Felix that I would bring him the money myself. It'll make him love me more, don't you see? He can't fall in love with a length of telegraph cable! I promised him!'

'That's all very fine,' said George, feeling that a man might indeed have strong emotions when a beautiful girl arrived on his doorstep with a fortune in her hand, 'but how are you going to get it back?'

'I'll find a way. I promised, didn't I? What would

Felix think if I got back to St Petersburg without the money? I'd be in the doghouse with no supper for days.'

'We have to give an answer very soon. By first thing this afternoon at the latest. Can't you see, Anastasia, that the wire is the safest way to do it? I promised the Prince to do all I could to look after his interests and to keep you safe. Won't you see sense?'

'I refuse to have the money sent by wire, George. I could ruin my prospects with the Prince. How can I hope to keep him faithful in the meantime if I do not return with the money?'

George Smythe thought that the chances of Prince Felix Peshkov remaining faithful to his beautiful ballerina were slim at the best of times, but he said nothing of that.

'You're being absurd!'

'So are you!'

'No, I'm not!'

One or two concerned glances were now being made at this young couple arguing so vehemently in French early in the morning. Well, they were known to be excitable people. One elderly Dowager began looking about her for a bell.

'For the last time, Anastasia, will you let me send word to Mr Elias Killick that he's to wire the money to the bank in Moscow? Yes or no?'

'No.'

'Is that your last word?'

'Yes.'

'Damn it all, Anastasia, can't you see that you're doing the wrong thing?' George looked really depressed. His latest possible time for arrival at the picture gallery was but fifteen minutes away. Maybe he could send a telephone message about a relation in distress. Then he remembered that he'd done that at least once already. He began wringing his hands. His sorrow and his concern seemed to touch something in Anastasia. She leant forward and held one of his hands briefly.

'George,' she said, 'there's something I haven't told you. Something I promised not to tell anybody.'

'What's that?' asked George petulantly.

'It's this. That money,' she was whispering now and the dowager returned her attention to the coffee and biscuits, 'it can't go near any banks. Not under any circumstances. This is what I promised not to tell. Oh, George, I wish I didn't have to break my promise. But I do, don't I?'

'I don't understand,' said George. 'What is it about a bank, for heaven's sake? One lot of depositors, one lot of borrowers, a lot of people running round in frock coats pretending to be more important than they really are. That's all there is, isn't it?'

Even the whispers were getting lower now.

'No, it's not.' The young man had to lean forward now to catch her words. 'It's a question of who owns the banks, isn't it?'

'I still don't understand,' said George, checking his watch again. 'Who owns the bloody banks anyway?'

'It's not the banks plural, George, it's bank singular.'

'Singular?'

'Why is this so difficult? The bank whose details we have, the one we gave to Mr Killick, is owned or part-owned by my friend Prince Felix's father. He has cut my Felix and his colleague out of all contact with the banks. Any transactions will be brought to his attention within the hour. Felix gave me the details of the bank before he realized how completely he and his friend had been cut off.'

'So,' said George, 'the father hears about the money coming in? He won't know how it got there.'

'He has drawn up a contract or something in banker language which states that any money going to that bank must be used to pay off some of the son's debts.'

'And is forty thousand pounds not enough to pay off the debts and leave some change?'

'I don't know. Prince Felix doesn't talk to me about money, only that bit.'

'I suppose he could find out where the money came from, diamond merchants out of Antwerp and London. You don't have to be a genius to work out what's been going on. Dear God, what a mess.'

'But do you see now that the money must not go to that bank? It must come here to me.'

'I do and I must go. I'll send the wire later this morning. And then, Anastasia . . .'

'Then what, George?'

'Then we'll have to begin all over again.'

*

Natasha Shaporova still kept open house for the corps de ballet. They were expected any minute now, for their timetables made them as punctual as clockwork. The girls still came, in the same numbers, some now refusing, very politely, to eat cakes or biscuits because of their weight. But Natasha, for the moment, was engaged in her correspondence.

She had decided, when *l'affaire Taneyev*, as she referred to it, began, that she would make enquiries at the other end, the Russian end. She did not have the resources of a police force, or even a determined newspaper reporter, but Natasha had something better than that, a host of relations who would know, or who would know who knew, any interesting details of the Taneyev family background. There weren't that many families in St Petersburg in which the mother was English – always a source of malice and gossip about Russian manners not being properly understood. She had written to her mother and her grandmother, and to two of her aunts and to the only one of her brothers she considered reliable. After that she had further cohorts of friends from school and cousins of every description. The replies were now arriving at regular intervals at her house in Chelsea. Gossip knows no boundaries.

The picture she was forming was orthodox (if you didn't count the English mother who had a habit of reading to some of her younger children in bed before they went to sleep, which was considered barbaric on the Nevskii Prospekt and the Fontanka Quay). Natasha had only two letters left when she found the hidden secret of the family Taneyev. It came in a long letter from her aunt, who prided herself on her knowledge of St Petersburg family history. After pages and pages of successful Taneyevs, soldier Taneyevs, banker Taneyevs, Admiral Taneyevs, drunken Taneyevs – far too many in Natasha's view, for she was growing rather fond of this family with a background rather like her own – Aunt Marie eventually came to the dead boy's grandfather, Josef Ilyich Taneyev, a middle-ranking Guards officer with a very beautiful wife.

This Taneyev was rather old when he married Anna Bulgakov, who was said to be one of the prettiest girls in St Petersburg. She had two sons when they lived in peaceful seclusion in Perm with the Guards Regiment, but very little society to speak of. 'And then, my dear, it all started to go wrong,' Natasha's aunt wrote. 'The husband was posted to St Petersburg. The duties weren't very serious so he wanted to live quietly in the country when he wasn't needed on military duties. His rank, however – for his was one of those fashionable regiments that are expected to appear at social functions in our capital – meant that he had to spend more time than he would have liked attending the great balls and soirees and parties of every sort. And he hated dancing, Josef Ilyich Taneyev – one of my closest friends had predicted that this would cause great trouble even before they were married – while Anna loved it.

She became reckless, dancing with the same partner all night sometimes, and causing great pain to the older man in the sitting-out area, who loved her and had married her. Eventually Anna became besotted with an artistic young man called Pyotr Solkonsky, who wrote a lot of poetry and whose interests and instincts were the opposite of Josef Ilyich's. You just had to see them together to see that they were having an affair – and they seemed not to care who knew it. She was, or she seemed to be, in love. But she forgot that she had married into a military family. The husband's fellow officers had been talking to him for weeks about challenging the poet-lover to a duel. Eventually he gave in, and the fateful day finally came: the meeting in a glade in a forest outside the city; the seconds in attendance; the carriages waiting to take the living and the dead back to their homes.'

150

Natasha was wondering at this point if her aunt hadn't missed out on a second career as a novelist. She read on.

'The result was a surprise, but perhaps a tribute to our military training. The poet fired first and missed. Perhaps he intended to miss, who knows? Josef Taneyev did not miss. His bullet struck the poet in the chest and did terrible damage to his lungs. They say the blood was pouring out of him in his carriage all the way back to his home. He died two days later. But, wait, Natasha, here is the point of this terrible story. The poet gathered his three brothers round his death-bed before he passed away. 'Revenge,' he whispered, coughing yet more blood onto the sheets, 'revenge, not in this generation but the next. Take my revenge on the generation after ours.' He died that evening. It took some time before the family Solkonsky realized what he meant. Any revenge in this generation would mean the death of one who might be the son or daughter of his lover. That was why the Solkonskys had to wait. Even in death he was trying to protect his Anna from unhappiness.'

Natasha knew from her other letters that Alexander Taneyev's siblings consisted of one older brother, Ivan, and three younger sisters: Marie, Elizabetta and Olga.

12

Arabesque

Arabesque is the position of the body supported on one leg, with the other leg extended behind the body with the knee straight. The standing leg may be either bent, in *plié* or straight. *Arabesque* is used in both *allegro* and *adagio* choreography. The working leg is placed in 4th open, *à terre* (on the ground) or *en l'air* (raised). Armline defines whether this is 1st, 2nd or 3rd *arabesque*.

Johnny Fitzgerald was meeting a stockbroker in the City of London, one of the money men recommended to him by Sweetie Robinson, who had played cards for money with Richard Wagstaff Gilbert. Two had declined very politely, but the third, Henry Wilson Pollock, senior partner of Pollock, Richards and Cork in Mincing Lane was prepared to talk to him.

'You're an investigator, Sweetie tells me,' Pollock began. He was a small, stout man who looked, Johnny thought, much as Mr Pickwick might have looked when he grew older.

'That's right, Mr Pollock. My current case involves a man you know well, I believe: Richard Wagstaff Gilbert.'

'That old bastard Waggers!' said Pollock, almost shouting. Johnny was surprised at the vehemence of his reaction. Most people would stick with the pleasantries of politeness for five minutes or so before showing their anger. This tubby little man launched straight in.

'I gather that you have had a lot of dealings with the gentleman in your time, Mr Pollock.'

'Gentleman is not a word I would use in connection with Waggers, Mr Fitzgerald, oh no. Definitely not.'

'Might I ask why?'

'If you had called ten or maybe even five years ago, I would not have told you. I would have been constrained by professional etiquette and what remains of the rules of society. But now? I am winding down my affairs. I shall keep a presence in the firm, but I shall not be here very often. I intend to spend my days looking after my garden and following the fortunes of Middlesex Cricket Club in the summer and Tottenham Hotspur in the winter.'

'What a pleasant prospect. I hope you will be able to watch one of the triangular Test matches between England and Australia and South Africa this summer. But for the moment, in a professional sense, you do feel able to talk about Mr Gilbert?'

'Let me begin with his business affairs. He specializes in new investment trusts and new offerings in general. Part of my business here touches the same areas. Now, I would have to say that there is nothing strictly illegal about what Waggers does. We have all done it up to a point, but not to the extent that he does.'

'What do you mean?'

'Word gets round every now and then about some new offering. It might be a cleverly constructed investment trust or a mining share or a brewer. The day before the company is opened for business, the men who know let it be rumoured abroad that this is going to be a winner. The recipients of this information make a mental note to recommend it to their clients in due course. Others, especially Waggers, make sure that they buy a large holding, and then sell it a few days later at a handsome profit. That was just the most obvious of his little schemes. The others are only understood by insiders in the City, which Waggers undoubtedly was.'

'And the cards, Mr Pollock, the cards?'

'The irregularities at whist only began about eighteen months ago, after he had a losing run that seemed to have gone on since Christmas. I hesitate to use that word beginning with "c", even in my own office, for fear it might come out and drench us all in scandal, Mr Fitzgerald. After Easter this year, several months ago, it was as if he had decided to take revenge on all those who play with him regularly. He always wins now, sometimes by a lot, sometimes by a little.'

'I have a little experience in cheating at cards, Mr Pollock, from a terrible case in the officers' mess at Simla years ago. A young subaltern took to cheating at whist to make amends for his overspending on the horses. He tried a variety of methods.'

'I would be most grateful for your inside information, as it were.'

'A pleasure, Mr Pollock. Tell me, what does the fellow wear?'

'I've often wondered about that, now you mention

it. He always wears long jackets – smoking jacket, Norfolk jacket with very deep pockets, that sort of thing.'

'And is there a certain amount of fiddling about with handkerchiefs, cigar lighters maybe, helpings of snuff?'

'There is sometimes, not all the time. Why do you ask?'

'If you're quick-fingered, you could whip the pack of cards you're about to deal into your right-hand pocket and substitute another one from your left. Do you see?'

'I do indeed.'

'Then there's the handkerchief on the floor midway between your chair and the chair next to you, either on the right or the left. You might be able to see your opponents' cards – only for a second, but long enough if you have a good memory.'

'He has an excellent memory, but I don't recall seeing that one in action.'

'Well-polished cigarette cases, perhaps?'

Johnny produced a handsome cigarette case from his breast pocket and gave it a quick polish.

'Do you have a pack of cards anywhere about the place, Mr Pollock?'

Mr Pollock did. Johnny was still polishing his cigarette case.

'Now then, Mr Pollock, this is my best bet – it's what brought down the man in Simla in the end. It only works on my deal, you understand, one hand in four. You keep up a flow of information as you go. And you place your cigarette case, which you have been fiddling with all evening, more or less in the centre of the table.'

'I see. Off you go.'

'J. Hobbs, W. Rhodes, R. H. Spooner,' Johnny began a recital of the England Test team due to play Australia at Lord's in the next few days, dealing the cards as fast as he could, but looking not at Mr Pollock or imaginary partners to the left or right, but at the reflection in the heavily polished case, 'C. B. Fry, P. F. Warner, F. R. Foster, nearly at the end now, F. E. Woolley, J. W. Hearne, E. J. Smith.'

Johnny pocketed the cigarette case with a flourish. 'I can tell you, Mr Pollock, you have four spades to the king, three small clubs, two diamonds to the ten and four clubs to the ace, king, jack and two.'

Henry Pollock picked up his cards. They were exactly as Johnny had said. 'My God, Mr Fitzgerald, you're a miracle worker. So that's how he did it! I remember a well-polished silver cigarette case from the last time we played.'

'Buy yourself a well-polished one, Mr Pollock, and play him at his own game. Maybe all four players should have polished cases and do the same thing each time a hand is dealt. It could be a sweet revenge.'

'I'm obliged, Mr Fitzgerald, it's more than useful in my profession to know how a man cheats at cards.'

*

'I've just come back from Blenheim Palace, Lord Powerscourt! It's fantastic! Amazing!'

Michel Fokine burst into the Powerscourt drawing room before Rhys had time to announce him.

'The stage for the orchestra is nearly finished. They've been laying long floorboards down on top of a whole series of staves sunk into the bed of the lake. There's a couple of musicians going up tomorrow to test out the acoustics.'

'Is Monsieur Diaghilev there in person, Monsieur Fokine?'

'He's there every other day, I would say. He cheered them all up when he told them the Venetians sank one million piles into the Grand Canal to build Santa Maria della Salute after some plague or other. I think there are two major churches in Venice built to commemorate victims of two different plagues. I sometimes think he's back in his beloved Venice, organizing for a troupe of dancers to perform in the middle of the Grand Canal. They're even going to have a bridge of boats to carry the performers onto their stages, like they do at the Feast of the Redentore when the great and good walk across the water to the church. The steward fellow is in charge of the whole thing. He seems to have even picked up a couple of words of Russian. He can say thank you very much and please don't drop that on my toe.'

'And all the rest of it? The caterers and so on?' asked Powerscourt.

'Fine, just fine. They've organized the local printers in Oxford to print little advertisements to go all over the place. Diaghilev suggested that they print a short guide to the ballets on the lake, so the audience can work out what's happening on stage. Only one person has fallen in so far – and he was carrying a very heavy beam – but he's all right.'

'And the seating?'

'That's going according to plan,' said Fokine, abandoning his seat by the fire and pacing up and down the room again.

'The people of Woodstock, my lord, have entered into the spirit of the thing with a vengeance. The hotels have ordered extra caviar from Paris and lashings of

157

vodka. One of them is planning to roast a couple of wild boar in their courtyard. The bakers have got hold of recipes for blinis, those little Russian pancakes, and are selling them in hundreds – a trial run, perhaps, for the big day. And beetroot for borscht, that Russian soup. I'm told you can't buy a beetroot within a fifty-mile radius from Woodstock.'

'And the big event in the evening in the Great Hall? I hope nobody's forgotten about that.'

'They wouldn't be able to, my lord. The Duke himself is taking a great interest in that, and in the affair by the lake.'

'Well, he is paying for it.'

'True enough, but every time he goes out on a tour of inspection, Mrs Duke – that's what the steward calls her when she's out of earshot, my lord – is by his side, urging him back to the big house. She spends a lot of time looking around – one of the dancers said she's checking to see if any photographers have arrived yet.'

'And have they?'

'We had a couple of enterprising ones yesterday, hanging so far over that Palladian bridge you'd have sworn they were going to fall in. One of them, a young fellow from the *Illustrated London News*, says his master at the magazine always believes the preparations are more interesting than the real thing.'

'He might well be right.'

'Indeed so, my lord. One thing they have done is to cut down the numbers inside the Great Hall. The steward, after a lengthy conference with Diaghilev himself, cane tapping regularly on the antique chairs, said that fifty to sixty would be the maximum number permitted to attend, and even that's a squeeze. Mrs Duke looked sad for a bit until the Duke himself rallied to the cause and told her it would be even more exclusive and even more highly prized.'

'And what of Diaghilev's finances, Monsieur Fokine?'

'Ah yes, the finances of Monsieur Diaghilev, my lord, I haven't forgotten. Where should I begin?'

The young man was now at the King's Road end of the Powerscourt drawing room, about to turn towards the fireplace end.

'The first thing I should say is that Diaghilev himself is not in the ballet business for money. Far from it. So what is he after? Glory, I think, fame certainly, but fame accorded to one who has changed the nature of ballet for ever. He wants to go down in history as the greatest impresario the world has ever seen. There is no limit to his ambitions. He wanted to conquer Paris and he has. They say there is another ballet being written by Stravinsky now that will change the whole nature and appreciation of ballet. And what does this mean when it comes to his finances? Total chaos is the answer. He does not distinguish between his own personal expenditure and the monies needed for the dancers and the stage sets and the artists who decorate them and design those fabulous costumes.'

'Are you saying that his personal account and the company's accounts are the same? No difference at all?'

'I am, my lord. Take the money he is getting from the Duke of Marlborough up there at Blenheim. That could go on paying the carpenters of the theatre in Paris, or the hire of theatrical costumes here in London, or on paying the bill for his last trip to Venice. And there's another thing. He is very successful at persuading the rich to sponsor his work. I bet Lady Ripon has had to put her hand in her pocket more than once on this trip to London. They give him cheques or banker's drafts. He then forgets he has them. Only recently he trotted into the accounts department with a huge cheque some rich backer had given him six weeks ago in Paris.'

'Is it therefore impossible to say at any given time whether he is bankrupt or not?'

'Quite impossible. One of the accounts people says they should turn him upside down every now and again and shake him vigorously to see what money falls out. People don't last very long in the accounts department, those young men with mathematical training from St Petersburg. There are a few who have stuck the course. One of the young men who has lasted longest claims he stays because of the excitement. He says it's like going over Niagara in a barrel all the time and hoping you're still alive at the bottom. Not necessarily what you'd expect to hear from an accountant. The other one also uses a watery metaphor. He says it's like keeping track of the flood before Noah decided to shove off in his Ark.'

'So there is no answer to my original question?'

'I'm afraid not. I know there's enough money to pay everybody till the end of next week. The Blenheim money may already have been spent paying bills in Paris or even St Petersburg. In two weeks' time, my lord, we all climb into the barrel and go back over Niagara again.'

*

George Walker the docker, Albert Smith from the railways, the brothers William and Thomas Baker and

Arthur Cooper were packed into Arthur Cooper's front room. His wife and children had been packed off to her sister's round the corner.

'Comrades, thank you all for coming. I have to report what our enemies would call a miracle. A miracle indeed. The long arm of Comrade Lenin has reached out across Europe to visit us here in Pentonville.'

He held up a very large envelope with pages sticking out of the top. 'This was put through my front door, and not by the postman, the day before yesterday.

'This is what the money is to be used for. Comrade Lenin wants us to print five hundred copies of his latest masterwork in English and five hundred in Russian.'

'How do you know that the work is from Lenin? That it isn't from our enemies, trying to trick us into printing literature that will not help our cause?'

William Baker was always suspicious. That, he often told his wife, was how he kept out of the authorities' files all this time. 'The courier who brought it gave very definite proof that it came from Cracow. He himself did not bring it all the way, he merely collected it from its temporary resting place elsewhere in London. I believe he is a courier acting for Lenin.'

'This isn't like the old days when you could print anything you liked and send it wherever you liked,' Albert Smith put in. 'They could have us all locked up for breaking that Official Secrets Act, so they could.'

'I do not see how the laws of the decadent bourgeoisie should be allowed to stand in the way of the advancement of the revolution, comrades.' Arthur Cooper felt that the revolutionary spirit seemed to be in short supply this evening.

'If you are opposed to this plan, I will proceed on my

own. Anybody who refuses to agree with my proposals will face reprisals from the party.'

'I think it's all very suspicious,' put in George Walker. 'A man arrives who says he is a colleague of Comrade Lenin. He gives you a sign. That's good enough for me. But that pamphlet, won't it have to be translated as well? That's another risk we are all taking.'

Arthur Cooper was growing more and more irritated.

'And can you not see that Comrade Lenin has thought of everything? He toils away in his lonely library and sends the next pamphlet to forward the cause of world revolution. All you can do is worry about some ridiculous law.'

'It won't be ridiculous if we end up in jail.'

'Comrade Lenin expected better from his colleagues in London. I was not meant to tell you this but I will. He thought you would agree to his wishes and carry them out without complaint. It seems he was wrong. He had given me the name of a translator and the name of a printing firm in Clerkenwell that will carry out the work. Comrade Lenin expected obedience. Do I have it?'

Reluctantly the revolutionaries agreed. Even then they weren't finished.

'What happens when they're all printed off? What do we do with them then?' asked William Baker.

'When the pamphlets are done, I will take full responsibility for their distribution. That matter is not for discussion either here or later.'

*

A rather different meeting was taking place upstairs in Markham Square. Lady Lucy, returned from nursing a sick aunt, was to be brought up to date by Natasha Shaporova, Inspector Dutfield and her husband.

'I don't think we have made much progress, really,' Powerscourt began. 'We are no nearer to solving the central problem of the case – who was the victim? Bolm or Alexander Taneyev? Personally, I have no idea. Inspector?'

'Well, my lord, my lady, I have to say, speaking as a policeman with some experience in these cases: statistically, it has to be Bolm.'

'How did you work that one out, Inspector?' Lady Lucy felt that she had made insufficient contribution to the case so far, even though she had the excuse of having been away.

'He's been around longer. He must be in his forties. He's had years and years to make enemies in the highly charged atmosphere of a company like the Ballets Russes. Maybe there's been some dispute about roles in the company we know little about.'

'There could be another reason you don't seem to have considered so far. *Cherchez la femme.* Jealous husbands, maybe jealous husbands come all the way from Paris to take their revenge on the man who took their wife. Is that possible, Natasha?'

'It certainly is. In Paris and London the women go mad for the ballet, possibly because it's not here for very long and the time for conquest and pursuit is short. Look at the way Lady Ripon and all the other Lady Ripons pursue them for afternoon tea and a spot of dancing after the muffins. I bet they have something more in mind. Maybe they don't do anything about it, but the dancers could become trophies, conquests to be shown off to your less or more fortunate friends.'

'And how do we find out if this is going on, or, or, perhaps more realistically, if it has been going on at Covent Garden?'

'I shall ask the corps de ballet,' said Natasha, 'though the gossip there might not be one hundred per cent accurate. I suggest you ask Sergeant Jenkins, Inspector. I believe he has good contacts now among the stagehands and the scenery people.'

'And what,' said Powerscourt, 'do we make of this story of the duel and the vow of revenge?'

'I think it should be taken very seriously indeed,' said Lady Lucy. 'Natasha is even now corresponding with her relations in St Petersburg. There may be more news yet to come.'

Lady Lucy did not care to mention it but she thought Natasha's network of contacts and relations in St Petersburg might be the equal of her own here in London.

'I find it all very strange,' Natasha said. 'The original duel must have happened fifty or sixty years ago. It could even have happened at the same time as the poet Pushkin's unfortunate end. But the authorities have always been very strict about duels and vendettas caused by duels. They have been known to send people to exile in Siberia for it.'

'But would those strictures apply if the revenge killing took place outside Russia?' said the Inspector. 'Suppose you are a male descendant of the victim. You come away on holiday. You carry out your killing. You go back home. Did you have a good time, the relations ask. London is a wonderful city, you reply. You expound on the changing of the guard or the shops on Oxford Street or the plays in the theatres. You don't mention the murder to a single soul, except your parents, if that.'

'There's one other thing that troubles me,' said Lady Lucy. 'You remember the Cossack dance in *Thamar*, the one where all the knives are hurled into the floor? Could the girls or one of the girls in the corps de ballet have become expert in those lethal instruments, so that she too would know how to kill Bolm or Taneyev, whichever was the victim.'

'Now I think about it,' said Natasha Shaporova, 'I think you're probably right. I suspect any of those girls could have done it; except, of course, that they were on stage at the time of the murder.'

'I shall make enquiries,' said Inspector Dutfield. 'Circus people, they're always throwing knives about. They should probably know.'

'I'm confused,' said Powerscourt. 'We just seem to have established a whole fresh lot of lines of enquiry, as if we didn't have enough already.'

13

Sauté

Literally 'jump'. As adjectives, *sauté* (masc.) or *sautée* (fem.). French pronunciation: [sote] are used to modify the quality of a step: for instance, "*sauté arabesque* indicates an *arabesque* performed while jumping.

By half past one in the afternoon, the crowds had begun to arrive at Blenheim Palace. The programme was due to start at three. They came through the main gate that led to Vanbrugh's triumphal entrance and the elegant courtyard within that led onto the front of the great palace. Small groups had already taken up their position by the edge of the lake and were having a picnic. Footmen and porters were on duty to show them the way to go. The wooden platforms for the musicians and the dancers were empty, a bare stage for the glories to come. Towards two o'clock, the crowds grew thicker. Powerscourt and Lady Lucy had a place reserved for them by Fokine at the rear of the Palladian bridge. There was a sort of throne area for the Duke

166

and his lady where they would be more visible than the dancers. Powerscourt suspected the steward must have been responsible for that part of the arrangement. He had made friends with a local reporter who was scurrying round the lake and the two entrances for information. The young man's name was Riggs, Benjie Riggs, and he told Powerscourt that he worked as a reporter on the Oxford newspaper and that his beat included Woodstock. 'It's going to be amazing,' he told his visitors. 'People are supposed to be turning up from the little towns and villages for miles around, not to mention Oxford itself!'

'Are you sure?'

'I am, sir. I asked in as many local pubs as I could contact last Thursday for a piece in the local paper. Some of the publicans are even thinking of closing down for the afternoon, and that's a fact.'

'Good God,' said Powerscourt. 'Do they know what to expect? I mean, they aren't going to be what you would call the usual crowd for a ballet, are they?'

'Well, it's free isn't it?' said Riggs. 'That's in its favour, for a start. The locals, some of them at any rate, even turn out to watch the arrivals when they have a costume ball up there in the big house, Marie Antoinette dancing with Napoleon, Nelson waltzing with Boadicea with his one arm. And that's just a glimpse of the participants from outside the front door. The ordinary people aren't allowed inside. Pardon me, my lord, there's a great throng just arrived at the main gate. They seem to have come in buses. I'd better find out who they are. I'll catch you up later.'

At two o'clock, Diaghilev himself waddled out of the main entrance to the palace. He appeared to wish to be incognito, for he had his hat pulled well down over his head. He strolled as far as the bridge and looked around. Powerscourt wondered if – even in his wildest dreams – he had ever thought of performing in such a place with such an audience. In spite of his hat over his eyes, a number of people recognized him from the newspapers.

'That's Mr Diaghilev!' 'Isn't that Diaghilev?' the sober whispered to each other. A rather inebriated fellow who had taken up position halfway along the lake roared out, 'Good on you Diaghilev! Well done mate!'

Diaghilev would not have understood a word. But he raised his cane as a gesture of politeness and hurried back to the safer quarters of the palace.

By a quarter to two all the seats at the edge of the lake on both sides were full. The new arrivals pitched camp on the ground. The footmen were stressing that all the area behind the seats was for sitting; the area behind a number of posts was standing room only, rather like a football match.

Benjie Riggs was back now. 'I'm on the way to that Palladian bridge now,' he said. 'It may be cut off by the crowds later on.'

'One question,' said Powerscourt. 'Who will the audience be? What will they have seen that's remotely like this before?'

'Well, no, they certainly won't have seen anything like this before. There's lot of the men, maybe most of the men, certainly the football-crowd people, who believe that the stage is full of virtually naked women all the time.'

'Just like in London at the opera house,' said Powerscourt.

'Francis,' said Lady Lucy. 'Behave!'

'There's some will have been to the circus with their children, some to the panto, a few maybe even to the theatre. For the ones from the countryside, the only thing like it will be an agricultural show with all those side stalls and jugglers and fortune tellers.'

It was now just after two fifteen. Another series of buses from Oxford deposited a hundred and fifty more.

*

A man in evening dress came down to the water's edge by the bridge and held his hand up, as if testing for wind direction. The musician's area was ready now, seats and music stands waiting for the men to play. Floating in the middle of the lake was an enormous platform for the dancers. This too, Powerscourt presumed, was secured with a series of staves to the ground at the bottom. A series of four wooden tongues, each wide enough for a couple of dancers, ran out north, south, east and west. There were two wooden bridges of boats, one for the musicians and the other for the ballet. There was one solitary boat on the far side of the bridge, furthest away from the house. Powerscourt reckoned that a giant might have been able to jump from the end of the tongue nearest the house onto dry land, but even for a giant it would have to be a prodigious leap.

At two thirty the huge crowd, increasing by the minute, had their first taste of action. The musicians, led by their conductor, the man who had tested for wind direction before, marched out of the main entrance, serenaded on their way by a couple of trumpeters on either side of the great doors. The crowd began to cheer. They carried on cheering until the musicians had negotiated their way onto their positions by the bridge. Above them was a canopy designed to stop too much of the sound disappearing into the sky above. The musicians began tuning up. On the signal from the conductor they all rose and bowed to the crowd. The cheering went on for some minutes.

'The crowd's well over two thousand now,' panted Benjie Riggs, fresh from a mission to the far side of the lake, where a group of Oxford football supporters were now waving their scarves in the air and chanting some impenetrable war cry. 'Policeman told me. The Duke and his party, including Diaghilev and his people, should be coming down about a quarter to three.'

The musicians were now playing a series of popular and patriotic airs, including a rather mangled version of 'Jerusalem'. Each was greeted with a wave of applause and roars of encouragement.

'I bet they learnt that on the bloody bus on the way down,' said Benjie. 'The footman from inside tells me they've hired an actor with a huge voice to be master of ceremonies. He's going to tell the crowd what each ballet is about before it starts. That way they shouldn't find it too confusing. My footman friend also told me he'd be able to tell them to shut up if they got out of hand.'

Just before a quarter to three, it was as if a dam had broken by the main gates. A large number of buses from Oxford brought another crowd of ballet lovers, ushered with great care to the seats on the far side of the lake. Picnics were being packed away. A small number of hardy souls came in by the rear gate, walking sticks in hand, wives and children straggling behind but still in attendance, the little ones frequently carried by a stronger parent.

The trumpets sounded again from the massive front door of Blenheim Palace. Diaghilev, wearing his best coat with astrakhan collar and what might have been a brand new cane, marched out of the main entrance, or waddled in Diaghilev's case, and led a party of his senior staff towards their position on the bridge. The dancers made up the rear with Nijinsky at the very back. Diaghilev waved happily to the crowds on his route as if he were royalty – which perhaps, for this brief spell in the Oxfordshire countryside, he was. His companions, Benois, Bakst, Nouvel, the entire Diaghilev gang, also waved to the crowds, but without the élan of their master.

'Go on Diaghilev! You show us mate!' rang out from the football supporters' end at the far side of the lake. It was acknowledged with a regal wave from the cane. As they took their places, a final burst of humanity swept through the main gates. The footmen were making valiant efforts to organize the standing sections of the crowd in order of height so everybody would be able to see. On the palace side the crowd were almost level with the path on top of the ridge that led from the end of Woodstock to the palace itself. On the far side they were almost level with the flat ground at the back as well. A couple of enterprising young men had climbed up a tree for a better view.

Powerscourt and Lady Lucy were on the far side of the bridge on the palace side, with a good view of the stage. They could hear the excitement coming from the slopes around the lake.

'For God's sake, William, whatever you do, don't fall asleep. I'll have nobody to talk to about it afterwards if you do.'

'Do you think the dancers are going to jump from the musical platform onto their own?'

'Is it true they've got one dancer who could leap from one end of the Palladian bridge to the other?'

'Have you any idea what they're going to wear?'

'Have you ever been to a ballet before? I expect it'll be like a circus with the humans taking the place of the wild animals.'

At ten to three, accompanied by a fanfare of four trumpets, and with a couple of footmen behind them, the Duke and Duchess, in their finest ceremonial robes, made their way arm in arm to their elevated seat on Vanbrugh's Palladian bridge. Behind them came a man in a lounge suit, clutching a bundle of notes. The late arrivals were shown unceremoniously to the nearest standing room to the gates they had come through.

'Who's that bloke with the notes? Is he another bloody duke?'

'Can't be. He'd have the fancy dress on.'

'Maybe he's one of Diaghilev's people.'

'Shut up, we'll find out in a minute.'

When the official party reached their seats, they all sat down. Everything seemed to have come to a complete stop. Then the bells of Blenheim Palace and the churches of Woodstock and Blaydon all struck the hour of three, not absolutely simultaneously. The man in the lounge suit stepped onto his podium.

'Ladies and gentlemen,' he paused, and said it again as the muttering died down, 'welcome to Blenheim

Palace. My name is George Foster and I am an actor from London come to act as master of ceremonies.'

It was easy to see why. The man had an enormous voice, easily capable of reaching those by the smaller gate and the football crowd on the opposite bank.

'Let me thank, first and foremost on this glorious afternoon, the Duke and his good lady.'

Lucy Powerscourt nudged her husband in the ribs, 'No "Her Grace", not even today.'

'It is thanks to their good offices,' the master of ceremonies went on, 'that Monsieur Diaghilev and his people are here today.'

'Not to mention the twenty-five thousand pounds,' Powerscourt whispered back.

'I'm sure you all know that the Ballets Russes have already made one prodigious journey, from St Petersburg to Paris and London. They have taken another shorter journey to be here with us today.'

Foster paused and looked down at his notes. The crowd were completely silent now. 'As most of you know, Monsieur Diaghilev and his ballet do not speak English. Let us, however, give them a very warm welcome to the heart of Oxfordshire this afternoon. And let us thank them for coming.'

Foster raised his hands as if conducting the entire crowd. Waves of applause rang out.

'Welcome to Oxfordshire,' they shouted.

'Thank you for coming.'

Only one voice from the football end struck a discordant note. 'Get on with it, mate! Bring on the naked women!'

Now George Foster turned to his right towards the palace. That seemed to be a signal. A group of footmen, stagehands and scene shifters carried a very ornate couch across a bridge of boats and placed it carefully at the very back of the ballet stage.

Foster waved a hand at the musicians. There was a long roll of drums.

'Ladies and gentlemen, all the way from St Petersburg, the capital of Russia, I give you: the Ballets Russes!'

14

Jeté

Jeté is a jump from one foot to the other similar to a leap, in which one leg appears to be 'thrown' in the direction of the movement (*en avant, en arrière* or sideways). There are several kinds of *jetés*, such as *petit jeté, grand jeté, en tournant, jeté entrelacé*, etc.

'Our apologies, first of all, to those of you who might have seen this first ballet at the Royal Opera House. Mr Diaghilev felt that it suits the setting here particularly well.

'So we begin today with the story of Thamar, Queen of Georgia, who rules her country in somewhat unorthodox ways. We see her first at her leisure. Then she orders a dance to lure a wandering Prince to her high castle. They dance together. They seem to fall in love. But they don't. Thamar the Georgian Queen is played by Tamara Karsavina and the Prince by Alfred Bolm.'

Foster sat down. A small procession of ballerinas, accompanied by the Georgian Queen, made their way onto the stage. The pale, brooding Queen languished on her couch as her maids began a dance to rouse her. Karsavina's clothes were a dark melange of Eastern promise, her dark-brown eyebrows a bewitching glimpse of Eastern beauty. Roused from her slumbers, she too joined the dance and waved a scarf out over the lake to entice a passing suitor.

The music rose to a crescendo as her suitor was ushered onto the stage from a bridge of boats. Alfred Bolm was brought forward to greet the Queen by two of her attendants. The Prince, her suitor, was lured in by the music and the dancing attendants; he wore a conical cap of astrakhan, a thick scarf wound round his neck and a great black cloak draped around him. With regal dignity and a smiling glance full of Eastern promise, the Queen advanced to greet him. The music swelled again as they drew close and her hands, half eagerly and half in a kind of caress, darted to his throat to loosen his scarf and show his face. The Queen summoned assistance to welcome her guest, and here Powerscourt realized how well Diaghilev's people had made use of the scenery. As she stamped her foot on the floor, two troupes of four guards, clad in Cossack uniform of red jackets with black trousers and long black boots, made their way onto the stage from the further end of the Palladian bridge.

They began a wild Caucasian dance, a blur of tossing sleeves and flashing boots. The men danced with a dagger in their right hand, whirling it up and down in a circular movement, then hurling it into the floor and leaping over it to drag out the quivering dagger and throwing it down once more. The daggers hit the floor with a thud that could be heard in the palace itself.

'Told you it would be like the bloody circus,' whispered a cynic a few rows in front of Powerscourt.

'Shut up! For once in your bloody life, just shut up!'

Two more guards crossed the little pontoon to wave their swords at the dancers' feet and make them leap even higher.

Bolm, the Prince, now performed a solitary dance to attract this Georgian Queen. It consisted of a series of leaps, each one higher than the last, one arm raised vertically above his head, his body arched like a string bow. As the dance ended, the Queen kissed her suitor on the lips and sped ashore, pursued by the Prince.

Some of the audience began muttering at this point, but the music was swelling louder and louder to tell that the end had not yet come. From opposite sides of the bridge, the Queen and her lover reappeared, the Prince staggering and gasping as he made his way back on stage. Then the Queen manoeuvred him right to the end of one of the wooden tongues that led to the pontoon. She too was menacing and wild-eyed. She slipped an arm around his neck, drew back his head and stabbed him in the chest.

A couple of the Caucasian dancers carried the body off stage, fake blood now dripping from his heart. The music stopped and the dancers bowed to the audience. Bolm, making a rapid recovery, slipped away from his guards and made his return to the stage.

Waves of applause and cheers rang out across the grounds of Blenheim Palace. Even the policemen were applauding. The football crowd were on their feet and shouting for more. There were cries of 'Bravo!' and 'Well done!' And a small boy, just next to Powerscourt, asked his mother, 'Is that man really dead?'

'Our second ballet,' George Foster repeated himself so his vast booming voice reached the farthest reaches of the lake, 'is set in ancient Greece at the shrine of Pomona, the goddess of fruit trees. The shrine is a wooded glade, rather smaller than here,' he smiled at his own witticism, 'where a spring feeds into a glassy pool. The story is of Narcissus.'

At this point Nijinsky pirouetted his way across the bridge of boats and bowed to the audience. 'A beautiful and self-indulgent young man, who spurns the advances of the beautiful mountain-nymph Echo.' Tamara Karsavina followed Nijinsky across the pontoon onto the stage and the huge pool of water surrounding it.

'Echo appeals to the goddess to send her a bacchante, a young woman with spells, to make Narcissus fall in love with her. Under the spell of the bacchante,' Nijinsky's sister, Nijinska was to join the stage a little later, 'he does fall in love; but not how Echo wanted.'

Echo was dressed in a violet robe, decorated with silver leaves, her hair loose and hanging down her back. The bacchante danced, sometimes holding a beaker of wine in one hand and a wine cup in the other, and sometimes playing with a red scarf that she held extended above her hands. All was in vain. Narcissus Nijinsky, now gazing at his reflection on one side of the lake, now on the other, now facing the bridge, now facing the town gate, was falling in love with one person only: himself. At the close he sank slowly onto his knees and leant over into the water, in love with his own reflection, eventually falling back in a sort of swoon.

'Bravo Nijinsky,' the football crowd hailed him as if he had just scored a hat-trick in a vital cup game.

178

'Bravo!'

Sections of the audience rose to their feet to cheer. On stage the Duke was seen to rise and join the cheering.

The third ballet was to have the most dramatic denouement of them all.

The audience were settling themselves back down on their cushions or on the grass or shifting from foot to foot if they were standing. Many were still discussing the ballet they had just seen. George Foster had them in the palm of his hand now.

'Our last ballet has a title that says it all. *The Spirit of the Rose*. A young girl, played by Tamara Karsavina, returns to her bedroom dressed in a white bonnet and ball gown. She has come home from her first ball. She holds a rose as a souvenir of the evening. She drops into a chair and falls asleep. The rose falls from her fingers to the floor. The Spirit of the Rose, Nijinsky, is seen at the window. He steps onto the floor and nears the young girl. Still asleep, she rises and dances with him. He leads her back to the chair, kisses her, then leaps through the window and into the night. The girl awakes and rises. She picks up the rose she dropped and kisses it. The curtain falls.'

The musicians began their romantic tunes and George Foster resumed his narration. 'The young girl walks slowly into the room and takes off her cloak. Underneath she is wearing white crinoline. She sinks into a chair and looks affectionately at her lover's gift, a red rose. She presses it to her lips, as though remembering the dances with her lover, which now seem so far away. As she relives her memories, her eyelids begin to droop and she falls asleep. The rose slips and the petals stain the floor.'

It was not the football section of the crowd but a different group on the opposite side who, as Powerscourt remarked to Lady Lucy later, must have been more accustomed to the world of panto.

'Look behind you! Look behind you for heaven's sake!'

The music changed. To an infectious whirl of rhythm, Nijinsky, curled up like a ball on the tongue behind the girl, rose to his feet and launched himself into the space in front of her. He was wearing rose-coloured tights and a cap and tunic of rose petals. He spun slowly round and passed his hands over the girl's head, as if summoning her back by some magical movement. Then he drew her from her chair as though she were guided towards him by some magnetic force, and led her into an ever-quickening waltz. Round and round they went, faster and faster, the audience beginning to clap in unison to the tune of the music. Then he returned the girl to her chair and danced to the opposite end of the room. He leapt out of the stage onto one of the tongues, took two steps forward and dived full length into the lake.

The audience were stunned at first. Then they burst into a long rolling round of applause that travelled right round the arena. Nijinsky rose from the waters of the lake and made his way to the edge, great drops dripping down his clothes. There was a long, slow gasp from the women in the audience as they watched him clamber ashore and be taken into the care of a stagehand who had arrived with a cloak and a dry pair of shoes. He squelched his way back to the main party at the Palladian bridge where Diaghilev and all the Russian party were standing to applaud him.

The dancers, the wet and the dry, took their places on the main stage once more. The musicians played an operatic adventure while the audience calmed down. Then, one by one, the dancers, major and minor, bowed to the audience and departed to the big house. The musicians too took up their music and their instruments and left their separate stage. The audience began to make their way home, discussing that final leap and the dive into the water. 'An act of such dramatic surprise that has not being witnessed in or around Oxford in living memory,' said the *Manchester Guardian*; 'a truly dramatic denouement to a truly dramatic day' was the verdict of *The Times*; 'a tour de force for M. Diaghilev,' said the *Illustrated London News*.

15

Pas de chat

'The step of the cat'. The dancer jumps sideways, and
while in mid-air, bends both legs up (two *retirés*) bringing the feet up as high as possible, with knees apart.
The Dance of the Cygnets from Swan Lake involves
sixteen *pas de chat*, performed by four dancers holding
hands with their arms interlaced.

Colonel Olivier Brouzet, the man in charge of the
French Secret Service, had the original of Fragonard's
The Swing on loan from the Louvre on the wall behind
his desk. Colonel Brouzet had never been a violent
man. One has to admit that the artillery of which he
was a noted exponent could cause frightful carnage
and terrible wounds, but Olivier Brouzet never saw
the damage his cannons created. Artillery men have
to be methodical and ruthless: methodical in ensur-
ing that their troop has sufficient time to reload properly according to the rule book; ruthless in pressing
home the advantage, even though there may be a

bloodstained slaughter of their enemies on the receiving end of their salvoes.

His guest this morning was in civilian clothes, a black frock coat, a linen shirt in pale blue, and an elaborate cravat that seemed to be based on a Japanese design. Colonel Maurice Martel Argaud was a star member of a fashionable cavalry regiment. He was serving a six-month attachment to the General Staff. He moved in avant-garde circles in the capital, consorting with Proust and being painted by Renoir with his friend Charles Ephrussi as guests at boating parties on the Seine.

And it was this link to the General Staff that had brought him to the attention of Monsieur, as he now was in his Secret Service role, Brouzet and his Fragonard on the Place des Vosges.

The prevailing military theory in the French Army at that time was that attack at all costs was the best policy. Its chief proponent was an officer called Grandmaison, who believed with all the passion of the convert that it was the only way to win wars. *L'attaque à l'outrance*, extreme attack, was the order of the day. It was the order of the revolutionary leader Danton to the French defenders at Verdun back in 1792: *il nous faut de l'audace, encore de l'audace, toujours de l'audace* (we must be bold, we must be bolder still, we must always be bold).

Colonel Argaud disagreed. He was a great believer in reading military history, a subject regarded as irrelevant and unnecessary by his opponents, who believed that truth was on their side and that this time things would be different. Wide reading in nineteenth-century battles convinced the Colonel that in the last century key battles, particularly those of Waterloo and Gettysburg, had been won by defence. And Colonel Argaud was convinced that mass slaughter of his fellow countrymen would result if a policy of all-out attack at any cost was pursued. He firmly believed that wholesale destruction of the French armies would take place on the battlefields of the next war if the military authorities followed the doctrine of '*l'audace*'. In French military circles, this was heresy.

*

Powerscourt was contemplating a piece of cheese with some interest when he noticed a commotion at the door of the hotel restaurant in Woodstock, the evening of the day of the ballet. A tall young man, wearing a dark grey suit and twirling his hat in his hands, was apparently asking a series of urgent questions of the nearest waiter, questions the waiter didn't seem capable of answering. He, in his turn, was gesturing towards the head waiter, who was advising an elderly couple about the wine list to accompany the sweet course.

'Hold on, Lucy,' said Powerscourt. 'I don't like the look of this one bit.'

Shortly the head waiter himself made his way over to the Powerscourt table. 'Lord Powerscourt? Please forgive me. The young man at the door wishes to speak to you. He says it is a matter of some urgency.'

'I'm sorry, Lucy. I'd better see what this is all about.'

Only in the street, when they were well clear of the hotel and its staff, did the young man – Sergeant Fuller – reveal his purpose. 'It's Inspector Jackson, my guv'nor, my lord. He wants to see you up at the big house at once. Inspector Dutfield told him you were here.'

'What's happened?' said Powerscourt, and something in the young man's demeanour implied that something terrible had come to spoil the day.

'There's another dead one, my lord. Dead ballet person, I mean, my lord, apart from the one you already have down there in London.'

'What sort of ballet person? Male or Female? Age?'

'Female, my lord, aged about twenty to twenty-five, my lord. My Inspector said I was to fill you in along the way.'

'You want me to come back to Blenheim Palace with you? Very good. I'll just tell my wife.'

It was only a short walk to the back gates. 'The time now is just after ten, my lord. We don't know yet when exactly it happened – some time after eight thirty at the earliest and nine forty-five at the latest. The girl was found by one of the footmen, my lord. She was lying in a pool of her own blood and stuff underneath the balcony in the Great Hall, my lord. The doctors say she'd have been killed instantly. We gather she was called Vera, Vera Belitsky, my lord.'

'Suicide on a day like this? With all that glory for the Ballets Russes? It seems unlikely.'

'My Inspector says he's had a case like this once before, in one of the colleges, my lord. High building: did he fall or was he pushed, that sort of thing. Only in this case it was a she.'

Powerscourt was thinking along similar lines. One case with a double possibility, dancer or understudy. Now a second. They did, however, have one thing in common.

'There's an old lady up there, my lord. Wants to speak to you as a matter of some urgency, she says.'

'Would you want this old lady as your grandmother, Sergeant?'

'No I wouldn't, my lord. Not at any price. You've caught me out there, my lord. We're not supposed to have opinions about members of the public, dead or alive, as you well know.'

They were now mounting the steps towards the Great Hall. A couple of constables waved them inside. Inspector Jackson, who looked even younger than his sergeant, came to greet them. One whole corner of the Great Hall was shrouded in sheets. The Inspector pointed up to the gallery.

'That's where she came from, right in the middle of that balcony. And that,' he pointed in the direction of the sheeted section, 'is where she ended up. The fall killed her. We're waiting for the undertakers to take her away. Some fool began babbling on about where on earth she is going to receive an Orthodox funeral and an Orthodox burial in the middle of Oxfordshire. I ask you.'

Inspector Jackson shook his head.

'Sorry, my lord. Let me tell you what we know. The ballet people danced here in the Great Hall, audience draped all the way up the stairs. The musicians were crammed in like mice on the balcony and the area behind, the dancers in the Great Hall down below. After the performance, the guests take a drink in the garden with the fountains out the back. Then they go in to eat in the State Dining Room with a few overspilling in the big room behind. They're all still there. The butler, a former military man, I understand, realized that they all had to be kept in the same place. That went down well, as you can imagine. My men are now working their way through them: invitation cards, please, name and address, where were you at the time of the murder?'

'Who found the body?'

'Sorry, my lord. One of the footmen found her. Thank God he had the good sense to go straight to the butler.'

An angry Lady Ripon was advancing towards them, brushing aside a couple of constables as if they were flies in her drawing room. She carried an enormous bag in her right hand – clutching it, Powerscourt thought, like a weapon of war.

'Good evening, Inspector,' she boomed, making the word 'Inspector' sound like an inferior sort of servant, somewhere between a sous chef and an under footman.

'My name is Lady Ripon, Patron of the Royal Ballet, I wish to speak to your companion, Inspector,' she carried on, 'the man called Powerscourt.'

Inspector Jackson showed that he might have met her type before.

'That won't be possible in here, Lady Ripon. This area is closed off. Perhaps you'd care to have your conversation outside. Our constables will be able to keep an eye on you out there.'

'Well, Powerscourt,' she began as they reached the bottom of the great steps that led into Blenheim Palace, 'I thought I had forbidden you entrance here this evening. But you turn up nonetheless. We'll let that pass for a moment. My people and I employed you to find out who killed that understudy down in London.'

She made the word 'understudy' sound like a packet of tea you might have to pick up at the grocer's when the Fortnum and Mason delivery hadn't arrived on time.

'You have failed. And now your prowess has led to a second murder, one you were powerless to prevent.

What do you have to say for yourself? If you were one of my servants or my staff, I should dismiss you on the spot. But I would have to consult with the board of the Royal Opera House who are, alas, not here at the moment.'

'I am truly sorry about the second murder, if murder it was—' Powerscourt began.

'Don't give me this if it was murder nonsense, Powerscourt. Everyone can see it was a murder. That's why all these policemen are charging about all over the place, making marks on the floors where they shouldn't, knocking over valuable pieces of porcelain, no doubt. You couldn't survive a fall like that onto a marble floor. It's not possible. Don't tell me all this would be going on for a mere suicide of a junior member of the corps de ballet.'

Powerscourt told her precisely that. 'And, let me tell you Lady Ripon, it is only right and proper that a young girl should receive the same attention if she was a suicide or a murder victim.'

'Your observations are outrageous, Powerscourt. Your performance is pathetic. Your record as an investigator is in ruins. Your future employment prospects are zero. Have no doubt that I shall tell all the society members – a select band in which you are not included – of your failures and your incompetence.'

With that Lady Ripon drew her cloak around her and swept back into the hall. Powerscourt had to admit that he was not sorry to see her go.

*

The French Secret Service believed that Argaud and his small band of confederates were passing their views on to a hostile power. Quite who this hostile power was, they were not entirely sure, but they felt it was unlikely it was to England, and possible but unlikely it was to Russia. Germany was the obvious place. If the German High Command knew that wave after wave of Frenchmen were going to pour out of their trenches in their ridiculous coloured uniforms and charge the German trenches, then victory would be assured. For a German victory, it would just be a matter of making sure there was enough ammunition for the machine guns.

Olivier Brouzet was certain that his visitor was passing secret information to the enemy. He did not know how or through whom the intelligence was transmitted. He intended to find out with his own very special form of torture.

'Come, *mon Colonel*,' he began, 'we both know that the French Army is always conducting manoeuvres, is that not so? Well, I have for you today details of a slightly unusual form of manoeuvre that could be repeated any time on those officers whose wives and daughters are living in the country. Plans have been laid, you understand.'

Brouzet knew that Colonel Argaud had a beautiful wife and two equally beautiful daughters. A slight look of alarm passed across his face.

Olivier Brouzet reached into a drawer on his desk and produced a large envelope. It contained a series of photographs, face down, all with a number written on the back in large letters. He brought out the first one. This showed an elegant *maison de maître* in peaceful rolling countryside. The proportions, with the double staircase and the large windows, were clearly those of the late eighteenth century.

'Look at this, my friend. It is a beautiful house with gardens and the odd statue on guard at the front of the house. But today there are visitors.'

He produced photograph number two, which showed a group of about twenty French soldiers marching along the road outside. They were not yet quite level with the entrance.

'Now we see, *mon Colonel*, who these visitors might be. It looks as if the men are on marching practice, but who knows what may happen? I wonder if the wife or either of the young ladies are on the lookout for visitors.'

Out came photograph number three, which showed that the little column had turned left and were now almost up to the front door.

'What can this be?' asked Brouzet, 'the soldiers have come to call. What on earth do they want?'

Photograph number four showed the men, still standing in line, listening now to an officer who seemed to be addressing them from the top of the steps. A sergeant and a private had been sent inside. 'See,' Brouzet purred, looking carefully at his victim, 'the Captain brings good news, a rare event for anybody to hear good news from their officers!'

Photograph number five showed the first detachment of soldiers making their way up the stairs. Those at the front had begun taking off their greatcoats; it looked to be a warm day.

Colonel Argaud was clasping his hands together and rocking slowly in his chair. The next picture was taken higher up and showed that the first four had taken their greatcoats off and were busy unbuttoning their trousers. To their left was a *madame*, traditional keeper of the rules in French Army establishments of this sort. She was knitting vigorously as she kept watch on her charges.

Photograph number six showed the men outside, chatting and laughing and punching their fists in the air. Half of them were making obscene signs with their hands and fingers.

Photograph number seven was not one of the clearest. It appeared to show a woman's knees, very indistinct, a couple of rough ropes they might have used to tie her feet to the bedposts at the bottom, and a second *madame*, also knitting happily in the corner.

'See how our French photographers take care not to show what should not be seen,' cried Olivier Brouzet. 'This photograph is not at all clear. I should have told you before that the men were told that this is a set menu here today: first the wife, then the beautiful daughters, with the youngest one last, if the *poilus* have any fire left in their bellies. It is customary, I believe, in these cases, to afford a pillow to the women to make life more comfortable and to drown out any screams. Even French privates can be squeamish at times. But the *madame* is keeping watch at all times.'

Colonel Argaud was sweating now, wiping his face with his monogrammed handkerchief.

Photograph number eight showed the first soldiers on their way out. They were laughing and joshing. One or two waved their rather limp equipment in the air, as if they had won a major victory. Photograph number nine showed the queue still waiting at the bottom of the steps.

'See, Colonel, the parade of the satisfied is now making its way down the stairs. But look!'

Photograph number ten showed the last group of soldiers kicking their heels outside, grinning and joking.

'There is more to come, Colonel, there is indeed more to come. The sport is only just beginning.'

The Colonel was turning pale. Brouzet moved in for the kill.

'We know where you live, Colonel Argaud. We know your son is away at St Cyr. How sad he will be to have missed all the fun this afternoon. We know the times the daughters are in the house and when they are away.'

Photograph number eleven showed a long queue coming down the stairs and only a few unfulfilled ones waiting at the bottom.

'Come, Colonel, this is only the first course. The men will receive some refreshment when have finished the hors d'oeuvres. Then it is time for the eldest daughter! She will be put in the same bed, of course. No point causing a lot of dirty washing for the staff, who are currently locked up in the basement. And then the youngest for pudding! What a feast!'

Colonel Argaud was not to know it, but Brouzet's photographs were beginning to lose their power. There were only a limited number of shots available on such an occasion, and most of them had been pressed into service.

'Photograph number eleven,' Brouzet began, but photograph number eleven never saw the light of day that afternoon. Colonel Argaud cracked.

'All right, Brouzet, all right. I give in. You really would carry out that awful ritual against my family, wouldn't you?'

'Of course,' Brouzet lied. 'We are all in the service of France.'

'If I tell you exactly what you want to know, will you promise never to interfere with my family in any way?'

Brouzet looked him coolly in the eye. 'I will.'

There was a pause while the two Colonels looked at each other, the girl in Fragonard's swing rising gracefully to the top of her arc on the wall behind Brouzet.

'These questions can be very painful,' said Brouzet finally. 'I apologize for that to a man of your military distinction.'

'There won't be much of that left after this afternoon,' Argaud said sadly. 'But carry on. You must do your duty.'

'Were you passing information about French military tactics to another power?'

'I was.'

'I am compelled to ask to whom you were sending this information, *mon Colonel*? To the Germans?'

Argaud was scornful. 'To the Germans? Me, an officer in the French Army? After Sedan? After their ludicrous Emperor had himself crowned in the Hall of Mirrors at Versailles? After Alsace-Lorraine? I thought you would have thought better of me than to ask that question.'

'Not to the English, surely? They probably know it already after all these joint exercises.'

'Not to the English, no.'

'The Russians? Surely not.'

'Surely so, Colonel Brouzet. They are not fools, these Russians. They know the problem facing Germany of fighting on two fronts. And it takes ages for the Russians to mobilize their forces across the vast space of the Russian interior with their ignorant peasants and their inefficient railroads. The Russian generals want to know how long they have got before the full might of the German Army comes to fight them. If the French hold out and win, as our generals are always telling the Russians they will every time they meet, then they may never face the full might of the German military machine at all. But if the French look like losing, it is a different matter. That is what I told the Russians, that the French would not win an immediate victory in the West.'

'The Russians are not stupid,' said Brouzet. 'This knowledge could impact on their military planning.'

'Such as it is,' said Colonel Argaud. 'One general told me the entire country would be paralysed by the effort of getting the troops to the front, wherever that might be.'

'I see. And how was your information sent on to St Petersburg, might I ask?'

'You will laugh when I tell you.'

'Tell me.'

'It was sent to St Petersburg through the Ballets Russes.'

'The Ballets Russes! When they were here in Paris?' Brouzet could see it all, the limitless possibilities of sending messages as they travelled from the Russian capital to Monte Carlo, to Paris, to London, now perhaps on to some cultural city in Germany. They travelled through and across the possible combatants in any future European war with their vast entourage and mountains of paraphernalia. This knowledge could occupy weeks and weeks of time for the customs men of Europe. There was somebody he knew in England to whom this information would be pure gold. He would send it on at once.

'That's a very imaginative choice, those ballet people; you could send anything down that route and not get caught.'

'Tell me, Monsieur Brouzet, what is to happen to me?'

'Well, I shall have to write a report, Colonel Argaud. Whether I ever send it anywhere is another matter. It seems to me, you see, that your sending this information to the Russians might work in France's favour. If they think the French are going to collapse early in the war, they will have to be ready sooner than they might have planned, and that could only work in France's favour if the Germans have to move divisions from the west to the east, if you follow me. I shall let you know what I decide. If I were you, *mon Colonel*, I wouldn't lose too much sleep over it, but I wouldn't do it again.'

'Thank you.'

As the elegant Colonel made his way downstairs, Olivier Brouzet put away his photographs. It was the fourth time he'd used them and they hadn't failed him yet. Not bad for an afternoon's work with some actors, a director, an experienced photographer and some props from the Comedie Française at his mother's house in the country.

16

Coda

Literally 'tail'. As in music, a *coda* is a passage which brings a movement or a separate piece to a conclusion.

In ballet, the coda is usually the 'Finale', a set of dances known as the *Grand Pas* or *Grand Pas d'action* and brings almost all the dancers onto the stage. A particularly large or complex coda may be called a *Grand coda*. If a large group of dancers are concerned, the terms *Coda générale* or *Grand coda générale* may be used.

In ballet there are many famous codas, such as the one found in *Le Corsaire Pas de Deux*. The so-called *Black Swan Pas de deux* from the ballet *Swan Lake* features the famous *coda* where the ballerina performs thirty-two *fouettés en tournant*.

Powerscourt thought there was something rather sad about watching the stages being dismantled shortly after seven thirty the next morning. Floorboards were being removed from the stages in the lake, the great staves that held them in position just visible beneath the water. He had already had a conversation with Inspector Jackson, who saw the logic, if not the practicability of his proposal.

'Let's try it by all means,' he said. 'Thank God it's a Sunday and there are no performances of the Ballets Russes in London. I've got a couple more translators, students at the medical school, coming to help with the translation. But they say Diaghilev was refusing to talk to anybody at all last night. He stomped off and looked at the pictures and wouldn't speak to a soul, even though the Duke's guests had a couple of fluent French speakers among them.'

Michel Fokine was looking troubled when Powerscourt found him drinking coffee in the State Dining Room.

'Of course I will take you to him. He is in a terrible mood. "The afternoon of my greatest triumph", he keeps saying, "spoilt by some silly girl who decides to throw herself over the balcony." For Diaghilev, my lord, art wins out over everything.'

They found him pacing up and down the Palladian bridge, as the planks and beams were being dismantled beneath him.

'Good morning, Mr Diaghilev,' said Powerscourt. 'May I offer my congratulations on your ballet yesterday afternoon. It was a triumph. It will live long in the memory of all who saw it.'

Diaghilev stamped his cane on the side of the bridge. 'They will remember it for the dead girl, that Vera Belitsky, not for the poetry of the Ballets Russes.'

'Mr Diaghilev,' said Powerscourt, 'I think you are wrong about that. But I wish to speak to you about matters of today. The local Inspector here will not let your people go until they have been questioned by the police. It is just not possible. You wish to bring your company back to London for tomorrow's performances in Covent Garden. As things stand, those interviews may still be going on when the curtain goes up. There will, inevitably, be one or two people to whom Inspector Jackson and his staff will wish to talk again. He is well aware of your problems, the Inspector. He has organized another couple of interpreters to come here with all speed from the Oxford Medical School. They are Russian born and one of them is also fluent in French from his time at the Sorbonne. If your people could be organized in groups of five or six, to be interviewed one at a time, of course, the process could be over by early afternoon, if not sooner.'

Diaghilev smacked his cane onto the bridge once again and muttered something to himself in Russian. Fokine kept his own counsel. Diaghilev began making short sorties away from the bridge as another three boards were carried off.

'Think of it, Monsieur Diaghilev,' said Powerscourt. 'If your dancers and your staff do not cooperate, you could still be here tomorrow or even the next day. You could miss out on two performances in London. Those who have bought the tickets, all people desperate to see your Ballets Russes, will be disappointed. Your reputation, so high after yesterday, will suffer. It's bound to.'

A rather chastened Diaghilev stopped walking for a moment. 'It is not my reputation I care about,

Lord Powerscourt, but my art; the art we create and take with us wherever we go. Art is the only thing that makes life worth living. The rest is all show and vanity.'

'Even art must go on,' said Powerscourt, sensing that somewhere there must be a key to unlock Diaghilev's intransigence, 'art must go on on Monday and art must go on on Tuesday and art must go on on Wednesday. There's another thing that would help mark the glories and the triumphs of yesterday.'

Powerscourt was to tell Lady Lucy later that he had no idea where this next suggestion came from.

'I have one further thought, Monsieur Diaghilev. Why not erect a plaque on this bridge in memory of Vera Belitsky, the dead girl? You could say her death happened after the performance. Maybe you should start collections after each performance for a fund to start a scholarship in her memory.'

M. Fokine suddenly sprang into life. 'It could be a scholarship for a poor dancer to attend the Imperial Theatre School back home, Sergei Pavlovich. That way her memory would live as long as the ballet.'

Diaghilev sighed. 'Sometimes I think I am like that man in Shakespeare who is surrounded by a sea of troubles which come not in a single one but in battalions. I have to carry the entire weight of the Ballets Russes on my shoulders and sometimes it feels too heavy to bear. But I like the plaque. I like the scholarship. We shall do as you ask. Perhaps you could see to it, Fokine.'

With that Diaghilev waddled off away from the house towards the great obelisk on the high ground above the lake. Powerscourt couldn't help wondering if he was going to take its measurements for an obelisk of his own.

*

Natasha Shaporova's train was leaving Cologne, the twin spires of the great cathedral still visible from her carriage window. Once she heard from one of the corps de ballet that Alexander Taneyev was always writing letters home, she did not hesitate. She caught the earliest express that could connect to St Petersburg and set off. She packed a bag and Tolstoy's *War and Peace*, which she had always meant to read but never got round to starting. She felt it would last her on the outward and the return journeys. Even as she read about the salons of St Petersburg, a part of her brain was saying to her: father, mother, three sisters, friends, sweethearts – was there one person Alexander Taneyev confided in? Who was it? She looked out at the German countryside now shooting past her window. Change in Berlin.

*

Arthur Cooper was as distressed as he had ever been in his new faith of world revolution, which had been inspired by the scriptures of Lenin and his followers. He had at last found the printer he wanted, a man who could organize the translation from the original Russian into English, and the printing of five hundred copies of each tract. 'What Is to Be Done Now?' he had learned, was the title of the latest gospel from Lenin's fertile pen in Cracow. The comrade, one Harry Smith, had a regular press in Clerkenwell, on which he would print all sorts of subversive literature. In Arthur

Cooper's world he should be offering to carry out the work for a nominal sum. But he wasn't. Cooper did not know it, but the tale of the roubles changed into pounds – and the very large totals of those transactions – was now common knowledge among a select few of the capital's revolutionary vanguard. And Harry Smith was one of them.

'It's not like it was in the old days, comrade. With these new laws they could lock me up in jail for a long time for spreading this kind of stuff around.'

'That's not the point,' replied Cooper, 'it's doing Lenin's work. That shouldn't be charged at your exorbitant rates and you know it.'

'I'll know it full well when the bloody policemen come knocking at my door. You've got to pay the going rate for the job. Why isn't he circulating the English pamphlet here in England, anyway? Answer me that.'

'Security, that's what.' All difficult questions were to be answered, Lenin's courier had told him, with that blanket response.

'If you don't like my price, go and find somebody else who'll do it.'

The comrades in Cracow, Cooper had been told, were most anxious that he should clinch the deal.

'All right. One thousand pounds for the lot. I can't say I'm happy with that, but it'll have to do.'

'Very good. I knew you'd come round in the end.'

'Who should I deliver the pamphlets to?'

'Bring them back here, heavily marked with the words Ballets Russes, Customs Requisitions and Clearances.'

'Very good.'

As Cooper showed his printer out of the back door,

he suddenly knew how he felt. It was if he was still a true believer in the Evangelical side of Christianity, who arrives at Heaven's gates only to be told by St Peter that a substantial entry fee would be required.

*

Lady Lucy had taken over the role of friend and counsellor to the girls of the corps de ballet. A translator was found among the great army of her relations in the capital. She had borrowed the samovar and a couple of icons from Natasha's housekeeper and was reading the notes made after each visit. She thanked her lucky stars that Natasha had written them in English.

'There's only one thing that hits you after you've read all these things, Francis,' she said.

'And what's that?' said her husband absent-mindedly. He was reading a selection of the newspapers and their coverage of the Ballets Russes's display at Blenheim Palace. Most of them were ecstatic; tactfully they had kept the story of the dead girl for the later paragraphs. Fokine had told him to look out for the photographs of the Duke and his lady. The photographers, unaware of the lack of title, had taken shots of them together all over the place, on the steps of the palace, progressing down the great sweep of the entrance court to the bridge, sitting applauding the performers. One inhabitant of Blenheim Palace, at least, would be happy with the coverage and consider the money well spent. Even though Gladys Deacon had still not been described as the Duchess.

'It's that man Bolm. He was after those girls like a man possessed. I'm sure one of them could have killed him. But there's a further complication, Francis.

You said that he pulled out about two o'clock in the afternoon because he was ill and Alexander Taneyev took over. So anybody inside the company would have known that the young Alexander and not the older man Bolm was to dance the Prince. But if you were an outsider, a man paid to do the job, you might not have known that. You could have lurked about in the scenic area and the backstage areas and gone to kill the chap who came down through the trapdoor. You mightn't even realize you'd killed the wrong man until you read about it the next day.'

'There is and there always has been,' agreed Powerscourt, 'a terrible question mark at the heart of the first murder. Did they kill Taneyev because he was Taneyev, or did they kill him because they thought he was Bolm? Or did Bolm take the evening off because he knew he or his associates would be able to kill Taneyev? Nobody backstage would have noticed Bolm at all. I think I'm going to ask the Inspector to make a further check on Bolm's movements for the whole day. He could, for example, have decided to kill Taneyev days before and laid his plans accordingly, only telling the theatre people after lunch.'

'I've rather grown to dislike Mr Bolm, making his advances on these young girls all over the place and at all times of day.'

'Doesn't necessarily make him a murderer,' said Lord Francis Powerscourt.

*

East Prussia stretched out in front of Natasha Shaporova's train. She was making good progress with *War and Peace*. Her knowledge of geography was poor and she wondered if Napoleon's armies had crossed the same space a hundred years before. She remembered somebody telling her that Tolstoy himself had seen military service in the Crimea. She hoped that there wouldn't be too much marching about and military manoeuvres. Never far from her mind was a family that might not be too different from *War and Peace*'s Bolkonskys and Rostovs: the family Taneyev, with its treasure trove of letters from the dead Alexander. Change in Warsaw.

*

Anastasia couldn't tell anybody in the Ballets Russes what had happened. She knew it would mean expulsion from the company, let alone possible prosecution for being an associate to theft in St Petersburg. She had cried so much and for so long that she thought there couldn't be any tears left in her little body. She found Lady Lucy's address and set out for Markham Square. Somebody had told her that the husband was a detective. Perhaps he would be able to help. She knew Lady Lucy's address and hailed a taxi to take her to Markham Square. Fresh reserves and reservoirs of tears overcame her so much in the cab that the driver leant back and offered her his best handkerchief, perfectly washed and pressed by the cabbie's wife in Harringey. He even forgot to ask her for the fare, but ushered her to the Powerscourt door and waited for Rhys to let her in. The butler had seen all sorts and conditions of visitors to Markham Square in his time but never one as distraught as this. Her whole life seemed to have come to an end.

'Anastasia from the corps de ballet,' he announced

to Lady Lucy, who was reading the forthcoming programme for the ballet.

'Anastasia, you poor thing,' said Lady Lucy. 'Your eyes are so red you must have been crying all afternoon.' She helped the girl into the large armchair by the fire. 'Would you like some tea? Something stronger? A glass of water?'

Through her sobs, the girl managed to nod for the glass of water.

'Now, Anastasia,' said Lady Lucy, who thought she had met the girl at Natasha's house in the early days, 'whatever is the matter?'

There was a prolonged burst of sobbing, broken only by further ministrations with the cabbie's handkerchief. Lady Lucy waited. Powerscourt had decided to let his wife do all the talking for now.

'There must have been something terrible,' said Lady Lucy. 'We're not the police, my dear, and we're not the Ballets Russes either. If you've got something to say, it need never go outside these four walls, I promise you.'

The answer came in a whisper. Powerscourt had often remarked how people thought they could minimize the effect of some terrible news by announcing it in the lowest of voices. He had decided it was the opposite of shouting at foreigners in English in the hopes that the volume might bring forth understanding.

'Jewels.'

'Jewels?' said Lady Lucy. 'Your jewels? Somebody else's jewels? You must speak up, Anastasia or we'll never hear you.'

Anastasia did not speak up. She spoke, if anything, even more softly than before.

'Not my jewels.'

'If they weren't yours, then why do you have to be so upset about them?'

'I don't have the jewels any more.'

'Do you mean that you were looking after the jewels for somebody else? And now they've gone, you worry you'll have to replace them?'

'No, no,' sobbed the girl, 'it's the money. The money from the jewels has gone.'

'Let's take this one step at a time, Anastasia? Have another glass of water. I'll order some tea in a minute. You had some jewels. You sold them one way or another. The money's gone. Is that it?'

'Yes, yes, that's it. That's right.'

'But whose were the jewels? Were they yours? Family heirlooms that would cause distress in your household?'

This brought a further burst of weeping, in which the words St Petersburg, George and something that sounded like Kollicky were all the Powerscourts could pick up.

Powerscourt now took over after a nod from Lady Lucy.

'Did the jewels come from St Petersburg, Anastasia?'

She nodded this time, relieved not to have to speak for a while.

'And you brought them here? Or did somebody else bring them here?'

The girl pointed at herself. Powerscourt hoped this unhappy experience hadn't left her partially dumb for the next half an hour.

'And who is George? A friend of yours?'

The girl nodded.

'Has he taken the money from the sale of the jewels?'

The girl shook her head.

'Did he organize the sale of the jewels for you?'

The girl nodded once more.

'You mentioned somebody who sounded like Kollicky just now. Were they Johnston Killick of Hatton Garden by any chance?'

Another nod.

'A very reputable and responsible firm they are too, Anastasia. I'm sure they will have done their best for you. Let me try to clear up the London end, if we may. You brought some jewels, which weren't yours, to London. I am guessing you were under instructions from St Petersburg to sell them during your stay here. You sold the jewels with the help of your friend George. You had the money. I am guessing when I say it was hidden among your luggage at the hotel. Now the money has gone. Is that right?'

The girl nodded.

'And the suitcase? The money was in a suitcase? Yes? So it is the suitcase that has gone missing?'

This time the girl managed a feeble, 'Yes.'

'Anastasia,' Lady Lucy moved back into command, 'I think you need to lie down and have a rest. I'll take you up to one of the spare bedrooms and I'm sure we can find some clean clothes that aren't stained with tears. We can move on to the St Petersburg end of things later.'

17

Entrechat

A step of beating in which the dancer jumps into the air and rapidly crosses the legs before and behind. For example: in an *entrechat-quatre* starting from fifth position, right foot front, the dancer will jump crossing her/his legs and beating first the right thigh on the back of the left thigh, then at the front of the left thigh, landing in the same position she/he started. Three changes of the feet in the air, ultimately changing which foot was front.

A battered Renault taxi-cab drew up outside 32 Place des Vosges, home of the European Art Exchange, the cover story for the French Secret Service Headquarters on the first floor. That taxi passenger must have pre-paid his fare, for he shot out of the Renault and into the building in a couple of seconds flat. The other visitor, the Préfet de Paris, or Mayor of Paris, had been shown in through the back door by the dustbin men, who voted for him regularly at election times. M. Dubois was their friend, and any friend of M. Dubois was automatically enrolled in their very own Legion of Honour.

So what brought this disparate group – three Frenchman, and an English Ambassador to France, Sir Miles Myddleton, just returned from attendance on his sovereign in Biarritz – together in a large, eighteenth-century room with high ceilings and elegant shutters on the windows one floor up in one of Paris's most elegant squares at seven o'clock in the morning? The answer was not long in coming. Colonel Brouzet made the introductions and summed up the reasons for their presence in a single word.

'Bonds, gentlemen,' he said. 'People have been selling French bonds in considerable quantities. If it goes on like this, it could cause a financial crisis all across Europe. It is French government-issue bonds that have brought us here together this morning.'

Outside the birds were still singing and one or two of the cleaning staff could be heard complaining to themselves down in the square. It was going to be a beautiful day.

'The movements in these bonds coincided with the presence in Paris of the Ballets Russes and their various appendages. I have to tell you that nothing would surprise me regarding the behaviour of the Ballets Russes.

'As you know, gentlemen, the French government has authorized, some would say organized, vast loans to Russia, many of them designed as bonds due for repayment at some date in the distant future. This, as we all know, messieurs, is war policy disguised as finance. The more Russia is industrialized, the more factories she can build with the money raised from these bonds. She can pay for new facilities to make armaments for use in any future war with Germany. A stronger Russia means a stronger France. Monsieur le Ministre?'

It was an unusual scene. Here, in the afterglow of the belle époque, the French Minister of Finance, M. Blanc, looked as though he should have been head of dustmen, and the leader of the dustbin men, M. Nivelle, looked as though he should be Minister of Finance. The minister was wearing an old suit, much frayed, with a wing collar that looked as if it had been made for his father at the time of the terrible days of the siege of Paris and the Commune back in 1870. The suit, like his vast estates near Chambord and in the poorer quarters of the capital, was part of his inheritance.

'War and a strong Russia, gentlemen,' he began, 'is in the hands of ministries other than my own.' The man sounded as if every single person in his own department was also part of his immediate family.

'We follow the instructions of the President of the Republic. It is now a good number of years since the great treaty between our country and Russia was signed. The President charged my predecessor with the task of binding Russia economically to us as part of the stance of the Republic towards our neighbours across the Rhine.'

It seemed that the poor man couldn't even bring himself to say the word 'Germans'. It was widely known how unpopular the Germans had been in Paris in 1870 and 1871, proclaiming the new German Empire in France itself, against the advice of Bismarck, who warned it could lead to a hatred that could last for generations. Well, that hatred had survived for forty years or more. It was still going strong. The scars had lasted till this day. The wounds were still suppurating.

'Perhaps you could give us a brief outline of your methods, Monsieur le Ministre?' Olivier Brouzet looked closely at the painting from the Louvre that had replaced the Watteau that had hung happily behind the director's desk for the past seven years. Now it was Fragonard's *The Swing*, the girl flying higher and higher, pushed from behind by an old man who must have been her husband, and watched from the front by her lover hiding in the woods.

'You've always done well with jobs for the workers, I'll give you that,' the dustbin men's leader, M. Nivelle, in his immaculate suit, suddenly made his first contribution of the day. 'The loans have made a difference. There are now lots of working class districts around St Petersburg and the great cities. My people are grateful for that, even if the wages are still terrible.'

'To our methods.' The Minister of Finance picked up where Brouzet had left off. 'Russia is not a democracy like we have here in France or in England.' He nodded at Ambassador Myddleton. 'Laws are passed by the Duma, the toy-town Parliament with no real powers, and sent to the Tsar. There they are either rejected or amended by the last person to talk to the Tsar. At the present time, that means the unspeakable Rasputin, or his lover, as St Petersburg gossip would have it, the appalling Alexandra, wife of the Tsar.'

'Why is she appalling?' asked the British Ambassador. He would have used a milder term himself.

'She is German,' the Minister replied, spitting out the word as if using a mouthwash at the dentist's. 'During the Terror here in Paris, the mob called

Marie-Antoinette "*l'Autriche*", which means either 'Austrian' or 'ostrich' – with its head in the sand. How right they were. It is the same in that vast Russian hinterland beyond the cities. Religious societies, like ours here in France, and in the Russian Orthodox Church, need a Holy Mary, a Madonna. They need the counterpoint too, the bitch goddess to make up their simple pantheon.'

*

'Lucy, my love, do you think she's telling the truth, that poor girl upstairs?' Lord Powerscourt asked his wife.

'Anastasia? Well, as a matter of fact, I do. Don't you? It's rather an odd question to ask, surely?'

'Well, I do think she's telling the truth. But what a fantastic story. It could almost be something to throw us off the scent. Whatever the scent is. At the moment I'm not quite sure. But think it has to do with jewels stolen in St Petersburg that have come to London, presumably in the luggage of the Ballets Russes. The jewels must have been sold through a dealer. And then the money itself is stolen. It's vanished. It's all too fantastic for words.'

'Do you think it has to do with the murders?'

'I don't, except for the Ballets Russes connection. I suppose I'll have to ask that poor man Inspector Dutfield to put his people onto the Premier Hotel.'

'But there's no mention in Anastasia's account of any connection with Bolm or Taneyev, is there?'

'If Natasha Shaporova finds any connection in St Petersburg to the stolen jewels, my love, I'll take you to New York for a fortnight.'

Lady Lucy and their eldest son Thomas had been

waging a persistent campaign for the oldest members of the Powerscourt family to go to New York and stay in a skyscraper. But so far the plan had failed.

'What would you do, Lucy, if your jewels were stolen?'

'Here in London?'

'Yes.'

'Go to the police.'

'And I suppose you'd do the same thing in St Petersburg, though by all accounts the police there aren't as good as ours. Would you employ a private detective to bring them back? Would you employ me?'

'Of course I would.'

'I'm not sure I would accept the case, Lucy. Count Powerscourtski would decline. Do you suppose that's why the Russians are so fond of detective stories? At least in the fiction the crimes get solved, which they don't in real life. Anyway, Inspector Dutfield will be here in a moment with his account of the movements of various people around Blenheim Palace on the evening of the murder.'

*

The Ambassador looked closely at Fragonard's *The Swing*. He felt that any society whose aristocrats and princes of the Church dabbled in art beyond baroque and beyond rococo must be on the brink of revolution. Art had lost its moorings with society. Fragonard, the Tiepolos, Boucher all lived in a pink universe that was not connected to the people, except perhaps in subject matter and the strings on the swing. He included Poussin in his charge sheet, a John the Baptist for the horrors to come.

'Perhaps we could return to the bonds,' growled M. Dubois.

'Of course, forgive me,' replied M. le Ministre. 'My young men with their degrees in mathematics from the École Nationale Supérieure and the other *grandes écoles* here in Paris have one thing in common. Their eyesight is already going from too many hours spent staring at figures. Many of them wear those owlish glasses you see on the Left Bank these days. They look out for hot spots or hot people, places where money well invested could increase and multiply and encourage the growth of other enterprises. Sometimes it works. Sometimes it does not. They spotted the sudden and apparently inexplicable sale of these bonds.'

'Thank you,' said Mr Brouzet. 'Now, Monsieur Nivelle, perhaps you could enlighten us about what is happening on the ground here in Paris?'

'It was one of Monsieur le Ministre's young men,' said Nivelle in the coarse accent of the suburbs. 'He was almost blind by the way, but he alerted us that many of the great finance houses here in Paris were selling French bonds – not in enormous quantities, but making substantial withdrawals nonetheless. We found the same thing happening on the ground in the poorer parts of Paris, people selling off their bonds. One week ago, it all stopped, as if some wizard had blown a whistle.'

'Forgive me for a moment, gentlemen,' said Colonel Brouzet, disappearing into a side room. He came back with an ornate ivory chess set, made in China centuries before. 'It's from the Louvre,' he said apologetically. 'They lent it to me along with the Fragonard. Perhaps these ancient warriors will help us.'

He placed the ivory chessmen carefully on a low table. 'Let us see,' Brouzet said, taking out one white castle and one black knight and placing them on the left centre side of the board. Here we have England and France, united by your King Edward's entente cordiale. Here, we have the German knight, right in the middle of the board. On the far side of the battle-field we have the black castle, the Tsar and his armies. Who benefits from the sale of these bonds? Sir Miles, perhaps you could bring some of your wisdom to the table here?'

The Ambassador hesitated before he spoke. Outside a party of raucous Americans were demanding of an unfortunate waiter why they could not have their breakfast at seven fifteen in the morning. That was what they did in Des Moines, Iowa where they came from, they proudly told the garçon.

'It all depends, doesn't it,' Myddleton said finally, 'as to why these people are selling their bonds; on whether they are selling them for their own use, or to some foreign agents who are lurking in the poorer parts of the city – forgive me, Monsieur Nivelle – and scooping up these bonds. Do we know what proportion of the total have been sold, by the way?'

'Just over six per cent of the total,' said M. le Ministre. 'That's a substantial percentage, by the way.'

'There is no evidence of a Monsieur Scoop operating anywhere in Paris,' said M. Nivelle firmly.

'It's worth remembering,' said the Ambassador, 'that there are only two finance houses in Europe that could mount such an operation as this. You would need offices right across the Continent and very large numbers of employees. You see, I don't think any of the governments would have the personnel to carry out such a conspiracy. They would turn to their bankers. After all, it was Rothschilds who financed Wellington's later years during the Peninsular War, and on to Waterloo itself. They are one of the houses. They control the bond market across the whole of Europe. The other family are the Ephrussis. They control the supply of grain across Europe from their base at Odessa in the Crimea, the breadbasket of central Europe, and like their rivals they have offices in London and Paris and in other capitals.'

'*Merde!*' said M. le Ministre. '*Merde alors!* What a thought! A cup final between the Rothschilds and the Ephrussis, fought out in the backstreets of the cities and in the Bourses and the Stock Exchanges of Europe, with a grand final between the Rothschilds and the Ephrussis played out on the finest tennis courts in Paris. What a prospect!'

Colonel Brouzet raised his hand. 'We play a little game, I think. We look at the hopes and fears of both sides. Then we think of who might want to buy these bonds. Sir Miles, I ask you to bat for England, as you say about the cricket in your country. What are her hopes? Fears come later.'

'The English politicians are preoccupied with matters at home, with strikes, with the problems of the House of Lords and the Irish question that never seems to go away. Her hopes are for a period of domestic peace and no change abroad. She worries that the great days of Empire may be over, that she could become one with Nineveh and Tyre.'

'And France, Monsieur le Ministre?'

216

'France hopes for *la revanche*, for revenge against Germany. Some of our monuments in the capital have been draped in black since we lost at Sedan in 1870. Nobody, man or woman, horse or dog has ridden through the great arch of the Arc de Triomphe since that date. La Gloire, l'Audace on the battlefield, the restoration of France to her rightful place as the cultural capital of Europe and the world: those are the hopes of France, Monsieur Brouzet.'

'Germany, Mr Dubois?'

'I didn't come here to speak for the Germans, Monsieur Brouzet, but I can speak to the question. We are in touch with our comrades in Berlin and dustmen everywhere. Germany means the Kaiser, a bundle of neuroses and vanities. He wants to be master of the universe. He wants peace with all the world. He is obsessed with the country of his mother and his grandmother Queen Victoria. He is the most unstable ruler in Europe.'

'I would dispute that, Mr Nivelle. I speak for Russia.' M. Brouzet was inspecting his ivory chessmen very carefully. 'I offer Tsar Nicholas the Second in place of the Kaiser. The Tsar is, even now, preparing to celebrate the tercentenary of the Romanovs next year. It will be a year of processions and parades and loyalty reaffirmed. Three hundred years of supreme power. He is probably waiting for some simple peasant being lined up to greet his Father, The Father of all the Russias, Nicholas the Second. Throw in Rasputin and the German bitch and the Tsar wins by several lengths. Above all, he wants no truck with Dumas and democracy. He wants to be an autocrat once again, to reclaim the past to secure his future.'

Colonel Brouzet paused for a moment and moved the white knight forward into an attack position. The black horseman went into the defence.

'Time is short, messieurs, eternity is long, Sir Miles. We have to grasp the nettle. Each of you has one sentence to explain why your country would want to buy up these bonds. England, Sir Miles?'

'England would buy the bonds to preserve the status quo and to prevent the Germans getting them.'

'Thank you. France?'

'France too would buy them for fear of the Germans having them.'

'Russia, that's me, is so preoccupied with the celebrations next year that it takes no notice of what might be happening in Paris.'

'Germany would buy them to throw a spoke in the wheels of the Triple Alliance and because some Germans want war now before the Russians become too powerful with their new industrial might.'

'Thank you all,' said Colonel Brouzet, moving a couple of Chinese pawns on his board. 'We may not have the answer, but at least we are better informed.'

Later that day, M. Brouzet sent the news of the vanishing bonds to his friend, the English investigator Lord Francis Powerscourt. There was only the most tenuous connection with the Ballets Russes – had one of their number brought word that the selling was to begin, perhaps? – but you could never tell.

18

Pointe work

Performing steps while on the tips of the toes, with feet fully extended and wearing *pointe* shoes, a structurally reinforced type of shoe designed specifically for this purpose. Most often performed by women.

They had most of the story now, Powerscourt and Lady Lucy. They knew that the jewels had been stolen in St Petersburg but they didn't know who had taken them or from whom they had been taken. They knew that Anastasia had been charged with the selling of them, but not by whom. They knew now about George Smythe, currently sitting happily in a Powerscourt chair and drinking some Powerscourt coffee. Anastasia's reluctance to name names did not extend to George's, possibly because he was English. At any rate, she had thrown him, metaphorically, to the wolves at the first available opportunity. Anastasia had been so upset after telling most of the rest of what she knew that she had been sent back to her hotel in a taxi-cab.

'Mr Smythe,' Powerscourt began, 'thank you for coming to see us so promptly. I appreciate that.'

'Thank you, Lord Powerscourt.'

'I'd just like to ask you a couple of questions, if I may. We are, as I am sure you know, engaged in the mystery of the deaths at the Ballets Russes, not into the thefts of large sums of money from a hotel in Russell Square. Let me begin by asking, who approached whom: did you get in touch with Anastasia, or did she get in touch with you?'

George Smythe paused before he replied. He was going to do a lot of pausing in the course of the interview.

'She got in touch with me, originally.'

'And how did she know to get in touch with you? Why you, George Smythe, and not anybody else?'

This question seemed to cause a certain amount of thought.

'I knew she would be coming.'

'How did you know she would be coming?'

'Somebody wrote to me from St Petersburg, saying that a girl called Anastasia would be in touch with me.'

'And are you prepared to tell us who that person is?'

'No, I am not.'

'Why not?'

'Because, Lord Powerscourt, if I may say so, you are, in effect, behaving like a policeman in this matter. I do not wish to incriminate anybody, even in a country very far away.'

'So the person who communicated with you came from St Petersburg?'

'I can say no more than I already have.'

'Very well. I can see your position. Would I be right

in saying that your role in all this was, quite simply, to sell the jewels for the best possible price?'

'Yes, my lord. It was.'

'Could I ask how you sold them?'

'I made enquiries. I found a firm called Johnston Killick in Hatton Garden. They took most of the jewels, as far as I know, to Antwerp and various places on the Continent where they had contacts. They offered to wire the money back to Russia. Anastasia wasn't having that. She wanted the money delivered to the hotel in a suitcase. I put her in a taxi after our last meeting and asked the cabbie to take her to the Premier Hotel.'

'You didn't want to be seen at the hotel with her, is that right?'

'It is.'

'Why not?'

'Lord Powerscourt, I'm sure you will understand. I'm not absolutely sure about the legality of my actions. I don't see how I could be breaking the law selling some jewels. But I wasn't sure. And I knew about the murders. It seemed to me the most prudent course would be to have as little as possible to do with the ballet people.'

'That's very helpful. And am I right in thinking that you are not prepared to tell us who contacted you from St Petersburg?'

'No, I mean yes, you are right in thinking that.'

'Not even if it was connected in some way with the ballet?'

'You said earlier that you did not think there was a connection with the Ballets Russes.'

'I did,' said Powerscourt, 'but now I'm not absolutely sure.'

19

Chassé

Literally 'to chase'. A slide forwards, backwards, or sideways with both legs bent, then springing into the air with legs meeting and straightened. It can be done either in a gallop (like children pretending to ride a horse) or by pushing the first foot along the floor in a *plié* to make the springing jump up. This step is generally found in a series, either with several of the same or a combination of movements. Like a glide.

A weary Inspector Dutfield arrived in the Powerscourt drawing room that afternoon. He carried a great bundle of notes in his briefcase.

'There's only one consolation about the second murder at Blenheim – always assuming it was murder,' he began.

'What's that?' asked Lady Lucy.

'Why, it's the fact that it happened at the evening rather than the afternoon performance. Think what it would have been like had it happened at the lake with all those people to interview. That could have taken days. This lot here –' he waved at the notes in his bag – 'were bad enough. I have to tell you, my lord, my lady, that we are no better informed at the end of the interviewing process than we were at the beginning. Certain members of the aristocracy might have been enjoying company they shouldn't have. That is not my business. It is impossible to establish any link with the previous murder, apart from the fact that they both involved the ballet people. What we hadn't realized was that the entire troupe, the men and the women of the corps de ballet, were on standby in case they were required to do an encore after supper. It was Diaghilev's idea. If you ask me, my lord, my lady, I don't think many of those people at the Great Hall concert were much interested in the ballet. It was a social occasion – see and be seen, that sort of thing.'

'But where were they all, all those Ballets Russes people?'

'Well, they were still in their costumes and they were wandering round all over the place. The footmen kept them out of the State rooms, the bedrooms and so on, but they were given the run of the rest of the place. None of them have watches so nobody has any idea of the time. So nobody can give any information about when they might have seen the dead girl, Vera Belitsky. She was killed from that balcony, thrown down a long way onto the marble floor to be precise. The balcony's the best place in the house to get a clear view of the hall; you can see up as well as down, which you can't do so well from the ground floor. Each and every one of them, I think, must have wandered onto that balcony to have a look at some time or other. There was one occasion when they all rushed off to the other side of the house for a peep into the dining room from the servants' passage, but I can't establish if the dead girl was left behind or not. And there's another thing.'

'What's that?' said Powerscourt, looking closely at the pages and pages of notes the Inspector had brought with him, all apparently useless.

'It's this, my lord. The whole place was wide open. Bits of the stage downstairs were being taken away. Bits of the stage from the open-air show were being brought back into the house for storage round the back. It's quicker if you go straight through the house rather than going round the back. There were carpenters and scene shifters and the like everywhere. A complete stranger could have walked in – a whole team of complete strangers could have walked in – and nobody would have been any the wiser. And all the while the guests were tucking into their caviar and whatever they had for the other courses.'

'Presumably,' said Lady Lucy, 'the Blenheim Palace people would have thought they were Ballets Russes and the Ballets Russes would have thought they were Blenheim Palace people.'

'You're absolutely right, my lady. Inspector Jackson is asking round about if people remember seeing any strangers on the day. Even he admitted it was a very long shot. The whole bloody place was full of strangers. So that's it, my lord, my lady. One last thing – Inspector Jackson, who is, I must say, a very capable officer, thinks that the answer lies inside the Ballets Russes. Like me, and, I suspect, the two of us, he believes the murders are linked. Is there a connection between Alexander Taneyev and Alfred Bolm and Vera, the poor dead girl in Oxfordshire? We shall do our damnedest to find out. And we still haven't had that interview with Monsieur Diaghilev that he promised us up there at Blenheim.'

'I shall have to leave you,' said Powerscourt. 'There is another complication in our relations with the Russians and the French and even, God help us, the Germans. French bonds have now taken a bow centre stage and I must go and talk to my brother-in-law.'

*

'You said you wanted to talk to me about the recent upswing in sales of French government bonds, Francis,' said his banker brother-in-law William Burke, now a mighty power in the City of London. Burke was sitting behind an enormous desk, operational headquarters of his financial activities. 'If it were serious, it could cause a financial crisis across Europe.'

'I do want to talk to you about French bonds, William. Thank you. Family well?'

'All well, even the eldest, wasting my substance at Oxford. Now then, the answer to your question lies not in the machinations of politicians or diplomats, the answer lies in the horses. I've got my principal witness right here somewhere in this building.

'I'll get our head porter,' said Burke, ringing a bell for service. 'Man by the name of Welby, Jack Welby. Former RSM in some bloody regiment to do with horses. Our friend Welby runs the most sophisticated betting syndicate in these islands.'

'Does he run the whole thing from here?' asked Powerscourt. 'Porter one minute, gambler extraordinaire the next? Your hat, sir, your coat. Put a tenner on

Island Queen in the three thirty at Doncaster, that sort of thing?'

'To the best of my knowledge, Francis,' said his brother-in-law, 'he never gives tips to any of the staff here. He's got contacts in all the major stables in Newmarket and Lambourn, the twin headquarters of English racing, and in the stables near the big meetings like Epsom for the Derby and Doncaster for the St Leger.'

'And is it all legal? Surely the Jockey Club and the other old relics who run racing must have been onto him?'

William Burke laughed. 'Two years ago a group of disgruntled bookmakers complained formally to the Jockey Club and the police. The Police Inspector told me afterwards that the Welby organization was like an old-fashioned friendly society, run for the benefit of its members. He said that if the gentlemen of the Square Mile here behaved like Welby's people' – Burke waved an arm at his window, which commanded a good view of the financial centre at the heart of London – 'the world would be a better place. He said he ended up congratulating our friend Welby for what he does, rather than leading him away to the cells. First time he'd ever done that in an investigation into the City and its activities, he said. If you're ill, Welby's outfit'll pay the bills. If your house is falling down, they pay for the repairs. The same if you're sick. If you're young and promising in the brains department, they'll see you get proper qualifications. He's devoted to the accounting profession, friend Welby. He's got two of his relations in the top stables in Newmarket now.'

'What's the secret?' asked Powerscourt.

'He doesn't cheat. He deals, he says, in the same kind of information any sensible man could pick up drinking with the stable lads. Which horse is off its food, which one is going well, which one looks like a winner this week. He's not fond of the jumps, Head Porter Welby. There's too much of the unpredictable about them, he says – stray horses, random collisions, that sort of thing. He punts a few pounds on the Grand National and the Cheltenham Gold Cup to keep up appearances, but his heart's not in it. He's a man for the flat. That's where he places most of his bets.'

'And what on earth has he to do with French government bonds, William?'

A pair of boots approached Burke's door; they heard a firm but polite knock.

'Come in, Mr Welby, this is my brother-in-law, Lord Francis Powerscourt.'

The two men shook hands. 'I want you to show off a bit, Mr Welby, if you would. I want you to run through the main flat winners this season. We'll leave the jumps out of it, as you're not that keen.'

'Just the major races, sir? I'm not sure I could manage the two forty at Salisbury last month if you follow me.'

'Just the big ones, here and in France.'

'Do you want me to start now? With our own ones here in this country?'

'Yes please.'

'In time order, sir, Two Thousand Guineas at Newmarket, early in the season, going's often a bit soft if you follow me, won by Sweeper II, jockey Danny Maher, trained by Atty Persse; One Thousand Guineas, also at Newmarket, won by Tagalie – strange name for a horse that and no mistake, sir – ridden by Les

Hewitt, trained by Dawson Waugh; Epsom Oaks, won by another bloody animal with a strange name, Mirska, ridden by Joe Childs and trained by Tom Jennings; The Derby, the big one as you know, sir, won by our friend Tagalie, ridden by Johnny Reiff and trained by Dawson Waugh. That's it for now, sir, the St Leger isn't till September.'

'My word,' said William Burke with a smile, 'that was very impressive. And across the Channel?

'Well, gentlemen there's really only one race over there that should concern you and that's the Prix de Diane, the equivalent of our Derby and also run in June. Horse called Qu'elle Est Belle won it this year. They're not so consistent over there as we are, sir. In 1848 they had one of those revolutions they're so fond of and the venue was switched to Versailles. And in 1871 they had one of their wars with the Germans and the race was cancelled altogether. There is one odd thing about the Prix de Diane I think you should know about.'

'What's that?' said Powerscourt.

'Well, sir, everyone likes to have a bet on it. In Paris the poorer people will sell some of their government bonds – they all seem to like buying government bonds over there – to have a bet. They say that the big-money men dip into their holdings so they too can have a flutter. Only happens with this one race, but they tell me it happens on a huge scale.'

'Thank you very much. That's it, Francis. That's where your great bond sale comes from. French gamblers.'

'I wonder if they won, the ones who cashed in their bonds.'

'History doesn't relate, my lord, 'said Head Porter Welby, 'and neither can I.'

*

Alexander Taneyev must have had plenty of practice at writing home to his mother, Natasha Shaporova thought, as she sat working her way through his correspondence with her in a little room full of icons that the family had lent her for reading. Sandra, the mother, had kept her letters from her son in a neat bundle in the table by her bedside. Other members of the family were even then searching for the various different places they might have left Alex's mail. Much of this correspondence touched on a mother's anxieties.

They had regular meals and attendance was compulsory. The food was very English with plenty of roast meats and rather disagreeable vegetables. The hotel looked after their laundry. Alexander, he told his mother more than once, was happy in London. It didn't have the gaiety, the élan of Paris, but he had seen plenty to admire. He was very excited about being chosen as understudy for the Prince in *Thamar*. This meant, he wrote, that the ballet authorities must think highly of him. He wrote rather dull accounts of the tourist delights he had seen – the Tower of London, too small to be a proper fortress, the queues at the fashionable shops in Bond Street too long, Buckingham Palace only impressive at the Changing of the Guard.

There was only one phrase that troubled Natasha and it troubled her greatly. It occurred twice, shortly before he was killed. 'What am I, Mama,' he had written, 'Russian or English?'

Why would a young man of about twenty years suddenly ask his mother that? She was certainly English, his mother, born and bred in fishing country in Hampshire, but surely he should have known the answer by now. Natasha could feel telegram number one coming on.

*

Johnny Fitzgerald was beginning to dislike Richard Wagstaff Gilbert and his habit of playing with his family's emotions. Powerscourt had reported on his morning visit, on the day the first murder had become known, and had described him as a cold fish. Among the many things Johnny didn't know about Waggers was how much money he was worth. He doubted if Waggers had ever told his relations. He would just have hinted at large sums, well worth waiting for. Johnny wondered how he was going to find the answer. He suspected an even larger contribution to Sweetie Robinson's funds might be needed. But for now he was in Richmond, about to call on Mrs Clarissa Cooper, mother to Nicholas and Peter, both potential winners in the lottery of Uncle Richard's will.

She showed him into a sitting room considerably smaller than her sister Maud's. Here there were no pictures that looked as if they might have been Impressionists on the walls, just routine reproductions you could have picked up for a song. Mrs Cooper was polite. She ushered him to a seat on the sofa by the window. She did not offer any refreshment. Johnny reflected rather cynically that the funds from Barnes might receive a warmer welcome here than they would in Chelsea.

'Mr Fitzgerald, my sister told me you would be coming. How can I help?'

'This is all rather disagreeable I fear,' said Johnny. 'Lord Francis Powerscourt has been asked to look into the demise of your nephew. Of course I do not need to tell you that. You already know it. But it is a sad but necessary part of those investigations to find out, however disagreeable this might sound, who might benefit from his will.'

'I do not imagine for one second that I will be a beneficiary of my brother's will. He keeps his own counsel in such matters.'

'I was given to understand from your sister that your brother was in the habit of telling his relations that his attentions had switched, first from one nephew, then to another, and so on. It all sounds very difficult for the families involved.'

'I do not see why I should have to talk about my brother's testamentary dispositions in front of a complete stranger, Mr Fitzgerald.'

'You are quite correct in that, Mrs Cooper. But the alternatives are somewhat worse – worse for you, I mean.'

'I'm afraid I don't follow you, Mr Fitzgerald.'

'Well, there's always the police, isn't there? When I walk out of here you could very soon have the Oxfordshire constabulary on the trail of your two sons, who both live near Oxford, I gather. They would make a lot of enquiries with neighbours, employers, friends and so on. There would be a lot of talk.'

'There are times when I really dislike my brother for the difficulties he has brought into this family. It is intolerable. What do you want to know, Mr

231

Fitzgerald? What do I have to tell you to make you go away?'

'Three things, Mrs Cooper, and thank you for deciding to be cooperative. First, if you would, do you know the size of your brother's fortune? I don't mean down to the last penny in the last investment trust, just a general sort of figure. Second, if you are prepared to give me your sons' addresses, I shall call on them and I can assure you of my discretion. And third, do you know if either of your boys went to the open-air performance of the Ballets Russes at Blenheim Palace?'

'As to your first question, Mr Fitzgerald, I think it is very difficult for me. I don't honestly know the size of my brother's fortune. But from your tone I suspect that the higher the figure, the higher the interest from investigators like yourself will be. Nobody's going to murder somebody for a couple of hundred pounds. But start talking of thousands, or tens of thousands, and the bloodhounds are on your trail. Am I right?'

'I would be deceiving you if I were to say that you were wrong, Mrs Cooper.'

'I shall give you the boys' addresses when you leave, Mr Fitzgerald. And I know that Nicholas and Peter were intending to go to the Oxford ballet and have their lunch on the grass in the park. I do not know if they actually went. They often change their plans, as young people do. Now it's my time to ask a question.'

'Of course, Mrs Cooper. Please do.'

'Am I right in thinking from your interest in rounding up potential suspects that you still do not know who killed my nephew?'

'That is a perfectly legitimate question. I shall tell you the truth. We don't know who killed him. If we did I wouldn't be here. We have a number of lines of enquiry running at present, but no, we do not know who killed your nephew.'

As he made his way back to the train station, Johnny thought she had told him one thing, even though she wouldn't have known it. Why would she have talked of tens of thousands of pounds if that wasn't something close to the real figure?

*

It was that time of the week again. Captain Yuri Gorodetsky was watching the telephone on his desk in the little office in Holborn. The windows were grimy, heaps of files packed up in disorderly fashion along the walls. It had always been one of the Captain's worst fears that his superior officer, the General from Paris with his passion for neat and exact filing, would pay an unexpected visit.

There it was! The Captain picked up his telephone. As ever, he suspected that the General was in the next room, shouting at him.

'Gorodetsky! Good morning to you. What news of the English Bolsheviks?'

'Very little, I'm afraid General. It all seems fairly quiet just now.'

'Come come man, you must have something to report, for God's sake! Every other day now I am bombarded with questions from St Petersburg. Every day I have to say we have no news.'

'Well, General, most of the money is still in that bank where it was last week.'

'Most of the money? Where is the rest of it, you fool?'

'It has gone to pay the printers, General. There are

233

to be two sets of five hundred copies made. They will be returned to Arthur Cooper and then he will decide what to do with them.'

'And you say this is nothing, my friend? This should keep them quiet for at least twenty-four hours, those jackals in Headquarters! What bloody language are they going to be in?'

'English and Russian, General.'

'It's the Russian one that is important. The English Bolsheviks can go and throw them across the railings of Buckingham Palace as far as I'm concerned. No doubt they think the waves of strikes in their country and over in Ireland will make people receptive to their cause. Are the Russian ones ready yet?'

'Not as far as I know, sir. The printer is a very sensitive man.'

'Title, Gorodetsky? Do we have a title for the bloody pamphlet? No doubt they intend to circulate it inside Russia as soon as they get their hands on it.'

'I think it's called "What Is to Be Done Now?" sir.'

'What indeed,' said the General, 'I think the bloody man Lenin wrote a pamphlet called "What Is to Be Done" some years ago. Sounds as if the comrades have been rather lax in the performance of their revolutionary obligations, if they have to get the same title twice. Repeat homework if you like. Pretty poor show.'

'Yes, sir.'

'Just get one thing into your head, Captain. You watch over this business as closely as you can with your English colleagues. When you know when and how the pamphlets are going to leave England, you let me know.'

'Are you going to have them picked up, sir?'

'We have had this conversation before, Captain. No, we are not going to intercept them. We are going to follow them to their destinations. I shall tell you more about this operation next week.'

'Yes, sir.'

'And remember, Captain. Any news of these pamphlets arriving, you get straight onto the telephone and let me know.'

*

Natasha Shaporova spent most of the afternoon reading through Alexander Taneyev's letters to his sisters. They were all younger than him, and Natasha felt that he would not be likely to confide in them. She had more hope of the elder brother Ivan, who was an officer in a fashionable regiment and liable to appear at any moment. The girls wanted to know about the fashions in London. The youngest seemed to expect her brother to inspect the clothes of the audience very closely during a performance and report back. The middle one seemed to think her brother should spend his time checking out the latest London fashions in the great shops of Oxford Street. And the eldest one wanted an impression of English men, their clothes, their manners, how they behaved towards the opposite sex. Alexander decided that this sister, Olga, must be planning a visit to England, well prepared for the young men she would conquer there, and intending to carry one of them back to St Petersburg. There was only one note to interest Natasha. 'Ivan has told me of the decision you may have to make. I think you should consult Papa as well as Ivan. That would be for the best.'

This too made its way to London down the telegraph wires and landed in Markham Square four hours after it had left St Petersburg. Mrs Clarissa Cooper's eldest, Nicholas, was a vicar. He was one of the more fortunate vicars in that distinguished community. His parish was owned by one of Oxford's richer colleges, and his parish came with a suitable endowment of between four and five hundred pounds a year. It was in the little town of Kidlington, between Oxford and Blenheim Palace, and its occupants were employed on the estates around Woodstock or in university business.

'Mr Fitzgerald,' he said, showing him to a seat in the parlour of his handsome vicarage. 'My mother sent me a wire. She said I was to be very careful what I say to you!'

He laughed and poured some tea. His wife was out, he said, handing out clothes to some of the poorer parishioners. She always did this, his Hermione, the first Friday of the month.

'Forgive me for plunging straight in,' Johnny began. 'I've talked to your mother and your aunt in London about this business of the inheritance from Uncle Richard. I thought it would be useful to talk to the surviving nephews as well.'

'Only too happy to help,' said Nicholas, 'but just let me say one thing at the outset. Both of those good ladies will have impressed on you that this doesn't matter at all, that it's all a whim of Uncle Richard's and nobody should pay any attention to it. They wouldn't want me to say this, but I do have obligations in my profession. All that stuff about it not being important is not true. It has taken up a lot of their attention for years now. Who's in; who's out: it could be a parlour game if it wasn't so serious. If Peter or I have fallen from favour – maybe my uncle doesn't approve of me being a vicar – who's going to inherit now? Mark? Is it his turn? Alexander can't any more because he's not here, God rest his soul.'

'Would you say they were obsessed by it?'

'I would, Mr Fitzgerald, I certainly would. Short of getting down on the floor and counting out the imaginary money, there isn't a lot else they could do.'

'Pardon me. Mr Cooper, do you know how much it is worth, this inheritance?'

'No.'

'Do they?'

'No. I don't think so, anyway. I've not been told, at any rate.'

'And how long was your time in the sun, as it were, when you were the favourite one? Of all the nephews?'

'I've followed the progress, Mr Fitzgerald. Alexander was the favourite at the moment. I suppose he'd been in place for about two months. My mother is always writing to keep me up to date. I'd say he had about one month to go. Three months is the average.'

'And there haven't been any times when one nephew stepped out of line, as it were, and was immediately sent packing from the top of the family tree?'

'It didn't work like that, Mr Fitzgerald. I don't think it would have made any difference if one of the cousins had married a parlour maid or eloped with a chorus girl – that wouldn't have changed a thing.'

'So, as far as you knew, these arrivals and removals, as it were, came completely at random?'

'For all I know, it could have happened when some financial deal came through or he lost heavily at cards.'

'So what would you think was the motive for all this? It must have caused a great deal of unhappiness among the relations.'

'Only if they let it. I know my brother is as bad as my mother and my aunt, pretending it doesn't matter, while following the story as closely as they do. You ask about motive, Mr Fitzgerald. It might be my profession, but I think he's a wicked old man. A lonely old man, with no family of his own, he likes teasing his relations with the one thing he has that they don't – and that's lots of money.'

'One last thing. I have to ask everyone this, Mr Cooper. Have you attended any of the performances of the Ballets Russes either here or at Blenheim?'

'I knew that question would come. On the day of the great concert at Blenheim I was here, pretending to tend my garden and thinking about my sermon for the Sunday.'

20

Tours en l'air

Literally 'turn in the air'. A jump, typically for a male, with a full rotation. The landing can be to both feet; on one leg with the other extended in *attitude* or *arabesque*; or down to one knee, as at the end of a variation. A single *tour* is a 360° rotation, a double is 720°. Vaslav Nijinsky was known to perform triple *tours en l'air*.

Inspector Dutfield brought news from Oxford.

'Let me bring you up to date with the news from Blenheim, my lord. Inspector Jackson has been most thorough. He asked the indoor staff, via the butler – as their head man – rather than through his own officers, how many strangers they thought they had seen about the place on the big day. They had met most of the technical people during meals in the servants' hall, and most of the dancers and suchlike getting ready for the performance. They thought there were four they had never seen before. All sounded Russian. Two of them had coats with those astrakhan collars.

One of them appeared to speak neither French nor English, so we can probably rule him out, assuming he wasn't pretending. One might have been a stagehand. Descriptions – imperfect though they obviously are – have been circulated round Oxford. I expect they'll ask on the trains as well. I don't think that takes us very far forward. We're still looking for two people on the relevant night in Covent Garden.'

Powerscourt felt glad, not for the first time, that he wasn't a policeman. All that leg work, all those questions, always the same as the ones you had asked five minutes before, the endless writing of notes. He'd have grown so bored he would have made a mistake.

'Well done, indeed, Inspector. At least that might produce something in the end. Please send our thanks to Inspector Jackson. We too have had some information. Two telegrams from Natasha Shaporova, reading Alexander's mail in St Petersburg.

'"What am I, Mama, Russian or English?" That's the first one. The second could be connected to the first, or maybe not.

'"Ivan" – that's the elder brother – "has told me of the decision you may have to make. I think you should consult Papa as well as Ivan. That would be for the best." Ivan is the elder brother. Lucy, what do you think?'

'They could be linked, as you say, Francis. Surely the first one could be something terribly simple, like who he should support in a football match between Russia and England, that sort of thing. But the second could relate to something more serious, as if there's something worrying him.'

'He may just wonder where his loyalties ought to

lie,' said the Inspector. 'He wants to take his bearings, which people he belongs with, that sort of thing.'

'I suspect we need something more specific, don't we?' said Powerscourt. 'And why, if we think it is serious for a moment, why would he want to know whether he's English or Russian? I don't see the context myself. It's not as if there's a war on and he has to decide which side to join.'

'Tell me this,' said Lady Lucy. 'Where are the letters Alexander Taneyev received here? There must be answers of some kind in there. They must be in police storage somewhere, is that not so, Inspector? Then we could read the correspondence at both ends.'

Inspector Dutfield smacked his hand very firmly on his knee.

'Of course, Lady Powerscourt. How right you are. Why didn't we think of that sooner? I'm sorry about that.'

'Never mind, Inspector,' said Powerscourt. 'I'm as guilty as you are. But you could lay your hands on them, couldn't you?'

'It'll take a day or two,' said Inspector Dutfield, 'but we can certainly locate them. I've got one other piece of news to impart. You remember that duel in the forest glade outside St Petersburg? A member of the Taneyev family and a member of the Solkonsky family? Well, we've checked the names of all the Russians staying in hotels in the capital for the past week or so. At Brown's Hotel in Mayfair there is at present a certain Mr Leonid Solkonsky, who gives an address in St Petersburg.'

'God bless my soul!' said Powerscourt. 'You've been keeping that one pretty close to your chest, Inspector.'

'You don't know yet if he is a relation, do you, Inspector?'

'I'm afraid, Lady Powerscourt, that as he is staying at a pretty expensive establishment, it might be better if your husband talked to him rather than a mere policeman.'

'Do Russians not like policemen, Inspector?' Lady Lucy was looking very determined all of a sudden. 'Do you think they are more suspicious than people here?'

'I asked one of the translators, Lady Lucy. They said people in St Petersburg would always be more suspicious of policemen than people in London.'

'I wonder why.'

'I don't think this is the best time for a discussion on the relative popularity of police forces, Lucy, interesting though that would be,' said Powerscourt, rising from the sofa to pace about his drawing room.

'I shall drop this fellow a note at his hotel, saying I propose to call on him tomorrow morning at eleven o'clock. Any change of plan to be sent back by the footman who brings the note. How's that?'

'Capital,' said Inspector Dutfield.

As he went down the flight of stairs to his study, Powerscourt wondered what would happen if he put the real questions directly. Are you a direct relation of the Solkonsky who fought a duel with a member of the family Taneyev all those years ago? How did you get into the Royal Opera House? Did you bring a knife or a dagger with you? Even as he signed his note, he realized there was one question that might make trouble for his cause. Why are you still here?

*

Peter Cooper had a pile of schoolbooks on each side of his table when Johnny Fitzgerald called. This particular

242

Cooper was not in a vicarage but in a spacious ground-floor flat in a large house off the Woodstock Road in Oxford.

'Mr Fitzgerald, how kind of you to call. I've been expecting you. As you can see, I'm a history teacher at the boys' school here in Oxford, and today is the day I mark the latest history essays.' He nodded at the two heaps of notebooks on his desk by the window.

'Are your charges doing well, Mr Cooper? Taking in what you have told them? Potential scholars all?'

'Would that they were, Mr Fitzgerald! I have watched them read the relevant pages in their history books about the French Revolution. I have talked till I am blue in the face about the potential causes. And what do I get? Some excellent work, I admit, but one of the wastrels – there are always three or four in any class, sending each other messages, looking out through the window, scratching signs on their chairs and desks – has said that the mob stormed the Bastille because they were bored and hadn't anything else to do. Another says that the King spent all his time on that damned tennis court where the oath took place and was so busy playing that he didn't pay any attention to what was happening in Paris.'

'I don't envy you,' said Johnny, 'but I think you look as if you might be a little over halfway through.'

'So I am, well, that's something. Now, Mr Fitzgerald, I understand you want to talk to me about Uncle Richard's will. Is that right?'

This was all pretty direct, Johnny said to himself. Take away the polite condolences and that was exactly what he had come for. 'Absolutely right,' said Johnny.

'I'm not going to beat about the bush, Mr Fitzgerald. I think it is most excellent sport. I drink in all the latest

243

news from my mother and my aunt. They all believe it's terribly serious, close the door to make sure the servants aren't listening in the hall – all that silly cloak-and-dagger sort of stuff. I think it's like being in a horse race – a very long horse race, mind you – where the favourite is in the lead for a while then he falls back and is replaced by one of the other runners. There used to be four of us in the race, now Alexander has fallen at one of the fences.'

'Becher's Brook, as it were.'

'Precisely so. And when the new position has been well established, that only lasts a certain amount of time before he too is replaced. My relations keep asking me how I feel about Alexander's death and I'm afraid I make the usual noises. But deep down, I'm rather intrigued in one sense. If you thought, Mr Fitzgerald, that you were one of four riders left in the big race, and that number was suddenly reduced to three, how would you feel? It's hard to get too upset about it when you think that your own chances have been improved by a third or a quarter. You were four to one in the big race. Now you're three to one. Don't you see?'

'That's all very interesting, Mr Cooper. Do you know who the new favourite is, by any chance?'

'No, I don't, as a matter of fact. I think I was in the lead until I was replaced by Alexander, so it's not likely to be me.'

'Do the changes in expectation, as it were, always follow the same pattern: A followed by B and B followed by C and C followed by D?'

'No, they don't. It's all completely random. There was once a period of A to D in strict alphabetic pattern, but it didn't last.'

'Does your uncle know you are a strict follower of form in this matter, Mr Cooper?'

'No, he doesn't. He hardly ever sees us at all. My aunt says he doesn't like young people as a rule, but that might just be camouflage.'

'Let's suppose, Mr Cooper, that you were in the preferred position, leading the field, and your uncle dropped down dead. What would you do with the money?'

'I'd get married for a start. I have been in love for six months or so with a young lady who teaches English at the girls' school here. We could buy a bigger house. Maybe I could give up teaching history altogether. The problem is, we don't know how much money there is. Do you know, Mr Fitzgerald?'

Johnny shook his head. 'No, I don't know exactly. I may have an idea quite soon.'

'Well, when you find out, and I'm sure you will, a resourceful chap like you, remember to drop me a line. Just the total will do. You needn't bother with the rituals of politeness.'

'Tell me this before I go, Mr Cooper. You say all your information about the places in the race comes from your mother or your aunt. You don't have any conversations with your uncle about the latest odds and so on?'

'That's right. It all comes from my mother and my aunt.'

As Johnny took his leave, a return to marking history essays calling on Mr Cooper's side, two thoughts would not leave him alone. The first was that he suspected Peter Cooper was probably more like his uncle than anybody suspected. And the second was that, in the discussions about what he would do with the money, there had been no mention of sharing it out with anybody else.

*

Natasha Shaporova was sounding depressed and frustrated in her room in the Taneyev household, surrounded by the family icons.

'Regret no further news to report here,' the telegram began.

Powerscourt was reading it aloud to Lady Lucy.

'Have read all letters to female members of the household. Nothing further to report. None of the men can find any of theirs. Alexander wrote more often to the women of the household than to his brother and his father. Both remember him referring to something very secret, something he shouldn't have seen at all, and what should he do about it. The brother doesn't remember replying, but admits he could have done. His father suggested that he send more details of what he'd actually seen. The brother thinks he may have left the letters in his barracks, the father thinks his may be in the yacht club. Both under strict instructions to carry out further searches. Regards Natasha.'

'That all sounds pretty miserable,' said Lady Lucy. 'I shouldn't like to be shut up in a room plastered with all those gloomy icons.'

'Think about it, Lucy. What could it refer to?'

'Well, it could refer to the future plans of the Ballets Russes. Further appearances in Europe cancelled because of lack of money. No return trip to London, perhaps.'

'Or it could refer to some affair happening inside

the company, something it would be very hard to cope with, if it came out.'

'Like what?'

'Well, like Diaghilev taking another lover apart from Nijinsky. That would put Nijinsky's nose out of joint for a while. He might even leave.'

'Perhaps it had nothing to do with the ballet and had to do with Ballets Russes being used as a sort of mobile post office, as Colonel Brouzet suggested from Paris. I can't see that at the moment, mind you.'

'Maybe what he wrote was proof that the company was bankrupt and he would have to go home.'

'Proof, certain proof, Lucy. There are no certainties here, none at all. We had better turn our attention to other things before we drive each other mad with speculation.'

*

Brown's Hotel, tucked away behind Piccadilly, prided itself on being one of London's most private and discreet establishments. It was not one of those hotels you would go to if you wanted to be seen. Leonid Solkonsky's suite was on the first floor. No shortage of funds, Powerscourt thought, back in the Solkonsky ménage near the Winter Palace or the vast estates in the interior. Any hope of solving the murder of Alexander Taneyev in one of London's finest hotels vanished when the footman opened the door of the sitting room and showed him in.

An old gentleman, with white hair and a small white beard, wearing some Russian military uniform covered with medals, walked very slowly to greet him. He was leaning heavily on a stick in his right hand.

'Lord Powerscourt,' the old gentleman showed him to a seat near the window, 'would you like some tea?'

'That would be very kind.'

'I always find English tea – well, English tea from Ceylon – so much better than the stuff we have at home.'

He rang the bell and lowered himself carefully into another armchair. 'You must forgive the uniform, Lord Powerscourt. For today only I have returned to my old role as Colonel Solkonsky of the Preobrazhensky Guards. I am an honorary Colonel of the regiment, having served in it all my life.'

'Should I call you Mr Solkonsky, or Colonel Solkonsky for today?'

'Forgive me if I opt for Colonel, Lord Powerscourt. It is only to honour an old man's whim. You see, I have to see three doctors this afternoon, all of them distinguished in their field. I always find the uniform brings with it a certain amount of respect. You're not likely to be left in the corner of some damned waiting room for most of the afternoon. Quicker service, that's the thing.'

'I hope the reason for the three doctors in an afternoon is not too serious, Colonel.'

'That is kind of you, Lord Powerscourt. They draw me diagrams on pieces of paper; they talk in some abstract medical language. I have had enough of the doctors of St Petersburg, so I have come to London.'

'Well, I hope your afternoon session is successful, Colonel.'

The tea arrived and the Colonel leant forward on his stick as it was poured. 'Well, that is kind of you.' He smiled at the waitress.

'It is my heart, Lord Powerscourt,' he continued as the waitress closed the door quietly behind her. 'I am short of breath all the time. I have great difficulty going up the stairs. This might sound like the normal condition of an elderly man whose time here is drawing to a close. But it has not happened gradually, as it does, I am told, in most cases. It has come over me in rather a rush in the last month or so. Then I would have made my way up the stairs – slowly, but without any strain. Now I have to take the lift, and even the walk to my rooms here leaves me exhausted and out of breath. That is why these London doctors think they may be able to reverse the position, at best, or slow the process down if total recovery is impossible.'

'I wish you all the best, Colonel.'

'But tell me, Lord Powerscourt, apart from the doubtful pleasure of taking tea with an elderly Russian Colonel in Brown's Hotel, what is the purpose of your visit here today?'

'I have come about the murders at the Ballets Russes, Colonel.'

'And what, pray, have they got to do with me?'

'This is rather difficult. We have learnt, Colonel, that there was an unfortunate link between your family, or what we think may be your family, and the family of the murdered young man, Alexander Taneyev, some years ago.'

'And what form might that unfortunate link take?'

'There was a duel, and some talk of revenge on generations to come.'

Colonel Solkonsky began to laugh. He began to laugh so furiously that Powerscourt feared he might be overdoing things in the heart department. Finally he clapped his hands together.

'Enough,' he spluttered through his tea. 'Forgive me for laughing, Lord Powerscourt. This is an old, old story in the Solkonsky family. I should point out that I am a second or third cousin to most of the family who were involved. Even the Solkonsky of the duel was only a distant cousin of mine. There are many branches of the family, and in my one we are about as far removed as it is possible to be from the family with the duel without turning into total strangers.'

'Why did you find the whole thing a laughing matter, Colonel?'

'Well, there has long been a family joke about the aftermath of the duel, the Solkonsky's Pushkin moment, if you will, since the great poet himself was killed in an unnecessary duel all those years ago. Nobody has ever given it any thought, that notion of revenge. But some family wit has always claimed that one day it would come back to haunt us all, and it has. Right here this morning. Forgive me if I find it amusing. On the day of my appointment with the three doctors too!'

'I can see that. Just tell me, Colonel, as far as you know, that there is no possibility of any member of the Solkonsky family having come to London to kill Alexander Taneyev.'

'I am the only member of the Solkonsky family here in London,' the Colonel told him. He raised himself very slowly to his feet and grabbed hold of his stick to steady himself. 'Do I look to you, Lord Powerscourt, like a man who is going to negotiate his way into the bowels of the Royal Opera House and kill somebody?'

*

250

Not for the fist time, Alfred Bolm was coming to the top of the agenda. Inspector Dutfield brought one small portion of new intelligence and some bad news to the Powerscourt household.

'One of my men following Alfred Bolm has reported that he is a regular visitor to the chess club,' he began.

'Chess club?' said Lady Lucy, as if this was some bastion of London society she had not yet encountered, 'what chess club? Whose chess club?'

'It's a small outfit, my love,' said Powerscourt, 'near the British Museum, full of intellectuals and scholars taking a rest from the Reading Room nearby.'

'Are you a regular attender, Francis?'

Powerscourt laughed. 'I've never actually been inside. I've passed it lots of times, but I've never looked in.'

'I see,' said Lady Lucy, who seemed convinced that chess clubs must be some form of den of iniquity, like those places where people went to smoke hashish and other illegal substances.

'The other news is not so good, my lord, my lady. It's this. We can't find any letters to Alexander Taneyev. They're not where they ought to be if they were there, if you see what I mean. Personal effects, that's our category, that's for passports, wallets, permits, small change, keys, letters, bus ticket stubs, they're not there. Valuables, that's different, that's a different category of item altogether. They're not there either. I've looked.'

Powerscourt had a sudden vision of the most unfortunate members of the Metropolitan Police, whose daily bread was earned filing all these belongings of the dead, the murdered, the victims of traffic accidents, into neat piles and then labelling them for a posterity that seldom came.

'Perhaps he hid them in his hotel room?' suggested Lady Lucy.

'We've checked there too,' said the Inspector. 'My Sergeant, still toiling away around the technical staff and possible visitors to the opera, tells me that his mama divides men into hoarders and throwers-away. It's quite a useful maxim in this case; maybe he just threw them away.'

'I think there might be something in that,' said Lady Lucy. 'Our eldest son, Thomas, is a thrower-away. So is his younger brother Christopher. Their father on the other hand is a hoarder; he never throws anything away unless you force him. I once found a Test match ticket in his jacket pocket three years after the match had taken place. I think Sergeant Jenkins' mother might have a point.'

'There is something else, mind you,' said Powerscourt, anxious to move the conversation away from long-forgotten Test matches, 'if Alexander thought the subject matter was highly confidential, he might not have wanted to leave it anywhere where somebody else might have seen it. That's why he might have destroyed it. Or hidden it, or possibly, though I think this is unlikely, given it to somebody else to keep. That way he could not be incriminated directly.'

'We shall go back to the dancers,' Inspector Dutfield sounded a little weary, 'and see if anybody was holding a number of letters from young Taneyev. He probably told them they involved affairs of the heart.'

*

Powerscourt had been summoned to the Royal Opera House and was being shown into an enormous box, close to the right of the stage on the circle level. A rather difficult rehearsal seemed to be in progress. And waiting for him in the corner seat was Diaghilev himself, hat and cane resting on the seat behind him.

'Welcome, Lord Powerscourt,' Diaghilev began. 'I promised to talk to you when we met by that bridge at Blenheim Palace. Well, here I am. Let me say at the outset that I hear you had a disagreeable interview with that woman Lady Ripon. Any enemy of that woman is a friend of mine, I can assure you. I presume she was the person who employed you to investigate this case?'

'That is correct, Monsieur Diaghilev.'

'I suspect my relations are more difficult with her than yours.'

'And why would that be?'

Down on the stage, the dancers seemed to be protesting very loudly about some move they were meant to make. Powerscourt noticed that M. Fokine was nowhere to be seen. Nijinsky himself was acting as choreographer for the day.

'I feel trapped,' said Diaghilev, leaning forward for a better view of the stage. 'On the one hand Lady Ripon is very successful at raising money to sponsor the Ballets Russes. But then she makes such unreasonable demands. We are to appear and dance for our lunch or our supper at her house and at the houses of her friends. Sometimes I think we shall never have any time off at all. Dancers need time to rest or they cannot give their best on stage. But I cannot say no to her, or the money may be withdrawn and the Ballets Russes may be unable to pay the bills.'

'I can see the difficulty, Monsieur Diaghilev.'

'I presume that in your case Lady Ripon is endlessly

asking why the case has not been solved, why you failed to prevent that second murder in the palace?'

'You are absolutely right.'

'I know you are going to ask me again about the murders. I repeat what I said before. I have nothing to say to you on that score. I live for my art. Nothing more, nothing less. I have asked my colleagues to cooperate with you. I was deeply moved by Blenheim Palace, I have to say.'

'Really?'

'I have arrived at the ballet by a roundabout route, Lord Powerscourt. I began with a minor role at the Imperial Theatre at St Petersburg. That didn't work out. My friends and I collaborated on a journal called the *World of Art*. About ten years ago I organized an exhibition of Russian painting, particularly portraits, at the Tauride Palace in the capital. To collect the portraits I travelled all over the country, deep into the interior, where nobody before had ever arrived asking for paintings of the ancestors. If you can imagine a run-down Blenheim Palace, its grand interiors left to rot slowly through the seasons, a couple of aged retainers and a part-time steward all that's left to look after the place, trying to hang on to the past and to hold back the future. Well, I must have visited hundreds of such places. After a while they can get under your skin.'

'How is that?'

'Well, when I thought about it, and it is a lonely business criss-crossing the whole length and breadth of Russia, I thought that all these palaces meant the end of a world. The end was there in front of me. Remote, boarded-up family estates with great houses frightening in their dead grandeur, inhabited by people who were no longer able to bear the weight of their past splendour. It wasn't just the men and women who were ending their lives here, it was a whole way of life. You could see it in their eyes. The eyes of the ancestors said that they were happy in their world, in a fully functioning estate like your Blenheim Palace, if you like. They were part of something living. The eyes of those remaining are dead; they have nothing to look forward to. I felt sure that we are living through a period of enormous upheaval, that there must be a new culture to replace the old one which is dying, if it is not already dead.'

'Was your exhibition a success, Monsieur Diaghilev?'

'It was a success of sorts, I think. People were fascinated by all these remote ancestors. People flocked to see them, many of them no doubt curious to see portraits of some of their grandparents; all of them agreed that it was a great thing to have assembled such a great many portraits. But I had not wanted it to be a clarion call for the past. I wanted people to see that it is up to our generation to build something new, something to replace all these fossils, their houses and palaces gradually falling down around them.'

'And is the Ballets Russes part of this new wave to replace the old, Monsieur Diaghilev?'

Diaghilev laughed and peered down at the stage where the dancers were still complaining about Nijinsky's teaching methods.

'I think the Ballets Russes are bringing ballet into a new world, a ballet very different to the one they teach at the Imperial Theatre School in St Petersburg. And ballet means so much more in Russia than it does here in London. Perhaps you could say we have made a start.'

Diaghilev picked up his cane and began twirling it round in his hand. 'I hope you can see one thing clear, Lord Powerscourt. Whether it was the magazine about art, or the exhibition of the ancestors, or my work here, I live for my art. It is everything to me. Nothing must be allowed to get in the way. That is why I have not taken as much interest as perhaps I should in the unfortunate incidents that have marked our stay in London. To me they are like brushing a fly off my face. We shall have to find replacement dancers. I have written to one or two people back home already. I say home, but it remains my greatest regret that we are not able to bring my ballets to St Petersburg. I hope you do not think me heartless, that is all. Even now, in the splendour of Imperial London, we all miss our homeland. Now, if you will forgive me, I have to go to another meeting. I shall leave my principal calling card behind.'

'Your principal calling card?'

'I have to go to see Lady Ripon at her house in Coombe. Nijinsky is my principal calling card. Don't think me so vain that I believe all the society ladies want to see me. They all want to see Nijinsky. He would be welcomed by every society hostess in London.'

*

'I say, look here, I can't talk to you now.' Mark Butler, the last of the cousins who might inherit the earth, had been tracked down to the croquet lawn of Trinity College, Oxford. 'This is a key match, you know, Trinity versus Balliol. Matches don't get much more important than that.'

With great difficulty, Johnny Fitzgerald managed to drag the young man away from his crucial game to answer a few questions about Alexander Taneyev and his uncle's will.

'Uncle Richard and his money?' he said a little wearily. 'Yes, Mama warned me that you were coming. No, I don't know how much money there is to come when the old chap pops off. And No, I don't know if I am now the chosen one or not. Is that enough for you? Can I get back to my game? My substitute doesn't seem to be doing very well.'

'No, you can't,' said Johnny, 'not yet. Believe me, I shall be as quick as I can. Did anybody talk to you about what you should do if you, Mark Butler, were to inherit all the money in the old man's will?'

The young man's eyes were still locked on the croquet game. A red ball, a Trinity ball apparently, had just been deposited with some force into a flower bed.

'Mama and her sisters had all that worked out. There was talk that Uncle Richard was going to insist that the money only went to one person and that it would be impossible to share it out. They had some legal scheme afoot to make sure that didn't happen. The three sisters had decided that the money should be divided out four ways, one quarter to each nephew. Sorry, that should be three ways now, shouldn't it? Sorry about that.'

'Did everybody know that was the plan?' asked Johnny, remembering that Mark's mother had definitely not told him about this scheme.

'No, they didn't,' said Mark Butler, 'it was meant to be a secret.'

He took his eyes off the croquet game for a moment. 'Oh God, have I said the wrong thing? I have a feeling I wasn't meant to tell anybody that. Will I get into trouble, do you think?'

'Well, I for one have no intention of telling your family any of what you just told me.'

'That's very decent of you. Is there anything else?'

'Yes, there is. Your mother tells me you have been going to the Ballets Russes quite regularly. Is that true?'

'It is,' said the young man, springing to his feet suddenly to applaud a particularly delicate shot by one of his teammates. 'Well done, William, well done! Sorry, Lord Powerscourt, three of us here have been going to the ballet but we always came straight back. We have to on this special course. I wouldn't even know where the room where Alexander was murdered is. We've got to be back here by a certain time, don't you see.'

Complicated mathematical questions about angle of strike seemed to be occupying the croquet players now. 'Have you finished with me now?'

'If you just give me the dates when you went to the ballet, that will be all.'

The young man fished out a small pocket book and gave Johnny the dates.

'Good luck with your game. Sorry for the interruption.'

'Not at all. Nice speaking to you. I say, you fellows, I'm back. You can send the substitute back to the sidelines now.'

As he departed, Johnny saw on a scoreboard that Balliol were leading Trinity College three to one. Perhaps it was all his fault.

21

Développé

A common abbreviation for *battement développé*. A movement in which the leg is first lifted to *retiré* position, then fully extended, passing through *attitude* position. It can be done in front (*en avant*), to the side (*à la seconde*), or to the back (*en arrière*).

Natasha Shaporova thought she had found something at last. It wasn't much and it was contained in a letter to his brother shortly before he was murdered. 'Thank you for your advice about those papers I should not have seen. People like me were certainly never meant to read them. Your advice is very sensible.' Natasha sent them verbatim to London.

'Why is nothing ever definite about this bloody case?' was Powerscourt's first reaction when he read them in Markham Square. 'Alexander could be talking about anything.'

'Let's just think about what he might be talking

about, Francis. You're usually very good at working out the possibilities in a case like this.'

'Love affair,' said her husband. 'Alexander has fallen for a married woman, or for a member of his own sex?'

'Can't we discount the last one about his own sex? Alexander would hardly be likely to ask his father, would he?'

'Or he could have discovered about a love affair in the Ballets Russes that could be very complicated. Tamara Karsavina fallen for the principal scene shifter, that sort of thing?'

'It's possible. Any more?'

'It has to do with the future plans of the Ballets Russes. They are totally bankrupt, perhaps, and are going to have to go back to St Petersburg on the next train.'

'Wouldn't that have happened by now, if it was going to happen?'

'Well spotted, Lucy. Maybe there's another change of plan with the Ballets Russes. They're going to rip up the timetable and go back to Paris immediately.'

'More?'

'Well, this is a bow drawn at a venture. Suppose what Colonel Brouzet said is true and there is a link between Russian spies using the Ballets Russes as a kind of postbox. I can't see it, myself. I can't see how young Alexander could ever have come to see something confidential.'

'You do know what all this means, Francis.'

'I do, Lucy, I do. It means we are still no further forward. I think I shall send a message to Michel Fokine asking him to drop by. He might be able to tell us if the information concerns the Ballets Russes or not.'

*

Johnny Fitzgerald had taken a generous helping of Treasury notes from the Powerscourt war chest in Markham Square. He did not believe Sweetie Robinson would talk about the size of Richard Wagstaff Gilbert's fortune out of the goodness of his heart. He had decided one thing about the nephews and the aunts. Four nephews being reduced to three was one thing. Three reduced to two would be something else again. If anything happened to Mark the Croquet Ball, as Johnny referred to him now, there would only be two – and two, moreover, in the same family. Four down to two would be more than suspicious; it would be a motive for murder.

Sweetie Robinson was doing further damage to his teeth with a large mint from the bowl in front of his desk.

'Ah, Mr Fitzgerald, fresh from your travels round the surviving nephews, I presume. What news of Mark the spendthrift, as I gather he is? The earnest vicar? The schoolteacher? All well, I take it?'

'All well, thank you, Sweetie. It won't take you long to work out why I have come today.'

'I can't imagine, Mr Fitzgerald. Put me out of my misery, please.'

'I won't beat about the bush, Sweetie.' Johnny was convinced that his man would have started to form an opinion of the wealth of Richard Gilbert the moment he had set his eyes on him. It was part of his trade, an instinct that would go with him whenever he met somebody new. Trading on this kind of knowledge, after all, provided a fairly large segment of his income. 'How much is he worth, our friend Gilbert?'

'You wouldn't expect me to hand that over without some kind of consideration for all the time spent working out the answer, would you now, Mr Fitzgerald?'

'No, I wouldn't,' said Johnny. 'How much?'

'I don't think I like to go in for that kind of arithmetic. I prefer a slower kind.'

Johnny had heard of this other kind, a sort of torture by money where the amount handed over had to increase with the value of the subject's financial position.

'All right,' said Johnny, 'let's say he's worth over a thousand and I'll give you ten pounds.'

'Thirty.'

'Twenty.'

'Done, he's worth more than a thousand pounds. Your next suggestion, Mr Fitzgerald?' Sweetie popped a fresh mint into his mouth. He was grinning with pleasure at his business.

'He's worth more than ten thousand pounds, Sweetie: how's that?'

'You're going rather fast for me. Shouldn't there be a bridge or two on the way? A calling station on the road?'

'OK Sweetie, he's worth more than five thousand pounds. Ten pounds, but we both think he's worth more than that.'

'I'll give you five thousand for twenty pounds, Mr Fitzgerald.'

'Done,' said Johnny. He took the money out of his pocket and laid all the notes spent so far on the table and pushed them over. In Sweetie's world you never knew when or indeed if people were actually paying you real money or not. Sweetie inspected the notes with great care. Forty pounds in notes were now by the side of the sweet bowl. Johnnie hoped their presence would make future transactions easier.

'Done, and another twenty for over ten thousand.' Johnny added another twenty to the pile.

'I agree. And seeing that you have been a man of your word, Mr Fitzgerald, I'll give you the total, as I understand it. Otherwise we could be here all day. You give me thirty pounds more and I'll tell you his worth and a little jewel for you to take away.'

Johnny had spent more or less as much as he thought would be necessary so far.

'You're a hard man, Sweetie.' He brought out another couple of notes and added them to the pile. 'I think that should do it, don't you?'

Sweetie Robinson grinned a rather terrible grin, revealing to a watching world just how much damage had been done to his teeth by his years of confectionery consumption.

'You're a hard man, Mr Fitzgerald, and that's a fact. I tell you that friend Richard Wagstaff Gilbert – Waggers to the City of London – is worth between ten and twenty thousand pounds. And closer to the twenty than the ten.'

That's enough to set a mother's heart racing, Johnny said to himself. 'And what's your little jewel, Sweetie, the one you've been saving up?'

'Wouldn't you like to know, Mr Fitzgerald. I told you before that he cheats at cards. This information is even more valuable.' Sweetie popped another humbug into his mouth and leant forwards across his desk.

'Richard Wagstaff Gilbert has been married. He married a girl called Katie Shore in a village called Blexham when he was in his twenties. He'll deny it, mind you. He keeps it very secret. That's all. I don't know if he has had any children with this Katie. Wouldn't those mothers and aunts just love to know?'

*

Powerscourt was looking forward to his visit to the chess club. He knew who most of the visitors would be. Scholars toiling during the hours of daylight to produce the definitive history of the English Civil War; imperial propagandists scribbling away on the divine providence that gave England her great empire beyond the seas; revolutionary foreigners, surrounded by the works of Karl Marx and Friedrich Engels, producing the definitive blueprint for revolution today or tomorrow, crackpots bent on proving that the descendants of Alfred the Great had settled in Weybridge and were awaiting the call to arms to save England from her troubles. When darkness fell in winter, or when the museum closed in the summer, a number of these citizens, supplemented by some mathematically minded civilians no doubt, crossed the road to the chess club in Great Russell Street.

There was a sullen porter at the door. Powerscourt was shown into a large room where there were no overhead lights. On each of the twenty chess tables was a lamp, lit if a match was in progress. One hundred and sixty pawns, forty castles, knights and bishops and twenty queens were ready for action to defend their king.

'Where's the manager, please?' Powerscourt addressed the nearest player, who looked like a schoolteacher fled from his marking and his preparations. He moved a knight forward to what looked to Powerscourt like a dangerously exposed position. He himself had given up chess since Thomas began defeating him every time at the age of twelve.

'In the office. Down there at the back.'

The office was small and looked out across all the various battlefields.

'Got to keep an eye on what's going on,' said the manager. 'We had a fight in here the other day about a disputed castling. Morgan's the name, by the way, James Morgan.'

'My name is Powerscourt. I am an investigator. I am looking into some strange circumstances at the Ballets Russes.'

'And how can we help you here? We offer recreation for the mind of a different kind to the Ballets Russes, but there must be some similarities.'

Powerscourt brought out a publicity photograph of Alfred Bolm and showed it to the manager.

'This man here, Alfred Bolm, does he come here at all?'

The manager looked at Bolm as if he were an old friend. 'Why, it's Mr Bolm. I didn't know he was in the middle of his dancing days. He came here last summer, certainly, and he has been here three or four times this year.'

'Is he a good player, the dancing Mr Bolm?'

'Well, he's good by our standards, he can beat most of the ordinary players here, but he's not very good by Russian standards. Most of them – and we have about half a dozen here – can beat Mr Bolm quite easily. Calm down over there! Calm down, for God's sake, or I'll have you expelled!'

A couple of foreign-looking players at a table by the corner were on the verge of a fight.

'Tell me, Mr Morgan, was there anything unusual about Mr Bolm? Did he play with anybody in particular?'

'Well, there is one thing. He's been in a couple of times with the same chap – they've signed in and paid their dues in the normal way. Mr Bolm always brings a briefcase with him. I'd say his partner was Russian, probably, with one of those little beards they go in for and a cap pulled down over the eyes.'

'And you didn't notice anything unusual about their game?' said Powerscourt.

'Not really, no.'

Before he left, Powerscourt scribbled his address in Mr Morgan's client book and asked to be kept informed about any further visits from Mr Alfred Bolm. Particularly ones where his companion was the same Russian as before.

*

Blexham is one of a multitude of English villages that have no claim to fame whatsoever. Its bulls win no prizes at agricultural shows. Its football team languishes at the bottom of its league. Even its wives and mothers win no awards for cakes or prize puddings. Its sons and daughters have brought no national renown in good works or politics or anything else back to adorn their village. It lies along a lengthy street with a couple of shops at one end, the pub – the Laughing Cow – in the middle and the church at the other end.

Powerscourt decided the church might provide a better chance than the pub, as this was late afternoon and the regulars were presumably still out in their fields. He found the vicar puzzling over the church accounts in his vestry.

'Powerscourt? Lord Francis Powerscourt, did you say?' The Reverend William Fortescue must have been in his late sixties, with white hair and very thick glasses. 'Forgive me, but a little Irish genealogy is a hobby of mine. Would I be right in thinking that you sold Powerscourt House to a member of a big brewing family some years ago?'

'You are correct, vicar. I am married to a lady called Lucy and we have four children, if that helps in your researches at all?'

'That is very kind of you.' The vicar pointed to his account books, full of details of church restoration and money for the repair of damaged tombstones. 'They used to balance, these books – what came in, what went out; but the population has dropped so much our income must have gone down; fewer weddings, virtually no baptisms, a lot of funerals. You can't ask a lot for funerals. Enough of our troubles here. How can I help you today?'

'I am looking into some strange goings-on at the Ballets Russes in London. As part of that investigation, we need some information about a man called Richard Wagstaff Gilbert, currently resident in Barnes in London. We believe he got married here some years ago.'

'I won't ask you why you are interested in this gentleman. That would be presumptuous. What age did you say he was?'

The Reverend Fortescue moved over to a shelf with large dark red ledgers labelled 'Births, Marriages and Deaths'.

'He is now in his sixties, must have been born in the eighteen fifties. We're not, you'll be relieved to hear, in quest of a baptism; only a wedding, which would have happened round about the eighteen seventies, if our man was typical of the time – though people in real life never are, in my experience.'

'This volume here starts at eighteen seventy, Lord Powerscourt. Perhaps we could begin our search here.'

Powerscourt wondered, as the vicar riffled through his pages, if all candidates for ordination for the Church of England had to take handwriting classes. For the writing was excellent, even as vicars came and vicars went.

'They say Blexham is a coming up and going down sort of place,' the Reverend Fortescue said, peering through his pages. 'The Bishop or the Dean or whoever sits in those glorious seats in the choir at Salisbury Cathedral up the road, sometimes they give it to a young man on the way up, his first parish – as it were; and then they give it to somebody on his way down, the last parish in a man's career. That's me.'

Powerscourt saw that his eyes read the entries a lot quicker than the vicar's as generations of Blexham hopefuls, Grants and Smiths and Hoopers and Farmers joined their lives together in Holy Matrimony. But of a Shore and a Gilbert there was as yet no sign.

The year eighteen hundred and seventy-six contained what they were looking for, a Katie Shore married to a Richard Gilbert. There were the usual attendant signatories. The vicar sounded relieved but tired.

'There we are, my lord, I'm so glad to have been able to find it for you. It wouldn't do to disappoint a member of the Powerscourt family.'

'I'm sorry to have to trouble you further, vicar, but could we check the births and the deaths register for the few years after?'

'Of course. It's likely that they moved away, mind you. A lot of people of their age moved away to Salisbury, or even to London to look for work that wasn't based on agriculture. That's why our local population keeps falling.'

An hour later, Powerscourt decided to call it a day. The unfortunate Sergeant Jenkins could begin his work at Somerset House at the year 1882, when Gilbert should have been thirty years of age.

'You could look in the graveyard here, if you like, Lord Powerscourt. I just hand over the money to the man who tidies up the grass and props up the falling headstones. I don't think I've ever read the names, now I think of it. There's enough to do, looking after the living.'

Powerscourt did indeed check on the headstones, the same names coming to meet him that he had seen born, married and buried in the register. If the little church of St Michael and All Angels Blexham had any secrets about the family of Richard Wagstaff Gilbert, it was keeping them close to its heart.

*

Captain Yuri Gorodetsky didn't have to wait for his master to speak this time. The General came straight on the line when he placed the call.

'Gorodetsky, you idler, what is going on in your neck

of the woods? What news of the Bolsheviks of Bethnal Green? What are the bastards up to now?'

'Nothing is happening here, General. The Bolshevik money remains in the capitalist bank in the City of London. There is absolutely no sign of any plans to move it just yet.'

'And the printer you wrote to me about, the rogue, overcharging like that? You'd think that an outfit dedicated to the equality of man could at least offer a decent price, rather than an exorbitant one for running off a few pamphlets. No intelligence there yet, I suppose. And what do our English colleagues have to say for themselves? I find it hard to believe that there is no activity at all.'

'They pay their informers well, as always, the English. They've had years of experience doing that. They say things do turn quiet sometimes. The comrades go about the place doing their work and recruiting for the cause. They still have the occasional meeting to rally support. I think they may be waiting for instructions about Lenin's pamphlet. I can't believe a number of those won't be left behind for the believers in Bethnal Green.'

'I have news for you, Captain, but you must keep it a secret. I am not meant to know myself. I only found out about it by accident and I don't propose to let you in on how I came across it.'

Most people lower their voices when speaking of secrets. General Peter Kilyagin raised his as far as it would go, so the Captain had to hold the instrument away from him.

'Headquarters, that's St Petersburg Okhrana, have sent a man to England. They sent him some time ago

– how long, I do not know. His mission is known only to a select few at the very top of the Okhrana. I know nothing about the details of his mission.'

'But why, General, why are we sending one of our top men to London? Why not to Berlin or Hamburg or Wilhelmshaven or one of those naval construction places?'

'Don't be absurd, Gorodetsky! Are you expecting our masters to behave rationally? Anybody who has spent time in the domestic department of the Okhrana knows only too well the fantastic lengths the revolutionaries will go to in order to blow up a train or a bridge. Their minds – I've always believed this – are shaped by that experience of bombs and explosions and they take it with them into the foreign service.'

'I still don't understand, sir.'

'Never you mind. You just keep your eyes fixed on those Bolsheviks. And remember the great maxim of intelligence gathering: 'Hold your friends tight but hold your enemies tighter.'

*

Michel Fokine was in cheerful mood when he called on the Powerscourts in Markham Square. Inspector Dutfield was organizing his forces, some to Somerset House, some to shadowing Alfred Bolm, some to search for more information about strangers on the night of the murder at the Ballets Russes.

'You'll never guess the success of those Blenheim Palace performances,' Fokine said happily. 'We've had invitations to come to all sorts of places: an Elizabethan jewel of a place called Montacute, wherever that is; a place with a room for every day of the year at Knole

271

(and I do know where that it is); and one from the Rothschilds at Waddesdon Manor. The Waddesdon people even offered to build a special replica of the Mariinsky Theatre in St Petersburg to be ready when we come back in the autumn. They said it wouldn't matter if it rained. Why, there was a rumour that the Queen, who is interested in these things, wanted to send an invitation for us to give a small evening performance at Buckingham Palace.'

'Was the rumour true, Monsieur Fokine? The one about Buckingham Palace, I mean?'

'No, it wasn't. People say that the King put his foot down. If I have this dancing lot in, he is supposed to have said, who the hell else is going to come through my doors and bore us all rigid? So that was the end of that.'

'Monsieur Diaghilev must be vey pleased with the way it went.'

'He is. But he says he'll never do it again. The whole event, he says, was much riskier than anybody thought. He hadn't counted on the people cheering and all that. Suppose they'd decided they didn't like it, he said, the good people of Blenheim Palace and Woodstock. We, the Ballets Russes – my Ballets Russes, as he refers to them – could have been booed off the stage and into the lake.'

Powerscourt told him in very general terms about Alexander's letters home and the messages they contained.

Fokine began pacing up and down the room again. 'The business about being English or Russian is something he talked to me about. I thought it perfectly natural. London is pretty overwhelming when you see it and its people in all their pomp at the ballet.'

'So what did you tell him?' asked Lady Lucy.

'I told him not to worry. I said it was perfectly natural to feel English in England – he's been here loads of times before seeing family and so on; he speaks English at home – and equally natural to feel Russian in St Petersburg or Moscow. I wouldn't worry about that if I were you, I told him.'

'And the other stuff, about the papers and so on?' said Powerscourt.

'I've been thinking about that, my lord, and my only useful thought is that it concerns the future of the Ballets Russes.' He paused for a moment and looked out into the square.

'He could perhaps have seen something on Bolm's desk when he was being made up; Alexander could have popped in to wish him good luck or some gesture like that.'

'And what could that have related to?'

'Well, Bolm is one of the senior dancers, so he's given a sight of some of the upcoming plans to make sure he knows what's coming. It could relate to one of two things. They might make a very small ripple here in Chelsea, Lord Powerscourt, Lady Powerscourt, but they could create a huge wave in the Ballets Russes.'

'Are you able to tell us what they might be?'

'Yes, I'll try. You've been more than generous to me while I've been here. The first could relate to the Ballets Russes going to perform back home in St Petersburg. We, the Ballets Russes, have never danced in our own country. Diaghilev had some fearsome row with the theatre authorities some years ago. Maybe he has sorted that out. Maybe I haven't been reading my mail, which I hate doing. That could be one surprise. It would cause a sensation all over Europe, the prodigal Diaghilev bringing his art and his artists home again.'

'And the other thing?

'I think the other thing would only make sense to somebody who lived inside the company, my lord. It concerns Stravinsky, the composer. There have been rumours for months now that he was writing the music for a new kind of ballet altogether, one that would change the rules. Nobody knows what it is called. Nobody knows when it will be finished. But it is going to be very different, composed to sound like some ancient dancing, and the music of Slav and peasant Russia, not the classical sound of the cosmopolitan elite of the great cities. It will be more primitive, more rustic. Many in the ballet do not like the sound of it. They prefer the classics like Chopin or Tchaikovsky or Rimsky-Korsakov. Stravinsky's music would bring out the tension between the western capital of St Petersburg and the peasant dances and folk music of the interior. It still has no name, this ballet – but, believe me, any news of its coming could rock the Ballets Russes to their foundations.'

'Does it have a date for the first performance, the opening night?'

'Nobody knows the answer to that, but if Diaghilev is in charge, and I'm sure he will be, the first night will be in Paris next year.'

22

Attitude

In ballet, an *attitude* has nothing to do with your personality. Actually, an *attitude* is a pose, a way that a dancer can hold herself. In order to perform an attitude, a dancer must balance herself on one leg while holding the other leg at a ninety-degree angle in a curved position. The raised leg can either be held to the back or the front. The arms of the dancer usually remain in fourth position, curved, one arm above the head, and one arm to the side.

Natasha Shaporova was coming back to London. She sent a very long telegram to carry her news before her as she left.

'Taneyev household hopeless. They must have had a family meeting and decided to get rid of me. This was after I had talked at length to the father and the brother. Both admitted that they had received the letters I spoke of before. Both had destroyed them. Both had agreed not to speak of the matter again to any living soul. They thanked me for my trouble and assured me that that was their final word. I might not have learnt the secret – if there was a secret – but nobody else would either. Alexander is in his grave, they said, and the content of his letters will stay with him there.

'Back to *War and Peace* on the Warsaw train. Precious little peace here.'

*

Harry Smith, the printer from Camberwell who was printing the Lenin pamphlets, felt rather guilty about charging so much money for the job. He was, however, well schooled in the revolutionary doctrine that emphasized the importance of cell structure, that a comrade in one department should not tell anybody else what he was doing in another part of the organization, in case of capture or interrogation by the agents of the capitalist class. So he had not told Arthur Cooper that he had two very urgent jobs for trade unionists in the docks and the railways and that he had urgent work to be produced for them. And speed in the printing business cost money. As a penance he was bringing a couple of proof copies of the latest 'Gospel according to Lenin' round, to show Arthur Cooper that work was indeed in progress.

'I've brought you these,' he said, when they were closeted in the front room well away from wife and children, 'a Russian one and an English one. These are just the first proofs. We've still got to check the translation and make sure that there aren't any mistakes.'

'Thank you very much,' said Cooper, picking up a page in Russian rather gingerly, as if it might blow up.

'I can't do anything with the Russian one. I tried once, you know, to teach myself Russian in the big library round here, but I couldn't do it.'

He stared rather helplessly at the page. He noticed that it seemed to contain a large number of explanation marks.

'Try this one,' said Harry Smith, producing a version written in the King's English. Looking down, Harry Smith noticed that it seemed to contain a number of old friends: the weak and vacillating bourgeoisie, the primacy of the working class and the importance of the revolutionary vanguard ready to lead and to speak and act in the name of the workers. He noticed too that the days of the capitalist class were numbered, the final crisis was at hand and that it just needed one final heave for the workers to triumph. Like some early Christian reading the Gospel of John some years after reading the Gospels of Luke and Mark, he felt that he had heard the main points before and, quite possibly, more than once. Like the Russian version, the English one contained plenty of exclamation marks. He wondered if there might be too many of them, as if the readers might not get tired of being shouted at all the time.

'This is very fine, Harry,' he said, handing back the proof. 'I presume I won't see any more of them until they are ready.'

'That's correct, if it's all right with you.'

Arthur Cooper nodded.

'There is the question of where I should deliver them to,' said Smith. 'I'm afraid I couldn't guarantee their safety or their security for very long. The police and their people are always sniffing around. I could keep them until a week today, if you like. They should be finished in a day or two.'

'That should be fine, but I might want you to keep them somewhere safe, if you see what I mean,' said Arthur Cooper, who was feeling slightly lost. You could hide revolutionary money in a capitalist bank, he said to himself. Where could you keep revolutionary literature? The British Museum? London University? The Bank of England? He rather thought not.

'That's fine,' said Harry Smith.

As he departed on his bus for the delights of Camberwell, a figure emerged from the shadows beside Arthur Cooper's house. The figure followed Harry Smith all the way home to his wife and his printing presses.

*

Sergeant Jenkins had never imagined there could be as many people with the surname Gilbert in the country. Surely, he thought, there can't be as many as this, and these were only for the year of 1882. There were another thirty years to go. He gritted his teeth and decided that he just had to carry on. He wondered if he should ask for assistance in this dreary business.

The Sergeant had also decided to abandon his attempts at learning the Russian language. He had only just finished the tricky business of the alphabet with all those extra letters. Even if this case lasted until the end of the year, he didn't think he'd be able to say any more than 'Good morning'.

Walter Gilbert, Maidenhead. Walter Gilbert, Gateshead, William Gilbert, Padstow, William Gilbert, Richmond. William Gilbert, Newark. Looking ahead he thought there must be another sixty or seventy Williams to go.

*

Lord Rosebery, old friend of Powerscourt, former Foreign Secretary, former Prime Minister, had sent a note round to say he proposed to call at three o'clock.

'How is your investigation into the Ballets Russes murders going, Francis?'

Powerscourt laughed rather bitterly.

'It's everywhere and nowhere, Rosebery. I don't think we even know who the murder victim was meant to be – the understudy, or the man whose name appeared on the programme. Sometimes I think the answer's to be found in St Petersburg, where we have been reading the understudy's letters to no avail; sometimes we think it may lie in the internal politics of the ballet. If you'd asked me when I took the case on if I thought I would have made so little progress after all this time, I should have dismissed it as an improbable fantasy. But there we are.'

'You must have some suspicions, Powerscourt? Surely, after all this time.'

'They are all like gossamer, my friend, one puff would blow them all away.'

'I have come with some intelligence that may help you in your cause, but I must tell you that it too is like gossamer waiting for that one puff.'

'There must be affairs of state involved, Rosebery, if you are coming to me with Delphic warnings like the Oracle.'

'I've always fancied the role of Delphic oracle myself,' Rosebery smiled. 'All those potions, all those desperate people coming to you for guidance and then the business of composing the riddle. You and I could have been rather good at riddles, Powerscourt; we could have been sitting there for hours talking nonsense while we worked them out.'

'We are, alas, in Markham Square, not on the mountainside at Delphi.'

'We are, that's true. Let me tell you a secret. Sometimes, if you have held my positions, those in the secret world – the diplomats, the spies, the people opening other people's mail – keep in touch with you. Sometimes it is for us elders to tell them that they have not gone mad. Sometimes it is for us to tell them they have gone mad. Sometimes it is to tell them that such and such an outcome is almost impossible. They only consult us when they feel the need for an outside eye, a final port of call before the Prime Minister.'

'This is all rather serious, Rosebery. Are you trying to tell me that the Ballets Russes may be involved in some diplomatic incident?'

'It could be. All I can tell you today is to watch your step. You may soon be embroiled in deeper waters than you bargained for when you took on this case.'

'Is that all you can say? I ought to watch my step? There is a killer on the loose out there, Rosebery: I am quite careful with my step already.'

'I have already said more than I should, my friend. If I have some more definitive news, I shall come straight over. I am staying in town for the present.'

'So you come to me, if you like, saying that you have received some form of Delphic message that you cannot yet decipher? Is that it?'

'You could put it like that. When I hear about your

need to trust in your wooden walls, or that the bull from the sea is coming at the time of the crescent moon, I shall let you know.'

*

Inspector Dutfield brought some ballet news to Markham Square later that afternoon.

'It's our friend Bolm, my lord. Or maybe he's not our friend after all. Twice in the last twenty-four hours he has gone up to my men who were following him and swore at them violently in French, or it might have been Russian. Detective Constables do not have to take any exams in foreign languages just yet. Then he spat on the ground. Maybe they'll get the evil eye next.'

'Where did this happen? It's certainly odd, Inspector, is it not?'

'Once near the front of the opera house, and once on the way out of the chess club. He should have been in a good mood then, for my man asked afterwards about the results of his last match. The manager said he'd beaten a man he usually lost to. And in less than fifteen minutes.'

'What do you suggest we do about it, Inspector?'

'I've changed the men over, my lord. There's a whole new detachment looking after Bolm now. It implies he's jumpy, but about what?'

'Or about whom? Why should he get jumpy about a couple of English policemen?'

'The only crimes such people would be interested in are crimes committed here. That would suggest that he's jumpy about the murder. Of course, you could say he would be quite right to be jumpy about the affair in

Covent Garden. He could have been the victim after all. But why now? Why not before?'

Inspector Dutfield was fiddling about in his notebook. 'I don't know. We shall just have to keep looking, I suppose.'

'Well, could you send my thanks and my best wishes to the two officers who received the treatment,' said Powerscourt.

As Inspector Dutfield departed for his duties, Powerscourt wondered if Alfred Bolm too might have had a message from the Delphic oracle. He wondered if the oracle might be an occasional visitor to the chess club.

*

Natasha Shaporova was deep into the family thickets of the Rostovs in *War and Peace*. The idea came to her from out of the blue. She hadn't gone looking for it. It just popped into her head. They couldn't all have missed it, the Taneyev family back there in St Petersburg, the Powerscourts in Markham Square, the English police. She thought about it from every angle she knew. Her train was slowing down for a change at Cologne. She checked her timetable. She should have over an hour to spare before the train made its connections and moved off. She shot into the telegraph office and sent a brief message to Powerscourt.

'Did Alexander Taneyev keep a diary? Regards Natasha. Cologne Station.'

*

Two senior porters had left their employment at the Premier Hotel, scene of the theft of Anastasia's jewel money. They had both been there for a number of years. Martin Magee and James Harding were reported to have been looking happy and confident before their departure. They had departed with such of their belongings that they kept on the premises.

This was the news that brought Inspector Dutfield hurrying round to Chelsea. 'They didn't bother to give notice,' he reported. 'They both seem to have left their lodgings in a hurry too. They paid up, mind you, for the remainder of their time before they left. Their landladies said they were both model guests in their establishments.'

'How long between their departure and your realizing that they had gone?' asked Powerscourt.

'It must have been a couple of days. We were trying to search the hotel to see if the money had been hidden away on the premises. Have you ever tried searching a hotel and its bedrooms, Lord Powerscourt? The guests were not cooperative at all. Two Americans threatened to call the police until we reassured them that we really were the police, if you see what I mean.'

'Will you call off the search, Inspector?'

'No, we'll have to carry on. There's no proof that they left with the money. Luckily we were able to get very good descriptions of the pair. Every policeman in London will be on the lookout for them soon. If that brings no answers, we'll circulate them round the country, concentrating on railway stations and ports. They could be on the Continent by now, my lord.'

'Where they could change the stolen money into foreign currency and nobody would be the wiser.'

'Absolutely correct. Our friend Killick didn't take the numbers of the notes, he didn't have time. I think I shall have to call in Mr George Smythe again, though I've always felt he was telling the truth.'

Inspector Dutfield began polishing his glasses with a fresh handkerchief. 'You've never really felt the robbery of the jewel money had anything to do with the murders, my lord, have you?'

'No, I haven't. And these revelations don't make me change my mind. Somebody had obviously stolen the jewels in St Petersburg and found they would be easily traced. So they transferred the deal to London to get the money.'

There was a knock and a cough at the door. It was Rhys, the Powerscourt butler-cum-chauffeur who always coughed before he came into a room.

'Telegram, my lord,' he announced. 'From Cologne Railway Station, my lord. I thought it might be important. For you, my lord.'

Rhys handed it over. Powerscourt read it aloud. 'Did Alexander Taneyev keep a diary? Regards Natasha. Cologne Station.'

'Good God!' said Powerscourt. 'We've never thought of that. Not one of us. Do you know if he kept a diary, Inspector?'

'Well no, my lord. We've concentrated our search on letters rather than diaries.'

'If it was one of those new ones, it could look like a book cover if it was lined up with other books.'

'I'll just have to go and take a look at his things, my lord. All of his stuff is still packed up at the station, as you know. I'll conduct the search myself. I'll come straight back if I find it.'

Fifteen minutes later another policeman found his way to the heart of Chelsea. Inspector Jackson made his apologies for arriving without notice. 'I had another piece of business to transact, my lord, but there is one thing in particular I felt I ought to tell you in person.'

'You're more than welcome, Inspector. Some tea?'

'Thank you, that would be kind. The thing is this. I've been reading all the accounts of the witnesses at the murder of Vera the ballerina. Not just the ones from the Ballets Russes, but from the invited guests as well. I tell you this, Lord Powerscourt. It was chaos backstage, as it were, in the other parts of the palace, while the guests were taking drinks and enjoying roast suckling pig and all the rest of it. There were two identified people milling around: one a tall, foreign-looking man with a dark coat and a hat who everybody thought was Russian, and one a middle-aged Englishman in a brown check suit carrying a walking stick – rather in the manner of Mr Diaghilev if you like, my lord, who everybody thought was a local, from Oxford, for he seemed to be able to speak Russian as well. Always assuming our constables are correct in identifying what he was saying as Russian, not French or German or Hottentot or what you will.'

'And what did your staff think they were doing?'

'This is the thing, my lord. Most of the domestic staff were in attendance at the dinner, serving out the peas or the parsnips or whatever they do on these occasions. For the rest, it was like a free invitation to wander all over the house. There was the odd footman about, and the occasional door closed to the Ballets Russes people, the dancers and the stage staff and so on, who were all well behaved. I come to my point, my lord.'

'Perhaps the gentleman with the walking stick was

just one of your extra translators brought in from Oxford?'

'That's very possible. We did conduct a fairly wide trawl to find those people. He could well have come from some department of the university.' Inspector Jackson paused to take a sip of his tea.

'It still must have been chaotic everywhere in the palace. The ballet people behaved as if they were visitors, as if they had been given a chance to look over the house like the other visitors the Duke of Marlborough and his lady let in during the year. One minute you could have been in the hall, another minute you could have been wandering round upstairs. And it's an enormous place. If we assume, and I grant you this is a pretty big if, that the murderer had come to kill the ballerina, he could have waited for ever in the wrong part of the palace. She could have been on another floor. She might have been out in the gardens looking at the fountains or that sort of stuff. My hunch is that he must have arranged to meet her on the gallery in a few minutes' time, that sort of thing. He wants to express his admiration in person. It will not do in the crowd. You can never underestimate vanity as a motive for doing things. So, when Vera arrives in the middle of the gallery, that's the end of her. The other man disappears back into the crowd and out the front door. It was murder by appointment.'

'God bless my soul, Inspector, that's a pretty fine piece of work!'

'I have to say I have no idea if it is true or not. There is one other thing. If a member of the Ballets Russes or anybody connected with the opera wanted to kill her in London, they'd have been liable to bump into a policeman or an investigator like yourself at any point and in any place. Up there in Blenheim Palace, there were only the footmen at that particular time. Not to mention our two strangers who had the great advantage that the Blenheim people thought they were Ballets Russes and the Ballets Russes people thought they were palace people.'

'And what have you done about the strangers, Inspector?'

Inspector Jackson finished his tea. 'We have circulated their descriptions all around Oxford and in all the towns and villages where the visitors could have come from.'

'How do you think the killer knew who his victim was, if you see what I mean?'

'I did think about that, my lord, but he could have asked any of the ballet people. You could have spotted a member of the Ballets Russes a mile off.'

'You have done good work, Inspector, well done.'

'Do you know, Lord Powerscourt, I've been an Inspector now for six years and this is the most unusual case I've come across in all that time. I think I may be able to tell my grandchildren about it in years to come.'

'Only "may" be able to tell them, Inspector?'

'That's right, my lord. I'm bloody well not going to tell them we've all failed to work out who the murderer was.'

*

'"London June the fifth. I wonder if it's extravagant and rather vain to buy another diary every time we move to a fresh city. Certainly there's still lots of room left in the French one. But I can always go back to that the next time I'm in Paris. I shall have in time a whole volume about Paris."'

Alexander Taneyev's diary had arrived by police constable late that afternoon. Inspector Dutfield had said he would come round later. Powerscourt maintained that his policeman colleague was feeling guilty about not having found it before. Lady Lucy told him he was being uncharitable.

'Do carry on, Francis,' she said.

'"Rehearsals start tomorrow with Monsieur Fokine. I have danced in all of these works before, mainly in Paris. My two understudy roles I have also danced before, both in Monte Carlo. I am lucky that I have been allowed to stay with my uncle, though they have told me at the hotel here that there will always be a room ready if I need it. It is two years now since I came to London with Mama and the girls."'

'I say Lucy, do you think I should skip a few bits and see how long before we get to the relevant parts?'

'I don't think you should skip anything just yet, Francis. I think it would be disrespectful.'

'"We were given half an hour today to walk around Covent Garden and take a full tour of the opera house. It's certainly grander than the ones in Paris, but nothing like our own place on Theatre Street back home. Maybe the fact that the Imperial Family come to see us in St Petersburg makes a difference. Everything has to be special all the time. I don't think the King here is very keen on the opera, even though they say he looks exactly like the Tsar. I think Mama told me they are cousins."'

'And that's the end of Wednesday June the fifth. What do you think of it so far, Lucy?'

'Promising start, I should say. It looks as though he puts down whatever comes into his head.'

'On we go. "Thursday June the sixth. Another rehearsal. Monsieur Fokine spends a lot of time shouting at the girls in the corps de ballet. I think they just find it hard to concentrate when they're left stuck in some position or other while he concentrates on something else. Mama and the girls always tell me how lucky I am to spend so much time with all these lovely young people. I tell them it's not like that at all. They're work colleagues, that's all. I just wish some other older members of the company behaved in the same way."

'Hello hello, Lucy. Do you think this is Bolm, enter stage left, as it were?'

'Probably, Francis. Just read on. There may be more.'

'"Monsieur Diaghilev looked in on the rehearsals today. He was talking to that composer Stravinsky, who looks very strange to me. People are already saying that Monsieur Diaghilev is about to run out of money, but they say that all the time."'

*

Sergeant Rufus Jenkins had taken up smoking again. He had managed to give it up at the request of Marjorie, his girlfriend from the Post Office – well, in fact, as the Sergeant told himself regularly, it was more of an ultimatum really – me or those damned cigarettes – and hoped that if he only smoked on duty and changed his clothes when he got home, he might get away with it. Marjorie couldn't stand the smell. She said it made her feel ill. The Sergeant rationed himself to one every half an hour. He was now in the second half of 1887, and had reached the letter P. Most of those letters were more than familiar to him now and he groaned as he reached the letter P. He knew it contained a good number of popular Christian names. Patrick Gilbert, Newcastle under Lyme, Patrick Gilbert, Wolverhampton, Patrick Gilbert, Southampton, Patrick Gilbert, Ludlow Shropshire.

Ahead were the Pauls and the Peters and God only knew how many of those. The Sergeant lit another cigarette in anticipation.

*

'"Friday June the seventh. Sometimes I find life in the ballet rather confusing. Our main purpose is our art, to produce the finest ballet in the world. M. Diaghilev keeps telling us that if we work hard we will reach that goal. It's the languages, really. With my uncle I speak English. With some of Diaghilev's people I speak French, as they prefer that to Russian. On my ballet work I speak Russian, like everybody else. The stagehands and everybody else speaks Russian. Which one do I belong to? At home I always feel Russian, even though Mama insists we speak English all the time, rather than French. My old nurse – I do hope she hasn't died yet, she must be well over eighty now – always spoke to me in Russian. She couldn't do anything else. But what am I? Am I Russian or am I English? I have spent a lot of time in England, with these two summers over here, and I find I can think in English. I can't do that in French, though I can speak it fluently. And of course I can think in Russian. I wouldn't like to lose the English bits of me if I was told I was Russian, any more than I would like to lose the Russian bits of me if I was told I was English. What am I to do? I shall write to Mama, although I know what she will say. She will say I am English. If I wrote to Papa he would say I was Russian. It's all very confusing."'

Rhys was coughing at the door. 'Urgent message from the Oxfordshire Constabulary,' he announced. 'From Inspector Jackson, my lord, my lady.'

'"We have received intelligence from a number of places concerning the Russian who might have been at Blenheim Palace,"' Powerscourt read, feeling rather like one of the slaves of some Eastern potentate whose sole job was to read messages or to tell stories to his master when the master was bored. '"The first one said that he had been seen entering the Ashmolean Museum. We have no reports of his coming out, but I doubt if he is still inside. The second sighting was of him at the railway station, about to board a train, presumably, unless he was meeting somebody. The third report, from rather further afield, has him walking through the village of Goring on the borders between Oxfordshire and Berkshire. They could, of course, all refer to the same man. Further reports as news comes in."'

'I can see that a man might want to catch a train or visit the Ashmolean Museum, Francis,' said Lady Lucy, 'but what on earth was he doing in Goring? What do you know of Goring, Francis?'

23

Bourrée

The word originates from an old French dance resembling the *gavotte*. In ballet, this denotes quick, even movements often done on *pointe*; the movement gives the look of gliding.

'What do I know of Goring?' mused Lord Powerscourt. 'Absolutely nothing, my love. I shall return to the diary.

'"Saturday June the eighth. I think the rehearsals have gone very well. This morning I had to take on the role of the Prince in *Thamar* in case Bolm should be indisposed or is too busy chasing the corps de ballet. I have watched Bolm perform this role so many times and I know, heaven knows I have been told often enough, that my role is to perform it in exactly the same way as he does. I am not to add any little touches of my own. The audience, Monsieur Fokine says, have come to see Bolm, not me, and the least I can do is to replicate down to the smallest movement what he would have done."

'There's a break here, Lucy, as if he added this last bit later in the day. Here we go:

'"Some of the girls are thinking of complaining about the way Bolm treats them all. They ask me for my advice! I agree that his antics, his endless approaches, sometimes physical, would be quite disgusting if you were a girl. Perhaps I am lucky in that I have sisters and I know how I would feel if anybody behaved like that with them. But I tell them that the Ballets Russes is more important than any individual. One of the girls told me that I sounded like Diaghilev when I said that. I told her I didn't care. One complaint of that nature could split the company apart, half for Bolm and half against Bolm. The performances would never recover. The unity of the company must come first. And I tell them that Fokine, for one, must know what is going on. If he knows, Diaghilev knows. Maybe somebody high up will have a word with Bolm. That, I tell them, would be for the best."'

*

Sergeant Jenkins was having another cigarette. He wondered if the smoke got into your hair. He could always say that he was surrounded by people smoking inside and outside the building. People were always smoking on the bus. He thought he could mount a reasonable defence against that charge. He was on the Rs now. He hoped for a moment that the entry might be for a Mrs Richard Gilbert rather than a Mrs Sophie Gilbert, née Shore. Ahead of them was another long line of Raphaels, Richards, Roberts and Ruperts. He consoled himself with the thought that the place closed in forty minutes' time.

*

'"Saturday June the eighth. The girls are still going on about Bolm. Don't they realize that if they go on and on about something it can get more than a little boring. I am in my room at the Premier Hotel now. The traffic is always very thick down our side of the square. I am feeling unsettled. There hasn't been time for a reply from Mama yet. I wonder how Papa is coping now Ivan is away on manoeuvres for a fortnight. Papa always says he finds it difficult being in a house full of women with no other man to talk to apart from the servants. That is why he always runs up those enormous bills at the yacht club when the men of the family are away. I wonder how he's coping now.

'"I have to say that I have not felt homesick since I have been here, not once. Just now I wish I was back home in St Petersburg, having family supper with some lively conversation going on."'

'Poor boy,' said Lady Lucy. 'He could have come round here if we'd known he wanted a bit of family life, couldn't he Francis?'

'He could have played a bit of chess with Thomas, though I wouldn't recommend it. We haven't heard anything like what we want, Lucy. Not yet anyway.'

*

Sergeant Rufus Jenkins was feeling like a lone fisherman who has taken his rods and his fishing basket and his rug to a remote riverbank and cast away all day. He finds nothing. Just when he thinks he might as well pack up and go home, he finally catches a fish. There it was! At last! He made a careful note in his notebook, including the entries on either side of it, and hurried off at full speed to Markham Square where he expected to find his Inspector. As he wished his bus would go faster, Sergeant Jenkins thought that the Powerscourt residence was turning into a sort of extra police station.

Rhys showed the panting young man, one or two buttons undone, hair dishevelled, gasping heavily, into the drawing room.

'Lord Powerscourt, Lady Powerscourt, apologies for bursting in on you like this, but I've got it! I'm sorry it's taken so long!'

'You are most welcome, Sergeant. We'll get you a cup of tea – or a bottle of beer, if you'd prefer. You've obviously come in a great hurry with your news. Tell us, pray, what sends you hurtling round the streets of London.'

'Sorry, my lord, I've come from Somerset House where I've been looking at the death certificates! Reverend Fortescue down in Blexham brought us the fist part of the story of the marital life of Richard Wagstaff Gilbert. Here comes the second.'

The Sergeant drew out his notebook. 'Mrs Sophie Gilbert, née Shore, Bermondsey, October the tenth, died in childbirth. The infant also died.'

'Was it a boy or a girl?' asked Lady Lucy.

'It was a girl.'

'Pardon me, my lord, my lady, a terrible thought occurred to me as I was walking upstairs here just now.'

'And what was that?' said Powerscourt.

'Why, my lord. Do you think he married again? And maybe he had another family we don't know anything about? No reason why he couldn't have had. There's plenty of time for him to have done that.'

'There are an awful lot of years,' said Powerscourt, 'waiting for you in Somerset House if I am wrong, but I don't think he did.'

'How can you be so sure, Francis?'

'Well, think of it like this. If you had a wife alive, you'd be leaving all your money to her first and then onto the children when she died. That would be the natural thing. But think of it. If you had a wife or children living, you wouldn't be able to torment your family with the question of who you were going to leave your money to. You'd feel you were betraying your own every time you mentioned it. It's only if you don't have any direct descendants that you could play these terrible games. And consider this as well. If you had a wife and children of your own, your sisters would know about it. They wouldn't take it seriously, all this talk of leaving the money to their children. I think you're clear of another thirty-year session down there in the archives, Sergeant. What do you think Lucy?'

'Well, he sounds a pretty odd sort of character, our friend Gilbert, with the dodgy money and the cheating at cards. You don't think he could have a wife tucked away somewhere in secret?'

'Oh ye of little faith,' said Powerscourt. 'As long as I have Thomas and Olivia and the twins I couldn't contemplate giving any serious money to any nephews or nieces. It would be impossible. I think that idea – of the second wife and family tucked away – can be removed from the investigation. It still leaves the three nephews with perfectly adequate motives for killing each other and increasing their chances of inheriting.'

*

Powerscourt and Lady Lucy returned to the diary of Alexander Taneyev, now at the National Gallery.

'"I went to Trafalgar Square this morning to the National Gallery. They certainly have a lot of wonderful paintings, but I don't think they are a finer collection than we have in St Petersburg. But the Claudes and the Turners are sublime. I so wish that either of them could have come to our city and painted the sunsets over the Neva. That would have been beyond anything here. It would have been so beautiful.

'"I had a long talk with my uncle over supper at his house last night. He says that he is going to leave me all his money. He's not going to leave a penny to Mark or Peter or Nicholas, which I think is jolly unfair. He kept going about it as if he were really enjoying tormenting my cousins. I think it's monstrous. If I ever do get that money I shall make sure I give it to Papa and get him to divide it all up between the four of us."'

*

Another telegram had arrived at the Savoy addressed to M. Diaghilev. 'Dear M. Diaghilev, It is my unfortunate duty,' wrote the General Manager of the Grand Hotel Monte Carlo, 'that the bill for your stay here earlier this summer has still not been paid. I enclose a copy for your convenience. Unless this is paid forthwith, the hotel will be unable to offer you or your associates any further accommodation in future.'

*

Colonel Olivier Brouzet spent the morning reading diplomatic telegrams in his office in the Place des Vosges in Paris. He wasn't only reading the telegrams sent from his own Foreign Office at the Quai d'Orsay in his part of the city, but the messages sent in and out of Paris by all the Great Powers: the Germans, the Austrians, the English and the Russians. He called it taking the temperature of the diplomatic circuit, and it enabled him to tell his masters which issues between the principal powers on the Continent were especially important. These, he would point out in his accompanying memorandum, might need a touch or two of diplomatic massage in the weeks ahead.

Earlier that summer, the French cryptographers had succeeded in cracking the codes of the Okhrana, the Russian secret police in St Petersburg, used in messages to and from their office in Paris. There was one particular phrase that caused him great concern. He telephoned his wife to say he would be out of town for a few days. He sent word to his masters that he could be found at the local Embassy. Then he went through to his inner office and demanded details of the train and boat services to London, departing immediately.

*

'I say, Lucy, we may be about to meet the Crown Jewels at last. There's a page here that the boy has tried to cross out, but he hasn't quite succeeded. I can still just

298

about read it. Thank God for the vanity of diarists. He could have ripped out the page but he didn't.'

Powerscourt leant forward to get as close as he could to the diary. '"I found a strange document on Bolm's desk this afternoon when I popped in to ask him about his performance. On the middle of the page, it said in English: This paper must not be shared with any third parties, none whatsoever. At the top of the first page of the document – the crossing out starts here – it says in English: Most Immediate and Top Secret. Not for Circulation. The next page was a report on some experiment or other; at least, I presume it was an experiment, full of equations and mathematical expressions, none of which I understand. It's like that all the way until the last page, where it said still in English: Next Experiment. Kingfisher. Goring June 28th. 0600 hours. There were so many equations and mathematical symbols I couldn't make any sense of it. I left Bolm's dressing room as fast as I could and came back here to the Premier Hotel. I think I shall go for a walk to clear my head. What am I to do? Who am I to tell? All that stuff about top secret and so on. I wish Mama or Papa were here to tell me what to do."'

'The date, Francis, the date at the end – that's three days from the opening night and *Thamar*, when the boy was killed. What do you think it means?'

'Well,' said her husband, rubbing his eyes, 'it's certainly not a recipe for making tea in a samovar, that's for sure. But all those equations and things, I'm at a loss. I wonder if it has to with guns and their alignment, some means for more accurate shelling of the enemy. Or it could have to do with the navigation of submarines, that's always tricky, apparently. Perhaps we'd better see what our diarist has to say when he comes back from his walk.

'Here we go. "There may be some spy ring centred on our ballet. I wonder if I shouldn't go to the English authorities at once. I think I should confront Monsieur Bolm this afternoon. I can't go round accusing him of things without hearing what he has to say."'

Powerscourt turned the page. It was blank. So was the rest of the diary. Alexander Taneyev had written his last entry.

'Look here, Lucy, I didn't put the date in when I was reading it out. As you said, this last page was written three days before he was killed.'

'So we don't know whether he talked to Bolm, we don't know whether he walked into a police station and asked to speak to somebody – we know nothing at all. He, in his turn, could also have done nothing at all, merely got so agitated that he forgot to put an entry in his diary that evening,' observed Lucy.

'The rest is certainly silence,' said Powerscourt, riffling through the empty pages. 'I know almost nothing of the secret world and the armaments race, though it is costing us all a great deal of money. I shall have to go and call on Rosebery at once. He knows even less about military equations than I do, but he knows people who do. And what of this entry at the end in three days' time. Kingfisher? Goring? Six a.m.? What on earth is all that about?'

*

Inspector Dutfield was told the secrets of the diary.

'Looks like that young lady made her journey all the way to St Petersburg in vain, my lord, my lady. I know nothing of the secret world, nothing at all. There's a whole department that checks out all the foreigners for coronations and royal funerals and that sort of major ceremonial event with lots of foreign leaders, but I don't know anything about that other world. I tell you what, my lord. I shall find out what I can about Kingfisher at Goring from the local force. I'll find out if the young man did go and call on any English authorities, police stations and so on. That should just take five minutes on the phone. With your track record as the chap in charge of Military Intelligence in the Boer War, my lord – well, at least that gives you a head start on the rest of us.'

'Inspector,' said Lady Lucy, 'do you think this knowledge is dangerous? For whoever comes across it, I mean.'

'I should say it's very dangerous, my lady. Two people have been murdered. We don't know whether this caused it or not, but it's the strongest lead we have got so far and that's a fact.'

*

Rosebery was reading the reports from his racing trainer when Powerscourt arrived in Berkeley Square.

'Bloody depressing news, Powerscourt. The one wretched animal I possess with a chance of winning the St Leger has gone lame. Unlikely to improve in time for the big race. Another year without a major winner.'

Powerscourt wondered if Rosebery had made the acquaintance of William Burke's head porter who carried racing results round in his head the way other people do football scores.

Rosebery looked very grave when Powerscourt told him about Alexander's diary entry and the secret papers.

'Equations?' he said. 'Pages and pages of them? God help us all. I was a History man, at Oxford, as you know. I know nothing at all about mathematics and all that stuff. Perhaps it has something to do with gunnery, naval gunnery maybe. They're always asking boffins who can't speak properly and never learnt how to hold a fork to produce different ways of firing guns. Accuracy, that's what they're on about, particularly when the ship may be going up and down in the swell and you can't actually see the enemy. And you say the poor boy might have been killed for his pains? Worse and worse. You've got the police working with you, I presume? They should be able to find out what Kingfisher Goring means. I suppose you want me to see if I can manage an invitation for you, would that be right?'

'Do you know, I hadn't thought of that, Rosebery, but that would be kind. Naval gunnery at dawn, what a prospect.'

'Let me go and knock on a few doors that a former Foreign Secretary and Prime Minister is allowed to visit, my friend. I can't promise you any kind of response in that time, but I'll try my best. Let's meet again tomorrow afternoon and I'll see how many doors I've been able to open. That is, if I've been able to open any at all.'

'Thank you so much. That's most kind.'

'Just one thing, Powerscourt. These people in this secret world are not to be trusted. They will tell me whatever it suits them to tell me. They will leave out whatever does not suit them. They will want to use you for their own purposes. They will not be concerned with your safety or your health, only what they can get out of you. It's important that you understand that right from the start. You probably remember it anyway from your time with the bloody Boer in South Africa and all those devious princelings you dealt with in India. Don't, for God's sake, forget it now.'

*

'Kingfisher Goring, my lord,' he began, 'is more usually known as the Kingfisher Hotel; it lies between Goring and the adjacent village of Streatley.' Inspector Dutfield was the first caller of the day at the Powerscourt residence.

'It is a handsome establishment with a number of the principal rooms, like the dining room and the drawing room, right on the riverside. The Thames flows right past the back door. You can, Inspector Huntley of the local force told me, watch one fish go past while you eat another. It is not cheap, my lord. It appeals to customers with high-quality food. But, just at the moment, the Kingfisher Hotel is closed to visitors. They are not allowed to return for a month. In the meantime the place has been taken over by some people holding a conference with a lot of important visitors from abroad. They've brought all their own staff. The locals have all been sent home on full pay. That's pretty suspicious for a start, if you ask me. That could mean anything: European criminals, money men planning their next raid on the financial markets; God only knows what's going on up there. But there are signs all the way from the railway station to the hotel that it is closed.'

'And the young man, Alexander Taneyev? Is there

any evidence that he might have walked into a police station and told them the contents of his diary?'

'None at all. We have checked all the central stations and the two closest to where his uncle lives, but no such call was made. No young man hurried away to the War Office or the Navy to tell his secrets.'

'Do you think he might have told somebody in the Ballets Russes; somebody like Fokine, for example?'

'You'd have to ask him, my lord. If it were me, I'd be too worried about who else might be involved in this business at the ballet. You could have been jumping right out of the frying pan into the fire.'

*

Colonel Olivier Brouzet of the French Secret Service was the next visitor to Markham Square that day. A note had arrived the previous evening. They spoke in Brouzet's immaculate English.

'Forgive me for taking up your time at this difficult point in your investigation. I felt bound to come, as I have some information which may be of some assistance to you.'

'Thank you so much for coming all this way.' Powerscourt told him about the diary and the strange symbols and the mysterious meeting at the Kingfisher Hotel at Goring. 'I suspect that these are state secrets; I just don't know exactly what Alexander Taneyev saw.'

'I too have some state secrets for you, my lord, ones that are more or less home-grown. Let me begin with the immediate reason for my visit. I recently had good reason to speak to a man who was suspected of sending secret military information to the enemy. We thought the fellow was giving it to the Germans, but this was not the case – it was the Russians who were to be the beneficiaries of his knowledge of French military tactics. When he was asked how he was supposed to send his knowledge to Russia, he was told to take it to the Ballets Russes.'

'Bolm perhaps, Monsieur Brouzet? Alfred Bolm?'

'We did not have a name. It appears that the ballet may be a clearing house for secret information of one sort or another. If you think of it, it's a very neat solution to an old problem. It has always been very difficult for a spy to get his message home. He may be watched. The boats and the trains may all have people looking out for him. But, my lord, if he has a clearing house – a post office, if you will, he can present his information there. There it is given to a different courier, or it is simply carried on to France or Germany or whichever country the ballet is going to next. They carry mountains of luggage of every shape and size: clothes, costumes, make-up. Maybe the agent just carries it in his head if it is a simple message. The information is then passed on, not in Britain where the authorities may be watching, but in another country where the authorities are looking for somebody completely different. It would all depend on the urgency of the information. If speed is of the essence, then a different courier might take it on. If it was very secret it may be carried on when the ballet moves on, the information, like your top-secret document, safely hidden in the luggage, described as a new part of a new script for the ballet perhaps, a ballet of spies and secrecy, who knows?'

'That is fascinating, Colonel Brouzet. So somebody like Alfred Bolm in the Ballets Russes might have been the spy carrying information on to France, or he could have been the intermediary who met the courier in his dressing room, or at his chess club, where he was a regular visitor.'

'Chess club? What is this chess club? You have chess clubs for spies here in London?'

Powerscourt laughed. 'It is near our British Museum, a place where historians and scholars go to write their books; it has an enormous collection of ancient statues and sacred figures from all over the world. That's where the Elgin Marbles are kept. A number of the people who work there – some Russians, a number of Eastern Europeans – go to this chess club and test their wits against the locals. Bolm was a regular customer in his time in London.'

'That is not all, my friend. What I am going to tell you now is much more serious. We have reason to believe that the Okhrana in St Petersburg recently sent a top man to London with the code name Andrei Rublev, who was – as you know – a famous painter of Russian icons back in the fifteenth century. Whether his namesake is going to carry out any religious artwork here in London, I rather doubt. He has been sent to secure the position of Alfred Bolm, if it is indeed Bolm who is responsible, and to make sure that none of those bothering him at present continue to do so. This is how they would do things in Russia, secure in the knowledge that nobody is going to ask questions about the doings of the Okhrana.'

'Do I understand that you think I would be regarded as one of those bothering Monsieur Bolm at present? And what would be my fate, do you suppose?'

'That I do not know. Beaten up, broken leg, face smashed in? Worse? Murder?'

'That's cheering news, Colonel Brouzet. But do you think this Andrei Rublev actually wants to kill me?'

'Without knowing how valuable the information hidden in those equations actually is, I cannot be definite. But I should definitely watch your step. I should watch your step very carefully indeed.'

'Thank you very much indeed. I was going to ask you a question about your source for this information and it seems to me that there is one route that is most likely. But it also seems to me that I should not ask you if you have been reading the Okhrana telegrams over there in the Place des Vosges.'

'You would be quite right not to ask the question. And I would be quite right in telling you that I could not possibly be expected to give you an honest answer.'

*

Natasha Shaporova arrived at the same time as a note from Rosebery saying he would be delighted to see Powerscourt at tea time in Berkeley Square.

'I am so sorry, Lord Powerscourt, I feel I have let you down over those letters and the diary.'

'Never mind, Natasha, I am sure nobody else could have done half so well. You did discover that there was something suspicious going on after all.'

He filled her in on all the details of what had happened since: the discovery of the diary and the secret meeting at the Kingfisher Hotel at dawn. He mentioned nothing of the warnings from Colonel Brouzet of the French Secret Service.

'Do you suppose you will solve the mystery as dawn comes up over the Thames, Lord Powerscourt? That would be an exciting way to put an end to our enquiries.'

'Who knows,' said Powerscourt, feeling that if the case went on much longer, he would have to apply to train as a Delphic oracle.

'But I am so glad you are back. I have an urgent task for you.'

'What's that?'

'Let me put it like this. When you discover a secret, or somebody tells you a secret, what is the first thing you want to do?'

'Tell somebody else about it,' said Natasha. 'It's quite hard to resist the need to share a secret so that you're not carrying it alone.'

'And who would you be most likely to tell the secret to?'

'To somebody you trusted,' said Natasha. 'That's what I would do, anyway.'

'Well, we have no way of knowing who, if anybody, Alexander talked to. He may have told his parents, but it's not the same as telling somebody in London. They were so far away. He would have been most likely to have told somebody in his immediate circle. Isn't that so?'

'It is. I think I see what you want me to do, Lord Powerscourt. You want me to go back to all those girls in the corps de ballet and ask if Alexander told them he had a great secret. People always get excited if they think they are about to be told something special. Am I right?'

'You are absolutely right, Natasha. But be careful not to give anything away. Not a word about mathematical equations or secret formulae, just general questions.'

'I was never any good at mathematics, Lord

Powerscourt. Even the simple things they tried to teach us. Two – no, three – governesses gave up on me completely about the nine times tables.'

*

Rosebery, it seemed to Powerscourt, had already been on a Delphic oracle course before Powerscourt called at his house in Berkeley Square.

'These matters around the Ballets Russes are difficult and dangerous, my friend. I have been able to discover a little more about the meeting at the Kingfisher. I presume you have discovered that is a hotel for the middle classes on the banks of the Thames. I have not, so far, been able to secure you an invitation, if that is the right word.'

'Come on, Rosebery, surely you can tell me something of what it is about?'

'That is precisely what I cannot do. I am told to warn you to be very careful. The whole thing could become very dangerous, especially for you.'

'Will you be able to obtain an invitation of sorts before the thing starts? There is only a day and a bit left, for heaven's sake. A man would want to get there the evening before, if possible. Or am I just to present myself at the gate and ask where the equations are kept?'

'Whatever you do, my friend, do not, I repeat, do *not* turn up at this place without an invitation.'

'And will my host be one person or am I going to meet a committee of some sort, advanced mathematicians all?'

'Powerscourt, I have known and respected you for a number of years. I value our friendship very greatly.

It would cause me considerable pain to have to call for Leith the butler and ask him to show you the door.'

'You're throwing me out?'

'It's only for your own good, I promise you.'

*

Natasha Shaporova went to the Royal Opera House early the following morning and took the first three members of the corps de ballet across to the Fielding Hotel. But she found that a change had taken place in the girls. They simply refused to speak about the murder at all. They changed the subject or they talked about that evening's performance. They complained about the English weather. Or they talked about how sorry they would be to have to leave London. But of diaries or letters or assignations or secrets, they would speak not a word. Even when Natasha tried another tack, asking who had spoken to them, emphasizing the virtues of silence, they would not break their silence.

'They're just not going to speak to me,' she told Powerscourt later.

'Can you guess who might have put the fear of God into them?'

'I think there's only one person who could have put the fear of God into them like this, Lord Powerscourt.'

'And who would that be?'

'Why, it's the person who controls their careers and their livelihoods, the person who can decree that they will never dance for him again.'

'I think I could make a guess, Natasha, but tell me who you think it must have been.'

'There's only person who could do it, and that is Sergei Diaghilev himself. He must have sensed that some strange things were happening in his ballet and he has sworn them all to silence.'

*

Rosebery came to Markham Square at eleven o'clock the next morning, looking grave.

'It's going to be all right,' he said to Powerscourt and Lady Lucy. 'I've spent a great deal of political capital getting the result you wanted. You are to present yourself early this evening at the Kingfisher Hotel which, strictly speaking, is in Streatley, not Goring. There's something about a bridge dividing them.

'Believe me when I tell you that I do not know anything at all about what you may find there. If you hadn't served as Head of Military Intelligence in South Africa, I doubt that these doors would have opened an inch. I told them that you were conducting an investigation into a recent murder and were not a contracted spy in the service of the German government. That much they did believe. That is all I have to say. May I wish you God speed and good luck.'

'You can't just slip away without answering a question or two, Rosebery,' Lady Lucy remarked as the former Prime Minister was picking up his hat and heading for the door. 'Is it dangerous? For Francis, I mean.'

'I would be failing in my duty if I did not say it might be dangerous. But it might not, Lucy. I'm sorry I can't be more specific than that.'

24

Frappé

A hitting or striking action of the foot where the foot
is directed toward the floor using a strong extension
of the leg. The foot starts in a wrapped position called
sur le cou-de-pied where the heel of the foot is placed
on the front of the leg directly below the calf, and the
toes of the foot are wrapped around the leg toward the
back, with the knee placed directly to the side. From
this starting position, the leg strikes forward, leading
with the heel, hitting the ball of the foot on the floor,
and extending to a pointed position with the foot. The
leg and foot then return to their original positions to
begin the *frappé* again.

You could hear it before you could see it, Powerscourt
said to himself, dressing reluctantly at a quarter to
four in the morning in his vast bedroom looking out
over the Thames. There they went, the dark waters of
the river, swirling and slapping and gurgling on their
long journey to the sea. The local birds were already

welcoming a new day. His reception on arrival late the previous evening had been curt.

'Ah, Powerscourt,' General Page had said as he presented himself, rather tired from his journey the evening before. There was a long pause. Page had been universally known as Silent Page, ever since his first days as a trainee Sub-Lieutenant many years before, when Lord Salisbury was Prime Minister. The pause went on.

'Sir!' Powerscourt replied, feeling that some form of dialogue might yet be possible. Page was now staring intently at a large black notebook in front of him. He made no entries.

'Good of you to come,' he managed at last, and sank back slightly in his chair, as if the effort of speech had exhausted him.

'Sir!' said Powerscourt, feeling that his replies in this attempt at conversation were somewhat limited. He waited. Silent Page was now looking intently at the river, as if enemy forces might suddenly disembark and seize the hotel. Then he inspected his pencil, as if it too might have hostile intent. Suddenly he leant forward and began inspecting a form in front of him. Powerscourt wondered if it contained the staff orders for the day or just the dispositions of his troops for the next twenty-four hours. Silent Page took a deep breath.

'Got to get you to sign this,' he managed at last. 'Official Secrets Act 1911, you know. You'll have seen about it in the papers.'

'Why?' asked Powerscourt, who had always had a reputation for questioning the orders of superior officers, especially when he considered them unnecessary. This time the pause was hardly there at all.

'Just sign the bloody thing, damn you. I went to a lot of trouble to get you here. Thought you might be useful.'

By Silent Page's normal standards, this was virtually the whole act of a Shakespeare play in one go. Powerscourt was so surprised he leant forward and signed it at once, without question. This time the silence reverted to its normal pre-Shakespearian mode. The General looked again at the river, checking perhaps for another arrival of enemy marines. He stared again at the black notebook in front of him.

'Breakfast's at four tomorrow morning. For God's sake don't ask me any questions. I might not be able to give you the answers. Official Secrets Act, don't you know.'

That breakfast was the strangest meal Powerscourt had been present at in all his years on the planet. The General was there, of course, conducting a silent reconnaissance on a pair of kippers. There was a German officer in civilian clothes and a monocle whose name, Powerscourt discovered later, was Ludwig von Stoltenberg, attached to the German General Staff. There was a sleek Frenchman, wearing the finest civilian clothes the Parisian tailors could provide, called Jean-Pierre Poiret. The two foreigners had taken to addressing each other in the other's language, so the Frenchman spoke to the German in impeccable German and the German spoke back to the Frenchman in near perfect French. A simple question of politeness about the direction of the marmalade became: *'Passieren die marmelade, bitte,'* from the French side of the Rhine, and *'Passer la marmelade, s'il vous plaît,'* from the other.

The usual strange Continental breakfast offerings of

cold ham and cheese were provided as a gesture of friendship towards the foreigners, but all three of them polished off a plate of bacon and eggs. When the marmalade had stopped travelling, Silent Page burst into speech again. Powerscourt noted with interest that the hostile kippers had been completely routed, with only a few bones left on the General's plate.

'Ahem,' he began, 'ahem, we leave in five minutes. I advise you to wrap up well.'

Each man travelled in his own car, a silent driver at the wheel. After five minutes or so they were deep in the English countryside and had to stop at a serious-looking gate, manned by a couple of soldiers, guns at the ready. As far as the eyes could see, a very tall wall, about eight feet high, guarded what looked like an enormous park. There were no buildings to be seen as the four cars set off up a long and winding drive that Powerscourt thought might lead to a Blenheim Palace or a Castle Howard. Instead they came to a second guardhouse, manned again by armed soldiers with sentries marching up and down the length of another wall, this time a little shorter, perhaps six feet high. Powerscourt wondered if these sentries were condemned to an everlasting patrol like the horsemen who rode round the Tsar's Palace at Tsarskoe Selo outside St Petersburg twenty-four hours a day.

The little fleet of cars finally stopped at what looked like a large birdwatchers' hide. Inside there were seats and binoculars and four telescopes and a grandstand view over the countryside. Silent Page suggested they make themselves comfortable.

'It should – ahem – be fully light in a few minutes. Then the action will begin.' There was a long pause, as

315

if he were a weatherman consulting his charts before producing the forecast for the day. He stared out at the fields in front of him. 'I'm told there will be no wind. We should – ahem – be safe here.'

Wind? Hostilities? Powerscourt felt a terrible apprehension running through his body. What on earth was going on? Why did they have to invoke the Official Secrets Act for something that was about to happen in the middle of a field in the middle of nowhere? He grabbed a pair of binoculars and stared straight in front of him. He saw, about two hundred yards away, a series of trenches dug in parallel with a series of connecting trenches at either end, like a child's parallelogram in a maths exercise book. He couldn't see how deep the trenches were. He noticed that the trench area was almost completely surrounded by trees or by man-made hillocks, which looked as if they had only been created very recently. The German began walking up and down, muttering to himself in French. The Frenchman began to rub his hands together, as if he were about to enjoy the best meal that the Savoy Grill could provide.

A gun went off, firing from the far side of the trenches, Powerscourt thought. He could see no sign of anything landing. Perhaps it was a blank. The shot had a dramatic effect on his two colleagues.

'*Achtung Achtung!*' said the Frenchman.

'*Merde! Attention! Attention!*' said the German.

Both whipped fresh notebooks from their pockets and proceeded to virtually glue themselves to the nearest binoculars. Powerscourt did the same, wondering if he would be reprimanded afterwards for not having a fresh notebook to hand. The other two were focused on the trenches. Powerscourt turned his glasses across the landscape and saw what the others didn't.

A young shepherd, complete with attendant sheep-dog, was driving a flock of about thirty sheep towards the trenches. Fiddling with the controls, Powerscourt saw that the young man – he didn't look more than twenty – was crying, and that the tears were running down his sweater as if he had been weeping for some time.

The sheep were driven into the enclosure surrounded by the trenches. They did not find them attractive, preferring to wander round their new enclosure. Powerscourt noticed that two large troughs of water had been placed at either end to keep the sheep in place. He glanced back up the hill. He thought he caught the glint of another pair of binoculars lurking at the edge of the trees. But however much he adjusted his controls, he never saw it again.

Looking to his left, Powerscourt saw that half a dozen goats were being driven down the little hill to join the party. They were roped together and their handler, a much older man, drove a post into the ground to keep them tethered as soon as they entered the enclosure. This man was older. He didn't cry. But he scuttled off back up the hill as fast as his legs would carry him. He seemed to be saying something to himself as he went, possibly praying, Powerscourt thought. For he was now certain that something terrible was about to happen in this parallelogram hidden among the green fields of southern England.

His two companions were scribbling furiously, though Powerscourt saw that their eyes never left the enclosure. Then the gun went off again. This time it seemed to land in the centre of the parallelogram. A thin mist, or fog, settled over the trenches and the grass. Thinking about it afterwards, Powerscourt remembered that the animals made no noise at all. Their fate was met in silence. One or two of the sheep tried to run back the way they had come, to the safety of the trees and their weeping shepherd. After a dozen paces they staggered to a halt and lay down. Other sheep and a couple of goats began slumping to the ground. The parallelogram was turning into a death chamber.

The German began saying '*Ave Maria*' very quietly in French, his eyes locked on the sheep; they were twitching furiously now, as if they could not control their arms or their legs. 'Hail Mary full of Grace, *Je vous salue, Marie, pleine de grâce.*'

The Frenchman replied with the Lord's Prayer in Luther's language. '*Vater unser im Himmel, geheiligt werde dein Name . . .*'

Powerscourt was certain that the animals were dying, killed off by some form of poison gas. He thought of his son Thomas, and all his friends and contemporaries who might man the British trenches in a future war in Europe, spread out in their innocence the length and breadth of England, and he put his head in his hands.

'*Mère de Dieu, Priez pour nous, pauvres pêcheurs, maintenant et à l'heure de notre mort.* Pray for us now, poor sinners, and in the hour of our death.'

All the animals were sinking to the ground now. Most of them lay flat on the ground, one or two still twitching feebly in their death agonies. The goats too were passing into the next world.

'*Und vergib uns unsere Schuld, wie auch wir vergeben*

unsern Schuldigern. And forgive us our trespasses as we forgive those that trespass against us.'

Powerscourt was close to tears. Why were his fellow countrymen preparing to use this terrible weapon, for he was certain that the animals were merely an alternative to humans who could not be found to volunteer for such a dreadful death. Who had approved it? The Prime Minister? The Chief of the Imperial General Staff? The Archbishop of Canterbury?

The Frenchman was stuck at the end of his prayer, saying it over and over again. There were only a couple of sheep still writhing on the deadly grass. The cloud of fog had passed on and was drifting slowly towards the hill where the shepherd had gone.

'*Denn dein ist das Reich und die Kraft und die Herrlichkeit in Ewigkeit*. Amen. For thine is the kingdom the power and the glory for ever and ever, Amen.'

Powerscourt promised himself that he would do all in his power to make sure that this gas was never used. Perhaps, he reflected ruefully, that was why he was here, to spread the word around the upper reaches of London society.

It was as they were leaving, the dead animals left in their place until the gas had totally cleared, that Powerscourt listened to what must rank as the most tasteless remark he had ever heard.

'We Germans are not good at tact or at jokes,' the German Colonel began, speaking now in perfect English, 'but it seems to me that the gas did not draw any distinction between the sheep and the goats.'

25

Pirouette

A *pirouette* is a turn on one leg, often starting with
one or both legs in *plié* and rising onto *relevé* (usually for men) or *pointe* (usually for women). The non-
supporting leg is held in *passé*. A pirouette may return
to the starting position or finish in *arabesque* or *attitude* positions, or proceed otherwise. It is most often *en
dehors* turning outwards toward the back leg, but can
also be *en dedans* turning inwards toward the front
leg. Although ballet *pirouettes* are performed with the
hips and legs rotated outward ('turned out'), it is common to see them performed with an inward rotation
('parallel') in other genres of dance, such as jazz and
modern. Spotting technique is usually employed to
help maintain balance. *Pirouettes* can be executed with
a single or multiple rotations.

Petroc Danvers Tresilian did not live up to the rich
promise of his name. Earlier Tresilians had made their
money through smuggling in the eighteenth century.

When large bribes were not enough to satisfy the customs men, it was rumoured that attractive young girls from the servants' hall or the more formal quarters upstairs were pressed into service. That never failed. Turn your faces to the wall while the gentlemen come in.

Later Tresilians, especially after their union with the Danvers at the time of the Repeal of the Corn Laws, had escaped from the clutches of the customs men into the great bosom of the English middle class. Amelia Danvers, who married Caradoc Tresilian, brought with her the virtues of High Church, high moral standards and a burning desire to make it into the upper reaches of society. One of her brothers became Governor of Bengal, another was a Fellow of All Souls and another kept up the family ambition by becoming a High Court Judge.

Petroc Danvers Tresilian did not seem to possess the buccaneering spirit of his ancestors. As the senior civil servant in the Cabinet Office, he glided around Whitehall, a couple of new recruits accompanying him on his progress. The cynics said he resembled nothing so much as a senior hospital doctor on his rounds, flunkeys and junior doctors in tow, as he pronounced the sentence of life or death on the recumbent forms (or government plans) as he passed on his way.

'Gentlemen,' he began, in a private lounge looking out over the river, 'thank you for attending our little demonstration. English is now the lingua franca of the day. From now on we are all complicit in these matters. We have all broken the Official Secrets Act many times this morning. It applies, as you know, to the clean shaven and the bearded, the washed and the unwashed, to foreigner and native Englishman alike.'

He's making them dip their hands in the blood, Powerscourt thought to himself. *We're all complicit now.*

'I would just remind you all of the dates we agreed at our last meeting at Baddesley Clinton. Three weeks from now we all travel to the desolate country behind Calvi in Corsica for the French demonstration. The Baddesley Clinton protocol –' Powerscourt could see how much Danvers Tresilian enjoyed the word 'protocol', which spoke, strictly speaking, of private clauses inserted secretly into treaties between states by their despotic rulers – 'makes it clear that our last demonstration should be in the Ardennes; close, appropriately enough, to the French border.'

The two foreigners nodded in agreement. Baddesley Clinton, Powerscourt thought. Baddesley Clinton. A little jewel of a house, with a perfect moat, in the English Midlands, it had been famous for concealing recusants in the reign of Elizabeth I. Perhaps they'd popped the two foreigners into the priest holes. They would naturally have been suspected of being agents of the Catholic faith – the fact they were foreigners was enough to rouse Elizabeth's spy master, Sir Francis Walsingham, into action.

'Now then, gentlemen, questions are allowed, although I cannot give any guarantees of my being able to answer them.'

That means he's not going to give any answers at all, Powerscourt said to himself.

'The wind,' said the Frenchman, 'would I be right in saying that there was virtually no wind this morning?'

'You would be right in assuming that,' said Danvers Tresilian.

'And there is still virtually no wind now, is that not right?' asked the German, peering out of the windows at the calm running of the river, swirling on its way to London and the sea.

The man from the Cabinet Office made a brief inspection of the Thames.

'You too are correct: there is still a dead calm here.'

Powerscourt had managed, with great difficulty, to clear his son Thomas and his friends from his mind. Now he was wondering what on earth was going on. What was this conspiracy all about? Why was the Frenchman here? And the German? Sharing secrets with foreign powers with whom we might be at war in a few years' time? Had Tresilisan permission from his political masters to be here, offering secret displays of the lethal properties of British poison gas? And if so, which masters? The urbane mandarins of his own department? The Generals in all their pomp and glory on the Imperial General Staff?

'The gas,' said the Frenchman, 'is a gas that could easily be manufactured through detailed knowledge of the more advanced forms of the chemical industry in all our countries?'

'You know the rules, Monsieur, I couldn't be expected to reply to such a question. Unofficially, and I shall not include this in the secret minutes of this meeting, unofficially the answer is yes.'

If they all know about how to make the stuff, what are these three doing here? Powerscourt asked himself. Then the answer came, or did it? For his theory was so bizarre that it seemed literally incredible. He remembered the Sherlock Holmes lines in *The Sign of Four*: 'How often have I said to you that when you have eliminated the impossible, whatever remains, however improbable, must be the truth?'

It couldn't be true, surely. Or could it? It was too improbable for words.

'I feel that we have probably exhausted the lines of enquiry that might be regarded as safe,' said the man from the Cabinet Office, gathering some papers in front of a very large and very expensive leather briefcase. 'Lord Powerscourt, you have been quiet ever since you arrived. You didn't even ask for marmalade this morning.'

That must be the Cabinet Office idea of a joke, Powerscourt said to himself. God help us all.

'Perhaps,' put in the Frenchman, 'you should tell our friend the real nature of our business. He was not at Baddesley Clinton. He does not know our purpose. If he does not know that, then why is he here?'

Danvers Tresilian slapped his hand on his brow rather dramatically. He's covering his tracks, Powerscourt said to himself. Maybe this is how the upper reaches of the mandarin class get themselves out of trouble in the discreet quarters of their Ministry or over a glass of something at the Athenaeum.

'The Baddesley accords,' Tresilian began – accords as well as protocols; Powerscourt's brain was working at full speed now, thinking of Metternich and Talleyrand and the intrigues that followed the war against Napoleon – 'state quite clearly that we gentlemen here are committed to our countries agreeing never to use poison gas in the event of war between us. We are neutral on the question of war or peace, though we would, naturally, prefer peace. But if there is to be a war, we see it as our duty to ensure that none of our countries use the dreadful stuff we saw in action this morning. How do we propose to secure this harmony? By lobbying as hard as we can with our political masters and their military counterparts to ensure that poison gas is never used. Lord Rosebery suggested you would be a very useful addition to our cause, Lord Powerscourt. That is why you are here.'

Powerscourt rose to his feet and bowed to those present. 'I am honoured,' he said. 'I congratulate you on your courage, to undertake such a mission that could well be laughed to scorn by our colleagues in uniform.'

'You will forgive me, gentlemen,' said the German. 'There is one further argument against the use of this poison gas. It only came to me as I watched the end of the demonstration earlier.'

'Do tell us your thoughts, my friend,' Danvers Tresilian was once more the perfect civil servant, not closing the discussion down, leaving avenues of exploration open to visitors, stones not left unturned, when a lesser man might have headed for the exit.

'We have to have the little game of war, gentlemen,' said the German. 'I am on the side where the guns were, the ones that fired a warning for the start and the one that fired the shell with the gas. Let's say I am the German officer commanding. My French friend here is the officer commanding on the other side. His men receive the full impact of the German gas, possibly even more powerful, having been made in Germany, than the one we saw earlier.'

'I and my men are in a state of complete chaos,' said the Frenchman, pulling a small cheroot out of his waistcoat pocket. 'My men are dying or dead. Some, no doubt, have gone blind or are going blind, and cannot see where they are. Others are running or stumbling away towards what they think is the safety of the rear lines.'

'Remember the weather,' said the German. 'It is still. Every bone in my body, every hour of training tells me that this is the moment to attack. The enemy are in trouble. Now is the time to strike. But I cannot.'

'Why not, pray?'

'The gas is still lying there. I cannot order my men forward into the same fog of poison that has decimated the Frenchmen. They too would suffer the same fate. It would be madness to follow up after a gas attack like this one.'

'Presumably,' said Powerscourt, 'if the wind changed it could blow your own gas back into the German lines. There again your troops would suffer the same fate as their enemies.'

'Exactly so,' said the German, 'it is yet another reason why this terrible weapon should never be used. It could boomerang back into the people who sent it there in the first place.'

There was a loud knock at the door and two well-built soldiers burst into the room. 'Begging your pardon, sirs, but we found this one sketching in his little book outside the plant where they make the stuff, sir.'

Powerscourt remembered the glint that could have come from the sun on a pair of binoculars on the edge of the forest. Perhaps they too belonged to this man, currently wriggling as hard as he could to escape his captors. He was wearing a very long greatcoat with a cap that could be pulled down low. He had a small beard and a great air of injured righteousness, as if he'd been caught defending the Holy of Holies.

'Let me go, you fools. You can't treat me like this. I am a diplomat accredited to the Court of St James.'

Powerscourt remembered Rosebery telling him during his time as Foreign Secretary that at least a third – if not a half – of those who presented themselves and their papers to the Court were spies of one sort or another.

The German and the Frenchman tried to make themselves as invisible as possible. They did not want to be seen by anybody outside their own circle. If their presence here was known to the authorities in their own country, they could be tried for treason and shot. They were very brave to risk the wrath of the authorities in their own military hierarchy. Visibility only added to the prospect of capture and exposure.

Then the stranger made his move. He seemed to slump down for a moment. As he rose he thrust his knee with all his power into the groin of the guard on his left and smashed his other elbow into the face of the guard on his right. They seemed to be holding him, but with one great heave he wriggled free and headed off down the corridor at full speed. Powerscourt set off after him, conscious – as he had been on more than one occasion on this investigation – that he was not as fast on his feet as he had been. Danvers Tresilian picked up the telephone and began barking out orders. He shouted to Powerscourt as he set off in pursuit of the stranger, 'For God's sake, man, whatever you do, don't go into the kitchen.'

26

Pulling Up

Pulling up is critical to the success of a dancer because
without it, the simple act of rising up would be
extremely difficult. It involves the use of the entire
body. The feeling of being simultaneously grounded
and 'pulled up' is necessary for many of the traditional
steps in ballet. To pull up, a dancer must lift the ribcage
and sternum but keep the shoulders relaxed and centred over the hips, which requires use of the abdominal
muscles. In addition, the dancer must tuck their pelvis
under and keep their back straight [so] as to avoid
arching and throwing themselves off balance. Use of
the inner thigh muscles as well as the 'bottom' is very
helpful in pulling up. Pulling up is also essential to dancers *en pointe* in order for them to balance on their toes.

The rag-and-bone man did not seem to be stopping at
very many houses in London's East End that morning.
Perhaps it was too early. Karl Lodost, Lenin's man
sent from Cracow to look after his business interests

in London, had called on Arthur Cooper two days before and informed him that he would be coming to take the pamphlets away in this unusual fashion and at this unusual hour. As he stacked the bundles of revolutionary rhetoric onto the back of the cart, Cooper wondered if this would be his moment in the great hall of historical fame, a revolution or revolutions started somewhere in Europe, inspired by Lenin's words that had been stacked for three whole days in the attic of his little house. The packets of pamphlets were all stamped 'BALLETS RUSSES, CUSTOMS CLEARANCE, ONWARDS DESPATCH'.

As he watched them trundle quite slowly up his street, he also wondered by whom and where they would be opened. When the cart had turned the corner into Union Street, he went back into his house to prepare some breakfast. He had not waited to see the milk float that seemed to follow Karl Lodost's rag-and-bone cart towards Covent Garden and the West End of London. The milkman didn't seem to be stopping to make any deliveries either.

*

Powerscourt hadn't time to wonder about kitchens or poison gas recipes as he set off down the passage. The stranger seemed to have vanished. The thump of his boots told Powerscourt he was moving up the corridor. A set of steps led down into a lower level of hell, beneath where he was now standing. There was a prominent sign at the top that nobody could have escaped: KEEP OUT! AUTHORIZED PERSONNEL ONLY! As he too turned the corner he saw his opponent making full speed towards a great set of double doors. Even at fifty yards, Powerscourt picked up the traces of a terrible smell and a dull noise that might have been machinery of some sort. Maybe, he thought, running towards the entrance, this was the Devil's Kitchen, where Lucifer or the Devil himself prepared menus of death for their victims. Human rather than crème brûlée, Enemy Flambé a speciality of the house.

It was the sound that struck Powerscourt as he made his way warily through the double doors. It was the throb of many giants hissing in unison, with the odd extra gurgle coming in from the side. The room was circular, about fifty feet by fifty. Great grey vats or silos lined the walls.

Powerscourt thought he could count thirteen of them. A series of pipes of varying shapes and sizes led down from each vat to the central section, a large open pit, the oven of the place. Very steep slopes led down to it from the main body of the death chamber, in case anybody needed to give the monstrous stew a stir or throw extra ingredients into the inferno. This was where the noise came from as the devil's brew marinated or stewed, surrounded by the waters of the Thames and the countryside of England. Powerscourt saw the advantages of the river setting – the Thames could carry away at full speed any amount of noxious leftovers, the debris of the kitchen that even the dogs and the local vermin wouldn't touch.

The Russian was right on the edge of the cauldron, sketching as fast as he could.

'Who are you?' asked Powerscourt.

'My real name is immaterial. I am a patriot. I love my country. On patriotic missions like this one, I go under the name of Andrei Rublev. When I have finished my work here, I am going to kill you.'

'That's very considerate of you,' said Powerscourt, feeling his feet going on the slippery floor. 'Might I have the honour of knowing which nationality is going to take me to the other side?'

'You may, you may indeed,' said the man, turning over another page of his notebook. He's a cool customer, this one, Powerscourt thought, finishing his work before he moves in for the kill.

'I come from Mother Russia, the land of Kievan Rus and the home of the holy monks.' Powerscourt wondered if he went to top-up courses in fanaticism with Rasputin in the Tsar's village after a session with the Delphic oracle.

'And what are you doing here?' asked Powerscourt, playing for time. Surely that bloody civil servant with the Cornish name could have sent some soldiers here by now?

'You do not understand. Russia may be building factories faster than any other power in Europe. But we do not have the knowledge acquired by you people in the decadent West. We have to steal to learn how to make the weapons of our enemies. We always have and we always will. Then Russia can take her seat at the top tables of the world. We would have the same weapons, including gas, as our enemies – and Mother Russia would not go naked to any conference table.'

'You can't build a plant like this with a few drawings,' said Powerscourt. His reply seemed to drive the Russian to fury. Powerscourt didn't think the man would have a gun, but knives, whips, steel knuckledusters that could smash a man's skull in?

'Listen, you fool Englishman! I will tell you the truth and then I will kill you. We have been looking out for you a long time, Powerscourt, We have kept abreast of your movements through compatriots in that silly dancing place.' The Russian had a heavy iron bar at his side to warn Powerscourt to keep his distance.

Powerscourt wondered what on earth Diaghilev and the Ballets Russes could have to do with this monstrous building on the Thames. Would Nijnsky and Karsavina dance a pas de deux in front of the devil's kitchen?

'The gas machines first,' said the Russian, 'you shall at least go to your well-deserved grave knowing the full extent of the power of Mother Russia. You think my work here,' he was still drawing furiously as he spoke, and had just gone to another new page, 'is the beginning. It is not. It is nearly the end. We have the formula for the gas from the French – there's nothing French engineers and chemists like doing more than boasting how their labours will add to the greater glory of France. This –' he waved an arm round the terrible silos – 'may be enough for our engineers, locked away in the interior where nobody could find them, a plan of this room and the disposition of the equipment may be all they need to complete the work.'

Where on earth were those bloody soldiers? There couldn't be much left to say about the pipes and the terrible cauldron at the centre. Only one card left to play.

'Why were your colleagues at the ballet reporting on my movements?'

'That has to do with the Ballets Russes. I shall tell you a little as you have less than five minutes left to live. We thought everybody would assume that Bolm was meant to be the victim. Everyone except you, my about-to-be-dead friend. I congratulate you on that.

The dead man was in fact who the dead man was meant to be, the understudy. He saw something he shouldn't have in Bolm's dressing room. He told Bolm he was going to report it to the English authorities. He told one of the girl dancers, Vera Belitsky I think she was called. She, in case you have forgotten, was the dancer I killed at Blenheim Palace. Taneyev may not have known much in the way of mathematics and chemical equations, but any fool can see the word "Goring" and the date. The other victim was also part of Taneyev's conspiracy. The little fool told the dancer all he knew and what he proposed to do about it. She had to go before she could tell the English authorities. We have a saying in Russia, *smert shpionem* – death to spies and traitors of every sort. That was what happened to Taneyev and his friend, and good riddance too.'

'So all of Bolm's bad behaviour with women was a red herring, as we say in English?'

The man was checking his drawings now. The end could not be very far away. Would he throw a knife or attempt to close in on him with the deadly weapon in his hand? Powerscourt had been fiddling about with his left hand among the materials lined up against the wall behind him. There was a square steel plate about the size of a dustbin lid that might do service as a shield. And there was a very long pole, slightly longer than the pole used to propel punts up and down the waters of the Cam and the Isis – though Powerscourt, for the moment, could not imagine what to do with it.

The Russian put his notebook and his pencil in his pocket. Even as he started, Powerscourt guessed what was coming next. He just had time to drag his steel shield in front of his body, up to the chin. He gambled that the man wouldn't try for his head, a smaller and more mobile target. The knife seemed to come simultaneously with the hand coming out of his pocket. It smashed into Powerscourt's shield and fell on the floor. Another followed, then a third, all repelled by the dustbin lid. The man began swearing viciously in Russian and started fiddling about with his right boot. Powerscourt saw his chance. He grabbed the punt pole, which had a sort of paddle at the end, as if for stirring the monstrous brew in the Devil's kitchen, and charged the thirty feet or so between him and the Russian. He felt, momentarily, that he was Sir Lancelot come to rescue the Lady of Shallot in some terrible jousting tournament. The paddle caught the Russian and pushed him backwards towards the pit. He staggered.

Powerscourt drew his weapon back and shoved again. He knew his strength was failing fast from inhaling these terrible vapours, but it was the best he could do. The man slipped and turned as he fell down the top of the slippery slope and began sliding down into the mouth of hell itself. Powerscourt moved in for the kill. Sliding down, the man made one last effort. He raised himself and sank his teeth into Powerscourt's arm. Gravity and the weight of the Russian were pulling them both towards the final vision of Hieronymus Bosch. It just needed a few splotches of brilliant red and some dancing flames in front and it could be hanging as the pride of place in some leading German art gallery, Powerscourt thought. He felt his arm might be about to break. He knew the fumes could overcome him at any moment.

334

There was a shot from near the door. The soldiers, Powerscourt whispered to himself, they've come at last. Two burly Corporals used their bayonets to free Powerscourt's arm – his left, he was glad to see. He was free. Everybody stood and watched in horror as the Russian began slipping down to hell. He was now out of human reach and nobody gave the order to throw him a lifeline. Four enormous steel plates appeared round the edges of the pit and began moving quite fast towards the centre. When they met, the Devil's saucepan would have a lid that admitted nothing into the mixture within. Somebody must have pressed a lever or a button to start the process off.

They watched in horror as the Russian – now slowly, now quite quickly – began to fall into the pit. He was swearing violently to start with. Then he managed to cross himself and began saying his prayers in Russian. He was going to need them now. Powerscourt found himself shuddering as he thought of what would happen to the man if he wasn't underwater by the time the square lids closed. He would be cut in half, or a quarter, or, maybe, God forbid, his head would be sliced clean off his body. One second the Russian would be winning the race towards total immersion. Then it would look as though the top of his face, maybe his hair, would be caught in the pincers of the steel plates.

Suddenly it was all over. Gravity won. The Russian was under the noxious mixture before the lid closed. But only by about ten seconds. Powerscourt thought a quick death by steel plate might have been the better option, but he was so glad he hadn't met the same fate. He realized that blood was flowing fast out of his arm where the spy had held on.

'We've sent for an ambulance, just breathe in the fresh air,' Danvers Tresilian said as he led him to a veranda looking out over the river. 'It'll be here in a minute. I hope to God you're going to recover fully. The doctors think that it would be impossible to survive in there for more than five minutes. You were in there for seven and a half. May the Lord bless you and keep you.'

27

À la seconde

To the side or in the second position. *À la seconde* usually means a movement done by the feet to the side such as a *tendu*, *glisse* or *grand battement*. A technically challenging type of turn is a *pirouette à la seconde*, where the dancer spins with the working leg in second position in *à la hauteur*. This turn is typically performed by male dancers because of the advanced skills required to perform it correctly. It is seen as the male counterpart of *fouettés en tournant*.

The four black funeral horses were standing very still outside Arthur Cooper's house. The driver, also dressed in black, waited at his post. The back of the hearse was empty. Inside, in Arthur Cooper's front room, three of his revolutionary colleagues were transferring money from a large container, sent under guard from the bank that held his account. In vain had the bank's manager pleaded with Arthur to leave some of the money behind. Nobody, he said, should leave their accounts completely empty. Surely, the bank manager had continued, Arthur would need some reserves for the inevitable rainy day.

It was all in vain. The three comrades had taken it in turn to guard the container all through the night.

'If you'd said to me when I joined the movement, Arthur, that I would spend an entire night guarding money from a bank rather than stealing it, I'd have said you were mad.'

'But it was stolen in the first place, liberated from the capitalist class in Russia,' Cooper had replied, 'and think of the good use Comrade Lenin will put it to when he gets his hands on it.'

'I tell you another thing,' said the comrade from Stepney. 'No customs man is going to be in a hurry to open this lot, I can tell you. I doubt if opening coffins is in their job description. Once it gets to the Continent, all those bloody customs men will be crossing themselves and saying their Hail Marys at top speed.'

Now the money was all tightly packed in the bottom of the coffin, with piles of bricks lining the upper levels. Very slowly, and with all due solemnity, the coffin was carried out of the door on four sets of shoulders and slid into position. On the top and the sides was a very clear description of the contents. Ballets Russes. Props Department.

Arthur Cooper took up his position beside the driver. Two other comrades rode at the back as the strange hearse with its four black horses set out west across London to the fruit and vegetable market at Covent Garden, where it would be stored along with all the other props in the Ballets Russes section of the storage facilities of the Royal Opera House.

*

General Kilyagin was tired of waiting for news from London. He rang Captain Yuri Gorodetsky at his post in the little office in Holborn.

'What on earth is going on, Captain?' he boomed down the phone line. 'It's days since I've had any news from London! What in God's name have you been doing? Inspecting the Tower of London? Going to the bloody ballet?'

'No, sir. I have news for you – important news that will change this case and take it out of my area of responsibility.'

'Out with it, man. What have those Bolsheviks been doing?'

'Everything is now secure in the luggage section of the Ballets Russes, General. Our English colleagues watched both consignments right into the building in Covent Garden.'

'You're still not making sense, Captain. What consignments?'

'Sir, both the revolutionary tracts and the money are now in the care of the ballet people. There they will remain until the whole lot moves off back to France or wherever they're going next.'

'You're sure of that?'

'Absolutely certain, General. Could I ask you a question?'

'With that answer you could ask me anything. Fire ahead.'

'What is going to happen to them now?'

'I do not have full authority to tell you that, Captain. They will be watched all their way to the final destinations. And by that I don't just mean Comrade Lenin and his revolutionary friends. We will watch the leaflets in particular right to their final destinations from Lenin's address list, be that in Moscow or Siberia or Kiev. Once they have been delivered, the recipients will receive a visit from the Okhrana. They may end up joining Lenin in exile, or, more likely, they will find themselves taking a long journey to Siberia.'

*

They kept Powerscourt in bed in a private wing of a military hospital for five days. The wing was sealed off. In that time a number of doctors came to see him, all in uniform. They listened to his breathing; they prodded his chest; they asked him to walk up and down. They were particularly keen to inspect the yellow pallor on his face. They didn't seem very bothered about his arm, though they did say it was healing well. They passed no judgement on his condition. They were waiting, they told him, for the man from London, who was a civilian and whose background had to be thoroughly checked before he was allowed to pass judgement. Dr Archibald Forester had a large and distinguished practice in Harley Street.

'Lord Powerscourt, I am delighted to make your acquaintance,' said Dr Forester, when he finally arrived.

'Perhaps you could enlighten me as to what is happening,' said Powerscourt, 'I have no idea where I am, apart from the fact that this is a military hospital. Nobody has told me what is going on. I feel like a parcel that is being passed round and round except that the music never stops.'

'Let me see what I can do to help. This hospital is near Aldershot. In spite of the best efforts of Mr Danvers Tresilian of the Cabinet Office and the military doctors, I have persuaded them to let me tell you what we know.'

Forester drew a chair up to the side of Powerscourt's bed.

'The problem with you, Lord Powerscourt, is that you are a medical freak. Indeed you are a freak in two ways, a double freak if you like. I don't mean that in any personal sense. I mean that you should not be alive at this moment. You should have been dead five days ago. According to the calculation of these military doctors, you stayed in that Devil's kitchen longer than anybody or anything, man or sheep or goat is meant to. Yet you are still here, and showing marked signs of improvement. You have caused a major headache for the military personnel preparing these lethal mixtures. Perhaps the dose is too small; let's not beat about the bush, if the gas needs to be made more potent to kill or maim a lot of humans, they are going to need the formula – the recipe if you like – to be made more powerful. That is going to cost money. I have no idea what our friend Danvers Tresilian is going to do about that.'

'Well, doctor, I am very pleased to be a freak. At least I'm still here.'

'I haven't finished yet, not by a long way. The other factor that makes you a freak is this. Nobody has ever tested this mixture on humans. Not properly. It's hardly surprising when you think about it. The staff at that Devil's kitchen have special clothes to wear, so they are protected. Because we have not tried these dreadful potions on humans rather than animals, we have no idea what treatment will work or what treatment will make it worse. If a patient comes into my rooms in Harley Street with a respiratory problem or a heart condition, we know what to do. There are textbooks. Among the medical fraternity there is a pool of educated knowledge. If I do not know the answer or an answer – God knows we're not infallible, however much we try to give the opposite impression – I can send my patient to a colleague or to a leading teaching hospital where they will know more than me.

'There is no medical textbook for you, Lord Powerscourt. You are first in the field. You are, quite literally, opening the batting. No doubt your case will feature prominently in the medical literature if anybody decides to use this form of warfare and our hospitals at the front are crowded out with victims. You are the first human, rather than animal, victim of gas warfare in this country. And, as far as I know, none of the animal victims has survived. So we are in *terra incognita*. We could try some form of treatment but we have no idea if it would work.'

'This is all very gratifying, to know I am first in the field, Doctor Forester, but can you tell me how much longer I have left to live? I have had enough of members of your profession inspecting me as if I were some form of freak in a circus. Do I need to revise my will today? Or tomorrow? Or can I leave it for a while?'

Doctor Forester laughed. 'That's a very good question, Lord Powerscourt. Indeed it may be the only question. I would not wish to insult you by putting a figure or a time on your life expectancy. The short answer is that I haven't a clue how long you will live after this ordeal. Neither has anybody else.'

342

Powerscourt thought he liked this doctor from London. At least he told you the score.

'To continue with my answer, you could live for years. Or the poison gas may carry you off rather sooner. These military doctors are keen to try out a number of different treatments. I propose to tell them that they could do more harm than good. Your arm will heal naturally over time, we believe.'

'So what are you going to suggest for me? What is the best treatment for a human guinea pig?'

'I am going to suggest that you go home tomorrow and rest. I don't mean that you should stay in bed all day. I'm sure you have had enough of that for now. Do whatever you would normally do, but don't for heaven's sake take any violent exercise just yet. It could be bad for your heart. I shall come and see you once a week. It may be that your body, like your arm, will try to heal itself, we just don't know.'

*

'I would ask you all not to look at me as if I were an exhibit in a zoo or some exotic animal in a circus,' Powerscourt began five days later, surveying his little audience in the drawing room at Markham Square. His left arm was still in a sling. Lady Lucy was in her favourite position, opposite her husband, on the other side of the fireplace. Natasha Shaporova and Inspector Dutfield were on the sofa. Powerscourt had told Johnny Fitzgerald the whole story the day after he came home from the hospital. His reaction had been typical. He was on his way back to Warwickshire.

'There you go again, Francis. How many times do I have to tell you that you mustn't go on these dangerous expeditions without me. I'm not saying you haven't come through it very well, mind you. But you'd have been a damned sight better off with me by your side.'

'I have to tell you,' Powerscourt continued, 'that I had to dissuade the authorities from making you all sign the Official Secrets Act before we met today. I told them that you were all responsible adults and would not dream of passing on anything that I say here this afternoon. And I have to say that a lot of the fresh information about events at the Ballets Russes comes from Inspector Dutfield and his police sources. And some of it comes from a mysterious gentleman at the Cabinet Office who is gatekeeper and guardian of most of the nation's secrets. Rosebery persuaded him to talk to me on the grounds that I had nearly been killed and deserved to know the full facts while I was still here, if you see what I mean.'

'I'm sure I can speak for us all, my lord,' said Inspector Dutfield, 'when I say you can depend on us, with or without the Official Secrets Act.'

'I have been thinking about the best way to describe this investigation,' Powerscourt carried on, 'and I think I would like to begin at the outsides and work in towards the heart of the matter.

'Consider first, if you would, the wicked uncle in Barnes, Richard Wagstaff Gilbert. A shady financier with a penchant for cheating at cards, a wicked uncle, a very wicked uncle, who liked to torment his nephews with the prospect of a glittering legacy when he died. Johnny talked to the remaining nephews and to the remaining sisters of Mr Gilbert. There was only one possible warning note in their evidence, that Mark the croquet player had been attending the Ballets Russes here in London. Johnny was convinced that the boy was not a killer, and he also believed his story that he had to leave as soon as the performance was over to get back to his college. The vicar and the teacher nephews need not detain us, but I must say my favourite memory of this investigation will be the thought of the vicar on the day of the great performance at Blenheim Palace attending to his garden and contemplating his sermon for the Sunday morning service as he pulled out the weeds. We can leave all that family in peace waiting for their inheritance.'

Powerscourt paused and took a drink of water. His bandaged arm was beginning to itch and he didn't think scratching it would be appropriate in the circumstances.

'There was the strange story of the French bonds being sold in large numbers but there was a perfectly sound reason for that. They too can be discounted.'

'And the jewels, Francis, the stolen jewels from St Petersburg? Can they too be discounted as being irrelevant to the murder?'

'How right you are, Lucy. There is a certain element of poetic justice in that affair. Inspector Dutfield told me yesterday that the thieves from the Premier Hotel have been apprehended and a lot, though not all, of the money recovered. I say poetic justice in that the money from the jewel raid was stolen, just like the jewels. Anastasia will just have to say that the money recovered was all they got from the sale of the diamonds and the rubies and so on. I'm sure she will be able to manage that.

'There are further Russian links I'd like to come to in a minute, but consider, if you will, the possibility that the first murder, the one here in Covent Garden, was carried out by a jealous husband, possibly even one from Paris who would have had to cross the Channel to restore the family honour. I didn't think there had been enough time here in England for Bolm to have his way with any compliant wives – the murder was committed shortly after the Ballets Russes arrived and Alexander Taneyev was killed during the first performance here in London. I didn't believe in the French connection either, so that trail can be discounted. The boy wasn't killed by a jealous husband.'

'But what about all the girls in the corps de ballet, Lord Powerscourt? Bolm was after them all the time.' Natasha Shaporova had collected the evidence on this count and she wasn't going to let it go just yet.

'I agree that Bolm behaved very badly with those girls. But there is only evidence of flirting, nothing more. Pretty serious flirting, by all accounts, but there was the added problem that those girls were on stage at the time the murder was carried out. So while Bolm is responsible for some pretty unacceptable behaviour – very unacceptable if you happen to be one of those girls – it wasn't Bolm who was killed. It was Taneyev.'

Powerscourt finally relieved some of the itching on his arm with a rub rather than a scratch. He didn't think the doctors would mind.

'We now come to a strange series of events that had nothing to with the murder. And while it may be too early to talk in detail about the Ballets Russes, they did have a key role to play in this subplot. Most of my information on this comes from Rosebery's friend in government intelligence, and the rest of it from Inspector

Dutfield and his colleagues. It helps, I believe, if you think of the Ballets Russes as a sort of glorified postbox. If you are a spy or a revolutionary, it's a perfect vehicle for your plans. There is a man called Lenin who is the principal revolutionary in Russia. He is, more or less, on the run. He cannot stay in Russia or he would be sent to Siberia or somewhere worse. He has stayed in Switzerland from time to time and he has stayed several times in Russia. He's even lived in London for a time and worked at the British Museum. He is currently in exile at a place called Cracow.'

'Why don't the Russians just go and arrest him? And take him back to Russia,' asked Lady Lucy.

'That's a good question, and I have to say I don't know the answer. Maybe the Russians think of him as a source for information or a point of contact for all the other revolutionary leaders he is in touch with. If they locked him up, this useful information would just dry up.'

'I'm sure Lenin's mail and his visitors are known to the Russian authorities at all times,' said Inspector Dutfield. 'They may even read all his letters before he does.'

'Several years ago,' Powerscourt continued, 'the revolutionaries organized a bank raid in a place called Tiflis. It was a bloody affair, but the raid realized an enormous haul of money for Lenin and his colleagues. Unfortunately most of it was in large denomination banknotes, and the banks knew the numbers. So the revolutionaries couldn't change it. They tried in a neighbouring country but that didn't work. Remember what I said about the Ballets Russes being a sort of postbox? Lenin or his cronies must have had a friend or a supporter in the company, not necessarily a dancer. They took the money to London in the Ballets Russes's luggage. It has been successfully changed into English pounds, and those will eventually return the way they came, in the Ballets Russes's luggage. They may even have done this by now.'

'From what you say, Francis, the authorities could have put their hands on this money any time they liked. Why didn't they?'

'I suspect, Lucy, that they are waiting to see where the money ends up. Then they may make their move, when they know the final destination. There is a further twist to the Lenin affair. He is a great scribbler, always producing pamphlets and books to enthuse his followers and keep them on the right course. You could regard them as the revolutionary equivalent of St Paul writing all those letters to the faithful across the ancient world – the Ephesians, the Corinthians and so on. It's to make sure there is no backsliding among the converts. Anyway, he sends a new pamphlet in Russian to London to be printed in Russian and English, five hundred copies each. I don't have to tell you how it's going to leave the country.'

'I believe, my lord,' said Inspector Dutfield, hunting through his notes, 'that the intelligence people think that these too will be waved through customs and everything else so that the Russian secret service, the Okhrana, can follow them, not just to Lenin in Cracow but to all the people he sends them to. That would provide a sort of *Who's Who* covering Lenin's revolutionary circle.'

'Exactly so,' said Powerscourt, 'exactly so. All of which brings us to the two principal characters in our

deadly drama. Alfred Bolm and Alexander Taneyev.'
He took another drink of water.

'Nobody who has seen Alfred Bolm dance can have any doubt that he is a complete master of his craft. He was trained in the classical tradition of the Imperial Theatre School in St Petersburg and has been delighting audiences all over Europe. The key question in this whole affair has been, Who was the intended victim: Bolm or his understudy Alexander Taneyev? For a long time I thought it must be Bolm. I was wrong. Bolm was not the killer either. If you think of him as a one-man version of the Ballets Russes postal system, you wouldn't be far wrong. One of the great difficulties for spies – I remember it well from the Boer War – is how to get your information back to your masters. Let us suppose we have Spy A, sent from St Petersburg in search of information about military experiments. He thinks he has some very important information. But he may be watched. So he takes his information to the postbox – Bolm, in this case – and the postbox passes it on to Spy C, possibly over games of chess at that club near the British Museum. Spy C might be thought of as a courier rather than a spy, perhaps. His job is to get the information home. The information about military experiments came to Bolm this way. It was Alexander Taneyev's misfortune that he happened upon this material while it was still in the postbox, as it were. Bolm had not yet had the time to pass it on to Spy C.

'We have all heard of the thought processes of Alexander Taneyev from his letters home, and that diary which ends so abruptly. We know that he was deeply worried about this information. I suspect that he confronted Bolm with what he had read. I believe he told him that he was intending to pass it on to the English authorities or, equally likely perhaps, that Bolm thought that was what he intended to do. Bolm passes this information on to Spy A, the most important link in the chain, who has already garnered crucial military intelligence. Spy A, operating under the pseudonym Andrei Rublev, kills Alexander Taneyev to shut him up. He can't talk to the authorities if he is dead. I suspect Andrei Rublev was rather good at that sort of thing. I would be surprised if Alexander was his first victim. Taneyev must have let slip to Bolm that he had told the dancer Vera of his plans. That was why Spy A went to Blenheim Palace to kill her too. He had to get rid of them both before they had time to walk into an English police station. After that, Spy A moved on to the experiment near Goring where he met me.'

'Do you know who the identity of the spy is, Lord Powerscourt?' Natasha had been staring at Powerscourt for some time, trying to work out what the yellow on his skin meant.

'I do not; I mean, I do not know his real name. Thanks to the activities of Colonel Brouzet in Paris, and what the man said to me when we met at Goring, we know his work name was Rublev, Andrei Rublev. But I have no more idea of what his real name is than I do the name of the man in the moon.'

'Andrei Rublev was a famous icon painter hundreds of years ago,' said Natasha. 'Would I be right in thinking, Lord Powerscourt, that you are unable to tell us anything more about the nature of that military experiment? I presume that was what caused the injuries to your arm and your skin.'

'I cannot say any more than I just have. It took me two and a half hours of argument before the secret people allowed me even to use the phrase "military experiment". I should say that Andrei Rublev is dead. He met with an unfortunate accident at the military experiment and will not trouble us any more. Inspector Dutfield is in the middle of a report to the Commissioner of the Metropolitan Police saying that the case of the murder of Alexander Taneyev and the poor girl at Blenheim Palace is now closed.'

'I see,' said Natasha.

'Perhaps I could reassure you, Mrs Shaporova,' said Inspector Dutfield, 'that even I have not been permitted to know what went on at that experiment.'

28

Fouetté

Literally 'whipped'. The term indicates either a turn with a quick change in the direction of the working leg as it passes in front of or behind the supporting leg, or a quick whipping around of the body from one direction to another. There are many kinds of *fouetté*: *petit fouetté* (*à terre*, *en demi-pointe* or *sauté*) and *grand fouetté* (*sauté*, *relevé* or *en tournant*). Similar to a *frappé*. An introductory form for beginner dancers, executed at the barre, is as follows: facing the barre, the dancer executes a *grand battement* to the side, then turns the body so that the lifted leg ends up in *arabesque*.

The silver hairs first appeared on Powerscourt's temples shortly before his birthday. For some days nobody talked about them in Markham Square. Oddly enough, it was Christopher, the reading twin, who had recently demolished *The Hound of the Baskervilles* over a single weekend when staying with some of his mother's more boring relations, who solved the problem.

'I know,' he said suddenly one morning after his father had left the house, 'let's call Papa Silver Blaze. You know, like the horse in the Sherlock Holmes story that is stolen but comes back to win the big race.'

'Didn't he kill somebody on the way?' said Thomas, who knew most Holmes stories virtually off by heart.

'He didn't mean to,' said Christopher, 'and they'd been cutting bits out of his leg or something.'

'I think it's horrid giving Papa a nickname, however nice it is,' Olivia complained.

In the end the Powerscourt young did what they had always done – they talked to their mother. Lady Lucy laughed. 'Well,' she said, 'you could ask him, couldn't you? I'm sure he would be rather proud to be known as Silver Blaze. The horse did win the Wessex Cup after all, didn't he?'

*

For his birthday, Powerscourt decided to reverse the usual order of celebrations. He handed out the presents early. He took the twins, Christopher and Juliet, fifteen years old now, to Paris for the weekend. They talked non-stop through all the delights of the French capital in English and French – Powerscourt, in his role of educating parent, was delighted to see that their French, which Lucy spoke a lot to them at home, was now almost fluent. Only one place reduced them to silence.

'Oh, my God,' Christopher whispered, and began writing in his notebook when confronted with the Hall of Mirrors at Versailles. 'Oh, my God.'

Christopher wanted to be a journalist. He really wanted to be an investigator like his papa, but he didn't think that would go down too well at the family

353

dinner table. Juliet, showing a greater maturity than people credited her with, wanted to be a doctor. Her fate had been sealed when she'd asked Lady Lucy if she could be a doctor and have lots of children as well.

'Why ever not?' her mama had said. 'You carry on. I'll back you all the way.'

Robert, Lady Lucy's son by her first marriage, was now First Lieutenant of a frigate on patrol in the cold grey waters of the North Sea, playing war games against Tirpitz's Dreadnoughts.

Powerscourt took the greatest care of his second child, Olivia. Caught between the precocious Thomas and the talking twins, she sometimes felt left out.

He asked Lucy to take Olivia shopping for some fashionable clothes. Although Olivia was young and coltish, Lady Lucy was correct in believing that Olivia would be the fairest of them all.

So here they were, Powerscourt and Olivia, drinking blanc-cassis in the dining room of the Ritz Hotel on London's Piccadilly, only open for six years, but already the place to be seen for the young and the fashionable. Olivia shared her father's intense dislike of champagne. Powerscourt suddenly thought back to when this about-to-be-very-beautiful young woman was small. Sometimes he would take a tiny Olivia out of the bath and wrap her in an enormous towel. Then he would write an imaginary address on her back with much tickling and thumps and bangs as the parcel progressed through the postal system. This process was usually punctuated by squeals and laughter. The whole event was characterized by a continuous running commentary by Olivia's papa. The parcel was always addressed to Olivia's grandmother. There, he was told later, she always behaved beautifully. As the only child in the house, she was fussed over at great length. She spent a lot of time talking to the animals. She had talked of a career with horses for as long as anybody could remember.

She still had not taken a sip of her blanc-cassis. There was a great sadness in her demeanour, as if she had been recently bereaved.

'What's the matter, my love?' asked Powerscourt.

'It's you, Papa. We're all so worried about you. You don't look well. You haven't looked well since you came back. And those doctors keep coming and they all leave looking like sick owls.'

Powerscourt saw at once that this was a crucial moment in his relations with his – as it were – adult children. Tell the truth? Procrastinate? Try to muddle through? In the end he knew he had no choice.

'I should have told you before,' said Powerscourt, taking a large gulp of his blanc-cassis. 'It's the gas, you see, the poison gas. I had to breathe in too much of it. The doctors have told me I should be dead by now.'

'Gas? Poison gas?' said Olivia. 'I don't understand.'

'If there's another war, my love, both sides are developing different forms of nerve gases which they say they would only use if the other side starts using theirs. They could kill people in enormous numbers. There you are, sitting in your trench or your tent. There's a slight breeze. Your enemies have shells and other forms of ammunition filled with this poisonous stuff. The Germans – let's not beat about the bush – the Germans are the best chemists in Europe and they are believed to have the most dangerous forms of gas. It can kill you. It can send you blind. It can destroy your mind but leave your body intact, or the other way round. It's

355

terrible stuff, my love. I just happened to inhale rather too much of it in my last investigation. I got caught up by accident in the British nerve-gas experiments. I sometimes feel as if I'm choking, as if the gas is going to pull my lungs out. It is getting better. It's just very slow.'

'And the scar on your arm, Papa, that terrible scar?'

Powerscourt told her of the death struggle in the nerve centre of the gas research establishment, hidden next to a hotel on the banks of the Thames so the toxic wastes could be carried away, and the Russian spy holding on to Powerscourt's foot and his arm as he was sucked into the terrible mixture in the middle of that vast laboratory.

'That's it,' said Powerscourt finally, 'but there's one thing above all else that is very important.'

'What's that?'

'I'm still here,' said Powerscourt with a grin. 'I'm bloody well still here!'

'So you are, Papa, so you are.' The girl's eyes were filled with tears. 'Thank God you're still here.'

'Don't be upset, Olivia, please,' said Powerscourt, noting that Olivia had still not touched a drop of her blanc-cassis. 'I give you a toast, my love. Raise your glass, please.'

Two glasses clinked together under one of César Ritz's more extravagant chandeliers.

'Your future, Olivia.'

The girl's eyes were brighter now.

'And yours, Papa. I love you so much. We all do, you see.'

*

This special birthday celebration was taking place at Powerscourt House in the Wicklow Mountains south of Dublin. When Lady Lucy realized that it was also twenty-five years since Powerscourt sold the family home in Ireland, she wrote to the new owners, a branch of the Guinness brewing dynasty, still there after all these years. Lady Lucy asked if the old owner and his friends could come back for a special anniversary and birthday combined. They replied that they would be delighted to welcome the Powerscourt family and friends back on this special day. Most of the invitations were carried out by telephone in case her husband became suspicious.

*

It was a beautiful summer's day, the sea sparkling in the distance, the mountains keeping watch over the great house. A couple of kestrels circled overhead and the seagulls seemed to be flying in relays from the sand dunes to the great fountain at the bottom of the steps.

There was only one person who held the threads or the skeins of Powerscourt's life in his hands, and that was Johnny Fitzgerald, a descendant of the famous rebel Lord Edward Fitzgerald, who had died of his wounds in the 1798 rebellion led by the United Irishmen. Johnny promised to bring one or two or three others who also claimed an affinity with the United Irishmen, a group composed of men of all religions who believed in the ideals of the French Revolution and freedom for Ireland. Their leader was Theobald Wolfe Tone, an unsuccessful Dublin barrister who had persuaded thousands and thousands of his illiterate fellow countrymen to sign the Oath of the United Irishmen.

Johnny was due in the early evening, bringing a man whose ancestors had betrayed the patriots for English gold, and another who said he was a direct descendant of Wolfe Tone himself. Then there was Lucy, love of his life, the only person who knew the complete guest list. After the party, Powerscourt was taking Lady Lucy back to the deep south of America they had seen on their honeymoon, to Charleston and Savannah and the antebellum mansions of the slave owners. Powerscourt himself wanted to see Atlanta, burnt to the ground by General William Tecumseh Sherman as his men went marching through Georgia. Powerscourt had secured a day pass for two trips related to the American Civil War, to Appomattox Court House where General Robert E. Lee had ridden through the cheering lines of the Confederate forces to surrender his flag and his country to Ulysses S. Grant. Powerscourt was also taking Lady Lucy to Gettysburg, where he proposed to find a forgotten corner of the battlefield and read the words that were among the many things that made Lincoln immortal, the Gettysburg Address. He thought they might both cry: for Lincoln; for the country he was never able to create because he was shot; for the arbitrary cruelty of history.

And hidden in the opening pages of his first edition of Gibbon's *Decline and Fall of the Roman Empire* were two tickets to cross Canada on the Canadian Pacific Railroad. They would go through the Rockies and end their journey in San Francisco.

Some of the key players in Powerscourt's previous cases had made the journey across the Irish Sea to join the celebrations. M. Fokine was temporarily confined to the ballroom in the big house, where he was teaching some of the girls the rudiments of ballet. Powerscourt hoped he wasn't going to shout at them too much.

Here is Powerscourt himself, sitting on a bench in the shade by the great fountain at the bottom of the cascade of steps that lead down from the back of Powerscourt House. Here he was born. Here he grew up, his boyhood marked by his father's worries about money, his mother singing with the young music teacher in the drawing room after dinner. He remembered the great parties for all of Dublin society, the bands, the dancing, all the Anglo-Irish excesses that his parents could no longer afford. It was the money or the lack of it that made Johnny Fitzgerald pull his friend from a place that should have been glorious – for its position, its history, the beauty of its interiors – but had turned instead into something like a prison house. Powerscourt had fled to London with his sisters and never looked back.

Now the house was owned by some obscure outriders of the Guinness brewing dynasty and had been perfectly restored.

Orlando Blane, the master forger from the investigation into a murdered art critic, was sitting at a temporary easel on the lawn, producing fake Renaissance-style portraits for all and sundry.

Lord Francis Powerscourt had brought with him for his birthday his son and heir Thomas, and Thomas's closest friend from Westminster School, Gabriel. The boys had gone off to climb Sugarloaf Mountain and enjoy the views. Also in the party were Powerscourt's brother-in-law William Burke's eldest son, a scholar of Merton College Oxford, and his girlfriend, the glamorous Contessa Eleanora Maria Paravicini, eldest daughter of an Italian duke, who had more titles than there are strands of pasta in a dish of spaghetti bolognese. The young Contessa, not yet in her twenties, looked like one of Botticelli's Madonnas, but a wicked smile hinted that earthly pleasures might not be out of bounds.

Coming down the steps, Burke's boy and the girl were as close as they could be without actually touching. Some way behind them was a smaller figure with an outlandish hat. It must be Lady Lucy, Powerscourt thought. He suddenly remembered her in an equally dramatic piece of headgear and an Anna Karenina coat, when she joined him in a box at the Albert Hall for Beethoven's Ninth Symphony twenty years before. Lucy had gone in as Lady Hamilton. She had come out almost somebody else entirely, as Powerscourt had asked her to marry him at the end of the third movement. He had written his proposal on a scrap of newspaper inside an advertisement for Bird's Custard. *Lucy, I love you. Will you marry me? Francis.* Back came the answer, *Of course I will. Lucy.*

The former Archbishop of Tuam, now Archbishop of Dublin, who led Powerscourt and his friends on the pilgrimage to Croagh Patrick in the case of the missing Irish ancestor portraits, was sitting quietly in the shade under a tree planted by Powerscourt's grandfather. He had promised to lead whoever might wish to join him in silent prayers at one of the most numinous holy sites in Ireland, Glendalough, the glen of the two lakes just a few miles away.

The young couple were holding hands now, in that surprised manner young people always have when they hold hands, as if they were the first humans to do so since God created the world all those years ago. They were now about a hundred yards or so from Powerscourt's position. He sat further back on his bench. He could see Lucy coming down the steps clearly now, waving a tiny wave. Behind her came a couple of waiters with ice buckets and glasses and a couple of bottles of wine. Sauvignon blanc? Pinot grigio? Powerscourt wondered if Lucy had remembered the cases of meursault he had shown her down in the dark Powerscourt cellars, the last wine his father had laid down before he died.

They were embracing now, the boy and the girl entwined in an embrace so passionate you felt as if you were intruding merely by looking at them.

One of the five Powerscourt bands began playing 'Tipperary, It's a long way to go'. The fountain dropped for a moment and he could see them very clearly. He thought of the Taj Mahal, another monument to the power of love. These young people – Patrick Burke always called his Contessa Els, to rhyme with bells, he remembered – were making a different sort of monument to love: less permanent but, perhaps, more brilliant. It would be made of crystal, or gossamer or dew, and would fade or evaporate as nature changed its courses. It was as if they were living inside one of John Donne's early sonnets, where the love burns so bright it could hurt your hands on the page.

Deus est caritas, Powerscourt remembered the young scholar saying the College Grace at a feast in Merton College Oxford that he and Lady Lucy had attended earlier that year, *et qui manet in caritate manet in Deo et Deus in illo*. God is love, and whoever lives with love lives with God and God lives with him.

The young couple, still graced with the drops and the spray from the fountain, turned into the Japanese garden.

Lady Lucy joined him and took his hand. This place will always be special, Powerscourt said to himself. It will be special for all members of the Powerscourt family and special for all members of the Burke family. Special, above all, for Patrick and Els and the brilliance of their love.

It was Natasha Shaporova who brought the news that finally closed this investigation. 'You'll never guess what Monsieur Fokine has just told me, Lord Powerscourt.'

'And what might that be, Natasha?'

'Well, you remember there has been a lot of talk about the music Stravinsky has been writing for the new opera?'

'I do.'

'Well, he's finished it at last. It's going to have its world premiere in Paris next summer!'

'Do you know what it's called, Natasha?'

'I do. Well, I only know it in French actually.'

'And?'

'It's going to be called *Le Sacre du Printemps*.'

'How would you translate that into English?'

'Some English professor has done that already. The new ballet is going to be called *The Rite of Spring*.'